I0763337

Other books by Keith Hoar

Zach Templeton Thriller Series:

EDGE OF MADNESS

RAGE

DEADLY SECRETS

HISTORICAL FICTION:

LEAGUE OF TRAITORS

NONFICTION:

DECEIVED The Assault of Revisionist History

COLD DARK LIES

A Zach Templeton Thriller

KEITH HOAR

First Edition

Zhetosoft Publications

Published by: Zhetosoft Publications

COLD DARK LIES is a work of fiction. Names, characters, institutions, places, and events are either the product of the author's imagination, or, if real, are used fictitiously without any intent to describe their actual condition or conduct. Any resemblance whatsoever to names, characters, actual events, locales, businesses, organizations, or persons, living or dead, is entirely coincidental and beyond the intent of the author.

All Scripture quotations are from the Holy Bible, Authorized King James Version.

ISBN(13): 978-1-7362761-4-3 (hardback)
ISBN(13): 978-1-7362761-2-9 (paperback)
ISBN(13): 978-1-7362761-3-6 (eBook)

~ For Kathie, my loving wife ~

Her amazing faith, selfless love, and
patient encouragement is my source of inspiration

[AUTHOR'S NOTE]

I fervently pray the novel you hold in your hands does not come true in your life time, at least, not as it is written.

While *COLD DARK LIES* is a work of fiction meant to entertain, it does contain a warning regarding events that *are* coming, perhaps soon. Will they happen next month; next year; five years from now; or longer? I do not know. No one does. However, Scripture is very clear that frightening times will, in fact, occur. "*This know also, that in the last days perilous times shall come.*" II Timothy 3:1.

Will the coming events occur exactly as written in this book? Very likely not. However, when the events prophesied do occur, they will be perilous and terrifying. The warning that begins in the above verse continues, "*For men shall be lovers of their own selves, covetous, boasters, proud, blasphemers, disobedient to parents, unthankful, unholy, Without natural affection, trucebreakers, false accusers, incontinent, fierce, despisers of those that are good, Traitors, heady, highminded, lovers of pleasures more than lovers of God; Having a form of godliness, but denying the power thereof: from such turn away.*" vss. 2-5. Verse three says, "*…despisers of those that are good…*" Would that not perfectly describe American society in the year just ended?

I did not write this novel to predict how future events will come to pass. I am a teller of tales and this novel is written primarily to entertain. However, you should ask yourself the question: *What If?*

DO NOT be distracted by the political rhetoric, false arguments, or "lies" that blind and divide so many of America's citizens. DO NOT fall victim to their never-ending hunger for more and more power with which they may control the ignorant and uninformed masses. There are far more pressing issues: Are *you* prepared? What will *you* do?

Arise from your slumber, get informed, and get prepared! A long-prophesied evil is rising. An evil that seeks to destroy that "Great Experiment" launched so many years ago by incredibly brave and honorable men. The air literally crackles with tension as we approach the "*Day of the Lord*", prophesied in Acts 2:19-20! Very often, that which is published as the truth is merely a cleverly veiled lie.

This novel is set in various locales in the United States and in other countries. Seemingly incorrect grammar that is contained inside quotes may reflect broken English. This is used by foreign characters. For example: "I zay again. Vere ess zee data?" would be typical speech for someone who has a poor command of the English language.

For a definition of world time zones used throughout this book, see the GLOSSARY at the end of the book.

Thank you for taking the time to read *COLD DARK LIES*. The author is very grateful for readers of his books. A sample prologue of this book and the prologue and/or the first chapters of current and upcoming books can be viewed on the author's website at https://keithhoarbooks.wixsite.com/home. You are welcome to reach out to the author through his personal email address at kahoarauthor@email.com.

Keith Hoar
October 2024
Northeast Oklahoma

Horror hath taken hold upon me because of the wicked that forsake thy law.

Psalm 119:53

Nearly all men can stand adversity, but if you want to test a man's character, give him power.

Abraham Lincoln

PART I

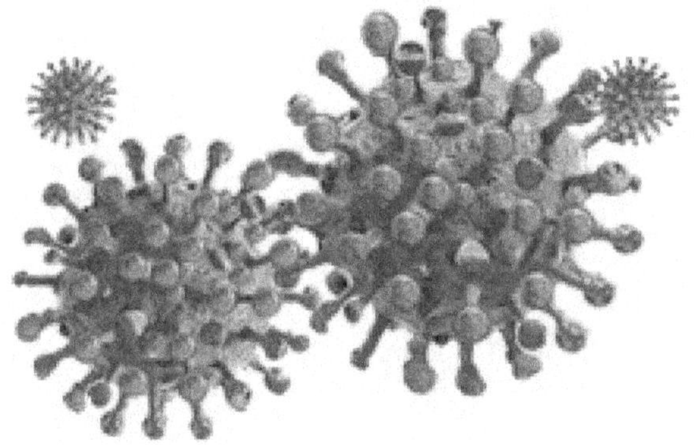

Prologue

David McClain sat in the semi-darkness, eyes glued to the television screen, unable to believe what he was hearing. His knuckles turned white as he gripped the television remote harder and harder. Never in a million years would he have believed it would come to this.

"Lies!" David exploded, shaking his head in anger and frustration. "Nothing but stinking lies! How can he sit there with a straight face and say that?"

David pointed the remote at the television, switched off the news broadcast, and hurled the remote across the room. Batteries and splinters of plastic bounced across the floor as the remote smashed into the wall, splitting into pieces. He pushed up off the couch and paced across the floor of his small condominium's living room. An angry resolve grew inside him as he paced. Knowing what he had to do, he turned and headed into the spare bedroom he used as an office.

"It's a very dark day. A very, very dark day," he muttered to himself as he sat down in front of his computer. He tapped the keyboard's space bar to awaken the computer, guided the mouse pointer to the icon for his email program, and double-clicked the left mouse button. After the email program opened, he clicked "Compose Email". He dug his wallet out of his hip pocket and slid out the scrap of paper hidden under his driver's license. He unfolded the paper, typed the cryptic address in the "To:" block, and typed an innocuous phrase in the "Subject:" block.

His fingers tapped hurriedly on the keyboard as he typed the message forming in his mind. Taking only a few seconds, he quickly read what he had typed. "Sounds good," he said. Guiding the mouse pointer across the screen, he clicked the Paperclip icon and navigated to a folder simply titled "Stuff" located deep in the computer's file directory tree. He selected three files and then clicked Attach. In a hurry to complete his mission, he clicked Send without double-checking what he had typed.

"Oh, good lord," David moaned when his eyes fell on the list of emails sitting in the Inbox. In his haste, with his mind clouded by anger, he had signed in using his normal email application and not the private, and secure, email application he had intended to use.

"Not Good. Not good at all," he fretted. He sat there for several minutes trying to decide what to do, but he realized there was absolutely nothing he could do. The simple email application he had used did not have a Recall feature. The email had already been sent, and that simply was that.

David knew the Foreign Intelligence Surveillance Act had given the U.S. government authority to collect the communications of Americans under a broad range of circumstances. Using, and more often abusing, that authority, the government watched online activity every minute of the day through automated methods and non-human, eavesdropping algorithms. The government had the resources necessary to dip into online communications whenever it deemed necessary — sometimes with a warrant, and more often than not without a warrant.

"Well, what's done is done. All that's left to do now is write my eulogy," David groaned as he ran his hand through his curly hair. He pushed his chair back, stood up, and started toward the door. Halfway across the room, he stopped and turned back toward the computer, deciding he should send a quick goodbye and warning to an old friend, someone he respected more than anyone else on the planet.

David signed out of the normal email application and started up the private, secure email application. Being more careful this time, he composed and sent a message that would get his friend's attention but would be meaningless to anyone else. He signed out of the secure email application, powered down the computer, and headed for the kitchen.

Assuming this could very well be his last enjoyment, he decided he would eat the last two remaining pieces of chocolate pie. "What difference does it make now?" he mumbled as he stuffed a large bite of the delicious pie into his mouth.

Early the next morning David McClain, Senior Intel Officer, United States Secret Service, got dressed and left for work just like any other morning. However, David never arrived at work. His closest friends never heard from him. David McClain simply vanished.

Chapter One

Wednesday Jan. 28th – 8:17 a.m. CET
Rungis International Market
Southern Suburb of Paris France

Recently arrived from Shanghai, China, Ling Jun Dong grabbed his bag, climbed out of the taxi, and handed a fifty Euro note through the open window to the taxi driver. "*Gardez le changement*," Ling said to the driver in broken French.

"*Oui monsieur*," the cabbie answered excitedly, delighted to receive such a large tip. Ling slammed the back door and the cabbie sped away from the curb in search of his next fare.

Ling, fifty-one, with salt and pepper gray hair, slipped the strap of his bag over his shoulder and headed for the entrance to the Rungis International Market. Stopping at the doorway, he waited for the line of people that had just gotten off a transit bus to enter the market. Nobody gave Ling more than a fleeting glance due in part to his small stature of five foot three inches. He deliberately wore drab, ordinary, casual clothes to avoid standing out. The four-inch gash that ran down the right side of his face had healed nicely leaving only a pencil-thin scar, hardly visible unless viewed up close.

To further mask his image, his hair had been cut short and he wore a ball cap pulled down low on his forehead. Certain that Interpol would have his photo stored in their database, Ling hoped the photo was old enough that he would not be recognized, allowing him to complete his mission and return home.

The people that he passed by or stood next to had no idea what a vicious criminal he was. Ling, a high school dropout from a tiny village outside of Changde in Hunan Province, China, began developing his career as a hoodlum while still a teenager. As he grew older, Ling descended deeper and deeper into the dark world of crime. While building his gang of criminals, Ling racked up a long list of crimes that included: mafia-style executions, assaults, theft, home invasions, extortion, illegal arms distribution, bribery, and many, many others. There was nothing Ling would not agree to in order to satisfy his lust for money. Well known in the depraved underworld of Chinese crime, Ling was cruel and without feeling. Even the smallest perceived insult would likely result in the six-inch blade he always kept hidden somewhere on his person being buried deep in the back of anyone foolish enough to cross him.

A job with an enormous payoff, to which he had finally agreed, had brought Ling to Paris. He could not believe his good fortune. One million dollars for one or two day's work. At first, Ling had been somewhat skeptical, but when he had been handed a stack of one thousand crisp one-hundred dollar bills, *in cash*, with the remainder to be paid upon his return to Shanghai, his skepticism immediately vanished. He smiled when he thought about what he would be able to buy with all that money.

Ling walked through the entrance of the market and stepped out of the main walkway to observe the market's activity. The noise level in the market was almost deafening. Thousands of shoppers lined the aisles in all directions, looking for bargains. Nearly as many shopkeepers, merchants, and vendors yelled to be heard over their competitors, creating a cacophony of sounds. Tourists twittered about the bargains they had managed to negotiate and stall owners noisily bartered the last of their greatly overpriced stock to anyone who stopped to look.

Browsing through an in-flight magazine, Ling had read about the market, located in a suburb on the south side of Paris called Rungis, during his connecting flight from Frankfort, Germany. From the description in the article, he had expected the market to be large. However, reading about it and actually seeing it and experiencing it were two entirely different things. The market was absolutely enormous. As the second largest wholesale market in the world, the whole market complex covered five hundred seventy-eight acres, slightly larger than the entire Principality of Monaco. The market housed nineteen restaurants, a bank, a post office, a hotel, and several gas stations. The market even had its own police force.

Thirteen thousand workers began flooding into the market at midnight each day to prepare for the day's activities. According to recent reports, just shy of forty-seven hundred tons of products passed through the market each and every day.

Stepping back into the aisle, Ling rejoined the flow of traffic entering the market. At the first aisle, he turned right and headed for the far end of the market. He had not gone far before the distinctive aroma of the seafood market filled his nostrils. Ling could hardly believe what he saw. Every imaginable kind of seafood lay heaped in various stalls, covering an area the size of a soccer field. Disliking the smell immensely and rather than continuing into the seafood market, he turned left. Three aisles deeper into the market, he passed the *Pavillon des Fromages*, the cheese market, with its rounds of cheese the size of wagon wheels. He walked past displays lined with hundreds and hundreds of different varieties of cheeses.

At the far side of the market he could see the produce hall, with its rows upon rows of delectable fruits and vegetables, artfully arranged to bring out their maximum visual appeal. Not seeing what he was looking for, Ling turned and scanned the market to his left. He needed to locate the meat market section, where he had been instructed to start. Fifty feet directly ahead, he spotted an information booth.

Ling hurried down the aisle, stepped up to the booth, and asked, "*Quel chemin vers le marché de la viande*?"

"*Le marché de la viande est à l'extrémité monsieur*," the young woman in the booth answered, pointing to her right.

"*Mercie*," Ling said.

Ling began walking toward the southeast corner of the market. As he strolled down the aisle, he first passed the perfumed splendor of rows and rows of exotic flowers, most of which Ling had never seen before. Shoppers bustled around the vast assortment of vibrantly colored flowers, occasionally purchasing an item that caught their eye. Next, Ling passed stalls piled high with a myriad of spices, filling the air with their sweet, fragrant aromas.

Finally, Ling spotted what he had been looking for. Being a strict vegetarian, he shuddered as he passed bin after bin of bloody, hanging carcasses of veal, beef, and various other animals that did not look particularly appetizing. He reached the end of the market, a section stacked high with white cartons stuffed with freshly slaughtered turkeys, pigeons, grouse, and wild rabbits, ready to be shipped or sold to passing shoppers.

Ling turned to his left and hurried to the far corner of the section. He slipped his hand into his pocket, feeling for the small rubber bulb. He was ready to begin.

Wednesday Jan. 28th – 3:47 p.m. ChST
Zhongnan University Xiangya Medical College
Tongzipo Road, Yuelu District
Ch'angsha, Hunan Province, China

Zhongnan University Xiangya Medical College, a division of Hunan Medical University, located in the Kaifu District of Ch'angsha, China, advertised itself as a multi-disciplinary and multi-specialty medical university, characterized by rigorous scholarship, advanced scientific research, and excellent medical technology programs. According to the latest marketing brochure, the university operated multiple research centers including centers for medical genetics, clinical pharmacology, medical instrumentation, and advanced surgical disciplines. The university boasted a large number of medical scientists, famous both at home and abroad.

Cutting edge biomedical and genetics research occurred two kilometers north of the university's main campus at the Xiangya School of Medicine, located on the north side of Tangzipo Road. An important piece of information *not* advertised in the university's shiny marketing brochure was the secretive genome editing and nanoparticle research that occurred in a highly secure, level-4 biolab, concealed deep in the basement of the advanced research building. Access to the biolab was limited to a very small handful of carefully selected researchers.

One of those researchers, twenty-seven-year old Chin Zheng Li, a post doctoral virology fellow, had awakened in the middle of the night, his mind churning over and over the same fear he had been wrestling with for over a week.

Ten days earlier Chin had overheard part of a heated conversation between Doctor Zhou, the Virology Department Director, and a Doctor Kenneth Thompson from the United States. Chin had noticed every time Doctor Thomson arrived at the university, he arrived early and always kept out of sight. On that day, Chin had also arrived early, intending to speak with Doctor Zhou in regard to some needed funding for an additional piece of laboratory equipment. Chin had walked into Doctor Zhou's outer office and had heard the two men arguing. At first, he had turned to leave, but something he heard made him hesitate. He had listened carefully until he heard a chair scrape on the floor. Chin rushed out of the office and returned to the lab, horrified by what he had heard.

After arriving home from work that evening, still frightened and horrified, Chin had contacted Tu Jin Lam, his wife's cousin, an epidemiologist in the United States. After Chin had recounted what he had overheard, Tu Jin had become alarmed as well. After much urging, Tu Jin had eventually convinced Chin to share additional details describing his research. Using a phony email username, Tu Jin had created a bogus account on a secure, online, file sharing service. Over the course of several days, at great peril, using that bogus account, Chin had smuggled out and uploaded a basic project description and some preliminary test results.

If he or one of the other researchers managed to develop a process to identify and limit off-target cleavage of the gene located at the targeted chromosome position, Chin's fears would no longer be just fears. They would become a terrifying reality. Using gain-of-function techniques they were to create the most lethal pathogen the world had ever experienced. Chin had become increasingly frightened over the following days. As he laid awake in his bed, his mind kept replaying the horrible things he had heard.

Anxious to determine if a solution to solve the off-target cleavage issue could be developed and if it would then produce the mutation he feared, Chin crawled out of bed early, showered, and ate a quick breakfast of cold rice with a little milk. He wrote a short note to his beloved wife, Min Ju Jiang, explaining his early departure. He bundled up in his heavy coat and began the long one and a half kilometer trek to the Shuiduhe metro rail station.

Chin would need to be extremely careful as he was already under increased scrutiny. Doctor Zhou had personally threatened him, telling him in no uncertain terms that if he did not complete his project tasks soon, he would face severe consequences. Delaying his assigned tasks to test his off-target cleavage theory could get him fired, sent to prison, or worse.

During the long eleven kilometer ride on Line 5 of Ch'angsha's metro rail system, Chin's mind churned with the fury of a hurricane. How could he devise a method to limit the off-target cleavage? At least a dozen times he asked himself the exact same question, "*What is effecting the target positioning?*" The answer always came back to the same answer—complexity. There were just too many pieces to control. How would it be possible to synchronize all the processes at once? Finally, the *proverbial* light bulb went on above his head. He could not believe he and the other researchers had overlooked such a simple solution. He felt certain he knew *exactly* how to solve the complexity issue.

The train's PA system announced the train was approaching the Wanjiali Square metro rail station. Chin stood, made his way to the doorway, and waited in line to exit the train. The doors slid open and as he stepped out onto the platform, he looked up and saw the train on Line 2 had already arrived. Racing across the platform, he slipped inside just as the doors closed. A quick ride across the Xiang River on Line 2 to the Yingwanzhen metro station, a quick connection to Line 4, then two more stops to the Liugoulong metro station. Chin exited the metro station and stepped out into the bitterly cold wind. He zipped his coat all the way up, stuffed his hands into his pockets, and hurried the remaining seven blocks down Tangzipo Road to his destination.

Arriving at the university's advanced research facility before the doors opened, Chin paced back and forth in the frigid air waiting for the night watchman to unlock the doors. Fifteen minutes later the night watchman unlocked one of the doors. Chin pushed through the door and dashed off down the hallway toward the advanced genetics laboratory at break-neck speed, in a rush to test his new hypothesis.

After four failed attempts and ready to give up, a simple mistake had resulted in unexpected success. Six hours later, Chin, deeply concerned and shaken that he had actually been able to solve the off target cleavage issue, stepped out of the level-four, high-containment area, containing the most exotic and deadly microorganisms known to man. Once outside the high-containment area, and having reattached his air feed line, he rotated the high-containment area's door handle to the locked position. Chin heard the inflatable gaskets of the shower room's double interlocking doors inflate, sealing the shower room completely. He punched a large button on the wall and waited while his positive-pressure breathing suit was sprayed with decontamination liquids. After a final rinse and unhooking the air feed line from his positive-pressure protective suit, Chin released the clear helmet's seal, pulled the gas tight zipper all the way down, and extricated himself from the bulky suit. He hung the suit on a hook near the shower room's exit to be scrubbed and sterilized by the lab's cleaning crew.

Chin made his way back to the advanced genetics laboratory. Stopping in front of one of the long, granite-topped workbenches, crowded with intricate glassware, microscopes, and sophisticated medical equipment, Chin cleared a spot just large enough for his laptop computer. He opened the laptop and sat staring at the screen trying to decide what to do. To make certain no one learned of the new technique he had discovered, he had dumped all printouts and test results of his successful process into the incinerator before leaving the biolab.

Chin had to make it look like he had been working on his assigned tasks or he would certainly suffer Doctor Zhou's screaming and ranting yet again. He opened his time log and began making fictitious entries, using the work codes for his assigned project. To match the fictitious entries, he opened his lab worksheet and typed in a matching, but fake, summary of work he should have completed. He hoped his fictitious entries were convincing enough that Doctor Zhou or Professor Yu would not discover his dishonesty. Chin did not like lying, but in this case he believed he had no other choice.

Worried his deception would be discovered, he knew he had to get word to Tu Jin soon that he had solved the off-target issue and the threat was real. He opened his word processor and began typing a complete description of the new process he had stumbled across that resolved the off target cleavage issue.

A cold, half-empty cup of coffee, Chin's second since he had returned to the lab, sat perched on the edge of the workbench. Chin's arm flinched, his fingers drooping and coming to rest on the laptop's keyboard. A string of v's began streaming across the laptop's screen. The laptop's "Sticky Keys" alert awakened Chin from his slumber.

Chin jerked upright and shook his head to clear the cobwebs of sleep from his mind. He grabbed the cup of coffee and took a sip. "Yuck!" Chin spit in disgust, as he swallowed a mouthful of the cold, bitter brew.

Chin slipped off the stool he was sitting on and headed for the sink on the other side of the room. He poured the cold coffee in the sink and tossed the empty cup in a nearby trash can. Leaning against the edge of the sink, he stretched his tired muscles and then returned to his work station. He struggled back up on the stool, feeling as if he had lead weights tied to his feet. Looking down at the laptop's screen, he grimaced when he saw the lines of gibberish his fingers had produced. Having arrived nearly ten hours earlier, and having worked right through lunch, Chin desperately wanted to just close the laptop and go home, but he knew he could not. He had to finish recording his notes and get them uploaded to the file-sharing site Tu Jin had created.

The process results he had started to record on his laptop before he drifted off to sleep proved his concern to be valid. To support his concern, he included the data confirming the four-fold reduction in off-target cleavage at the targeted chromosome position he had obtained by simplifying the CRISPR Cas9 System. He explained that he had selected an enzyme from a different process by mistake. When the mistaken enzyme, a GAAA linker, was added to the process, it acted as a spacer sequence and the two nucleotide chains linked into a single chain. When the artificially created Cas9-sgRNA enzyme was introduced into the target cell, the modified Cas9-sgRNA complex successfully cut the cell's DNA, inducing the desired genomic mutation. When one of the other researchers happened across the same process, as they surely would, the university would be able to create the most lethal bioweapon ever conceived.

Chin believed his documentation thoroughly described and substantiated his premise. At the end of the document, he added the conversation he had overheard in Doctor Zhou's office. He reread the document and corrected several typing errors. Satisfied with what he had typed so far, he began to explain how he believed a Doctor Kenneth Thompson from the United States and whoever else was involved intended to use the new bioweapon soon.

Concentrating on his typing, Chin did not notice the figure that entered silently through the laboratory door and walked up behind him.

Wednesday Jan. 28th – 12:22 a.m. PST
Mueller Residence
Shearwater Lane,
Pajaro Dunes, California

Doctor Robert Mueller, President and Chief Medical Officer of Biogen Pharmaceuticals, leaned against the highly polished, marble-topped bar in his home office. Using his new found wealth, he had purchased the palatial home three months earlier. After his requested upgrades and renovations had been completed, the final price came in at a little over six million dollars. Taking in the exquisite, hand-crafted cherry bookshelves on both sides of the bar, he smiled and thought to himself, "*It was worth every penny.*"

Doctor Mueller lifted two crystal tumblers from a glass shelf, set them down on the countertop, dumped two ice cubes in each one, and poured some very expensive, single-malt scotch whiskey into each tumbler. He grabbed the tumblers and strode across the dimly lit room to the large bank of windows overlooking the Pacific Ocean.

Fifty-one year old Doctor Mueller, owner of fifteen patents at Biogen Pharmaceuticals, had amassed a small fortune. The six million dollar, privately-gated home perched on the cliff above Monterey Bay clearly evidenced his success. Everything he owned was of the finest quality, selected to impress and intimidate. Dressed in worsted wool, gabardine trousers, a midnight blue, cashmere turtleneck sweater, a custom-tailored wool blazer, and finished off with a pair of Italian designer oxford shoes, his wardrobe alone cost more than most people's cars. To Mueller price was of little concern. He was the personification of success and he dressed to prove it.

Another man stood gazing out the panoramic windows at the ocean below. The sound of the waves crashing on the beach drifted in through a partially open window. A full moon hung in the clear black sky like a giant pearl, its light reflecting off the water's rippled surface.

"Beautiful view isn't it," Doctor Mueller said, handing one of the tumblers to the other man.

"Breathtaking would be a better word," Doctor Chandan Chaudhari, Clinical Project Manager for Biogen Pharmaceuticals, answered.

"Well, Doctor Chaudhari, we have business to discuss," Doctor Mueller said, pointing toward the limited edition Eichholtz sofa he had imported from Italy at a cost somewhere above fifteen thousand dollars. Doctor Chaudhari eased down onto the couch, being very careful not to spill a drop of his drink on the elegant fabric.

Doctor Mueller took a seat in a cobalt-blue side chair sitting opposite the sofa. He set his tumbler on a glass-topped side table, leaned forward, and said, "I need to know how the work in Ch'angsha…." Doctor Mueller stopped mid-sentence, hearing a knock on the front door.

"Were you expecting someone else?" Doctor Chaudhari asked.

"No. Stay put. I'll find out who it is."

Doctor Mueller pulled the curtain back to see who had knocked on the door. A look of surprise mixed with disgust clouded his face when he recognized the man standing on the other side of the door. He opened the door and waited for the man to enter.

"Good evening or should I say morning Doctor Mueller," the man said, stepping inside.

"Doctor Thompson," Doctor Mueller greeted, trying to keep the annoyance from showing on his face. "Doctor Chaudhari is in the office. Follow me."

The two men walked through the living room and into the office.

Doctor Chaudhari stood up, offering his hand when the two men entered. "Doctor Chaudhari, this is Doctor Kenneth Thompson. He is Director of Microbiology, Immunology, and Genomics at the Beckman Institute for Cell Engineering. Doctor Thompson is the project broker here in the US." Doctor Mueller winked quickly at Doctor Chaudhari and continued, "Please gentlemen, sit. Doctor Chaudhari, please give us an update on the activities in Ch'angsha."

"I am afraid the project has hit a roadblock. It has… Ah…"

"Out with it, Doctor," Doctor Mueller snapped. "It's late and I have early meetings tomorrow and I imagine Doctor Thompson would like to hear your update and be on his way."

"I am told there is still a problem with the propensity for off-target cleavage," Doctor Chaudhari responded.

"That issue was supposed to have been solved last week," Doctor Thompson exploded. "The first phase is being implemented as we speak. We cannot move on to the next phase until the off-target cleavage issue has been solved."

"Sir, I am aware of that," Doctor Chaudhari answered in defense. "As you know, the introduction of the synthetic Cas9 nuclease enzyme is a highly complex process and must not be hurried. Doctor Zhou informed me they have been unable to mitigate the off-target cleavage. That disrupts the transsection of the DNA sequence, resulting in an unsuitable alteration. When the DNA-binding seed sequence is introduced it completely misses the target recognition region. The end result is that the cell's Brownian motion repair mechanism fails and the mutation becomes uncontrollable."

"Did Doctor Zhou give a timeframe for when he thought they would have a solution?" Doctor Thompson asked.

"No. Not in so many words. He said they are working around the clock but they have limited resources. The researchers must not only be highly educated they must pass a rigorous security screening."

"I do not want to hear any more excuses, Doctor Chaudhari," Doctor Thompson threatened. " I want..."

"But, Doctor Thompson," Doctor Chaudhari interrupted. "The editing and target selection must be approached with extreme care. Only then..."

"That is enough," Doctor Thompson bellowed. "Mister West is furious over these repeated delays. Call Doctor Zhou and inform him this issue must be resolved within three days. If not, I will personally see to it that he is stripped of any and all university positions and I will have him thrown into prison and then I will have Doctor Mueller send you to Ch'angsha to oversee the project. Is that clear?"

"Yes, Doctor Thompson. I will personally call Doctor Zhou and warn him of what will happen if he does not solve the off-target cleavage issue within three days."

"Very well. By end of day tomorrow, I expect to hear that results are being made."

Doctor Thompson turned and headed toward the door. He hesitated, turned toward Doctor Mueller, and said, "A word in private."

Doctor Mueller rose from his chair and followed Doctor Thompson into the living room.

Fifteen minutes later, a door slammed and Doctor Mueller returned to the office.

"Who is Mister West?" Doctor Chaudhari asked.

"He is the Deputy Assistant to President Borden," Doctor Mueller replied.

"And what authority does Doctor Thompson have?"

"He answers directly to *Marduk*, Prince of the Golden Serpent, the only survivor of the Supreme Council of The Illumined Elite. *Marduk* answers directly to Herr Schechter, Eminent Grand Commander of the L'Ordre de la Lumière. You would be wise to follow Doctor Thompson's orders. He has very powerful allies and is not to be trifled with. Eagle said to follow his orders implicitly."

Having been led to believe all members of the Supreme Council had died, Doctor Chaudhari's eyes grew wide with fear upon hearing a name he thought he would never hear again.

"I see it in your eyes. You are surprised to hear he is alive."

"I was told all members of the Supreme Council were killed two years ago during their botched attempt to release the virus they created."

"A necessary deception, Doctor. What I am about to tell you must *never* leave your lips. If you reveal even one word, you will be found floating in the ocean you were so fondly gazing at earlier. Only a very select handful of adherents were allowed to know of his existence. He has now joined with the Committee of 300, the most powerful men in the world. The ten individuals that rule the committee not only have enormous wealth, they can trace their lineages all the way back to the ancient gods, who entrusted Earth's leadership to their offspring. We have a plan and we *will* succeed."

"You said 'we'?" Doctor Chaudhari asked, a puzzled look clouding his face.

"Yes, Doctor Chaudhari, you are correct. I have joined in alliance with the council. This is our opportunity to overthrow their government, to destroy their culture, to destroy their customs, to destroy their Constitution, and finally, to destroy their people. We will destroy everything that is important to the capitalist dogs. I assure you this time our plan *will* work!"

Doctor Mueller had inched closer and closer as he raged, exposing the venom and hatred he carried inside for the very system that had made him not only rich but *very* rich. Doctor Chaudhari slid sideways on the sofa to avoid the spittle that flew out of Doctor Mueller's mouth.

"Are you afraid, Doctor?"

"No, but I have never seen you so angry."

"Well, you should be afraid. Anyone that dares challenge the new order that is coming will be hunted down and executed."

"Understood, but why will your plan work this time? A group of extremely powerful men failed the last time."

"Do you know what a chimera is, Doctor?"

"Yes, from mythology, a chimera is a monstrous, fire-breathing hybrid creature, but from a biological standpoint, a chimera is a hybrid composed of cells from two or more individuals that are genetically distinct, so that the chimera appears as a different individual."

"Correct. The virus that will be created in Ch'angsha will be no ordinary virus. It is only half of the chimera. By its design, it will circumvent every known channel of control. As Doctor Thompson said, the first half is already being spread. To maximize the virus's mobility, the mortality has been minimized, but it is extremely contagious and, therefore, it is easily spread. It will appear deceptively mild for most of its life, mimicking the symptoms of the flu or a common rotavirus. The virus created in Ch'angsha will be the second half of the chimera, provided Doctor Zhou's team can solve the off-target cleavage issue."

"But once it is combined, it will still just be a single virus," Doctor Chaudhari challenged as Doctor Mueller took a sip from his drink.

"Yes, but starting with a virus from the filovirus family, specifically the Marburg virus, Ch'angsha will mutate the virus so that it will attach itself to the first virus and become a totally unknown virus with not only high mortality but also an extremely high mobility. The incubation period for the virus is six to twelve days. Those infected will be contagious without any clinical signs. This is the key to its mobility because it will go entirely unnoticed. Ninety percent of the people who come into contact with an infected individual will be exposed without knowing it. The world's virologists will be totally baffled by its behavior because it will violate the well-known and accepted viral model. You are familiar with the term R-naught, are you not?"

"Of course," Doctor Chaudhari answered. "It is a measure of how many people can typically be infected by one sick person. Most viruses have an R-naught of two point six or less."

"Correct again, Doctor. The chimera virus will be ultra contagious because the mutated virus will be created as a sticky virus. This virus will be able to live outside a person in the air or on surfaces for up to nine days. That will give the chimera virus an R-naught of somewhere around eight. So, one infected person can be expected to spread the virus to eight other individuals. The virus will have an eighty percent infection rate. That means that if one hundred people are exposed, eighty will get sick. We expect that of those who get sick, about ninety percent will get so sick, they will need hospital care. At least half of those will die. Using those estimates, for every one hundred people exposed, thirty-six will die. That is a catastrophic level of contagiousness. We expect that once medical facilities become overwhelmed, the percentage of those that will die will be far higher. This new disease will be an absolute nightmare in its ability to spread. The result will be absolutely horrifying."

Doctor Chaudhari shuddered as the picture of the suffering and death he had just heard described filled his mind. "How will we escape this new disease?" he asked.

"Do not worry, Doctor. We will be inoculated against both virus strains before the final product is released. Would you like your inoculation against the first virus now?"

"Yes, Doctor Mueller, I would," Doctor Chaudhari replied enthusiastically.

"Come over here by the bar."

Doctor Chaudhari rose from the sofa and hurried over to the bar, stripped off his jacket, and started rolling up his sleeve. Doctor Mueller retrieved a doctor's bag from a cabinet in the built-in shelving unit. He set the bag on the bar and took out a syringe and a square packet containing an isopropyl alcohol wipe. From the refrigerator under the bar, he grabbed a small vial of colorless liquid. Doctor Mueller slid the syringe's needle into the vial's rubber seal and withdrew two milliliters of the liquid. After thumping the syringe to remove any air bubbles, he swabbed Doctor Chaudhari's arm, and inserted the needle.

"All done," Doctor Mueller said as he withdrew the needle. "Your arm might be stiff and sore for a few days. I will let you know when it is time for the next inoculation. I believe you know your way out."

Doctor Chaudhari rolled down his sleeve, slipped on his jacket, turned, and headed for the office door. He stopped beside the sofa, gulped down the last swallow of his drink, and set the empty tumbler down on the end table. He exited without saying a word.

Doctor Mueller shook his head as he picked up the tumbler and looked at the water ring on the end table. He walked back over to the bar, set the tumbler down, and grabbed a bar towel. Returning to the end table, he wiped up the water ring. On his way back to the bar, he heard a car engine start up. He stopped and watched Doctor Chaudhari's BMW drive thru the gate and turn left onto Shearwater Lane. The BMW drove a short block, turned left onto Rio Boco Road, and disappeared from sight.

Chapter Two

Wednesday Jan. 28th – 4:47 p.m. ChST
Zhongnan University Xiangya Medical College
Tongzipo Road, Yuelu District
Ch'angsha, Hunan Province, China

Professor Yan Ling Yu tapped Doctor Li on the shoulder and scolded, "Doctor Li, you are late for your meeting with Doctor Zhou. This is the second time this week you have been late for a meeting. Doctor Zhou will be furious. You must hurry."

Chin Li flinched when he heard Professor Yu's voice. He quickly closed the document he was typing, hoping Professor Yu had not been able to read any of the document. He glanced at his watch, shook his head and groaned as he pushed himself up from the lab stool. He snatched his notebook and scurried out the door right on Professor Yu's heels. Both men stopped at the security desk, signed out of the secure lab, and made a beeline for the elevator. Arriving first, Chin Li punched the elevator's Up button. The two men stepped inside as soon as the elevator's doors slid open. Chin Li reached out with his right hand and jabbed the button for the fourth floor multiple times, trying to make the door close sooner. The door closed and he leaned against the back wall.

Neither man said a word as the elevator made its ascent to the fourth floor. The elevator doors slid open and Chin Li and Professor Yu stepped out into the foyer of the fourth floor. The two men hurried past portraits of former Chinese leaders hung on the walls of the dimly lit hallway.

The hallway widened into a larger foyer, with three separate offices opening off of it. The walls of the foyer were covered in matching panels of tight-grain mahogany, giving the room a rich and aristocratic atmosphere, like an elite men's club that Doctor Li would never be allowed to join. Two secretaries' desks faced each other, forming an aisleway leading directly to the door of the office of the Director of Clinical Operations and President of Hunan Medical University.

"Doctor Li," Professor Yu goaded in a low voice. "Straighten your tie and do something with your hair," he advised as they approached the aisleway.

Not taking the time to button the top button of his shirt, Chin Li pulled his tie up tight to his neck and quickly ran his hand through his coal-black hair. Feeling uneasy, as if he were passing through some type of gauntlet, Chin Li took a deep breath, trying to quell the ominous feeling growing deep inside him.

Without knocking, Professor Yu pushed the door open and together both men hurried into the receptionist's office.

"Go right in," advised a well-dressed, young woman in the inner office, sitting behind a large oak desk piled high with stacks of papers. "Doctor Zhou is waiting for you and he is very angry."

Professor Yu tapped three times on the door to Doctor Zhou's office, pushed the door open, and waited for Chin Li to enter. Chin Li took a deep breath and walked into Doctor Zhou's office. Doctor Zhou looked up and scowled, waiting for Professor Yu to enter and push the door shut.

"Professor Yu, please sit," Doctor Zhou said, pointing to a tan side chair sitting at the right side of his desk. "You, Doctor Li, may stand right here in front of the desk."

Doctor Zhou rose, stared directly into Doctor Li's eyes, and said nothing. Doctor Zhen Ping Zhou, fifty-three, tall but slightly stooped, had striking, prematurely white hair. Despite his stooped stature, he exuded a commanding presence. Attired in a long white doctor's coat over green scrubs, with a surgical mask dangling around his neck, he was overdue in surgery and furious that Doctor Li had been late yet again.

Chin Li's heart rate increased and beads of sweat began to glisten on his forehead. Terrified Doctor Zhou might have discovered his sneaking information out of the lab, he pressed his hands against his legs to keep them from shaking. Doctor Zhou placed his hands on the desk and leaned forward, still staring directly at Chin Li. Doctor Zhou's eyes narrowed, anger clouding his narrow, craggy face. Chin Li could feel the sweat running down his neck but he could do nothing about it. Visions of being thrown into prison danced before his eyes.

"Doctor Li, your project is behind schedule," Doctor Zhou shouted. "Phase one has already started. We *must* have a solution from you soon. What is causing the delay?"

Chin Li felt as if he were frozen. Overwhelmed with fear, he stared at Doctor Zhou, his jaw locked, unable to answer.

Doctor Zhou straightened up and walked around the desk, stopping directly in front of Chin Li. "It is answers I want and it is answers I will get," Doctor Zhou bellowed, his face turning red, the veins in his neck bulging.

Chin Li was petrified. He still could not speak. Blood pounded in his ears. He felt dizzy.

"Well, Doctor Li?" Doctor Zhou screamed. "Do I need to replace you? Would you like to be transferred to the sanitation department? I can certainly do that."

Sweat dripped from Chin Li's chin onto his tie. "I am sorry I am late," Chin Li stammered. "I…."

"Professor Yu, get Doctor Li out of here!" Doctor Zhou roared. "I have heard enough of this imbecile's excuses."

Professor Yu jumped up, grabbed Chin Li's shoulder and pushed him toward the door. They had taken only one step when Doctor Zhou reached out, grabbed Chin Li's arm, and spun him around.

"Doctor Li," he seethed. "You will be here in my office tomorrow morning at 8:00 am sharp. Not one minute later. Be ready to describe all your documentation and work papers. The project will be turned over to someone else and you will be terminated and reassigned. Is that clear?"

All Chin Li could do was nod in acknowledgment. Professor Yu pulled the door open and shoved Chin Li through the doorway. Professor Yu grabbed Chin Li's arm and literally dragged him to the elevator.

As the elevator began its descent to the laboratory level, Professor Yu turned toward Chin Li and asked, "What is wrong with you? Why didn't you speak up?"

Chin Li opened his mouth to speak, but simply shrugged and stared at the floor. Upon reaching the laboratory level, Professor Yu pushed Chin Li out of the elevator and directed him to the security station.

"When Doctor Li has gathered his materials, he is to turn his laptop, workbooks, and security access card over to you," Professor Yu informed the security guard. "You will then escort him out of the building."

Professor Yu signed them both in and escorted Chin Li into the lab. He followed Chin Li to the workbench where he had been working.

"I just don't understand," Professor Yu said, shaking his head. "You are a highly skilled researcher and showed much promise. You could have gone far. Oh well, what's done is done. Gather up your workbooks, sign out of any systems you were signed into, then turn everything over to the guard on your way out. When you arrive in the morning, have security call me and I will come and escort you to Doctor Zhou's office. I would suggest that you not be late."

Chin watched as Professor Yu turned and left the lab. Chin slumped down on the stool, dug a handkerchief out of his pocket, and mopped his face and neck. He turned and looked at the laptop, wondering what to do next.

"*Why didn't I speak up*?" he asked himself.

Totally by accident, he had stumbled upon a solution to the off-target cleavage issue. It would be the key that would allow the university to create any number of chimeric viruses. He was absolutely certain of that. If he had spoken up and told Doctor Zhou of his success, he would have been rewarded, and possibly promoted. Instead, he was now headed for some menial, backbreaking job, if he did not end up in some filthy prison. But there was something more than just fear and Doctor Zhou's overbearing personality that had kept him from speaking up.

If he had revealed the solution he had discovered, the bioweapon he had overheard being discussed in Doctor Zhou's office would become a reality. It would be the most lethal virus to ever exist. Upon graduation, he had wanted to go into pediatric research, but university officials had noticed his stellar qualifications. They suggested he apply to Doctor Zhou's virology research team. In China there was no such thing as a suggestion. You did not say no. You simply did as you were told and that was that. Now, his career was over. Chin's thoughts returned to the present and the task of gathering up his materials.

Amazed that Professor Yu had left him alone, he looked around the lab to make certain he was completely alone. Satisfied, Chin opened an internet browser, intending to upload the summary document he had typed earlier and several key work files to the online file sharing service Tu Jin had created. He waited for the browser to connect. Twenty seconds later a dialog box appeared indicating no internet connection. Chin tried two more times with the same result. Doctor Zhou must have already had his network privileges revoked. Once he signed off the server, he would not be able to sign on again.

"What do I do now?" Chin muttered under his breath, knowing he was running out of time. He would have to sign out soon or the security guard would come looking for him. "*What? What? What?*" he screamed silently in his mind, desperation setting in. The notes he had typed fully described the solution he had discovered. He could not leave that behind. He had to get it to Tu Jin. But how? He was out of ideas.

Scanning the lab, he racked his brain for an idea, any idea. "That's it!" Chin exclaimed when his eyes fell on his shoulder bag lying on one of the lab stools. He remembered the USB flash drive he had stashed in one of the bag's interior pockets.

He would have to make a physical copy of the project and hope he could get it to the right people. He pulled the USB flash drive from the pocket and inserted it into the laptop. To protect his prior work, Chin had created a temporary folder for testing his new hypothesis.

Chin opened a file browser, clicked on the project's master directory, and dragged the folder over onto the flash drive. Once the file copy process completed, he verified the file count, making certain all the files had been copied. Inside the master folder, he clicked on the temporary folder, clicked Delete, and then clicked Okay on the warning dialog box. He opened the Recycle Bin and deleted the folder there as well to make certain there would be no record of the solution he had discovered.

After ejecting the flash drive, he removed it and started to slip it back into the pocket inside the shoulder bag but stopped. Concerned the bag would probably be searched as he left, he slipped the flash drive into his sock and pushed it all the way down under his foot. Chin signed off the server, powered down the laptop, and disconnected the network cable.

Chin checked all the drawers and the countertop for any personal items, knowing he would not be returning. After stuffing his few personal items into his shoulder bag, he grabbed the project notebooks and the laptop. Balancing the items with his left hand, he opened the door, and exited the lab. He walked over and set the items on the security guard's desk.

"Ming, here are the items Professor Yu said I should turn over to you."

"Your shoulder bag, please," the security guard said.

Chin slid the strap off his shoulder and handed the bag to the security guard. The security guard took the bag and made a thorough search, inspecting the contents of all its compartments.

"Now, you must stand over here," the security guard ordered.

Chin walked over beside the security station as ordered.

"Sorry, Doctor Li, I am required. Turn out your pockets," the security guard said.

Chin pulled out his left pocket which was empty. His right pocket contained only a few coins. The security guard got up from his chair, walked over beside Chin and patted him down sliding his hand all the way down to his ankles. Believing Doctor Li had no university property, the security guard pointed at the logbook and said, "Sign there."

Chin signed the logbook and waited.

"Follow me," the security guard said, pointing toward the elevator. Up one level, at the east entrance, the security guard looked sternly at Chin and said, "Doctor Li, tomorrow you will not be allowed to enter this door. You must go to the main entrance."

"I understand," Chin answered.

Without another word, Chin turned, exited the building, and started walking down Tongzipo Road toward the metro rail station. As soon as he was out of sight of the university, Chin leaned against a street sign, pushed his sock down, and retrieved the flash drive from under his foot. He placed the flash drive in a pocket inside his shoulder bag and zipped it closed. He flipped his coat collar up to protect him from the cold wind and continued his walk to the Liugoulong metro station. Arriving at the metro station between trains, Chin sat on the cold bench and waited. Nearly frozen, Chin stood up and stamped his feet to stimulate the circulation in his feet. Hearing a train approaching, he stepped over to the loading area and waited for the train to stop. As soon as the last passenger stepped off, he rushed onto the train and its soothing warmth.

Chin located an empty seat and sat down. Before leaving the university, he had decided he was not going to return in the morning. When the university officials realized he was not returning, they would notify the police. Soon after that, the police would show up at his apartment and he would be arrested. If the university discovered he had taken the project data, he would not live long enough to make prison.

Chin felt sick that his decision would also put Min Ju, his wife, in danger. Knowing the Chinese police, he was certain they would refuse to believe she was not involved. Min Ju would be subjected to the same brutal interrogation he would. He vowed he would not allow that to happen. That meant he needed a plan to escape and soon. Chin's mind raced through one possibility after another as the train sped down the track. When the train pulled into the Shuiduhe metro station, the final stop on Line 5, Chin had concocted a plan of sorts. It was not a terribly well-thought-through plan. Fighting panic, he was running on instinct and his instinct told him to flee the city. But where? How? An idea began to form in his mind. Chin thought it might just work, but only if everything went perfectly.

Chin hurried off the train and raced through the Shuiduhe metro station, exiting on the east side of the building onto Wanjiali North Road. He turned east, following Panlong Road. Two blocks to the north he could see the seven-story, four-star Vienna International Hotel. Seeing the hotel, reminded Chin of a happier time three months earlier when he and Min Ju had splurged for their anniversary, spending an entire week's budget to dine there and experience the lavish buffet everyone raved about.

He pushed that thought out of his mind and concentrated on working out the remaining details of his escape plan. Continuing east on Panlong Road, he turned north on Tenghui Road. With the bitterly cold wind blowing against the left side of his face, he slogged another ten blocks and then turned east again on Laodaohe South Road, the final segment of his long journey home. At least he now had the biting, cold wind at his back.

Arriving at the apartment building on Huayuanli Third Street, where he and Min Ju rented a tiny one-bedroom apartment, Chin pushed the door open and entered the building, worried about how Min Ju would react when he explained what had happened at the university. Climbing the stairs to their third floor apartment, he decided the best thing to do was to come right out and tell her, especially considering the escape plan he had concocted would need to begin immediately.

Across the Xiang River on the west side of Ch'angsha, in the Xiangya School of Medicine's computer center, a scheduled control routine opened up and began running comparison algorithms across the university's many servers. Several minutes into the routine, Chin's unauthorized deletion triggered a call to a subroutine that would execute a deeper analysis of the server that stored Chin's project. When that subroutine compared Chin's current work product to his previous day's work product, it exposed a major variance. The subroutine sent a high priority email to the university's laboratory director and to the chief of security and popped up an "Unauthorized Deletion" warning dialog box on one of the screens in the bank of monitors located in the security control room.

Wednesday Jan. 28th – 10:05 a.m.
Rungis International Market
Southern Suburb of Paris France

Ling Jun Dong, pretending to browse the various booths and displays of wares, had worked his way around the entire market. As he walked by, pretending to inspect a particular display, he had squeezed the rubber bulb in his pocket, causing a fine, and barely noticeable, mist to settle upon the display. At the seafood section on the north end of the market, his final stop, squeezing the bulb no longer produced any mist. Having completed his mission, he was eager to return home and collect the large sum of money he had been promised.

As he turned and started toward the market's exit, he was suddenly overcome with an attack of chills. Shivering almost uncontrollably, he leaned against the upright support of a stall lined with white cartons packed with freshly caught shrimp ready to be sold to eager customers. He sneezed repeatedly. A merchant rushed out from behind the stall. Standing as far away as he could, the merchant reached out with a box of tissues, and yelled something in a Chinese dialect that Ling did not understand.

Ling pulled several tissues out of the box and wiped his nose. The merchant yelled again, pointing excitedly toward the exit. Ling nodded his head in understanding and started walking toward the exit.

Still fighting the chills, Ling stopped several times as he made his way toward the exit. The tissues had become completely soaked and useless. He located a trash receptacle two aisles away. He lurched over to the trash receptacle and tossed the tissues, fighting another sneezing fit. Left with no alternative, he wiped his nose and chin on the sleeve of his coat. "*Who cares. I'll buy a new one when I get home,*" he thought.

As he neared the exit, he remembered seeing a restroom on the right side of the exit when he had entered the market. He hurried into the restroom, selected a stall at the far end, and locked the door. Turning his head, he listened for several seconds to see if there was anyone else in the restroom. Hearing no one, he stripped off his jacket and then his shirt. He loosened his belt and pulled the rubber bulb through the hole he had made in the pocket of his trousers. Ling unbuckled the rubber bladder strapped around his chest. He hung the bladder over the hook on the back of the stall door. He pulled on his shirt then his jacket. Hit by another sneezing fit, he rolled off a handful of tissue and sat down.

Shivering violently, he braced himself against the wall of the stall as yet another wave of chills swept over him. He felt as weak as a kitten. The man who had paid him the first installment of his money had promised he would not get sick. The man had jabbed a needle in his arm and pushed in a clear liquid he had called an inoculation. The man had said the shot would protect him. Convinced he could not be affected by the liquid he had dispensed around the market, Ling decided he must have picked up a cold on the flight from Shanghai or maybe the flight from Frankfort.

Instead of returning on the early afternoon flight to Frankfort and then on to Shanghai, Ling decided he would return to the hotel he had stayed in the previous night. He would check in, get some medicine for his cold, and then call the airline and change his flight to an early flight the following morning.

Ready to leave, he listened for activity in the restroom. Hearing the door open and close, he waited. He heard the sound of running water, and then someone pulling paper towels from a dispenser. Once he heard footsteps leaving the restroom, he opened the stall door a crack and peeked out. Seeing no one, he hurried over to the trash receptacle and stuffed the rubber bladder down into the receptacle as deeply as he could.

Standing at one of the sinks, he leaned over and splashed cold water on his face. He pulled two paper towels from the dispenser, dried his face, opened his eyes, and looked in the mirror. Red and puffy eyes stared back at him from a face that looked pale. He wiped his nose on one of the paper towels and noticed a dribble of blood. He felt absolutely horrible. All he could think of was getting to the hotel and climbing into bed under a mountain of blankets.

He shuffled out of the restroom, down the first aisle, and out of the market. Stepping out into the bright sunlight, he squinted, barely able to keep his eyes open. To his surprise, he found no one waiting at the taxi stand. He hurried over, stood beside the sign, and waved at a taxi. The next taxi in the queue roared up to where Ling was standing. Ling opened the door and crawled inside.

"*Novotel Paris Coeur d'Orly, veuillez,*" Ling croaked as another wave of chills swept over him.

"*Oui Monsieur,*" the cabbie answered as he slid the clear plastic window behind him closed.

The cabbie stomped on the accelerator and sped away from the curb. Soon the taxi was speeding down Autostrada 106 toward the Novotel hotel located on the Orly Airport property. After a short, but agonizing, fifteen minute ride, the taxi pulled up to the hotel's front entrance. Ling crawled out and tossed the driver a one hundred Euro note through the open window. While Ling stumbled toward the hotel, the cabbie pulled up to the taxi parking area, grabbed a can of aerosol disinfectant, and sprayed the back seat down until it was dripping wet.

Ling sneezed and again wiped his nose on the sleeve of his jacket. He pushed through the inner door and walked over to the registration desk. Ling had only one thing in his mind: getting some medicine, reaching his room, and crawling into bed.

Wednesday Jan. 28th – 5:25 p.m. ChST
Chin Li Apartment
Huayuanli Third Street
Ch'angsha, Hunan Province, China

"Chin, what have you done?" Min Ju Jiang, Chin Li's wife, wailed after hearing Chin's explanation of what had happened at the university. "You have stolen their data. The university will find out and they will tell the police. They will hunt us down. We will be beaten and we will be sent to prison."

"I am sorry, Min Ju," Chin consoled. "I had no choice. I told you what I overheard in Doctor Zhou's office. What they are planning to do will kill millions of people. I cannot let that happen."

"Chin, you are just a researcher. What Doctor Zhou or the university does with your research is not your responsibility. You only do what they tell you to do."

"But Min Ju, I will know," Chin asserted. "How can I live with myself if I allow millions of people to die. Their deaths will be slow and painful. There will be much suffering. They said doctors will give inoculations for the virus, but to a body's immune system the combined virus will look like a completely different disease. They are lying, Min Ju. I do not believe the inoculations will provide any protection. What about you and me? What about your family and our friends? Do you want to see them suffer?"

"I will tell my family to wear masks."

"But, Min Ju, you do not understand. Doctor Zhou told the doctor from America it will be a sticky virus and it can live on surfaces for over a week. All you have to do is touch an infected surface. It will then be absorbed through your skin."

"Oh, Chin, why would anyone create such a horrible thing?"

"Min Ju, do you not remember the news program we watched about some kind of new order or something? There are very evil men in the world who believe they are smarter than everyone else. They want to reduce the world's population by over one-half."

"I did not believe it. I thought it was just nonsense."

"No, Min Ju, it is all true!" Chin snapped, letting his rising anxiety get the better of him.

"Chin, do not be angry with me," Min Ju sniffled, grabbing for a tissue and dabbing at her eyes.

"I am sorry," Chin apologized. "I am frightened and I am angry. I agree with you. I cannot understand how anyone could do such a thing. Before I left the lab, I promised myself I would not allow this thing to happen. That is why I took the data. I *must* get it to someone that will understand it and will be able to do something to stop those evil men."

"But how can you do that?"

"I have already talked with your cousin, Tu Jin Lam. You remember. He is an epidemiologist in America. He was horrified when I told him what I had overheard in Doctor Zhou's office. I explained the project's off-target cleavage issue. He understood the issue exactly and agreed if my research was successful, it would be the key that would allow them to create the chimera virus. I left early this morning to test a process I believed would solve the issue. Well, my idea failed, but later I made a mistake and I injected a wrong enzyme, but the process worked. Min Ju, if the university had found my work, they would have everything they needed to make this terrible virus. Tu Jin has created a fake account on a file sharing service. When I attempted to upload the explanation of my solution and examples of the data, I could not. My access had already been revoked. I was locked out of the university's systems and could not get back in."

Min Ju's eyes grew wide with terror. "What will you do now? How will you let anyone know?"

"I copied the entire project onto this flash drive," Chin answered, holding up the small, black USB stick. "All the work I completed today I put in a temporary folder. I deleted that folder before I left. Even so, I believe it will only be a matter of time before one of the other researchers discovers the same process. That is why it is so important for me to get this to someone quickly."

"We will run away," Min Ju said. "We must find a way to escape."

"Yes, Min Ju, I agree," Chin responded, nodding his head repeatedly. "I remember at supper two days ago, I think you said your uncle was visiting from America. Is that true?"

"Yes. His mother is very sick. He has been here for several days. I think he is still here. His mother lives here in the apartments. Only two buildings away."

"Great!", Chin burst out. "Then the plan I came up with while I rode the train home might work."

"But Chin, when you do not go to the university in the morning, they will notify the police and they will come looking for you."

"We cannot wait until tomorrow. We must go now. Gather only what you can put in one small suitcase. Hurry, we must go quickly."

"Oh Chin, what about all our things? You have worked so hard. We have just begun to have some nice things."

"We have no choice. We must leave them behind. Come, we must go."

Chin and Min Ju raced into their tiny bedroom. While Min Ju rummaged through the small closet, Chin ran to the chest in the corner and pulled out all the drawers, dumping the contents on the bed. Picking through the pile, Chin separated out the items that he would need for two or three days, limiting them to what would fit into the small suitcase he had pulled from under the bed.

Chin looked up and saw Min Ju holding up the beautiful dress he had given her to wear for their anniversary, the night they went to the fancy, four-star hotel. Chin shrugged, shook his head, and went back to picking through the pile of clothes on the bed. With tears in her eyes, Min Ju let go of the dress, letting it drop onto the floor. She turned back to the closet and continued selecting items. Finished, she dumped the items she had gathered into a small suitcase from the closet.

Chin saw Min Ju struggling to close the suitcase. He stepped around the bed and tried to get the suitcase to close. No matter how hard he pushed, the suitcase just would not latch closed. Chin waited while Min Ju picked through the items and removed one item. He pushed the top down and put all his weight on it while Min Ju closed the latches.

Back on his side of the bed, Chin looked at his pile of selected items and thought it would fit in the suitcase. He shoved the rest of the items on the floor and set the open suitcase on the bed. He crammed his items into the suitcase and mashed the lid down and latched it closed. With the suitcase in hand, he started to leave the bedroom, but stopped when he noticed Min Ju standing at the head of the bed staring at the exquisite, porcelain figurine that had belonged to her mother. The figurine was of a beautiful Chinese woman with long, delicate fingers holding a lotus blossom. The figurine was the only thing Min Ju owned that had belonged to her mother, who had died three years earlier after a short illness.

The despondent look on Min Ju's face broke Chin's heart. Some things were just too much to bear. He set his suitcase down on the bed, unlatched it, and pulled out several items. He gently lifted the figurine off the shelf and carefully wrapped it in one of his shirts and placed it in the middle of his suitcase.

"No, Chin Zheng," Min Ju said, laying her hand on Chin's arm. "You must not. You might need those things."

"I will buy more if I need something," Chin said. "It is the only thing that reminds you of your mother. Please, let us talk no more of it. It is going with us. Come, let us finish. We must go."

Chin closed and latched his suitcase. He grabbed his and Min Ju's suitcases and nudged Min Ju toward the door of the apartment with his shoulder. Min Ju opened the door and stepped into the hallway. Chin followed, stopping halfway out the door. He turned and looked back at their apartment. Five years of their lives lay before his eyes. He shook his head and pulled the door shut.

"Down the back stairs," Chin urged. "Quietly, we must be careful. There are eyes everywhere."

Chin and Min Ju eased slowly down the three flights of stairs being as quiet as they could. Stopping at the back exit leading to the trash bins and parking lot, Chin asked, "Which direction is the building Ning Bo's mother lives in?"

"Two buildings to the south," Min Ju answered.

"Let's go. Stay in the shadows as much as possible."

They exited the building and crossed the parking lot, walking behind the trash bins. At the edge of the parking lot, Chin stopped and looked back at the apartment building. He did not see the curtain in a second floor window swing shut.

Wednesday Jan. 28th – 5:50 p.m. ChST
Zhongnan University Xiangya Medical College
Tongzipo Road, Yuelu District
Ch'angsha, Hunan Province, China

The security guard in the university's security control room sat motionless in a swivel chair before a bank of eight monitors displaying feeds from video cameras monitoring the perimeter of the building. Snoring softly with his feet up on the desk, he was jarred awake by the ringing of the telephone. His feet hit the floor as he scrambled to grab the phone, snatching it from its cradle on the fourth ring.

"Yu Chang, security control room. May I help you?"

"This is Doctor Zhen Ping Zhou. My dinner was interrupted by a warning from the automated server control check routine. Why have I received this alert?"

"Doctor Zhou, the monitors for the university servers are in the other room," the security guard answered. "I will go check them right now."

"Well, be quick about it. My dinner is getting cold," Doctor Zhou yelled into the phone, but it did not matter. The phone was lying on the desk. Yu Chang, the security guard, had already rushed off to the server room to determine what had triggered the alert.

Doctor Zhou grew angrier with each passing minute as he waited for the security guard to return.

"Sir, I have found what triggered the alert," the security guard panted, gasping and out of breath from his run to the control room and back.

"What took you so long?" Doctor Zhou screamed.

"I am sorry, Doctor Zhou," the security guard stammered. "There are eight monitors. They were all asleep. I had to wake each one individually and see if it had an alert on the screen. When I found the one with the alert, I had to open the master panel and..."

"I don't want to hear excuses," Doctor Zhou shouted. "Out with it. Just tell me what triggered the alert. I don't have all night."

"The alert log said there was a suspicious deletion on server ZL6."

"What server is that?"

The security guard grabbed the control notebook lying on the table and flipped it open to the page that listed all the university's servers. He ran his finger down the list until he came to ZL6.

"The control notebook says that server ZL6 houses the databases for the genome editing and nanoparticle research lab and the biolab."

"Who was signed on the server when the deletion took place?"

"The event log indicated there was only one person signed on at that time. A Doctor Chin Zheng Li."

"What?" Dr. Zhou screamed. "Contact security police and have him arrested immediately. Give the police my contact number. I want to be informed immediately when he is arrested."

"Yes sir. I will call them immediately. Is there anything else?"

All the security guard heard was dial tone because Doctor Zhou had already hung up. The security guard reached out and depressed the hook switch to be certain the line was clear. He released the hook switch and punched the number for the Ch'angsha metro police department.

A desk sergeant answered on the second ring. The security guard explained that a university employee had destroyed vital university data and may also have stolen sensitive property. He informed the desk sergeant that Doctor Zhou, Director of Clinical Operations, had requested that Doctor Chin Zheng Li, the person responsible, should be arrested immediately. He informed the desk sergeant that Doctor Li lived in apartment four-zero-seven in building three located on Huayuanli Third Street. The desk sergeant advised the security guard that a patrol car would be dispatched immediately.

The security guard thanked the desk sergeant and hung up the phone. He propped his feet up on the desk and returned to his duty of monitoring the security cameras.

Chapter Three

Wednesday Jan. 28th – 11:02 a.m. CET
Novotel Paris Coeur d'Orly Airport
5 avenue de l'Union
Val-de-Marne, France

Ling Jun Dong reached out and took the key card the hotel's desk clerk held out and slipped it into his front trouser pocket. "*Où puis-je obtenir des médicaments*," Ling Jun asked, suffering from chills and a fierce headache.

"*Dans le couloir à droite*," the desk clerk answered.

Ling Jun grabbed the strap to his shoulder bag and slipped it over his right shoulder. "*Merci*," he mumbled as he turned and headed for the gift shop.

Ling Jun shuffled off, turned right, and headed down the hallway past the elevator to the gift shop located at the end of the hallway. Stopping at the sales counter, he asked the woman sitting beside the cash register where the cold medicines were located. The woman pointed toward the back corner of the shop. Standing in front of a rack full of various types of pills and syrups, Ling Jun scanned the various items. He grabbed the first cold medication he saw, paid for the item, and made his way back to the elevator. He punched the Up button and waited.

Mercifully, the elevator arrived quickly and the doors slid open. He stepped into the elevator, jabbed the button for the fifth floor, and leaned back against the wall. The elevator arrived at the fifth floor without making any stops. Ling Jun pushed himself off the wall and exited the elevator. Directly in front of him a sign advised that his room was down a hallway to his left.

Standing in front of the door for room five-twenty-one, he jammed the key card into the reader. A green light above the door handle came on and he heard a loud click. He pushed the handle down and shoved the door open. He stumbled into the room, tossed his shoulder bag on the bed, and rushed off to the bathroom in search of a glass. Desperate to get the cold medicine into his system, he grabbed a glass off the counter and tore off the protective paper wrapping. He held the glass under the faucet, filled it with water, and set it back down on the counter. Ripping at the package of cold medicine like a madman, he tore the box into pieces, scattering the contents on the floor. He kneeled down, picked up one of the cards lined with capsules, and punched out two of the large green capsules.

Shaking violently, he slopped water all over himself as he downed the capsules. There was only one thing left to do before he could crawl into bed. He still had to call the airline and change his flight to early tomorrow morning. He left the bathroom, walked over to the table, picked up the phone, and dialed the airline. Interrupted twice by sneezing fits, he finally managed to communicate with the airline representative and get his flight changed.

Feeling woozy, he put his hand on the table to steady himself. He felt hot and disoriented. Never in his entire life had he felt so miserable. Putting the back of his hand to his forehead, he thought this had to be more than just a cold. Far more. But the man that had promised him the money had said the shot he gave him would protect him and he would not get sick. "*If that were true why do I feel so sick*," he wondered. Ling Jun had made a terrible mistake when he took the word of another criminal. Not only did the injection not contain any protection against the virus he had spread, it contained a substance that had quickly destroyed his body's immune system.

Ling Jun was certainly not the sharpest pencil in the drawer, wasting the first two years of high school while failing the majority of his classes. Dropping out of high school early in his junior year, Ling Jun found the quick and easy money gained from crime much more to his liking. Starting his life of crime as a small-time thief, he had quickly morphed into a sadistic animal. He had risen quickly, becoming a major player in the sordid underworld of Shanghai, not because of his intelligence but because of his propensity for violence. Ling Jun had put two of his criminal associates in the hospital for nothing more than a simple, perceived slight. Anyone that knew Ling Jun feared him and with good reason.

Failing every science class he ever had, Ling Jun was ignorant of even the simplest concepts of science. It was that ignorance that likely put him in the horrible situation he now found himself. The man that had given him the shot, had told him to be careful handling the liquid when he filled the bladder. Ling Jun had barely listened, his mind fixed on the large sum of money he had been promised. The man had tried to explain what the liquid was and why it was dangerous, but Ling Jun had no idea what he was talking about. So, he had quit listening.

Ling Jun had quickly agreed to take the job and had picked up the liquid and the rubber bladder. Ecstatic with the first payment in his pocket, he had rushed home and placed the materials on the rickety table in what his landlord called a kitchen. Ling Jun had stared at the crystal clear liquid in the container, wondering how it could be dangerous. Not having listened to what the man had said, he had screwed off the lid and sniffed at the liquid. It did not smell bad. While filling the bladder he had made the worst mistake of his life, sloshing some of the liquid onto his hands and onto the table. Wiping his hands on his trousers, Ling Jun had laughed, thinking the man must be stupid to pay such a huge sum for such a simple job, but the sum of money was huge so he would do as the instructions said.

Ling Jun staggered and fell against the bed, sinking to his knees. With great difficulty, he pushed himself up and staggered into the bathroom. Leaning over the sink, he splashed cold water on his face. He grabbed a washcloth, dampened it, and mopped his face. Looking in the mirror, he groaned in horror. His face was ashen and pale. His eyes were red and puffy and so swollen they looked like mere slits. He felt nauseous and dizzy. Squinting because the bright light blinded him, he staggered and fell hard against the wall. Losing his balance, he cried out in pain, turned, and reached out for something to keep him from falling. Blinded by the tears in his eyes, he snagged the shower curtain instead of the wall. The curtain rod ripped loose from the wall, scattering curtain rings and screws onto the floor.

Ling Jun, still grasping the shower curtain, fell into the bathtub with a loud thump. He moaned and tried to get out of the tub. A sudden, uncontrollable spasm contorted his body as he was racked with another round of intense chills. With what little strength Ling Jun had left, he struggled and managed to slip his left arm out from under his body. He grabbed one corner of the shower curtain, pulled it over himself, and drifted off into unconsciousness.

Early the next afternoon, housekeeping would discover his stiff, dead body, a victim of his own ignorance and greed.

Wednesday Jan. 28th – 5:09 a.m. EST
Adam West Residence
Fulton Street NW
Washington, DC

A sprawling three-story home on Fulton Street NW, overlooking Palisades Park, stood out from the rest of the houses along the street. The enormous pie-shaped, half-acre lot, the largest on the street, was immaculately manicured. Even in the dead of winter, the landscape, designed by one of Washington DC's leading landscape architects, was stunning. The distinctive bark and vibrant berries of the ornamentals along with the colorful evergreens stood out against the dazzling white blanket of snow that had fallen overnight.

All was quiet inside the seven thousand, nine hundred square foot house, sunrise still nearly two hours away. In the master bedroom, located on the southeast corner of the second floor, the ringing of a cellphone interrupted the quiet. Adam West groaned as he slipped his arm out from under the down comforter. Annoyed by the early-morning disturbance, he grabbed the ringing cellphone off the nightstand, intending to reject the call and go back to sleep. Jolted awake upon seeing the caller's name on the cellphone's display, he swiped the screen and said, "Why are you calling so early?"

"What is it?" his wife mumbled.

"It's just business," Adam West answered, covering the cellphone with his hand. "Go back to sleep. I'll take it in the study."

"Hang on. I'm on the way to my study."

He threw the comforter aside and slid his legs out of bed, easing his feet into the lambs-wool slippers sitting beside the bed. Without turning a light on, he stepped out into the hallway and eased the bedroom door shut. With his hand against the wall for guidance, he made his way down the hallway and into his study. He turned on the light and pushed the door shut.

"Why are you calling so early?" West grumbled, glancing at the desk clock. "You are never to call me unless it has been arranged in advance."

"I know," Doctor Robert Mueller protested in defense. "I believe this is important enough to call you immediately. We have a problem. Doctor Zhou just called me. He believes there might have been a leak."

"A leak," West shouted. "How could that happen. They have sophisticated containment systems. Doctor Zhou assured us that a leak could not happen."

"No. No," Doctor Mueller responded. "Not a leak of the virus. He is worried that someone, a Doctor Chin Li, has stolen project data."

"What makes Doctor Zhou think that?"

"Earlier in the afternoon Doctor Zhou reprimanded Doctor Li for being late to meetings and for poor quality work. Doctor Zhou informed Doctor Li he would be reassigned to a menial position. Forty-five minutes later Doctor Li exited the lab and turned in his laptop and all project notebooks. A security guard searched him and escorted him out of the building."

"If the guard searched Doctor Li and found nothing, why is Doctor Zhou worried?" West questioned.

"Doctor Zhou received an automated alert from the university's computer system later in the evening. The security guard said a scheduled check routine detected an unauthorized deletion from the server that housed the project on which Doctor Li worked."

"Go on."

"Doctor Zhou called the on-duty database administrator and instructed him to do a deeper analysis of the affected database. A few minutes later, when the administrator called him back, he said the amount of data deleted was quite large. Doctor Zhou said it would likely represent an entire day's work."

"Can we recreate the data that was deleted?"

"No. I asked Doctor Zhou that. He said the discrepancy routines only track file sizes. His excuse was that to track at a deeper lever would require huge amounts of storage."

"Imbeciles," West muttered under his breath. "Well, can we at least determine what he was working on?"

"From what Doctor Zhou told me all they can tell is that he worked in the level-four biolab for nearly the whole day. Doctor Zhou also said that employee internet usage reports indicated that Doctor Li attempted to make an internet connection just before he exited the lab."

"So, Doctor Li tried to connect to an internet site and couldn't. Then he deleted a large amount of data."

"Why would he delete data?" Doctor Mueller asked.

"Think about it, Doctor. He spent most of the day in the biolab. He deleted a large amount of data because he did not want anyone to see it. We must assume he was successful in mutating the target virus and he then deleted the record of that. Flash drives are very small and easily concealed. Was Doctor Li strip searched?"

"I do not believe so."

"Then, we must also assume he might have had a copy of that data on him when he exited the lab."

Doctor Mueller audibly groaned at the thought of that data getting into the wrong hands."

West continued, "Has Doctor Zhou called the police to find Doctor Li?"

"Yes," Doctor Mueller replied. "He said as soon as the deletion was discovered, the security guard called the Ch'angsha Metro Police."

"All we can do is wait," West remarked. "I need not tell you what will happen if that data were to fall into the wrong hands."

"I am fully aware."

"Call Doctor Zhou and inform him the Ch'angsha Police are not to harm him. He is to be searched and interrogated. We must find out if he has contacted anybody. Doctor Zhou is to call you the instant the Ch'angsha Police have him in custody. Understood?"

"Yes, sir, I will call him immediately."

West ended the call and dropped the cellphone on his desk. He walked behind his desk and stepped to the window that overlooked Palisades Park. In the distance, just beyond the park, he could see the lights of Georgetown Cemetery. To his right he could already see a long line of cars building as they headed down McArthur Boulevard toward the city. Worried about the latest development, he turned and paced back and forth between the desk and the window. To be prepared, he would need to start damage control in case the data had already leaked out.

"How could they be so careless," he snarled, stomach acid backing up in his throat. Knowing it was going to be a very bad day, trying to get back to sleep would be useless. He decided he just as well get dressed, head into work, and face Eagle, but first he needed to get his acid reflux under control. If it got any worse, he would end up with a full-blown ulcer. He turned off the light and headed toward the bathroom for some antacid tablets.

West swore and slammed one drawer after another in the bathroom vanity as he searched in vain for the antacid tablets.

"What's the matter, Adam?" his wife asked, having been awakened by the slamming of drawers.

"Sorry," Adam West scowled. "Where are the antacid tablets? I can't find any."

"I just bought some more yesterday," his wife answered. "I haven't brought them up from downstairs. They're still down in the kitchen. I'll go get some."

"Never mind, hon. I'll go down and get them. As wide awake as I am I'll never get back to sleep. So, I'm going to go into work early. I'll start the coffee before I come back up to get dressed. Why don't you just go back to bed."

"Okay. Adam, you really need to do something about your acid reflux. You know what the doctor said."

'Yeah, I know. Maybe next week."

He walked over and kissed his wife on the cheek and headed for the kitchen down on the first floor.

"There're in the cabinet by the garage door. On the bottom shelf," his wife called out to his disappearing back.

West walked into the kitchen and flicked on the light. Barefooted, he padded across the gleaming white oak floor to the coffee station at the side of the kitchen. He punched the coffee brewer on, turned, and walked over to the counter closest to the entrance from the garage.

"*Which cabinet*," West wondered as he stood in front of the bank of custom crafted cabinets. Starting at the first cabinet on the left, he swung open the door.

"Well, that's not it," he grumbled, seeing his distorted reflection in the stainless steel mixing bowl sitting on the middle shelf. He closed the door and tried the next cabinet in line. "Nope. Not that one either," he complained, finding a cabinet filled with assorted sizes of drinking and wine glasses.

"Finally," he snapped.

Just as his wife had said, sitting on the bottom shelf were two bottles of antacid tablets. He snatched one, twisted off the lid, ripped off the seal, dumped two tablets out into his hand, and tossed the tablets into his mouth. Making a face of disgust, he chewed the chalky tablets as he walked back over to the coffee brewer.

Making quick work of adding coffee grounds and water to the brewer, he punched the Brew button and headed back upstairs to get dressed.

Reaching the top of the stairs, he started down the hallway but stopped when he thought he heard a floorboard creak. He stepped backward, then stepped forward again, and there it was again. Already angry from the earlier phone call, he vowed he would call the builder and demand he return to fix the floor. A brand new house should not have squeaky floors. Shaking his head, he continued on to the bedroom to get dressed.

Twenty minutes later West emerged from the bedroom dressed in a black Brioni, hand-tailored, virgin wool suit that cost more than most people's salary for an entire a month, a perfectly knotted red silk tie drawn up tight to the collar of an Alan David custom-tailored white shirt, and completed with a pair of twelve hundred dollar black Ferragamo loafers, polished to a high sheen.

Anxious to be on his way, he hurried down the stairs, grabbed his travel mug, and poured it full of coffee. Rather than sitting and reading the morning newspaper like on a normal morning, he decided he would grab the newspaper on the way out and read it at work if he had the time. He switched the coffee pot off and exited the kitchen into the garage.

He tapped the control that raised the garage door. Bending over slightly, he slipped under the partially-open door and retrieved the newspaper. Back in the garage, he slipped into his car, inserted the key into the ignition, and started the engine. He shifted the car into Reverse, backed out, and pressed the garage door remote clipped to the sun visor. Once in the street, he shifted the car into Drive and roared off down the street.

West loved the look and feel of the Dark Emerald Green CT5-V Blackwing, the most powerful Cadillac luxury sedan ever built. Normal individuals could only dream of owning this sedan aka sports car because of its extremely limited availability. When Adam West, Deputy Assistant to the President of the United States, had walked into a local Cadillac dealership, the owner had scrambled out of his office, promising him anything he wanted. "No obstacle is too great. We will find you the exact model you want in the color you want," the dealership owner had quickly promised. Three weeks later, as promised, the Dark Emerald Green CT5-V Blackwing was delivered right to Adam West's door with a full tank of fuel.

West cruised down Fulton Street NW, turned left onto Dana Place NW, and two blocks later stopped at the traffic signal. When the light turned green, he made a quick left onto MacArthur Boulevard and pressed down hard on the accelerator, the tires squealing in protest.

Seeing the speedometer reach sixty miles per hour, West eased off the accelerator, not wanting to get a ticket. He inhaled deeply, smelling the rich aroma of the expensive leather interior. He allowed his speed to drop to the posted limit as he settled in for the five mile, twenty-plus minute ride to the White House.

Gripping the car's steering wheel tightly in his hands, he could feel the restrained power of the CT5-V. West's luxury vehicle and his impeccable, and expensive, wardrobe bespoke of the power of the office he held. Literally, he felt himself to be the fourth most powerful man in the United States, and like most extremely powerful men, he used that power for self-advantage, and, in many cases, for illegal purposes. West smiled as he veered left onto Reservoir Road NW, halfway to his destination.

Wednesday Jan. 28th – 6:16 p.m. ChST
Ning Bo Chai Apartment
Huayuanli 3rd Street
Ch'angsha, Hunan Province, China

Chin Zheng Li and Min Ju Jiang reached the apartment building Min Ju's uncle lived in. Pausing at the edge of the building to catch their breath, they huddled together in the cold, frightened and near panic. Chin shoved Min Ju further back into the shadows when he heard police sirens in the distance. Chin stepped back and leaned forward, peering around the corner of the building. Fearing they had been found out, his heartbeat raced and his mouth felt as dry as dust. Flashing blue light lit up the sky behind the trees lining the street. The wailing sound of the sirens grew louder and louder.

Chin sucked in his breath when he saw two police cars emerge from behind the trees and skid around the corner. His first thought was to run, but where? He knew they could not outrun the police cars. He reached out and grabbed Min Ju's hand, believing they were doomed.

The police cars roared past the building and disappeared from sight, their sirens growing fainter. Shaking like a leaf, Chin slumped back against the building and slid down the wall until he was sitting on the cold ground. Sucking in deep gulps of air, slowly his heart rate began returning to normal as his body burned off the flood of adrenalin coursing through his bloodstream.

"Chin, we must go," Min Ju urged. "We will be suspicious just standing here. Hurry. We must get inside the building."

"You are right, Min Ju," Chin answered, pushing himself up off the cold, frozen ground.

He took Min Ju's hand and, together, they sprinted around the corner and raced into the building.

"Which floor," Chin asked, puffing and out of breath.

"Fourth floor. Apartment number fourteen."

Chin stopped at the bottom of the stairs, looked up, and groaned, wondering if he had enough strength left to climb up three flights of stairs. In China, only the wealthy lived in buildings that had elevators. He inhaled deeply and slowly blew out the air. Motioning to Min Ju to follow, he started up the stairs.

Using the railing, Chin literally pulled himself up the last six steps. His muscles burned as much from the effects of the adrenalin as from the physical exertion. Also breathing hard, Min Ju reached the top of the stairs.

"Which way now?" Chin asked.

"That way," Min Ju responded, pointing to her left. "The next to last apartment on the right."

Chin and Min Ju walked softly down the hallway, stopping in front of the door to apartment number fourteen. Chin reached out and rapped on the door. Receiving no response, Chin rapped harder. After a few seconds, he could hear footsteps approaching the still closed door.

"Who is it?" a male voice called out from the other side of the closed door.

"It is Min Ju, your niece, and my husband Chin Zheng," Min Ju replied.

The door swung open and a slightly built, older man, in his late fifties, with a narrow, weathered face stood waiting for Chin and Min Ju to enter. He was casually dressed, wearing faded jeans and a one-size-too-large sweater. The man had a shock of deep black hair hanging over his forehead that frequently needed to be pushed up out of his face or snapped back with a sudden toss of his head. Surprised by his visitors, he said, "Min Ju, I did not expect you. Come in."

"Thank you, Ning Bo," Min Ju said as she and Chin stepped inside the apartment.

"You look as if you had seen a ghost," Ning Bo commented when he looked over at Chin. "What is the matter?"

"It is a long story," Chin answered. "May I have a glass of water please?"

"Of course. You and Min Ju come into the living room and sit down. I will get water for both of you."

Ning Bo turned and hurried into the apartment's tiny kitchen. A few seconds later he returned with two large glasses of water and set them on a small table sitting in front of the dilapidated old couch where Chin and Min Ju were seated.

"You must excuse the mess," Ning Bo said. "As you know my mother is terribly sick. She requires much care. I am not able to keep up."

Chin nodded understanding as he reached out and picked up one of the glasses. He had difficulty holding the glass to his mouth his hands were shaking so badly. He swallowed several large mouthfuls of water and set the glass back on the table, nearly knocking over the other glass of water.

"Chin you must tell me what has you so scared."

Chin took two large breaths and asked, "How much do you know about the CRISPR-Cas9 gene editing process?"

"I believe I understand its basic concepts. I am a charge nurse on the vascular surgery floor of New York Presbyterian Hospital. I remember seeing a report about it on the television."

"That is great," Chin said excitedly, knowing the story he had to tell would be somewhat easier to explain. He inhaled deeply and began the explanation of what had brought him and Min Ju to his apartment. Ning Bo stopped Chin several times during his explanation and asked questions about the process of combining and editing the chemically modified, nucleotides.

Chin stopped his explanation and took another drink of water. About to continue, Ning Bo interrupted, "I am afraid I do not understand. Please explain again about what you called a chimera."

"When I overheard Doctor Zhou and an American Doctor by the name of Kenneth Thompson talking, their…"

"Doctor Kenneth Thompson," Ning Bo blurted out, a look of utter shock on his face. "I can't believe it. I know that name. He is a leader in the immunology and genomics field. He is one of the most respected doctors in America."

"Yes, I am certain it is him," Chin continued. "I see him many times. He hurries in the back entrance and always goes straight to Doctor Zhou's office. As I was saying, their plan is to increase the lethality of the new virus they intend to create. Doctor Zhou said the behavior of the virus will be designed so that it will circumvent all normal channels of control. They will do that by separating the chimera into two phases. I believe the spreading of the first phase may have already begun. The first virus is extremely contagious but shows no outward symptoms for seven to ten days."

"How is this virus to be spread," Ning Bo asked, sitting on the edge of his chair.

"Sorry, I do not know," Chin answered. "I have not heard anyone talk about that. Very likely they would use some kind of aerosol dispersal in a crowded public place. As contagious as the virus is, it will spread like a wildfire especially if it is released where there are a high number of international travelers. By the time the first symptoms begin to show, it will have already spread around the entire world. Any vaccine they attempt to engineer would be totally ineffective. The two viruses will combine to create the chimera. It will contain the attributes of both viruses and when combined it will be *completely* unknown to the body's immune system. The chimera will have extreme mobility *and* extreme mortality. Ning Bo, this new disease will be unspeakable! Millions of people will die!"

"Chin, that is terrible," Ning Bo exploded. "Have you told anyone?"

"Yes," Chin replied, "I had contacted Min Ju's cousin, Tu Jin Lam. He's an epidemiologist in the United States. He gave me a login to a file sharing site. I shared only some basic project descriptions and preliminary test results, but I never heard from him again. I dared not tell Doctor Zhou that I had discovered a method to link the second virus. He got very angry because I had made no progress. He said he was going to transfer me to some menial position. When I got back to the lab to gather my things, I found out my internet access had already been revoked. I could not allow the method I found to be discovered. I copied the entire project folder onto a flash drive. Then I deleted the folder that contained today's work."

"Chin, they will find out," Ning Bo gasped. "You will be arrested and beaten. Then they will throw you into prison. And what about Min Ju?"

"I know," Chin responded. "but I had no choice. That is why Min Ju and I are here. Doctor Zhou and the others must not find out about what I learned today. Someone must stop them. You must help me get this information to Tu Jin or to someone who can prevent this madness."

"What can I do? I am only a nurse."

"But surely you must know someone," Chin pleaded.

"Well," Ning Bo responded, his eyes gazing up at the ceiling while his mind searched through his acquaintances, trying to identify anyone that might be able to help. "Maybe… Ah… No, I can't use him."

"Who are you talking about? Can he help?"

"Someone I treated when I served as a hospital corpsman aboard a Navy frigate. An officer reinjured his ankle very badly. We became friends when I directed his physical therapy. Three months of intense physical therapy did not help. Left with no choice he accepted a medical discharge."

"Why can't you ask him?" Chin pleaded. "Do you know where he is?"

"That officer left the Navy and went into politics. He was very successful. He became President of the United States."

"The President!" Chin exclaimed, a stunned look of disbelief on this face. "Is that really true?"

"Absolutely. It is all true." Ning Bo asserted.

"Do you think you could reach him?"

"I doubt it, but I do know someone that I think might be able to reach him. He is an admiral in the Navy. His name is Admiral Charles Hadley. He knows lots of important people."

"That is great. I typed a document and had it ready to send to Tin Ju but found my internet access revoked. It is on the flash drive with the rest of the project notes, test results, and also the full sequence of the process I discovered that would allow Doctor Zhou and the others to create the monster virus. I beg you. You must help me get this information to someone that can stop this."

"After hearing what you have described, I agree with you. We must get this information to Admiral Hadley."

"Yes. Yes. As soon as possible," Chin urged. "How do we contact this admiral?"

"First, we must make a copy of this data for safekeeping," Ning Bo remarked. "Do you have this flash drive with you?"

"Yes, Ning Bo, here it is," Chin answered as he smiled, pushed his sock down, and slipped out the flash drive.

"Very good," Ning Bo said. "My laptop is in the bedroom. I will get it and we will make a copy. Then I will see if I have the Admiral's number in my Seldom Used contacts list."

Ning Bo rose from his chair and disappeared into the bedroom. Chin, his hands shaking less, grabbed the glass of water and took another long drink. He set the glass down and looked up at Min Ju. She reached out and took Chin's hand.

"I am very proud of you, Chin Zheng Li. Many other men would have done as Doctor Zhou ordered and allowed many innocent people to die."

Chin turned and kissed the wife he loved so dearly. He hugged her tightly and whispered in her ear, "I love you my beautiful, Min Ju." Chin held the embrace tightly as Min Ju's shiny black hair caressed his face. He could smell the slightly sweet fragrance of jasmine blossoms and coconut that came from her shampoo.

"Chin, we have work to do," Ning Bo advised as he stepped back into the living room. "Quit smooching your wife. Come, sit at the table. We will make a copy of the flash drive."

Chin kissed Min Ju's cheek, rose from the couch, and joined Ning Bo at the kitchen table. Chin watched as Ning Bo inserted the flash drive into one of the empty USB ports, created a new folder on his hard drive, and began the copy process. Both men watched as the progress bar slowly crept toward one hundred percent. Three minutes passed. The copy process completed and the dialog box disappeared. Ning Bo ejected the flash drive and removed it from the USB port.

Ning Bo grabbed the computer bag he had laid on the table and dug around inside. He pulled out a blank flash drive, shoved it into the empty USB port and reversed the process. As soon as the copy process completed, he ejected and removed the second flash drive. Guiding the mouse pointer over the new folder he had created, he clicked on it. About to press the Delete key, he moved the mouse pointer to an open application and typed furiously for thirty seconds, completely ignoring his spelling errors. Without taking the time to proofread, he clicked several icons and then exited the application. He clicked on the temporary folder he had created, pressed the

Delete key, double-clicked the Recycle-Bin icon, and also deleted the folder there to be certain the data Chin had smuggled out of the university existed nowhere but on the two flash drives.

"Now, we have only your flash drive and this backup flash drive," Ning Bo advised, slipping the newly copied flash drive into his pocket. He turned back to the laptop, opened his Seldom Used contacts list, and started scrolling down through the entries. "Here it is," he remarked with surprise. "Admiral Hadley's number is here. It is only five in the morning in Washington, DC, where the admiral lives, but I know he is an early riser. I will call him right now."

Ning Bo lifted his cellphone off the kitchen counter and tapped in the number listed in his contacts file. After double checking the number, he tapped the call button and waited. The phone on the other end rang five times and then went to voice mail. Ning Bo frowned and hung up.

"I will try the admiral later," Ning Bo said. "Now, we must decide on a way to get you and Min Ju to safety. It must be immediately. Once the university finds out what you have done, they will call the police. All the airports and metro and bus stations will be notified. There will be no way out."

"What will we do then?" Chin quavered. "We *must* get this information to someone who can help."

Ning Bo's brow furrowed as his mind raced, trying to think of a way to get Chin and Min Ju safely out of China. He shook his head, grimaced, and grunted "I don't know. I just don't know."

Ning Bo leaned over and stared at the floor. Abruptly, he straightened up and looked at Chin. "The only way I can think of is to drive you to Hong Kong myself. I know someone there that may be able to sneak you out of the country."

"But I have no money," Chin exclaimed.

"That is no problem. The man owes me a favor. I will call my brother to come and sit with my mother. Quick, get Min Ju ready. I will try the admiral one more time. Then we must leave."

Ning Bo jumped up to his feet and hurried into the bedroom. He kissed his mother's forehead, fished his cellphone out of his pocket, and made two quick, and very short phone calls. Ending the last call, he walked over to a small closet and grabbed his coat.

"Come on, let's go," Ning Bo urged as he returned to the living room. "Now, before the police come."

Chin grabbed Min Ju's hand and the three of them left the apartment and headed for the stairs. They reached the bottom of the stairs and raced to the building's front door. Upon opening the door, they stopped dead in their tracks, hearing the sound of screaming sirens. Three police cars roared into the parking lot and screeched to a stop. Six officers piled out of the cars and rushed toward the building.

"I'm sorry Min Ju," Chin said with tears in his eyes.

"Chin, take Min Ju and go out the back door," Ning Bo ordered. "Run through the woods. If I can, I will contact you later. I will try to hold off the police as long as I can. Go Now. Hurry!"

Wednesday Jan. 28th – 5:38 a.m. EST
Hadley Residence
Wisconsin Avenue, Unit 1101,
Chevy Chase, Maryland

Rear Admiral Charles Hadley, retired, opened his eyes in the semi-darkness and stared at the swirling shadows dancing on the ceiling of his condo's first floor bedroom. For over an hour, he had tried to get back to sleep but had failed. After many long years of rolling out of bed at zero five hundred, his body had become conditioned to wake up at the appointed time.

Admiral Hadley stretched, letting his arm fall on the opposite side of the bed. The emptiness his arm found reminded him of his much-loved wife, Jean, gone now for just over a year. Despite the passage of thirteen months, the terrible emptiness still lingered, especially at night during the quiet. Jean had suffered horribly during the last few months of her life as cancer ravaged her body. During the last two weeks of her life, Admiral Hadley had spent all his waking hours sitting at her bedside as she grew weaker and more frail. On the day she breathed her last breath, he had held her hand and wept for a long time. He knew she had been released from the pain of this life and was in the arms of her Blessed Savior. He tried to focus his mind on that assurance but still the deep sense of loss hovered over him like a dark thunder cloud.

Returning from his sad reverie of the past, he rolled over and picked up his cellphone from the headboard. He squeezed the power button to awaken the display. The display indicated five thirty-eight AM. He noticed a voicemail icon at the top edge of the display. Accustomed to receiving many voicemail messages, he turned off the display, peeled back the covers, and swung his legs over the edge of the bed. Sitting there in the semi-darkness with his elbows on his knees, he stared at the floor, praying silently that today would not be the same emotional rollercoaster ride as the previous day, and too many days before, had been. For Admiral Hadley living without his beloved wife, a good day was defined as one that was just less bad.

He pushed himself up from the bed and stretched again to relieve his stiff muscles. Barefooted, he plodded over to the south window, eased back the drapes, and peered out at the pool eleven stories below. Rather than reflections from sparkling water, the admiral saw the black canvas cover stretched tightly across the pool. An arctic cold front had moved in overnight, but so far, it had only deposited a thin skiff of snow which was being blown around by a strong north wind. If the weatherman was correct, there was much more to come.

Hoping the weatherman was wrong, the admiral let go of the drapes. Stopping at the foot of the bed, he eased his feet into a pair of old, worn slippers, and headed toward the kitchen to make some much-needed coffee.

Admiral Hadley flicked the hall light on, squeezed past a jumble of partially-filled boxes, and walked down the hallway. Stopping at the thermostat, he raised the temperature two degrees. Continuing on into the kitchen, he flipped the light switch on and headed for the coffee maker sitting at the far end of the counter. Several cabinet doors stood open, having been emptied of their contents. Pushing a stack of packing paper aside, Admiral Hadley loaded the coffee maker with grounds, poured in water, and punched the On button.

Admiral Hadley dropped two pieces of bread into the toaster and pushed the lever down. Becoming even more depressed, he could hardly believe his eyes as he looked at the disarray. Half-filled boxes, stacks of dishes, rolls of tape, and piles of trash were scattered everywhere. Shaking his head, he thought the room looked in as much disarray as his life.

After months of insistence from his son, the admiral had finally agreed the time had come to sell the condo. He could no longer argue against the reasons his son gave him: the condo was too big for him, it contained too many memories, having been forced to retire he no longer had any need to remain in the Washington, D.C., area, and Florida's great weather.

Rather than just stand at the counter and wait for the toast to pop up and the coffee to brew, he walked into the living room, stopped by the front closet for a robe, then opened the front door to get the morning newspaper. He grabbed the newspaper lying in front of his door, stepped back inside, and pushed the front door closed. Dropping the robe on the couch as he passed by, he walked back into the kitchen. The toast was up and ready. He grabbed butter from the refrigerator, slathered it onto the toast, placed the toast on a small plate, and set the plate on the small table that sat in the breakfast nook. At the coffee maker, he filled his favorite mug with the steaming brew, returned to the table, and sat down. He blew across the hot coffee, steam curling up into the air.

After taking a careful sip of the hot coffee, Admiral Hadley slid the newspaper out of its pink, protective bag. Unfolding the newspaper, he laid it out flat on the table, and began reading. Fifteen minutes later, the toast finished and only a swallow of lukewarm coffee remaining in the mug, Admiral Hadley pushed the empty plate aside. Rather than deal with the mess in the kitchen, he decided to clear out his voicemail messages.

He refilled his mug with coffee, picked up his cellphone from the counter, and headed into the living room. Seated on the couch, he tapped the phone app icon, and selected the voicemail entry from his contacts list. After the automated spiel completed, he tapped in his pin number and waited.

"Six voicemails," Admiral Hadley blurted out, shaking his head.

He tapped One on the cellphone's on-screen keyboard and began listening. One by one he listened to the voicemail messages while sipping his coffee, occasionally pressing Seven to delete a message. When the cellphone began playing the sixth, and, final message, Admiral Hadley's hand stopped halfway to his mouth. He set the coffee cup down and concentrated on the message. The voice recorded in the voicemail was so excited he could only understand a few words. As the message concluded, Admiral Hadley saved the voicemail so he could listen to the message again.

After listening to the message three more times, he could not recognize the voice and still only understood a few words. He listened two more times, grabbed a pad of paper from the side table's drawer, and wrote down the few words he could understand: horrible - *?????*, *?????* - dead, crisper – *?????*, the name *?????* Thompson, *?????* - mile or maybe file, and something that sounded like a website name.

Admiral Hadley exited the voicemail system. Returning to the phone app, he tapped Recents and looked at the first entry in the list.

"Ning Bo Chia," Admiral Hadley said out loud, feeling there was something familiar about that name. He repeated the name two more times, trying to trigger his memory. Nothing. A search through his contacts list revealed nothing. The name was not there, meaning the person was likely not a friend or acquaintance. Still, something about that name nagged at him.

Determined to solve the mystery, he ripped the top page off the pad, he refilled his mug a second time and headed upstairs to his office. He poked the monitor's and computer's power buttons, and waited. He entered his computer pin number and waited for the boot-up process to complete.

After opening an internet browser, he performed a quick search for the name "Ning Bo Chia", and scrolled through three pages of results. Nothing.

"But that name is familiar," Admiral Hadley complained. "I know that name. Why can't I remember who it is? It has to be someone familiar. So, why is the name not in my contacts list?"

Staring at the computer screen, he ran the name over and over in his mind. Still nothing. Thinking it had to be a really old acquaintance, he decided to check the file where he kept names and phone numbers of businesses and people that he seldom contacted and, therefore, did not keep in his phone contacts list. He located the file, opened it, and scrolled down the list. There the name was on the second page.

"Of course," Admiral Hadley exclaimed, slapping his forehead. "He was the charge nurse when I had my left-side, carotid bypass surgery. I was certain I knew that name."

Admiral Hadley and Ning Bo Chia had had coffee numerous times during the admiral's recovery and had become friends. The two men had even met for dinner once after the admiral's discharge from the hospital. Phone numbers were exchanged and promises made to keep in touch, but as often is the case, when Admiral Hadley had returned to his demanding work schedule, the memory of those promises quickly faded.

A quick check of the cellphone's call log indicated the call had come in an hour and fifteen minutes earlier. Assuming Ning Bo would still be on duty at the hospital, Admiral Hadley selected the call record and tapped the Call icon. The phone on the other end rang three time. A man's voice speaking Chinese answered, shouting in a demanding tone. When Admiral Hadley did not answer, the man switched to broken English.

"Who is call?" the man demanded. "We must know who is call."

Admiral Hadley still did not answer.

"Ning Bo Chia is much trouble. Is Ch'angsha China police. Who is call? You must answer!" the man screamed.

Admiral Hadley hung up and stared at the cellphone. "*Why would Ning Bo call me from China? And what kind of trouble is he in?*" Admiral Hadley asked himself.

Admiral Hadley returned to his voicemail and played the message three more times, but still could not understand any additional words. Rather than listening to the message over and over, he tapped the message and sent it to his email. In addition to an attached mp3 audio file, a new cellphone app feature also sent a transcript of the message. Hoping the transcript would help him make sense of the message, he exited voicemail and laid the phone aside

Admiral Hadley turned back to his computer and signed into his email system. The message he had just sent sat at the top of the Inbox. He detached the mp3 audio file, then clicked on the email, and began reading the translated text of the voicemail. The text contained mostly dashes where the speech-to-text transcription had been unable to decipher the excited speech. Surprisingly, the transcription had filled in three additional missing words in what he had written down. The partial sentence now read: "horrible - *disease*, *thousands* - dead, crisper – *Cas9*, *?????* Thompson, *?????* - file, and EasySend.com".

"What does horrible disease, thousands dead mean?" Admiral Hadley asked aloud. "and what is crisper cas9? Who is *?????* Thompson? What does file and EasySend.com mean?" But a bigger question nagging at the admiral's mind was, "*Why would Ning Bo send a message like that to me?*"

Admiral Hadley stared at the text on the screen for several minutes trying to understand its meaning. The words, "horrible disease and thousands dead" were clear enough, but what they applied to was as yet unknown. The next group did not make sense, so he copied the words "crisper cas9", pasted them into an internet search engine, and pressed ENTER.

The very first item in the search results instantly triggered Admiral Hadley's memory. "Of course," he muttered. The speech-to-text process had mistranslated the word to "crisper" when it should have been "CRISPR", an acronym that stood for a gene-editing tool that used a type of modified protein to act like a pair of scissors that can snip parts of DNA strands into pieces. He remembered it well, but hoped he would never hear of it again. Not two years ago, a violent criminal at the behest of an evil, secret society had nearly succeeded in releasing a deadly virus created with that process. His dear friend, Zach Templeton, had nearly lost his life battling that monster.

The admiral now knew "horrible disease" and "thousands dead" likely meant some new and unknown virus. He moved on to the next unknown word, obviously someone's name. In the search engine, he typed five question marks and the word "Thompson", returning thousands of results. Adding the word "virus" still produced far too many results. Substituting the word "doctor" for the question marks, produced another hopelessly long list of names. With no way to narrow the list down, he moved on to the remaining unknown words.

Assuming the words, "*?????* – file" and "EasySend.com" pointed to some kind of file sharing website, Admiral Hadley typed www.EasySend.com on the URL line of the internet browser and pressed ENTER. Just as he thought, he was now staring at the login page of a file sharing website. The cursor was blinking in the email address entry box. He retrieved Ning Bo's email address from his contacts file and pasted it into the block. Having no idea what Ning Bo might have used for a password, he began trying various guesses: his wife's name, the city where he lived, the street where they lived, his house number, and a dozen other guesses. None of the guesses worked.

"What else is there to try?" Admiral Hadley grumbled, clenching his fists.

He glanced at the contacts file for more information and entered the words 'nurse', 'vascular', and 'surgery'. "Still nothing," he shouted, banging his fist on the desk.

He glanced at the contacts file again, entered the word 'Presbyterian', and pressed ENTER.

"Well, what do you know," Admiral Hadley exclaimed, as the login screen disappeared and the file access screen appeared, displaying a page full of filenames.

He selected the most recent file at the top of the list, titled Project, right-clicked, and selected download. A dialog box appeared displaying the file download's process. Admiral Hadley watched as the progress bar expanded slowly toward the one-hundred percent mark. The download took nearly two full minutes to complete. After signing out of the website, he double-clicked the downloaded file and extracted its contents to a temporary folder.

Admiral Hadley's eyes grew wider and wider as he quickly read through some of the contents, a sense of alarm growing within him. A word processing document was the most frightening. It contained an alarming description of some disturbing virus manipulation that was occurring in Ch'angsha China. He did not understand a lot of the medical and technological jargon, but he understood enough to appreciate the hideous threat it represented. In addition to the description of the overall project, there was reference to a successful genomic manipulation run by a scientist by the name of Chin Zheng Li. The file contained the names of the viruses and enzymes used and a narrative of how Doctor Li had happened upon the proper nucleotide, linker enzyme to trigger the mutation.

Admiral Hadley quit reading and sat back in his chair, stunned and frightened by what he had read. "*Why would anyone even consider such an unspeakable thing,*" he asked himself.

The packing could wait. Meeting with the realtor could wait. Literally, everything could wait. There was nothing of his career left to salvage after the confrontation with that evil witch, Hayworth.

The only order of business left to accomplish was to get the information he had to someone and quick, but who? He rummaged around in his mind looking for a name. Someone. Anyone.

"That's it!" he exclaimed, realizing the exact people he needed to get the information to as two names popped into his mind. About to rise from his chair, he heard a loud knock at the front door.

Peeking through the front door's peep hole, he saw two men. As one of the men turned sideways, the grip of a pistol was clearly evident when his jacket swung open. Admiral Hadley carefully eased the coat closet door open and lifted his weapon from the shelf. He crept back over beside the front door and waited.

Wednesday Jan. 28th – 7:00 a.m. EST
Hadley Residence

After hearing nothing for several minutes, Admiral Hadley flipped off the lights, hurried over to the large, south-facing window, pulled the curtain back an inch, and watched two men walk across the parking lot, get into a black Suburban, and drive away. Assuming the men would come back, he knew he had to protect the information by sending it to someone else.

He grabbed his phone from the table, searched through his contacts list, and dialed the number for his old friend, Edgar Cordell, the former White House Communications Director under then President Paul Cantwell.

After five rings, an out-of-breath Edgar Cordell answered, "Admiral Hadley, I was about to leave for work. I'm surprised to hear from you."

"Sorry to call so early, but this is important," Admiral Hadley said. "Are you where you can talk privately?"

"Hang on while I go to my office."

Admiral Hadley heard a door slam and the sound of footsteps. Then several squeaks as Edgar Cordell made his way up a stairway. Another door slammed.

"Okay, Admiral. Go ahead."

"First off. I'm not an active admiral anymore," Admiral Hadley said. "I had another run in with that witch Hayworth. She said if I didn't have my retirement papers on her desk by the end of the day, she would have me arrested."

"Arrested," Edgar Cordell exclaimed. "For what?"

"Doesn't really matter," Admiral Hadley grumbled. "It was time. I was more than fed up with the lunacy going on in that Borden administration. I had plenty of years in. So, I did as the witch requested and now I am Rear Admiral Charles Hadley, Retired."

"I was going to say I'm sorry, but I guess that's not the case."

"Absolutely. Believe it or not, the next day I felt better than I have felt in months. I sold my condo and am moving to Florida to be closer to my son."

"Well, congratulations Admiral. That sounds terrific. I bet you won't miss DC."

"You've got that right. Not in the slightest. Now for the real reason I called, but first you had better sit down."

Edgar Cordell pulled his office chair out, sat down, and said, "Okay, Admiral, I'm listening, but first I need to share something I have learned in the past few days. Data proving there was massive election fraud during the last election has come into my possession. It was passed to me and a reporter for The Liberty Times by a data analyst in Washington. He is now scared to death because he knows the people behind this will try to silence *anybody* that has knowledge of the fraud."

"You're kidding," Admiral Hadley exclaimed. "Does anybody other than you, the reporter, and the analyst know about this?"

"I don't think so. I have to get this to somebody for safe keeping."

"Okay, but first, about two hours ago, I listened to a voicemail from a friend of mine by the name of Ning Bo Chia. He was my nurse, when I had my bypass surgery. He had called me from China."

"From China. What was he doing in China?"

"I don't really know. I assume he must be visiting family. I couldn't make sense of the voicemail he left. I could only understand a few words here and there. So, I called his number back. Someone from the Ch'angsha China police answered. The man said that Ning Bo was in much trouble. Then the man screamed and demanded I tell him who I was. I hung up without saying a word. I sent the voicemail to my email, hoping a transcription of the message would help me understand it."

"Did that help? Were you able to understand any of it?" Edgar Cordell asked.

"Only a little," Admiral Hadley replied. "The transcription filled in three additional words. The message said something about a horrible disease, thousands dead, somebody named Thompson, a file name of some kind, a file transfer site named EasySend.com, and, worst of all, CRISPR Cas9.

"Crisper cas9? What is that?"

"It's a gene editing tool scientists use to manipulate DNA. You won't believe what that thing can do, but the *really* scary stuff is in the file I downloaded from Ning Bo's transfer site once I was able to guess his password and get logged in."

"What is scary about it?"

"It's much too complex for explaining it over the phone. I put the files in our standard, password-protected ZIP protocol. I will send the ZIP file to you over the encrypted transfer protocol. Do you remember it?"

"Yes I do. I have the URL, username, and passwords saved in my encrypted contacts file. I'll read it as soon as I download it."

"This is a world threat like nothing I have seen before. Be extremely careful. I am certain the people behind this will do whatever it takes to keep this from getting out. Once you have it, you will understand its importance. Contact Bigdog and make arrangements to send him the fraud data. Do you understand?"

"Yes, I understand."

"It was great to talk to you," Admiral Hadley said as he ended the call and returned to his packing.

PART II

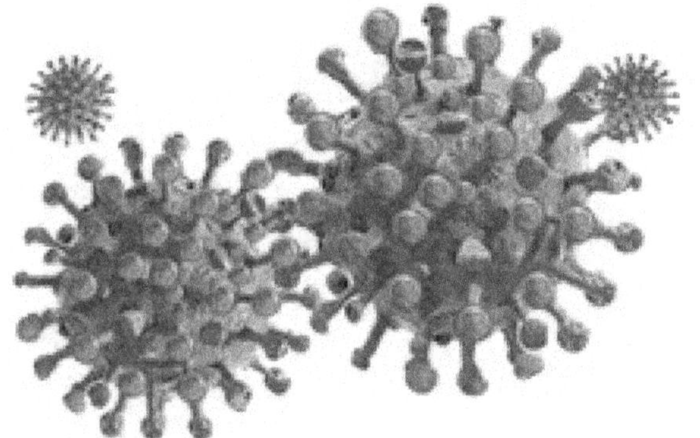

Chapter Four

Wednesday Feb. 4th – 6:15 p.m. EST
East Broad Street
Falls Church, Virginia

Melvin Hartman cranked the windshield wipers up to their highest speed, but the car's windshield wipers scraped hopelessly back and forth, batting at the fast-falling snowflakes. Melvin knew that, at any moment, if he did not slow down, he would lose control on the slick, snow-covered street. Disregarding common sense, Melvin pushed even harder on the accelerator, afraid to speed up, but terrified not to. "*Why wasn't I more careful?*" Melvin, senior reporter for *The Liberty Times*, lamented, angry with himself.

Marvin had jumped at what he believed to be the story of a lifetime – a stolen election and now someone could prove it. As he constructed the outline for his expose, he had begun to believe it might actually be the story of the century. Visions of receiving the Pulitzer Prize had danced in his mind when he had gone to bed that night four days ago. He was to meet his contact the next day for the rest of the proof. What Melvin had failed to consider was what the evil men behind the stolen election would do to him if they found out he knew.

Glancing upward, he stared at the rearview mirror. Snowflakes drifted in through several two inch holes in the rear window where bullets had passed through. Unable to see anything through the shattered rear window, he returned his attention to the street in front of him. Crouching down to peer through a small, clear spot in the snow-streaked windshield, he gasped, seeing a busy intersection appearing just ahead.

"Oh, God!" Melvin cried, knowing he would not be able to stop in time. "I'm going to die!"

Losing the battle with the panic flooding his mind and unable to control his involuntary reaction, Melvin jammed his foot on the brake pedal. He sucked in his breath and prayed harder than he had ever prayed in his entire life. The brakes had little effect on the slick, snow-packed street. To Marvin, the car seemed as if it were sliding even faster.

"Move! Move! Move!" Melvin screamed at the large semi-truck that had just entered the intersection. "Faster! Faster!" Melvin shrieked, but the huge truck seemed frozen in place. Melvin's jaw went slack, knowing it would be impossible to stop. Melvin closed his eyes and waited for the crash.

Wednesday Feb. 4th – 6:20 p.m. EST
Zach Templeton Residence
Big House Plantation Road
Bluffton, South Carolina

Zachariah James Templeton sat at his desk unseeing, nodding off again, unable to keep himself awake after working nonstop for the past six hours on the redesign of the data acquisition system for a new microwave system slated to be installed in just six weeks. Sometime around mid-morning, he had received a frantic phone call from Grant Hollins, his boss and CEO of Silverline Communications, detailing several major changes the client had demanded. Compounding the problem, purchase orders for the data center equipment were scheduled to be released in just five days. For the changes to be verified, approved, and signed off on in time, Zach would have to complete and deliver the updated diagrams no later than noon the following day. Hoping to finish the required changes before supper, he had not even taken time for his and Anna Mae's afternoon coffee time together.

Zach jerked upright, startled by his wife, Anna Mae, yelling up the stairway, "Supper is almost ready. Are you coming down soon?"

"Yeah," Zach hollered down the stairway, leaning his head sideways as he rubbed his sore neck. "I'm not finished, but I need a break. I'll be right down."

Zach pushed away from the desk and began to stand up. He groaned, rubbing his aching left knee. Zach was in reasonably good shape except for his knee, severely damaged during an encounter with a violent terrorist. Sitting for long periods of time always caused the damaged knee to stiffen up.

"Huh, what's that?" Zach exclaimed, noticing a small pop-up window flashing in the lower-right corner of the monitor screen.

He sat back down, grabbed the mouse, and guided the pointer over the pop-up window. He double-clicked the right mouse button and waited. His primary email application opened, displaying a new email at the top of the Inbox. Zach clicked the new email and quickly read the short message. The automated message indicated that a new email had just arrived in his classified email account.

"*That's odd*," Zach thought. Having given his private, classified email address only to a *very* select handful of people. Not currently involved in any classified projects, he had no reason to expect any activity on that email account.

He opened a new instance of his internet browser and typed in the URL of his classified email server. He entered his username and anchored the cursor in the password entry block. It had been months since he had accessed his classified email account. He stared at the blinking cursor. His mind was blank. He could not remember the password.

He had written the password down and had hidden it somewhere. But where? Opening the middle drawer of his desk, he stared at the various items. "Nope, not there," he grumbled. A search through the rest of the desk drawers also yielded nothing. "Where is it?" he grumbled, thumping his temples with his knuckles.

"Aha, that's it!" Zach exclaimed, suddenly remembering where he had hidden the password.

Zach stood up and made a beeline for the closet. He lifted a biometric lock box off the top shelf and laid it on the bed. He pressed his thumb on the fingerprint scanner and waited. The lock box clicked and the lid popped up. Zach flipped the lid completely open and lifted out his Secret Service credential wallet. Slipping his finger behind the ID photo, he eased out a small scrap of paper.

Back in front of the computer, he typed in the password written on the scrap of paper. The encrypted email system opened and Zach saw one new flashing email at the top of the Inbox. He recognized the domain name displayed in the "From:" box as coming from an end-to-end encrypted email service, but he did not recognize the username — *BlackCobra.*

Feeling confident that the classified email server would have blocked any incoming computer viruses, Zack clicked on the email and began reading.

> *Hey Zee:*
>
> *Haven't talked since your birthday party. The <u>T</u>riple <u>F</u>udge cake was <u>d</u>elish. Going out of town. Remember Senator Cantwell? He sends kind regards.*
>
> *Curly,*
> *mc*

"Huh, that doesn't make any sense at all," Zach shrugged, furrowing his brow while rereading the odd message, trying to decipher its meaning. The name "Curly" at the bottom he recognized as David McClain. Zach had met the curly-haired Secret Service agent when he was in Washington, D.C., to be awarded the Presidential Medal of Freedom. Agent McClain had been assigned to Zach and Anna Mae as security. Having both served in the U.S. Navy, Zach and David had quickly become close friends.

The rest of the message made absolutely no sense. David had never called him "Zee". Zach had not had a birthday party since he was eleven years old. He had never had triple fudge cake. And Paul Cantwell was *not* a senator. He was the former President of the United States.

"What on Earth is he trying to tell me," Zach mumbled out loud. "And why are five random letters underlined?"

"Zach," Anna Mae shouted up the stairway for a second time. "You said you would be right down. Supper is ready and Mazie is hungry."

"I'm sorry," Zach answered. "Something strange came up and I need to figure out what it is. You and Mazie go ahead and start without me."

"Okay, but don't be too long."

Zach's attention returned to the odd message. He stared at the words on the screen, but nothing in the message made any sense. All the things David mentioned were untrue except, perhaps, for the *going out of town* part.

"There *has* to be some hidden meaning here," Zach muttered. He copied the entire message and pasted it into a blank document in his word processor. After selecting all the text, Zach increased the font size to make it more readable. Only then did he notice the long string of odd symbols under the signature.

mc [illegible]

Something about the odd symbols seemed vaguely familiar, but what did the two letters "mc" at the beginning of the line mean? "*Why are they different than the rest of the symbols*?" Zach asked himself, leaning closer to the screen. "It's obviously some kind of code. Hmm… 'c' for code? m-code?"

"That's it!" Zach blurted out. "Now, I recognize it. It's the Masonic Code. I knew I'd seen that before."

He selected all but the first two letters and converted the symbols to a standard font.

imaunfejckbmzmyrpmypabxefkawbwvlipz

"Good grief," Zach moaned. "It's just another code."

Zach stared at the string of letters for another ten minutes. In frustration, he swiveled his chair and stood up. Desperately needing a break, he decided to go downstairs and join Anna Mae and Mazie for supper.

"What are you thinking about?" Anna Mae asked several minutes later, noticing that Zach was distracted. "You haven't said three words since you sat down and you have a far-away look in your eyes."

"Do you remember David McClain?"

"Yes, of course I remember him. He's the Secret Service agent that was assigned to us when we were in Washington, D.C."

"I received an email from him, but it doesn't make any sense."

"What do you mean?"

"He called me Zee. Said he hadn't talked to me since my birthday party. He even called President Cantwell a senator. None of those things are true and he knows it."

"Why would he do that?"

"I have no idea unless it was just to get my attention. Even more strange is the string of strange symbols under the signature. It's a code within a code."

"How do you know it's a code within a code?"

"The first two letters are 'mc'. Turns out they stand for Masonic Code."

"You're kidding," Anna Mae remarked. "You mean like…"

"Yes," Zach interrupted. "Exactly like the code that led us to that bizarre statue in the false room in the basement."

"Oh, Zach," Anna Mae cried. "I don't even want to think about that horrible time. You almost died. It was awful."

"I'm sorry," Zach said, reaching out and taking Anna Mae's hand. "David would know I would recognize the symbols. If he went to the trouble to use a double code it has to be important and something he wanted no one else to see. I will have to determine what the key is to the second code."

"Why don't you call him?"

"Of course. I'll do just that," Zach said as he dug in his pocket for his cellphone.

Zach tapped the Phone icon and then the Contacts list. He selected Agent McClain's official number and tapped Call. The call went immediately to voicemail and an automated voice advised Agent McClain was out of town and would be unavailable until further notice. Not to be deterred, Zach went back to the Contacts list and selected the personal cellphone number Agent McClain had given him and tapped Call.

Zach heard a distinctive warble tone then a recorded voice announced, "You have reached a non-working number. Please check your number and try again."

"That's bizarre," Zach said, looking up at Anna Mae with a puzzled look on his face.

"What's bizarre?"

"David's official number went straight to voicemail and the recording said he was out until further notice. His personal cellphone number said it's a non-working number. I don't believe that. There's something fishy going on."

"So, what do you do now, Zach?" Anna Mae quizzed.

"I start digging," Zach answered. "First, I have to determine what cipher he used for the internal code."

"How do you do that?"

"That I don't know. There are literally hundreds of ciphers and code systems. It would take weeks or even months without some way to narrow down the search."

"Well, David gave you a key so you would recognize the Masonic Code," Anna Mae suggested. "Wouldn't he also give you a key to identify the internal code?"

"Exactly!" Zach shouted, a smile spreading across his face. He jumped up, grabbed Anna Mae's face in his hands and kissed her forehead. "What would I do without you?" Zach chuckled. He turned and raced toward the stairway. Hurrying as fast as his knee would allow, he made his way up the stairs, limped over to his desk, and flopped into his chair. He jiggled the mouse to wake up the sleeping computer.

"Yep, that's it," he affirmed, staring at the email message on the screen. "The letters 'T r i f d' are underlined. It must be a trifid cipher."

The trifid cipher had been used extensively by the military in the past, but had fallen into disuse due to the availability of more complex ciphers that were much harder to crack. Zach opened a file browser, searched his hard drive, and opened a trifid decryption application. He copied and pasted the string of letters into the on-screen text box and clicked the Decrypt button.

"Holy moley," Zach gasped, his voice edged with fear as he stared at the decrypted message.

Zach looked down at the leather credentials wallet he had left lying open on the desk. On the right side, a gleaming gold shield with a silver star in the center held his attention. Reaching out with his hand, he ran his finger across the blue enamel banner with raised letters that spelled out "Special Agent". He had wanted to resign his position with the US Secret Service, but then President Paul Cantwell had refused, saying as President he had the authority to make the appointment permanent.

The badge, glaring back at him in the reflected light from a desk lamp, reminded him of his battle with one of the most evil men to walk the planet, a battle that had nearly cost him his life. Even worse, Anna Mae Watts, who later became his wife, had been put in serious danger as well.

An ominous feeling settled over Zach as he looked back up at the message displayed on the monitor. A soldier's instinct warned him he was being dragged into yet another clash with evil, but this time it was not just about him. What about Anna Mae and his sweet little Mazie? He vowed no one would hurt even one hair on the head of his beautiful little girl.

"No one!" Zach snarled as he stared at the message.

Wednesday Feb. 4th – 6:21 p.m. EST
East Broad Street
Falls Church, Virginia

Swirling yellow flames had leaped high into the air, igniting the wooden poles supporting the power lines crossing Broad Street. Globs of blazing, molten oil dripped from a power company transformer that had burst due to the intense, blistering heat. Fire crews, positioning their trucks two blocks away, unable to approach the scene due to the intense heat, sprayed water on the surrounding buildings in hopes of containing the firestorm and keeping it from spreading. Spectators lining the streets blocks away watched in horror as burning fuel from the ruptured tanker truck consumed all vehicles unfortunate to have been within a block when Melvin Hartman's vehicle, still travelling in excess of forty miles per hour, slid into the intersection.

Had Melvin been just five seconds later, he would have missed the East Coast Transport fuel tanker fully loaded with fourteen thousand gallons of gasoline. As it was, Melvin's vehicle slammed into the tanker slightly in front of the rear wheels. The collision ripped open a large gash in the transport's tank. Sparks or, perhaps, heat from the vehicle's engine instantly ignited the fuel spilling out. One second later the entire tank erupted, spewing burning fuel one hundred feet into the air. The concussive blast shattered windows two blocks away and killed those drivers or pedestrians close to the blast instantly. The occupants in burning vehicles further away had not been so fortunate.

Trailing four blocks behind Melvin's fleeing vehicle, a dark blue Chevrolet Malibu with two men inside had quickly pulled over to the curb and stopped when the driver saw Melvin's vehicle sliding toward the tanker. The man seated in the passenger side of the vehicle pulled out a cellphone, pressed a speed dial number, and waited.

"Yes," a deep, husky voice answered on the third ring.

"Hartman's dead."

"Are you certain?"

"Absolutely. His vehicle just slammed into a fuel tanker. The entire block is on fire. No one could have survived that."

"What about the leaked information?"

"He had already left his apartment when we got there, so he had to have had it with him. When we started tailing him, we had other assets turn his apartment. They found nothing. No computer. No laptop. No flash drives. If he had a laptop, he must have taken it with him. I assure you anything he had in the car with him will be melted beyond recognition."

"Did Hartman talk to anyone else?"

"We have been listening to his phone and monitoring his email for the last three days. Nothing on the phone, but there was one suspicious email that we believe mentioned the information."

"What about the recipient of the email?"

"We put him under surveillance as soon as the monitoring team saw the email."

"And?"

"So far, we're just watching him."

"There absolutely cannot be any more leaks. See that it goes no further. Take care of it tonight!"

"Yes sir," the man acknowledged. He ended the call, turned, looked at the driver, and said, "The boss said the leaks go no further. He emphasized the word 'tonight'."

"Got it," the driver replied.

The driver slipped the SUV into gear, made a wide-sweeping u-turn, and headed the other way to follow the boss's orders.

Wednesday Feb. 4th – 6:52 p.m. EST
Zach Templeton Residence
Big House Plantation Road
Bluffton, South Carolina

Zach leaned forward and stared at the string of characters for several minutes, trying to decipher its meaning. The words were all smashed together because the encryption process had removed all the spaces.

extremecautionJFTpeopledisappearing

To help understand the message, Zach placed the cursor between the obvious words and added a space.

extreme caution, JFT, people disappearing

The words and their meaning were plain enough, but what did the three letters in the middle of the message mean? "J F T," Zach pondered, repeating the letters out loud. "What do they mean?"

With nothing to lose, Zach opened his internet browser, typed the three letters into a search engine, and pressed Enter. He browsed through the entries on the first page of results. Finding nothing of interest, he clicked for the second page. Scrolling down the page, he stopped halfway down at the entry for James Bugental. The very first line of the result started with, "James Frederick Thomas Bugental…"

Zach started reading aloud, "James Frederick Thomas…" He stopped and repeated the letters, "J F T. James Fredrick Templeton. Could it really be that simple?" James Frederick Templeton was his father's name. Zach grabbed his cellphone off the desk and dialed his father's number.

"Hey son," James Templeton greeted. "This is a pleasant surprise. I didn't expect a call from you."

"Something came up. Are you in a place where you can talk safely?"

"Ah… yes," James Templeton hesitated, wondering why his son sounded so rattled, detecting the nervous tone in his voice.

"Are you absolutely certain?"

"Yes, I'm certain. I'm sitting in my office alone. What is it Zach? What has you so rattled?"

"Do you know David McClain, the Secret Ser…,"

"Yes, I know Agent McClain very well," James interrupted. "Why are you asking about David?"

"I received a short and very suspicious email from him. It arrived in my classified email server. The main part of the email didn't make sense. It said things that David absolutely would have known were not true. The most frightening thing was a string of symbols under the signature."

"How so?"

"The first two letters below the signature were 'mc'. I determined it was encrypted using the Masonic Code. Remember that?"

"I certainly do. Please, go on."

"Well, when I decoded the symbols it was just a string of meaningless letters. So, the line was a code within a code."

"A code within a code? It must be important. Did you figure out the second code?"

"Yes, I did with Anna Mae's help," Zach answered.

"Oh, really. How did Anna Mae help you?"

"I couldn't figure the message out and was getting frustrated. I needed a break. So, I went downstairs and joined her and Mazie for supper. I mentioned the message and that I hadn't been able to decipher it. She said if David had given me a key to the first code he would probably have also given me a key to the second code. I raced back upstairs and looked at the message again. She was exactly correct. There were some random letters underlined. Turns out it is a trifid cipher. Once I decoded it, your initials are right in the middle of the message."

"A trifid cipher. You're kidding," James exclaimed. "We used to use trifid ciphers back in my early CIA days. I haven't seen one of those in years. So then, I assume part of the email mentioned a fictitious birthday party. Is that correct?"

"Yes it does," Zach stammered. "How on Earth did you know that?"

"Zach, listen *very* carefully. Do not say another word."

"But, I need…"

"I already know what it says. Not one more word. It's not safe." James urged.

"But I…"

"I said not *one* more word," James snapped. "Do you understand me?"

"Yes sir, I understand," Zach answered.

"Do not, I repeat, *do not* talk to anyone about that email or this phone call. I'll be in touch."

The connection terminated. Zach pulled the phone away from his ear and stared at the silent cellphone. Something was seriously wrong. Only once before had his father snapped at him like that. Zach had no idea what had caused it, but something about Agent McClain's message had set his father off. How did his father know about the birthday party? More importantly, what did the message's warning mean? Desperately wanting to know what Agent McClain's message meant but left with no further clues, Zach returned to the analysis of the changes to the data acquisition system he had been working on earlier.

An hour later, he leaned back in his chair and shook his head, having made very little progress on the data acquisition analysis. No matter how hard he tried to concentrate, his mind kept drifting back to the odd messages. How did the second message relate to the first message? What was the reason for extreme caution? Who was disappearing? Was his friend, David McClain, one of those that were disappearing? And why had his dad been so short with him on the phone?

For over two hours, Zach forced himself to concentrate on the analysis, finally finishing it at ten thirty-five. He attached a cost overrun summary to the analysis and emailed it to his boss. Dead tired and bleary-eyed, he dragged himself off to bed with the unanswered questions still swirling in his mind.

Thursday Feb. 5th – 12:27 a.m. EST
Wagner Residence
Oak Ivy Lane
Fairfax, VA

"Huh, what's that?" Secret Service agent, Jeffery Wagner, mumbled, jolted awake from a sound sleep by the sound of breaking glass. "Jen! Jen! Wake up!" Jeffery urged as he shook his sleeping wife. "Go hide in the closet! Hurry! Now!"

Jeffery threw the covers back, slipped out of bed, and grabbed his service weapon from the top drawer of the night stand. Both hands gripping the weapon tightly, he eased the bedroom door open with his foot and crept slowly down the dark hallway. Arms shaking as much from anger as from fear, his lungs begging for air as he tried not to breath.

During the past two days, fear had been building in Jeffery's mind because of what he knew. On his way to lunch on Thursday, he had noticed someone following him. "*How had they found out so quickly*?" he had wondered. Now, somebody was here, in his house. He was certain. He could feel it. His fear *was* justified, and now he was going to catch whoever it was and prove to everyone someone was silencing people.

Jeffery tried to swallow but his mouth was cottony dry. "*Almost to the doorway*," he urged himself as he inched along in the darkness. "*Just a few more steps*."

BANG!

Someone kicked the hallway door open. Blinding pain exploded inside Jeffery's mind before he could use his weapon. Everything went black. Jeffery fell onto the floor, twitched several times, and then lay still. The pistol slipped out of his hand, slid across the floor, and bumped up against the opposite wall.

Two men, dressed in all black, ski masks covering their faces, and black surgical gloves on their hands, rushed into the dark hallway.

"Find out who he's talked to," the taller of the two men commanded. "I'll go see if anyone else is in the house."

The shorter man kneeled down, grabbed Jeffery under the arms, and lifted his shoulders up off the floor. "Wake up," the man demanded as he shook Jeffery's limp body. Getting no response, the man let go with his right hand and slapped Jeffery viciously across the face. "Wake up," the man snarled. The man let go, Jeffery's head banging on the hard floor. The man drew back his arm and slammed his meaty fist into the center of Jeffery's chest.

"Oomph," Jeffery gasped, air exploding from his lungs. He fought to regain consciousness but overwhelmed by the blinding pain in his head he lapsed back into unconsciousness.

"Wake up I said," the man screamed as he slapped Jeffery again.

Jeffery jerked and tried to rise up on his elbows, but before he could, the man grabbed Jeffery's shirt and pulled him up close to his face.

"Who have you talked to?"

"I… huh… what… can't…," Jeffery groaned as his eyes opened briefly and then fluttered closed.

"Wake up! Wake up!" the man shouted as he slapped Jeffery yet again.

Jeffery's eyes opened to narrow slits as he tried to focus on the face in front of him. He opened his mouth to speak but nothing came out.

Infuriated at being unable to get the information he wanted, the man reached under his jacket and pulled out a semi-automatic pistol with a sound suppressor screwed to the muzzle. He jammed the end of the suppressor against Jeffery's forehead, determined to extract the information he wanted.

"Tell me who you've been talking to or you die right now!"

"Cr... Cro...," Jeffery wheezed, trying to form a word.

"What did you say," the man demanded, leaning closer so he could hear. "Repeat that. Say that again."

Jeffery's breath escaped from his lungs in what could only be described as a death rattle. Repeated shaking and slaps to Jeffery's face produced no response. Pressing his fingers against Jeffery's neck, the man felt for a pulse. He swore as he straightened up, kicked Jeffery's lifeless body, and headed down the hallway in search of the other man.

The taller man turned and waited for the other man to speak. When the man did not speak, he asked, "Well, what did he tell you?"

"All I got was a name or part of a name. At least I think it was a name."

"What do you mean you think?" the taller man grumbled. "We were instructed to find out what he knows and who he has talked to. Go back there and find out. Now!"

"Won't do no good," the shorter man stammered. "He's dead."

"Great! Just great. You idiot!" the taller man fumed. "You shouldn't have hit him so hard. Let's find the woman. Maybe she knows something."

Both men flipped up their night-vision goggles and the taller man turned on the light as they entered the bedroom. He reached down, grabbed the edge of the mattress, and flipped it up and off the bed.

Nothing.

He nodded toward the closet door. Slowly he turned the door knob and yanked the door open. Stepping inside, he quickly checked both sides of the closet. He kicked at a pile of clothes lying on the floor.

Nothing.

"Didn't the boss say he was married?" he asked the shorter man.

"Yes," the shorter man answered. "Medium height with blond hair."

Jen had had sense enough to grab her cell phone from the nightstand as she scrambled out of bed. Disregarding her husband's instruction to hide in the closet, she had rushed into the bathroom and had crawled under the sink. When she heard the men enter the bedroom, she had dialed 9-1-1. She desperately wanted to speak, but terrified she would be overheard, she froze. She heard the sound of footsteps coming closer, her heart beating faster as terror gripped her heart. Repeated demands from the 9-1-1 operator to answer went unanswered.

The taller man flipped on the light and looked around the bathroom. He grabbed the shower curtain and jerked it, one end of the curtain rod ripping loose from the wall. The loose curtain rod and curtain clattered noisily as they fell into the bathtub.

Nothing.

The man turned and started toward the door.

Nearing full-blown panic and startled by the sound of the falling curtain rod, Jen flinched and knocked over a bottle of shampoo. She tried to grab it, but it fell against some other bottles which clattered against the wall of the cabinet.

Hearing the sudden noise, the man stopped and stared at the long, oversized, double vanity. The man reached for the door pull and yanked the cabinet door open. "Aha, there you are," he sneered, grabbing the terrified woman's ankle. "Come out of there," he roared as he dragged her out forcefully.

Jen laid on the floor quivering, icy dread gripping her heart.

"What do you know about who your husband has been talking to?"

Paralyzed with blind terror, Jen did not answer.

"I asked you a question," the man shouted. He stepped closer and kicked her in the ribs. "I said who has your husband been talking to."

"No! No!" Jen wailed. "Please don't hurt me!"

The man crouched down and grabbed a handful of Jen's blond hair, jerking her head up to within an inch of his face. So close she could feel the man's hot breath on her face.

"I'm only going to ask you once more. Maybe this will help convince you I mean what I say." He pulled a gun from his waist band and pressed the muzzle of a sound suppressor directly against her forehead. "Who has your husband been talking to?"

"I don't know," Jen sobbed.

"I don't think I believe you."

"You have to believe me. He's very secretive about his work. I don't know anything."

"He must have said something. A name? A place?"

"No," Jen howled. "Nothing. He always…."

"Well then, you're useless to me," the man interrupted. He pulled the trigger and stood up. As he walked out of the bathroom, he pulled a washcloth off the towel bar and wiped the end of the suppressor.

"What now?" the other man asked.

"Toss the place. Pull out every drawer. Go through the closets. Gather all the computers and any watches or jewelry that look like they might be worth something. Make it look like a robbery. Do it quickly. We need to get out of here. The woman had a cellphone in her hand."

Both men busied themselves hurriedly dumping drawers, overturning furniture, and ripping clothes from hangers. Their search netted nothing of any value except one laptop that had been hidden under a pile of clothes in the back of a closet in the spare bedroom. The taller man shoved the other man through the hallway door and pulled the mangled door closed. After exiting the house's back door, they trotted quickly between the neighboring houses to a car parked a block away on the opposite street.

"Hurry. In the car. I hear sirens," The taller man barked as he slid into the driver's seat of a dark blue Chevrolet Malibu. He started the engine, shifted it into gear, and pulled away from the curb as the other man pulled his door shut. The driver barely slowed for the stop sign at the intersection, turned right, and disappeared into the dark night.

Friday Feb. 6th – 1:40 a.m. EST
FBI Headquarters
900 Block Pennsylvania Avenue, NW
Washington, D.C.

Forty five minutes later a black SUV drove across the Theodore Roosevelt Bridge and entered Washington, D.C. Upon reaching the end of Interstate 66, the driver veered right and continued east on Constitution Avenue. A little over one mile later, he turned left onto Sixth Street NW, then left onto Pennsylvania Avenue NW. Three blocks later he turned right onto Tenth Street NW. In the middle of the block, he turned off the street and into the entrance for the underground parking garage for the J. Edgar Hoover Building.

The driver, FBI Special Agent Martin Williamson, slipped his credentials wallet out of his jacket pocket and held it out to the security guard on duty. The guard compared the ID photo in the credentials wallet to the face in the car. Satisfied, the guard opened the gate and waved them through.

Special Agent Williamson wound his way through several rows of empty parking spaces and parked close to the secure elevator. Both men climbed out of the car, Williamson waiting while the shorter man, FBI Field Agent Andrew Tiner, opened the trunk and stuffed two black, hooded sweatshirts and two pairs of surgical gloves into a gym bag. Special Agent Williamson slipped a cellphone out of his pocket, typed a short message, and hit Send, alerting the "Boss" that they had arrived.

FBI Field Agent Tiner poked the elevator's Up button. The door to the secure elevator slid open and both men stepped inside. Special Agent Williamson pulled his credentials wallet out, held it up next to the proximity reader, and pressed the button for the building's top floor. The elevator's doors slid shut and it began its ascent to the top floor.

"I tell you, I don't like killing a fellow agent," Field Agent Tiner admitted.

Special Agent Williamson turned, glared at Tiner, and said, "Do you want to stand in front of Eagle and tell him the information leaked out because you felt bad?"

"No answer I see," Special Agent Williamson mocked. "Well then. Keep your mouth shut."

"Ugh," Special Agent Williamson grunted, glancing at his watch. One forty-five A.M. It was going to be a very long day. The boss's nocturnal habits were legendary throughout the Bureau. It was well known he often worked at his desk through the night. Despite that fact, no one had ever caught him nodding off or complaining about being tired. And no one had ever seen him without a jacket and tie, always looking like his suit had just come off the rack from some high-end men's clothing store.

The elevator lurched to a stop, the door slid open, and Williamson shoved Tiner out into the executive floor's foyer. The lights were dim and the hallway deathly quiet. The plush, burgundy-colored carpet absorbed all sound as the men made their way down the silent hallway. They stopped in front of a highly-polished mahogany door. At eye level, a gleaming brass name plate read: Jerome Conroy, Director, Federal Bureau of Investigation.

Special Agent Williamson raised his arm and rapped softly on the door three times with one knuckle, waited a few seconds, then rapped twice. Twenty seconds later the door swung inward and Director Conroy waved the men inside and quickly pushed the door shut.

"In my office, gentlemen," Director Conroy said, pointing toward the inner door leading to his private office.

Director Conroy waited and followed the men inside. He pushed the door closed, walked around behind his desk, unbuttoned his jacket, and sat down. Despite sitting behind his rather large desk, his height of six foot, five inches presented an intimidating image. Even at one-forty-five in the morning, everything about Director Conroy bespoke his brusque demeanor: his neat and meticulously arranged desk; close-cropped, dark hair; ruler-straight posture; and close-set, penetrating eyes.

"Well, Agent Williamson," Director Conroy began. "Did you get the information we have been tasked to obtain?"

"We think so," Special Agent Williamson answered uncomfortably.

"You think so!" Director Conroy challenged, tensing in his chair, his voice rising in pitch. "What do you mean you think so?"

"Agent Tiner here got part of a name, we think. When Agent Tiner was questioning him, he ah… ah…"

"Out with it," Director Conroy barked. "You may speak freely. I assure you there are no listening devices in this office. I check myself *every day* and the walls were double sound proofed at my request!"

"As I was saying," Special Agent Williamson said. After clearing his throat he continued, "When Agent Tiner was questioning him, Wagner died. He must have hit his head when he fell. I found his wife hiding in the bathroom but she didn't know anything."

"And?"

"She's dead also. We tossed the place. Made it look like a robbery gone bad. We heard sirens as we were leaving but we cleared the area before they arrived."

"What about the vehicle you were driving? What if someone saw you?"

"We used a former drug dealer's car. We ditched it in a mall parking lot. Even if they find the car, it can't be traced back to us."

"Okay. So what was the partial name you got?"

"It started with C-r or C-r-o. Oh, and we found this hidden in a closet," Special Agent Williamson added, holding out the laptop they had found.

" I assume it is password protected."

"Yes sir, it is. Agent Tiner tried to boot it up but got nowhere."

"Okay," Director Conroy acknowledged as he stood up and took the laptop. "I'll have my IT guy take a look at it. Tell me that name again."

Special Agent Williamson repeated what they had heard. Director Conroy, with no change in expression, spun his chair around, and unlocked a drawer in the credenza sitting against the wall behind him. He rifled through a group of hanging folders and pulled out a photo.

"Could this be the name you think you heard?" Director Conroy asked, sliding the photo across the desk.

"Croft. Eugene Croft," Special Agent Williamson mouthed as he stared at the photo. "Could be. The first letters of the name certainly fit."

"Croft is an independent data analyst with a sub-specialty in pattern recognition," Director Conroy elaborated. "Supposedly, he is one of the best in the field. He worked with Huffman and Wirth at Mitchell Analytics. An election fraud investigator by the name of Kevin Hunt has been nosing around where he doesn't belong. It seems Hunt has also been communicating with Mister Croft. Yesterday Hunt made a frantic phone call to Croft to warn him, but Mister Hunt did not get to finish his phone call."

"Do you want us to find out what Croft knows?" Special Agent Williamson asked.

"No," Director Conroy answered, staring directly at Williamson. "Croft has an early morning flight scheduled on Monday to fly to DC. You and Tiner fly out to Phoenix and see that he does not make that flight."

"With so many individuals from the same organization ending up dead, won't someone get suspicious?" Special Agent Williamson asked.

"Doesn't matter. The election data should *never* have leaked out in the first place. *Marduk* said these leaks must be sealed. *All of them*. He said no matter what it takes. Understand?"

Both men nodded their agreement and stood to leave.

"One more thing," Director Conroy called out as Special Agent Williamson put his hand on the door knob. "I have learned that Edger Cordell,

White House Communications Director for former President Paul Cantwell, has received information from Hunt that will expose the manipulation of election results. When you return from Phoenix, find Cordell and find out if he has shared that information with anyone. Then see that Mister Cordell takes a permanent vacation."

"Yes sir," Special Agent Williamson acknowledged. "Consider it done."

Chapter Five

Monday, Feb. 9th - 3:14 a.m. MST
Croft Residence
East Thunderbird Drive
Phoenix, Arizona

Eugene Croft, a highly-skilled, independent virology researcher, had climbed into bed jumpy and on edge. On Sunday as he returned from shopping for a few things for an upcoming trip, he had seen the same car trailing behind him enough times to become suspicious. The car had turned off on another street five blocks before he arrived home. He had tried to convince himself it was just a coincidence, but his uneasy feeling would not go away.

Gene, as he was known to his friends and colleagues, was five days past his thirty-eighth birthday. Gene, often contracted by medical research companies, had an uncanny ability to understand and identify problems in the most complex research processes.

On the road at least forty weeks a year, he had become a well-seasoned traveler. After enduring a number of very unpleasant experiences, he had developed an aversion for taking the first flight out in the morning. He much preferred booking mid-morning flights which did not require middle-of-the-night dashes to the airport.

Four days earlier, alarmed by a phone call from a contact from the past, Gene had reached out via email to Kevin Hunt, an old friend and colleague who lived in Washington D.C. Gene had asked Kevin if he knew anything about the previous election results, specifically if it had been manipulated to change the ultimate winner.

The following day Gene had been surprised and more than a little alarmed by the frantic phone call he had received from his old friend. Kevin, one of those people with a soft voice who talked a mile a minute, had always been somewhat difficult to understand, but Kevin had been so frantic all Gene heard over the phone was gibberish. After several minutes of listening to Kevin's high-pitched ranting, Gene had only been able to calm Kevin down enough to grasp a few words.

Gene heard, "*...Bill Huffman...killed...suicide bomb blast...,*" before Kevin lapsed back into panic. Asking Kevin to repeat slowly, Gene had managed to pick out a few more snippets, "*...must tell no one...extremely careful...do not...,*" before Kevin lapsed into near hysteria. Ten seconds later,

Gene heard a loud clunk and banging sounds, then the phone went dead. Three attempts to call Kevin back went straight to voicemail.

Gene had remained seated at his desk for several minutes after the abruptly-ended phone call trying to make sense of his friend's panicked warning. "*What was he not to tell anyone about? Why should he be careful? Did it have something to do with being followed?*" he wondered. He replayed the conversation, such as it was, over and over in his mind. There were just too many gaps. The conversation just did not make sense. Over the next five hours, Gene had become increasingly concerned about his friend's welfare as repeated phone calls continued to go straight to voicemail.

Spooked by recent events and the panicked warning from his friend, Gene had decided to change his scheduled flight to an earlier day. After an hour of fruitless searching through airline schedules, he had learned all mid-morning or later flights were already oversold. Rather than risking the standby list and hoping to snag a cancellation or a no-show, Gene had reluctantly booked the next to last seat on the 6:05 a.m. nonstop flight to Washington Dulles.

Lying awake in the darkness, Gene opened his eyes and glanced at the bedside clock for the tenth time in the past hour. The alarm was set to go off in just over twenty minutes. Rather than lie there awake in the darkness any longer, he carefully slid out from under the covers and stood up.

His wife, Shannon, groaned, muttered something unintelligible, and pulled the covers up over her head. At thirty-four, she was pregnant for the third time. Her first two pregnancies had resulted in miscarriages early in the third month. The last time she had been nearly inconsolable. After more than a year of counseling and much encouragement, Shannon had agreed to try for a baby one last time. She was now five months pregnant. It had been a very grueling five months for Shannon and for Gene. Every pain or unexpected cramp would terrify Shannon, making her think it was another miscarriage. It had been one of those rare nights when she had slept well. For what had seemed like hours, Gene had lain awake listening to Shannon's soft, rhythmic breathing. He certainly did not want to wake her and risk another argument.

Over the past week, they had had several arguments regarding Gene's sudden decision to meet with his old colleague in Washington. Shannon was also concerned over recent events and the growing violence. She reminded Gene of his promise to not travel during the last half of the pregnancy. Despite Gene's attempt to explain the urgent, and unexpected, need to meet with his colleague, Shannon had refused to budge. She had accused him of not caring and refused to talk about it any further.

Frustrated that he could not convince Shannon of the critical importance of the hastily arranged trip, he had sat on the living room couch too agitated to consider sleep. Finally, nearing midnight, he had pushed himself up off the couch, knowing he had to at least try to get some sleep or the trip would be miserable. He undressed, slid into bed, and stared at the ceiling.

Having already packed early the night before, his suitcase sat beside the dresser waiting. The shocking and incriminating analysis he had prepared and the flash drive containing the supporting project data were safely stored in his laptop bag. To avoid waking Shannon, he decided to use the downstairs bathroom to get ready. He extended the suitcase's handle, set his laptop bag on the suitcase, and grabbed the handle. About to step through the bedroom door, he reached into the dish on the dresser where he always dropped his loose change and car keys.

"What?" he muttered angrily under his breath when he discovered the car keys were not there. "Where are they?"

He set the suitcase upright, slipped into the master bathroom, pushed the door shut, and flipped on the light. After scouring the vanity's countertop, he pulled open every drawer and searched its contents. He looked on the floor, in the linen closet, and behind the commode. Nothing. The keys were nowhere to be found.

"*This is exactly why I don't like booking the early morning flight*," he growled to himself as he grabbed his laptop bag and suitcase and headed downstairs to continue his search for the missing car keys.

He set the suitcase by the front door, dropped the laptop bag on the living room couch, and hurried into the kitchen. After poking the coffee brewer's On button, he slid open the storage tray and selected a French Roast coffee pod. Disappearing into the downstairs bathroom, he continued his search for the missing car keys. The keys were not there either. Back in the kitchen, he rummaged through the junk drawer. Still no keys. He checked the pockets of all his jackets hanging in the coat closet. He searched the side table by the front door, the entertainment center, and the dining room table. He had searched everywhere he could think of.

"Why can't I find the stupid keys?" he fumed, returning to the coffee brewer. He dropped the coffee pod in the brewer, slipped his travel mug under the dispenser, and jabbed the brew button. While the brewer went through its cycle, he glanced at his watch still trying to remember where he had put his car keys. Nothing. His mind was blank. He didn't have a clue where the car keys could be. With no idea where else to look, he walked into the living room and lifted his wife's purse off the closet door. He located her key ring and slipped off the spare key to the Chevy. He would call Shannon when he landed and explain why he had taken the spare key.

Back in the kitchen, he grabbed the travel mug, turned the brewer off, and discarded the used pod in the trash can. Having risen well before the alarm was set to go off and having packed the night before, he still had some time to kill before he needed to leave. He turned off the kitchen light, walked into the living room, and sat on the couch. Sitting there carefully sipping the hot steaming coffee, in his mind he replayed his old friend's revelation about Bill Huffman's sudden death.

Gene unzipped the laptop bag, pulled out his laptop, and turned it on. A quick internet search revealed that Bill Huffman had been killed in the violent blast of a suicide bomb. Most disconcerting of all was the fact that the blast had occurred only ten blocks from the Capitol Building in Washington D.C. According to the AP news story, the damage from the huge blast had been so widespread, the authorities had, so far, been unable to pinpoint the exact target.

About to close the internet browser, he noticed another name he recognized. He clicked on the link to the article and began reading.

> *At 1:47 a.m. on February 6th, Fairfax, Virginia, police reported they responded to a shooting in the 1300 block of Oak Ivy Lane, where they found two victims, Jeffery Wagner dead from a blow to the head and his wife, Jennifer, dead from a gunshot wound. The house had been ransacked. At this time police believe it was a robbery gone bad. Later reports indicated both had been pronounced dead on the scene at 2: 08 a.m.*
>
> *Police told reporters on the scene they are searching for two men who were last seen fleeing the scene in a dark black or blue mid-size Chevrolet. "Do not approach or take any action," police said as a public warning for anyone who might come across the getaway vehicle. The two men are considered armed and extremely dangerous.*

One of his old friends seemingly missing, one killed by a suicide bomb, and now a Secret Service agent and his wife had been murdered in their home. Not only were these men friends, they had all worked at the same data analytics firm until two and one-half years ago when Gene had left to start his own consulting business. The last time Gene had spoken with the two men that had been murdered, they both had still worked at that same firm.

The baffling warning from his friend, news of the suicide bombing, and the murder of a second friend set off multiple alarm bells in Gene's mind. Given Gene's analytic mindset, he found it hard to believe that these events could be mere coincidences. Adding the latest events to the troubling demonstrations and violence occurring across the country because of the disputed election, had it not been for his old friend's pleading request to meet him to discuss the results of his discovery, Gene would have refused.

Gene slid his finger across the touch pad and hovered the mouse pointer over the Start button, about to power down the laptop. He furrowed his brow for a few seconds, then slid his finger across the touch pad and opened a file explorer session. After expanding the file tree, he right-clicked on a file, and clicked on a command listed in the speed menu. He waited for the command to complete, closed the explorer session, powered down the laptop, and shoved the laptop back into the bag.

"Good grief," Gene squawked. A quick glance at his watch revealed he had spent way too much time reading the news articles. Now, he would have to scramble to make it to Phoenix's Sky Harbor airport in time to catch his flight.

Gene scooped up his laptop bag, grabbed his suitcase, and flew out the door. He tossed the laptop bag and suitcase on the back seat and jumped into the front seat. After jamming the spare key into the ignition, he twisted the key to start the engine.

"*That's odd. I've never heard that funny sizzling sound before*," he thought, tilting his head to the side.

That was the last thought that ever passed through Eugene Croft's mind.

Heard more than a mile away, the force of the thunderous blast shattered windows for two blocks in all directions.

Chapter Six

Monday, Feb. 9th - 11:00 p.m. CET
Hotel Rixos Fluela Davos
Tschuggenstrasse at Bahnhofstrasse
Davos, Switzerland

Gerard Schechter, dressed in a perfectly tailored, dark suit, sat alone in the hotel's upscale lounge. The double-breasted suit, hand crafted from a luxurious blend of the finest Italian wool and silk with a tight-checked pattern, sported the label of the most prestigious tailor in Milan, Italy. Gerard always wore the suit with all three buttons of the double breasted jacket buttoned up. An elegant red silk tie with a perfectly tied double-Windsor knot drawn up tight to the collar of a white silk shirt completed his stylish appearance.

Gerard drained the last swallow of his drink and gently set the heavy crystal glass on the gleaming, mahogany bar. He spun around on the bar stool, stood up, and headed for the lobby. Crossing the elegantly decorated lobby, he detoured around a group of men speaking a language he did not understand, walked down a short hallway, and stopped in front of the elevator. About to punch the Up button, he stopped, turned, walked back into the lobby, and stepped up to the front desk.

"Guten abend, Herr Schechter," an impeccably dressed young man greeted, bending slightly at the waist.

"Irgendwelche nachrichten für mich?" Mr. Schechter asked, in perfect German.

"Ich glaube schon. Lass mich nachsehen," the front desk clerk answered, stepping sideways to the far end of the counter. He slid open a drawer and flipped through a stack of numbered divider cards. Holding a folded piece of pink paper in his hand, he returned and handed the message across the counter.

"Danke," Mr. Schechter said as he grabbed the message, turned, and walked back to the elevator. A man dressed in a striking, black tuxedo and a woman in a dazzling, green evening gown with a snow-white, fur stole draped over her shoulders stood waiting for the elevator to return to the ground floor. Mr. Schechter nodded at the couple and waited.

A bell rang, the Up arrow above the elevator door turned green, and the elevator doors slid open. The couple stepped inside and leaned against the back wall. Mr. Schechter followed. The man reached out and punched the button for the third floor. Mr. Schechter fished his room key out of his trouser pocket, shoved it into the VIP access slot, and punched the button for the sixth floor, the top floor of the hotel, reserved strictly for premium guests. The couple spoke softly in French as they waited for the elevator to reach the third floor. The elevator stopped and the doors slid open. Mr. Schechter smiled and nodded at the couple as they exited the elevator.

The elevator doors slid closed and the elevator continued its ascent to the top floor. The elevator doors slid open, revealing the sixth floor's grand foyer. To the left were three one-bedroom presidential suites. On the right side of the foyer was the hotel's two-bedroom royal suite which covered half of the top floor. Mr. Schechter turned right and slid his room key into the door's access slot. The light blinked green and he pushed the door open. He stepped inside, flipped the light switch on, and let the door swing closed.

Mr. Schechter eased his slightly overweight six-foot frame onto the cushion of an elegant, mulberry-colored MacKenzie-Childs designer sofa that cost more than most people's cars and kicked off his shoes. He slipped off his jacket, removed the message from the left inside pocket, and draped the jacket across the arm of the sofa. Leaning back against the sofa, he unfolded the paper and read the handwritten note, a frown immediately clouding his face.

Two months shy of his sixty-seventh birthday, Gerard Schechter had been born György Ábrahám Szabó in Budapest, Hungary. Kázmér Szabó, his father, had actively collaborated with the Germans during the World War II occupation of Hungary, often meting out severe punishments to the locals for a violation of some Nazi rule or edict. Kázmér Szabó enjoyed his role as a Nazi enforcer far too much, earning him the well-deserved title—The Butcher of Budapest.

When Kázmér Szabó learned Germany was losing the war, he fled Hungary and moved the Szabó family to the United Kingdom. Soon after arriving in the UK, he had changed the family name from the Hungarian-Jewish Szabó to Schechter to hide from his responsibility for the appalling war crimes he had committed.

Unlike most children who despised the heritage of their Hungarian-Jewish parents that had aided the Germans and became wealthy during the war, Kázmér's oldest son, Gerard, reveled in it. Gerard thought it especially appropriate that the German surname 'Schechter' was actually derived from the Hebrew word 'shachat' which means to slaughter or butcher.

A brilliant student, Gerard fervently applied himself to his studies, eventually earning a Doctor of Philosophy degree from the University of London. Gerard began his financial career as a teller in one of London's largest banks. Plying his acumen of the banking world, he advanced quickly, becoming a senior vice president in less than five years. He started a small pooled investment fund which grew more quickly than any of its rivals. Reinvesting all the profits from his first fund and adding some highly illegal manipulations of currencies, he became the senior advisor to one of Europe's largest investment funds.

Gerard's motives went far beyond just the acquisition of wealth. He used his wealth like a giant club to badger people and companies into submission. When his great wealth did not work, he resorted to threats, intimidation, and physical violence. In the criminal underworld of London, just like his father, he was quickly becoming known as The Butcher.

Easily manipulated as a young man because his family had been a non-practicing Jewish family who never spoke of God or their faith, Gerard's mind had been easily poisoned by the radical, atheistic philosophy professors that taught at the university. Gerard became an avid supporter of radical, progressive movements and ultra-liberal political causes, to which he donated hundreds of millions of dollars.

Gerard's positions on the governing boards of several large investment funds and membership in the World Economic Forum (WEF), was what had brought him to Davos, which hosted the World Economic Forum's annual meeting of globalists, political activists, and business elitists. Another reason that brought Gerard to Davos was its favorable microclimate. Located in a high valley in the Swiss Alps, Davos was a popular destination for the sick and ailing, especially recommended for lung disease patients. Since childhood, Gerard had been somewhat sickly which drove his decision to maintain a semi-permanent residence at the Hotel Rixos Fluela Davos.

Gerard Schechter, as demanding as he was wealthy, would fly into a tirade if a room was not available when he demanded one. Because he made many trips to Davos, he booked the Royal Suite for an entire year at a time, never giving the exorbitant cost of $1.35 million Swiss Francs a second thought. His immense wealth, hard to quantify accurately, by most estimates, exceeded $45 billion dollars.

Gerard sighed deeply, put both hands on the exquisite mulberry-colored tweed fabric, and pushed himself up from the sofa. He ambled across the room, his feet sinking deeply into the soft, plush carpet. Stopping at a small desk in the corner of the room, he lifted the receiver off the phone, dialed an international number, and waited.

"Hallo," a thick, guttural voice answered.

"Why did you call me at the hotel?" Gerard asked, switching to German upon recognizing the voice.

"It is important. We have located what you are looking for."

"Very well. Hang up. I will call you back on the *other* phone."

Gerard dropped the receiver back on the phone and hurried over to a large bookshelf built into the west wall. Reaching up to the top shelf, he removed a book titled, *The History of the Grecian War*. The book, covered in rich wine-colored leather with gold leaf stamping on the spine, had the outward appearance of a very old and valuable book. Gerard flipped open the cover and thumbed a five digit code into a cipher lock. With a soft click, a small drawer slid out of the end of the book. He lifted a shiny, gold-colored cellphone out of the cutout and laid the book on a small table standing beside the bookshelf. While dialing an international number from memory, he returned to the MacKenzie-Childs sofa and sat down.

After three rings, the same thick, guttural voice answered, "We are ready, sir."

"What about the fool in Arizona?"

"Someone must have warned him. He changed his flight but we ordered our *friend* to see to it that he never got on it. I assure you the stupid fool will *not* be talking to anyone. He and any information he might have been carrying was incinerated."

"The person who warned him?" Gerard questioned.

"He and his friend, both eliminated."

"Have you located the original source of the information?"

"No, sir, but we have men searching. It is only a matter of time."

"You must have some idea."

"Yes. We….,"

Gerard heard a loud clunk and then silence. "Hello. Hello. Are you there?" Another clunk. Gerard heard scraping noises and what sounded like a muffled voice.

Hans Pfitzner swore out loud, struggling to grasp the slick cellphone with his gnarled, claw-like left hand, the result of a botched arson attempt early in his criminal career. He had tripped over a chair in the darkness as he ran out of the building. A careless mistake that had nearly cost him his life and had left him with only a thumb and two fingers on his left hand, earning him the nickname—Two Fingers. After spending five days in the hospital, Two Fingers had served ten years in prison.

"I am sorry. I dropped the phone," Hans Pfitzner grumbled, resting the edge of the phone against the red, rippled scar that started above his left eye, ran down along the side of his nose, and ended at his chin. The ugly scar, a permanent reminder of what his carelessness had cost him, stood out like a flashing red light, requiring Hans to always wear a hooded sweatshirt to avoid being recognized.

"Have you located the source or not?" Gerard asked again.

"Yes, we have the person you described in sight. Gustav is following him. What do you wish us to do?"

"Has he communicated with anyone else?"

"We do not believe so. We have tapped his phone. He has only talked with family, he has not been out of town, and he has not met with anyone."

"That is not good enough," Gerard scolded. "He would never be so stupid as to contact anyone openly. You must find out what he knows."

"He will not give up that information easily."

"I pay you to get results," Gerard shouted. "Do whatever it takes, then silence him."

"Ja, mein Herr," Hans Pfitzner answered.

Gerard ended the call and returned the cellphone to the fake book.

Monday, Feb. 9th - 6:10 p.m. CST
Woodland Hills Mall
South Memorial Drive at East 71St. Street
Tulsa, Oklahoma

James Frederick Templeton pushed himself up from the hard metal bench he was sitting on, walked a few steps to a trash receptacle, and dropped his empty coffee cup in. Slowly he walked back toward the bench, his eyes flicking back and forth scrutinizing the other early-evening shoppers. The phone call from his son regarding the encrypted message contained within an email from Secret Service Agent David McClain had awakened his old CIA senses. He hated to have been so abrupt with his son Zach, but the less he knew the better at least until he knew what had spooked Agent McClain. He stopped, turned, and watched the traffic flowing up and down the mall. Seeing nothing unusual or suspicious, he turned back toward the bench.

"Are you ready to go?" James asked, holding his hand out to help his wife, Margaret, up.

"Yes, I'm ready," Margaret answered, taking hold of James's hand and pulling herself up.

They turned left and headed down the corridor toward the mall's south entrance. James took the empty coffee cup from Margaret's hand and tossed it into the trash receptacle as they strolled by.

"I'm sorry the fabric store didn't have what you wanted," James offered, patting Margaret's hand. "Seems like we wasted a trip."

"That's alright," Margaret remarked. "You've been so busy in your office the last few days, it was nice to get out of the house and do something different. And the coffee was really good."

Arm in arm they strolled into the JC Penney store, browsing the aisles as they meandered toward the exit. Suddenly, James let go of Margaret's arm and turned back to get a closer look at something that had caught his attention. The change of direction was so sudden he bumped into the tall, thin man walking behind them.

"Sorry," James offered as he stepped around the man, quickly making a mental note of the man's characteristics. He had seen the man before out near the food court. He remembered because the man had the hood of his sweatshirt up and kept his hand stuffed in his coat pocket. James continued his quest and hurried off toward a display of men's ties.

"I like that," he remarked as he stopped and admired a vibrantly colored purple, silver, and gray tie looped around the neck of a display manikin.

"Why don't you buy it," Margaret said as she caught up to her husband.

"I don't know," James shrugged. "I have plenty of good ties at home."

"Oh, James, for Heaven's sake. You're as bad as old Mister Scrooge. We can afford it. If you like it, just go ahead and buy it."

"Yes, Ma'am," James smiled. "I believe I will."

James located an identical tie in the piles of ties arranged below the display dummy, turned, and searched the store for the nearest checkout register. Seeing a register just two aisles away, he hurried over and stood behind a woman just finishing up her transaction. He quickly paid for the tie and rejoined Margaret, waiting by the exit door. Together, they pushed through the exit doors and hurried through the cold air toward their car.

"Brrrr," James exclaimed as he jumped into the driver's seat. He jammed the key into the ignition and started the engine. "You want to grab something to eat on the way home?" he asked, while waiting for the engine to warm up.

"I'd rather not," Margaret answered. "I'm kind of tired. I would just as soon go straight home."

"Your wish is my command, milady," James joked as he shifted the car into reverse and backed out of the parking space.

James followed the parking access road around the southern perimeter of the parking area, watching to see if anyone followed them. He turned right onto the exit road. At the stop light, he turned right onto Seventy-first Street and immediately shifted over into the left lane, preparing to turn south onto Memorial Drive. James noticed a dark gray Toyota Corolla that had followed them out of the parking lot also pulled into the left-turn lane three cars behind them.

The left-turn arrow turned green and the line of waiting vehicles sped through the intersection, heading south on Memorial Drive. Two impatient drivers moved over a lane, zoomed past the Corolla, and dove back into the left lane.

"You're going to lose them," the Corolla's passenger shouted.

"Do not worry Gustav," the driver replied. "I already know exactly where they are going."

Staying under the speed limit and not in a hurry, two blocks later, the occupants of the Corolla lost sight of the Templeton's white Chevrolet SUV in the heavy traffic. The Corolla continued south for nearly a mile then turned right onto East Ninety-First Street. One quarter mile after crossing South Sheridan Road, the Corolla turned left onto South Lakewood Avenue. A short block later the Corolla turned left onto East Ninety-Second Street then right onto South Maplewood Avenue, pulled over to the curb, and stopped. The driver turned off the headlights, looked toward the middle of the block, and watched as the garage door on the Templeton's house closed.

"I told you I knew exactly where they were going," the driver said.

The two men sat in the car and waited as several other cars drove down the street and pulled into driveways. After waiting several more minutes, all seemed quiet. The driver reached inside the left side of his jacket. He slipped a Ruger MK II, .22 caliber pistol out of his shoulder holster. From another pocket, he retrieved a sound suppressor and screwed it onto the muzzle of the MK II.

"Quick, let's go before another car comes" the driver said as he opened the door and climbed out. "You go around back," he instructed the other man.

He gently pushed the car door closed, pulled the hood of his sweatshirt up over his head, and trotted across the street. Holding the MK II pistol under his jacket, he walked to the middle of the block and stopped even with the Templeton's front door. A quick glance in both directions revealed the street was deserted. The driver jerked his head to the left. The other man ducked between the houses and eased himself up and over a fence separating the houses.

The driver turned and walked up the sidewalk, stopping in front of the door. He eased the MK II out from under his jacket. Holding the pistol down at his side with his good hand, he reached for the doorbell with the misshapen index finger on his left hand.

Monday, Feb. 9th - 7:35 p.m. EST
Zach Templeton Residence
Big House Plantation Road
Bluffton, South Carolina

Zachariah James Templeton yawned as he turned off Laurel Oak Bay Road onto Big House Plantation Road. Returning home after the weekly staff meeting at Silverline Communications in Savannah, Georgia, he had nodded off several times. Zach was physically and mentally exhausted from the long hours working at his position as a senior data analyst. Sudden and troubling changes to a project demanded by an important client had only added to his workload. After turning off the Okatie Highway, he had stopped along the side of the road and had walked around the car twice to clear the cobwebs from his mind.

Zach yawned as he turned off Big House Plantation Road onto the lane leading to his house. The tires of his light gray Buick Encore crunched loudly on the gravel driveway as he approached the house. He pulled up to the parking area adjacent to the front porch, stopped, and switched off the engine. Leaning his head against the steering wheel, he wondered if he had enough energy to drag himself out of the car. He took a deep breath, straightened up, and pushed the door open. Grabbing the top of the door frame, he hauled his five foot nine inch frame up and out of the car.

Yawning deeply again, he stepped up onto the porch and pushed the front door open. A reddish-brown blur hurtled across the room and smacked into him, nearly knocking him backward out the door.

"Tripp, stop," Zach yelled, pushing the excited redbone hound away. "What is the matter with you?"

Zach set his laptop bag on the floor, pushed the door closed, bent over, and grabbed the hound's head with both hands. He ruffled the hound's ears and patted him on the back. The hound wagged his stub of a tail madly and proceeded to wash Zach's face with his wet tongue.

"Stop, Stop," Zach laughed. "Come on you silly dog let's go into the kitchen."

Zach tossed his jacket at the couch and limped toward the kitchen with Tripp bounding along beside him, growling and tugging at his sleeve. Zach had always been a "dogs belong outside" kind of guy, that is, until he met the lovable redbone hound named Tripp. Zach had encountered Tripp the first day he had moved into the two-story farmhouse on Big House Plantation Road. It had taken a lot of coaxing, but the hound had finally given in, lured by the two slices of bread in Zach's hand. At that time, Tripp belonged to Miss Anna Mae Watts the landlord and owner of the property.

Nearly two years had passed since Zach and Anna Mae had stumbled across a trail of baffling clues that had helped them hunt down a vicious terrorist known by everyone in the terrorist world as *al-Ta'abin*, an Arabic nom de guerre which meant—The Snake. Zach had been recruited a second time to serve as a special agent answering directly to the President of the United States. He and Anna Mae had tracked the deadly terrorist to a location where he was preparing to release a deadly virus with a nearly one hundred percent fatality rate. A horrendous and nearly fatal encounter with the revenge-crazed madman had ensued. Had it not been for Anna Mae's bravery *and* a little bit of stubbornness, *al-Ta'abin*, would have killed Zach that day. Even though Anna Mae's desperately fired shot had killed *al-Ta'abin*, Zach's injuries had threatened to take his life as well. On that terrifying day, the EMTs had told Anna Mae they did not hold out much hope as they had loaded Zach onto a gurney and had rushed him off to a nearby hospital.

After a long and complicated emergency surgery, Zach had spent nearly ten days in the hospital. Even though Zach's parents had arrived and agreed to stay, Anna Mae had insisted she take care of Zach until he was able to manage on his own. Over the following weeks, Zach had mostly recovered. The only lingering evidences of his encounter with the evil madman were a nasty scar running from the center of his chest to nearly the center of his back and a pronounced limp, the result of a severely damaged knee when *al-Ta'abin*, had viciously stomped on it.

One day during his long recovery, Zach had been sitting on the back porch enjoying the warm morning sun. He had finished his cup of coffee and had struggled to stand up with the assistance of his cane. As Zach had pulled the screen door open, Tripp, the redbone hound, an ever-present companion to Zach during his recovery, had managed to sneak halfway into the house before Zach had stopped him. He had blocked the hound's way with his cane and had shooed the hound back onto the porch. Inside the house, Zach had turned and looked back at the sad, dejected face peering at him through the screen.

"*He was very well behaved and he had been such a good friend what could it hurt?*" Zach asked himself.

Zach had turned and discovered that Anna Mae had been watching the whole time. "It's fine with me," she had said without being asked.

The instant Zach's hand had touched the screen door, Tripp had leapt to his feet and stood at the door, his stubby tail wagging wildly. After Zach had opened the door, Tripp had raced into the house and had stood right beside Zach. As the weeks had passed, Zach and Tripp had become inseparable. When Zach moved, Tripp moved.

"Daddy. Daddy," four year-old Mazie shouted as she ran out of the bedroom. "Look what I did. Is it pretty?"

Zach took the crayon drawing Mazie held out with her right hand and said, "It's beautiful. Let's put it where everyone can see it." Zach walked over to the refrigerator, pulled off an unused magnet, and used it to hang the drawing in the middle of the door. He bent over and picked Mazie up and squeezed her tightly, then pretended he was waltzing her around the kitchen floor. Nearly losing his balance when his lame knee protested, he put Mazie down.

"More. More. More," Mazie squealed.

"Sorry, Sweetie," Zach said, "Daddy's knee hurts. I can't. Let's get ready for dinner."

Anna Mae smiled at her husband, thinking how blessed she was. Six months after the Presidential Medal of Freedom with Distinction awards ceremony in Washington, D.C., Zach had married Anna Mae Louise Watts in a very small, very private service attended by Zach's parents, Rear Admiral Charles Hadley, Kip Johnson, Admiral Hadley's pilot, Zach's boss, Grant Hollins, Owner and CEO of Silverline Communications, and former President of the United States Paul Cantwell and his wife, Christine.

Soon after the wedding, Zach's and Anna Mae's adoption of Mazie, Margaret Jean Pickett, had gone off without a hitch. The death of both of Mazie's parents to the deadly virus left only one living relative, her eighty-one year-old grandmother. Living in a nursing home, she was unable to care for herself let alone her two year-old granddaughter and she had voiced her full agreement with the adoption. So, Margaret Jean Pickett became Margaret Jean Templeton.

Zach hugged Anna Mae and kissed her on the cheek. They both looked down when Tripp squeezed between them.

"Yes, I love you too," Zach chuckled as he reached down and rubbed Tripp's ears. "Sorry, I'm so late. We had some data transmission issues earlier in the week and the discussion about a necessary solution to correct them ran a little long."

"Well, I was beginning to wonder if the meatloaf was going to survive," Anna Mae quipped, turning toward the stove. "Set the table while I get things out of the oven."

"Yes, ma'am," Zach chimed as he turned toward the cabinet where the dishes were stored. "Tripp, go lay down."

Tripp curled up on his rug but kept his eyes on Zach as he gathered plates, glasses, and silverware and set the table. Mazie, sitting in her booster seat, grabbed her plastic spoon and was about to attack the meatloaf and mashed potatoes on her plate.

"Wait Mazie. We need to ask the blessing. Bow your head," Zach said as he began to ask the blessing. "Heavenly Father, we thank you for this wonderful meal, for the hands that prepared it, and for the love we share as a family. Amen."

With the blessing finished, Mazie attacked the food on her plate with a vengeance. Zach and Anna Mae loaded their plates and as they ate, they discussed plans for their garden as soon as the weather warmed up enough.

With dinner finished and Anna Mae in the bathroom giving Mazie a bath, Zach was busy gathering up the dishes. He bent over about to load the dishes into the dishwasher when his cellphone rang. He set the dishes on the counter, dashed into the living room, snatched the cellphone off the end table, and swiped the screen to answer the call.

"Hello," Zach answered cautiously, suspicious when he did not recognize the number displayed on the screen.

"Is this Zach Templeton?" a female voice asked.

"Yes, this is Zach Templeton."

"Wait one, sir."

Zach stood waiting, hearing muffled voices in the background. A few seconds later, Zach heard an excited male voice.

"Zach, are you there?"

"Admiral Hadley, is that you?" Zach asked, recognizing the voice of his old friend.

"Sorry, but I had to know it was you before I took the phone. I'm at the home of a friend."

"A friend?"

"Yes, a friend. She was my secretary."

"Was your secretary?" Zach answered in a questioning tone.

"Yes, was," Admiral Hadley repeated. "I was forced to retire. I guess I crossed that evil witch, Vice President Hayworth one too many times. She demanded I put in my papers. I did and they were accepted immediately. I was escorted out the door a civilian."

I'm sorry, Admiral," Zach offered.

"Don't be. It was time, but that is not the only reason I called. I...," Admiral Hadley quit talking.

"Admiral Hadley?" Zach asked when the admiral did not continue. "Admiral, are you still there?"

"Yes, Zach. I'm still here. I'm just not sure I should continue. I don't want to put you and Anna Mae in danger."

"Does this have something to do with your being forced to retire?"

"No. Ah... Well, maybe yes more than no."

"Admiral, we have been friends for a long time. More than friends, actually. Anna Mae and I consider you family. If you are in trouble, you need to tell me."

"Okay. Sit down. You aren't going to believe this."

Zach sat on the couch and listened to Admiral Hadley's strained and emotional voice.

"You're kidding!" Zach choked, the color draining from his face.

Monday, Feb. 9th - 6:58 p.m. CST
James Templeton Residence
South Lakewood Avenue
Tulsa, Oklahoma

Hans "Two Fingers" Pfitzner shifted his weight impatiently and pressed the doorbell a second time. He had watched as the garage door closed and he could hear a television playing, so he knew the Templetons were home.

James Templeton saved a draft of the email he had open and rushed out of the back bedroom he used as an office when he heard the doorbell ring for the second time. Glancing into the kitchen and not seeing Margaret, his wife, he hurried toward the front door. James grabbed the doorknob and eased the door open a few inches. Having noticed movement in the front door's frosted side panel, Pfitzner tensed. Seizing the opportunity, he kicked the door open and pointed the muzzle of the sound suppressor directly at James's face. James backed up into the living room as Pfitzner pushed the door shut.

"Vere ess vife?" Pfitzner snarled.

"Huh, what are you talking about?" James stammered.

"Vife," Pfitzner shouted. "You know. Voman live here vif you."

"Oh, I don't know exactly," James gulped. "Somewhere in the house."

"Do not be smart," Pfitzner warned. "Find vife."

With the sound suppressor jammed firmly against the back of James's neck, Pfitzner followed James as he poked his head into each of the bedrooms. Finding each bedroom empty, the two men moved through the living room and into the kitchen just as Margaret came up from the basement with a jar of spaghetti sauce in her hand. She shrieked and dropped the jar of sauce, sending the bright red sauce and shards of glass splattering across the tile floor and onto the lower cabinets.

"What is the meaning of this?" Margaret wailed.

"Shut up voman," Pfitzner yelled. "Go sit at table." He grabbed James and shoved him toward the door leading to the backyard. "Open door," Pfitzner ordered.

Not seeing any safe alternative, James complied. He unlocked the back door and pulled it open. Gustav Tiedemann, Pfitzner's accomplice, barged into the room, slammed the door, and locked it.

"Vach her," Pfitzner yelled at his accomplice. "If voman moves, kill her." He took a step closer toward James and growled. "Vere ess zee data?"

"What data?" James responded. "I don't know what you're talking about."

Pfitzner drew back his right arm and slammed the pistol against the side of James's face. James recoiled and fell against the wall. Pfitzner grabbed James by the shirt and drew him close until James could smell the man's hot, foul breath.

"Du hältst mich für dumm?" the man exploded.

James looked at the man and shrugged, having no idea what the man had said.

"You thinkink I am stupid?" Pfitzner repeated in broken English. "I zay again. Vere ess zee data?"

"I'm telling you I don't know what you're talking about," James groaned, rubbing the angry, red welt coloring the side of his face.

Red-faced, Pfitzner shoved James against the wall and screamed, "Am losink patience. You vill tell me now."

Pushed beyond his limit, anger boiled up inside James causing him to lash out at the man. He lunged for the pistol, but missed. Pfitzner kicked James's right leg out from under him. James lost his balance and landed flat on his back, knocking all the air from his lungs. Wheezing and trying to scramble backward, James failed to avoid Pfitzner's large, size thirteen foot. The large square-toed boot crashed into James's ribs. James cried out in pain, reeling from the vicious jolt.

Filled with rage, Pfitzner took hold of James's shirt, lifted him up, and hurled him toward the table. Unable to maintain his balance, James crashed into a chair and fell onto the floor.

"Töte die Frau," Pfitzner yelled at his accomplice in German.

The man named Tiedemann extended his arm, pointing his pistol directly at Margaret Templeton's forehead.

"No, stop," James gasped, trying to dislodge himself from the tangle of overturned chairs. "Don't hurt her. She doesn't know anything."

"If you not vant voman to die, you vill tell me vere ess data," Pfitzner growled.

Bargaining for time, James sputtered, rubbing his painful ribs, "Computer. Back room."

"Show me now or voman dies!"

Struggling up from his knees, James leaned on the table for support. He let go of the table and stumbled toward the back bedroom.

"No, James," Margaret stuttered, shaking with fear. "They will kill us when they get what they want."

"But Margaret, I don't have any choice."

James touched Margaret's shoulder, winked, and started down the hallway with Pfitzner following close behind. After walking into the bedroom, James pulled the desk chair away from the desk and collapsed into the chair.

"Hurry up," Pfitzner urged, poking James in the back of his head with the sound suppressor.

James slid open the middle drawer of the desk, fished out a small flash drive, and held it out.

"How I know vhat ess on zis?"

"Here, let me show you," James grunted, grabbing the flash drive out of Pfitzner's hand.

James pushed the protective cap back and shoved the flash drive into an empty USB slot on the front of the computer. He jiggled the mouse, waited for the computer to wake up, opened a File Explorer session, and then clicked on the flash drive's main folder.

"See, it's all there," James said, pointing at the list of file names displayed on the screen.

"Not mean nothink," Pfitzner shouted. "Show me vhat zis means."

James drew in a breath, knowing he was only going to get one chance. As he slid the mouse across the surface of the desk, he deliberately tapped a pencil cup, knocking it off the edge of the desk. With Pfitzner momentarily distracted, James made his move.

Chapter Seven

Monday, Feb. 9th – 8:25 p.m. EST
Blue Crab Restaurant
Fifth Street South
Arlington, Virginia

Edger Cordel, former President Paul Cantwell's White House Communications Director, held up his hand and signaled the server that had just dropped off food at a nearby table. The server leaned the large, round serving tray he was carrying against the wall of the restaurant's serving station and hustled over to Edger's table.

"May I take that?" the server asked, pointing at what was left of Edger's dinner.

Edger wiped the corners of his mouth with his napkin and nodded. The server stacked the bread plate and silverware on the plate. Balancing the dishes on his left hand, he asked, "Can I get you some desert?"

"No thank you, but I could use some more coffee," Edger answered.

"Right away, sir," the server advised as he turned and disappeared into the kitchen.

Edger felt faint buzzing coming from his jacket pocket. He reached his hand into his jacket pocket, pulled out his cellphone, glanced at the number displayed on the screen, then swiped the screen to answer the call.

"Hang on," Edger said, seeing the server approaching his table, coffee pot in hand. Edger placed his hand over the cellphone and waited while the server refilled his cup. He took a sip of the steaming coffee, held the phone up to his ear, and continued, "Go ahead but be careful. I'm at the restaurant. I've been waiting for your call."

"Sorry, I got delayed," the man on the other end explained. "Do you have it?"

Edger grabbed the napkin from his lap and wiped small beads of perspiration from his forehead, his eyes surveying the nearly empty restaurant to see if anyone was listening. Only one person seated four tables away had noticed Edger pull the cellphone from his pocket. As soon as their eyes met, the man looked away and resumed his conversation with the woman seated across from him.

Edger lowered his voice and answered, "Yes, I have it. I'm going to secure it in my wall safe as soon as I get home."

"No, that's no good," the man objected. "Huffman and Wirth are both dead. You've got to….,"

"Dead? When? How?" Edger interrupted, his voice rising."

"Keep your voice down," the man snapped. "Yesterday. They were both murdered."

"Do the authorities know who's responsible?" Edger questioned, his voice filling with emotion.

"That's not important right now. I think someone is on to us. You must deliver it tonight. Can you do that?"

"Yes. I have it with me. I can deliver it as soon as I leave the restaurant."

"I don't have to tell you how critical this is," the man cautioned. "Meet me at the usual place."

The call abruptly ended. Edger cleared the screen, dropped the cellphone back into his jacket pocket, and mopped his forehead again. He shook his head. Things were happening much sooner than he expected. Eager to be on his way and not wanting to wait for the server to show up again, he dug his wallet out of his hip pocket, selected a couple of bills, dropped them on the table, and placed a glass on top of them.

The man that had looked away when Edger glanced in his direction, fished a cellphone out of his pocket and hurriedly dialed a number. "He's on his way out," the man said. Not waiting for an answer, he ended the call, stuffed the cellphone back into his pocket, and watched Edger out of the corner of his eye.

Struggling, Edger pushed his two hundred sixty-five pound, five foot eight inch frame up from the table and headed for the door. Passing the server on his way to the exit, he called out, "In a hurry. Money's on the table. Keep the change."

Two men in a dark green Lexus GS had followed Edger to the restaurant. Parked on a side street half a block from the restaurant, the two men had waited for instructions. The passenger in the Lexus, Andrew Tiner, FBI Field Agent from the FBI's DC office, scrambled out of the car and headed for Edger Cordell's brand new, white Cadillac XT5 SUV, parked across the street from the restaurant.

Edger exited the restaurant, crossed the street, and hurried toward his car, deeply concerned by the murder of the two men he had met with just a few days earlier. Distracted by his troubled thoughts, Edger did not see or hear the man slip up behind him.

Edger unlocked the car and pulled the door open. About to climb in, Edger flinched when Agent Tiner shoved the muzzle of a pistol into his ribs.

"Don't be stupid," Tiner warned. "If you try anything, I *will* kill you."

Edger started to turn, but Tiner punched Edger in the ribs with his free hand and shoved him into the car. Tiner opened the rear door and jumped in behind Edger. Tiner pressed the muzzle of his 9mm semi-automatic against Edger's neck and ordered, "Close the door and drive."

As Edger drove out of the parking lot, the driver of the Lexus, Martin Williamson, FBI Special Agent also from the FBI's DC, office, pulled away from the curb and followed the Cadillac as it drove north on Glebe Road toward Interstate Sixty-Six.

The man that had watched Edger in the restaurant had exited the restaurant and watched as Edger was shoved into his car. He pulled a cell-phone from his pocket again and pressed the redial key.

"Yeah," Special Agent Williamson answered.

"Cordell said he has it with him. You *must* get it. Once you have it, make certain he tells no one."

"Yes, Sir," Special Agent Williamson answered. "Consider it done," Williamson added as he ended the call.

After driving out of the parking lot, Edger Cordell drove north on Glebe Road for several miles. Agent Tiner, in the back seat, ordered Edger to turn left onto the entrance ramp for westbound Interstate Sixty-Six. A few seconds later the dark green Lexus GS, turned left onto the interstate entrance ramp, and merged into traffic several cars behind Edger's Cadillac. Special Agent Williamson kept Edger's Cadillac XT5 in view as they passed through Falls Church, Virginia, and entered rural Fairfax County. The traffic thinned out quickly after the two cars left the suburbs surrounding Washington, D.C.

For twenty-five long, grueling minutes, Agent Tiner kept the muzzle of his pistol pressed against Edger's neck. Afraid to take his hands off the steering wheel to adjust the temperature, the interior of the Cadillac soon became overly warm. Drops of perspiration rolled down Edger's neck, soaking the collar of his shirt. He swallowed hard as he passed the exit ramp for Highway Twenty-Eight, his usual exit.

Two miles later, Tiner tapped Edger's neck and ordered, "Exit here. Turn right at the end of the ramp."

"Where are we going? What do you want?" Edger stammered.

"Shut up and drive," Tiner shouted, pushing the pistol harder against Edger's neck.

Edger stopped at the end of the exit ramp, looked left, and then turned right as instructed. He drove north on Virginia State Highway Two-Thirty-Four and entered Manassas National Battle Park. One-half mile into the park, he stopped at a stop sign, crossed US Highway Twenty-Nine, and continued north, exiting the park three-quarters of a mile later. The Lexus had lagged back, already knowing where the Cadillac XT5 was headed. Special Agent Williamson glanced in the rear view mirror to check traffic. Being

Tuesday night past nine o'clock, traffic was very light, especially considering the park had been closed for several hours.

"Turn left on the next road," Agent Tiner ordered Edger Cordell.

Nearly missing the unmarked gravel road, Edger had to stomp on the brake and turn the steering wheel sharply to make the turn onto the gravel road. Two hundred yards from the highway, the rutted gravel road narrowed and changed to nothing more than a pair of worn tire tracks through the weeds. Edger stopped when the tire tracks ended.

"What now?" Edger stammered.

"Turn into the opening, there between the trees," Agent Tiner instructed, pointing to his right.

Edger turned right, passed through a narrow opening in the tree line, and followed two barely visible tracks leading to an old, abandoned barn.

"Drive behind the barn and turn off your lights," Tiner ordered.

Edger drove behind the barn as instructed. He shifted the Cadillac into Park and turned off the headlights. Several minutes later, the Lexus pulled up beside the Cadillac and turned off its headlights. Special Agent Williamson climbed out, walked beside the Cadillac, and yanked open the driver's door.

"Get out," Williamson barked.

"No. You can't do this," Edger wailed.

Williamson pulled a semi-automatic pistol from a shoulder holster, pointed it at Edger's face, and bellowed, "I said get out!"

Edger scrambled to release his seatbelt and nearly fell out of the car when the seatbelt released. "What do you want?" he grunted as he slid out and stood up. Edger's fear turned to shock when he recognized the man standing in front of him. "I know you," Edger stammered. "You're an FBI agent. This is against the law. You can't do this."

"Where is it?" Williamson yelled, ignoring Edger's complaint.

"I don't know what you are talking about," Edger exploded.

"Convince our friend here we mean business," Williamson shouted, looking over at Tiner.

Agent Tiner, also standing beside the Cadillac, shoved his pistol behind his back and stepped in front of Edger. He grabbed Edger by his jacket, slapped him, punched him in the stomach, and slammed him against the car. Edger fell in a heap on the ground.

"Get him up," Williamson ordered. "Let's see if he's ready to talk."

Tiner dragged Edger to his feet, pinning him against the side of the Cadillac. "Where is it?" he yelled in Edger's face.

"I'm telling you I don't know what you're talking about."

Williamson made a show of deliberately and slowly screwing a sound suppressor to the muzzle of his pistol. He pushed Tiner out of the way, stepped in front of Edger, and jammed the sound suppressor against Edger's cheek. Leaning to within an inch of Edger's face, he snarled, "We know you have it. Somebody listened to your phone call at the restaurant. You told whoever you were talking to that you have it. I want it now!"

"No," Edger shrieked.

Williamson exploded with rage and shoved Edger against the car, tightening his finger against the trigger.

Monday, Feb. 9th – 7:30 p.m. CST
James Templeton Residence
South Lakewood Avenue
Tulsa, Oklahoma

James Templeton made a made wild grab for Pfitzner's gun. Unfortunately, the wheeled office chair James was sitting in scooted backward because of the force of his lunge. He desperately grabbed at the gun, but his fingers missed by two inches. Grasping at empty air, James lost his balance and fell off the chair, landing hard on the floor.

As he banged up against the desk, James kicked at Pfitzner's legs, landing his foot two inches above Pfitzner's left ankle. Pfitzner yelped and fell to his right. James scrambled to his knees and pounced on top of Pfitzner. Having managed to hang onto his gun, Pfitzner swung his arm upward and smashed the gun against the side of James's head.

Stunned by the vicious blow, James crumpled and fell sideways. Before James could clear the fog from his brain, Pfitzner was up on his knees, pointing his gun at James's face.

"I vill kill you right now," he hollered, a maniacal look on his face.

James cringed, waiting for the sound that would mean the end of his life, but the sound never came. He looked up and saw Pfitzner struggling to his feet, still pointing the gun at him.

"Get up, unwissendes schweinegesicht," Pfitzner snarled. "Sit in zee chair and do as I zay. Do zat again, and I vill make you and your vife's death very painful."

Rubbing the side of his face, James pushed himself up and slumped heavily into the chair. Pfitzner shoved the chair with his foot, sending James crashing into the desk.

"I am askink for last time. Vere ess zee data?"

James dragged the keyboard back in front of the monitor and laid his right hand on the mouse.

"Careful, I am watchink you," Pfitzner warned.

James slid the mouse across the pad, moving the pointer up and toward the left side of the screen. As the pointer crossed over a rectangular, gray button, James clicked the mouse button. The open window closed, revealing the screen underneath.

"Vat vas zat?" Pfitzner demanded. "Vat happen ozer screen?"

"I just closed it to show you what's underneath," James lied. "Now, I have to close this screen to show you the file listings.

James slid the mouse again, moving the pointer to the top right corner of the screen. He clicked the "X" and closed the email application that had been open, revealing the desktop screen with various icons scattered across it.

"Stop stallink," Pfitzner shouted. "Show me zee data files now!"

"But you won't recognize the data even if I show it to you," James blurted out, turning toward Pfitzner.

"Vell then, dummkopf, I vill takink all of computer!" Pfitzner bellowed, succumbing to the rage boiling inside him. He raised his arm and pointed the 9mm pistol directly at James's forehead.

James saw a flash of movement at the doorway. A dark, hooded figure wearing a Halloween mask rushed quickly into the room and bludgeoned Pfitzner in the side of the head with a large semi-automatic pistol. Pfitzner's 9mm pistol fell from his hand as he crumpled to the floor, a dark, red stain spreading out on the carpet.

"Be quiet. If you want to live, do not say a word," the hooded figure whispered, holding his finger to his lips.

The hooded figure bent down, picked up Pfitzner's pistol, unscrewed the sound suppressor, dropped it in his jacket pocket, and shoved the pistol behind his back.

Gustav Tiedemann, Pfitzner's accomplice, hearing the commotion, called out from the kitchen, "Hans, was ist los. Was war das für ein Schläger??"

The hooded figure put his finger to his lips again and waited.

"Hans, geht es dir gut," Tiedemann hollered.

"Gustav, hilf mir. Ich bin verletzen," the hooded figure croaked, making his voice sound gravelly. He pushed Pfitzner's body out of the way, stepped over beside the door, and waited.

The wait was short. A few seconds later Tiedemann ran into the room and bent over his partner. An unsuspecting Tiedemann received the same vicious slam to the head as had his partner. Tiedemann fell over his partner and lay still.

"Say nothing and do *exactly* as I tell you," the hooded figure commanded. "We must get you out of here quickly. Do you understand?"

James nodded his head up and down acknowledging that he understood.

"Where is the data?" the hooded figure asked.

James pointed at the computer.

The hooded figure bent over and pulled the computer out from the lower compartment in the desk. Not bothering to power down the computer, he grabbed various cables and yanked them out. Holding the computer under his arm, he pointed toward the door. With James in the lead, he pulled the door shut as he exited the bedroom and together they headed for the kitchen.

"Oh, James you're okay" Margaret cried out as James peeled the duct tape off her mouth.

"You must be quiet and do exactly as I say," the hooded figure demanded, pointing the menacing pistol at her.

"Margaret, do as he says," James urged.

The hooded figure walked to the back door, switched off the lights, and ordered James and Margaret to step outside and wait. He pushed the door closed and locked it. Standing in the shadows, the hooded man watched and listened. No sounds of traffic. The streets were quiet.

"Hurry, we must go quickly there's a storm coming," the hooded figure said, hearing the loud rumble of a freakish, mid-winter thunderstorm. "My car is two blocks away."

A dazzling explosion of white-hot light produced by one hundred million volts of electricity came first, lighting up the neighborhood in a dazzling flash of blinding light. A sizzling crackle followed as a jagged spear of lightning knifed through the humid air, striking in the center of a playground less than a block away. About to step out of the shadows, they all cowered as the sharp crack of thunder literally shook the ground.

"Hurry, we must go, now before it gets worse!" the hooded figure urged as the first drops of rain began to splatter upon the ground.

Poking the gun in Margaret's back, he pushed her out into the rain, going in the opposite direction from which Pfitzner and his accomplice had come. Upon reaching the car, the hooded figure pulled the back door open and grabbed two pairs of handcuffs from the floorboard. He threw one pair to James and said, "Sorry, you must put these on your wife. Then take that duct tape and put it over her mouth. Be quick about it. The storm is about to let loose."

James wondered if he should make an attempt to overpower this new hooded assailant, but ultimately, he complied, afraid he would get Margaret hurt or killed. James took Margaret's hands, placed them behind her back, and clicked the handcuffs around both wrists. "*I'm, sorry*," James mouthed as he ripped off a six-inch piece of duct tape and placed it over Margaret's mouth. Margaret lowered herself onto the backseat and slid over to the passenger side of the car.

"Put one handcuff on, then put your hands behind your back," the hooded figure ordered, handing James the other pair of handcuffs. "Don't try anything and you won't get hurt."

The hooded figure stuffed his weapon behind his belt and quickly snapped the free handcuff over James's wrist and pushed him down onto the backseat beside his wife. A piece of duct tape went over James's mouth.

The wind shifted direction suddenly and increased dramatically as torrential rain began pelting the ground. The hooded figure yanked the car door open, jumped into the driver's seat, started the engine, and checked the street in both directions. Finding the street still quiet and deserted, he slipped the car into gear. Another bolt of lightning streaked through the sky, illuminating a blinding wall of water, driven sideways by the intense wind. The car rolled slowly down the street, the windshield wipers thrashing back and forth at top speed, barely able to keep up with the deluge of rain drops. The car reached the intersection, turned the corner, and disappeared into the dark, rainy night.

The residents along South Lakewood Avenue, sitting in their living rooms munching snacks and watching their favorite television programs, had no idea their friends and neighbors, the Templetons, had just been kidnapped.

Monday, Feb. 9th – 8:01 p.m. EST
Riverside Flight Center
Tulsa, Oklahoma

During the nineteen minute ride from the Templeton home on Lakewood Avenue across the south side of Tulsa to the Riverside Airport, the hooded figure that had saved James and Margaret Templeton from certain death had revealed himself to be Secret Service Agent David McClain. David and James were old friends, having worked together in the past. David McClain's duty in the White House allowed him to often overhear many things. When, quite by accident, he overheard that James and his wife were to be silenced by a pair of contract assassins, he had not hesitated to get involved.

When David bailed out of the car and started to transfer some luggage to a small Cessna, James Templeton hurriedly dug his cellphone out of his jacket pocket and dialed his son, Zach's, number from memory. The things he had learned from his friend during the ride to the airport, frightened him and he had to warn his son.

As soon as his son answered on the third ring, James disguised his voice as best as he could and said, "Don't talk, just listen."

"Who is this?"

"I said just listen," James insisted. "This call must be short."

"I'm listening," Zach grunted.

"Bill Huffman and James Wirth were murdered. Gene Croft died this morning in a car bomb and now Kevin Hunt is missing. You may be next. Watch your back."

James ended the call and powered the phone off, praying the short call would not have been intercepted.

"Hurry up," David McClain yelled over the sound of the Cessna's engine noise. "We have to get out of here, *now*."

James dropped the cellphone back in his jacket pocket and grabbed Margaret's hand. "Come on. Let's go"

Together, James and Margaret rushed over to the small plane and clambered inside. They had barely settled back into their seats before the pilot released the brake and began taxiing toward the runway. Three minutes later the Cessna turned onto the runway and lifted into the dark sky.

Monday, Feb. 9th – 9:11 p.m. EST
Zach Templeton Residence
Big House Plantation Road,
Bluffton, South Carolina

Having finished putting Mazie to bed, Anna Mae climbed the creaky stairs to their upstairs bedroom, slipped into her pajamas and robe, and made her way back down the stairs. She walked into the living room and found Zach sitting on the couch gazing blankly off into space.

She started across the room, hesitated, and stared at Zach, former US Navy SEAL turned senior communications analyst. Zach was the bravest, most fearless man she had ever met. She remembered the first time he had touched her hand and how gentle he had been as he dressed the wound she had gotten from falling on an old tree stump. That first day, deep down inside, she knew this brave but gentle man was the person she wanted to spend the rest of her life with. Now she could not imagine her life without him. She continued across the room and stopped beside him.

"Zach, I know you're tired, why don't you come to bed," Anna Mae urged.

Zach did not answer. He sat rigid, unmoving, frozen in place like a marble statue.

"Zach," Anna Mae called out a little louder as she tapped him on the shoulder.

"Huh? Oh, Sorry, I didn't hear you come into the room," Zach offered in defense, turning toward Anna Mae.

"Zach, what's wrong?" she asked, concerned by the look of distress on his face. She always knew when something was troubling him.

"I just can't believe it," Zach shrugged, shaking his head. "I just can't believe it."

"Can't believe what? Zach, talk to me. Tell me what has you so upset."

"Admiral Hadley called while you were giving Mazie her bath and putting her to bed. He's not an admiral anymore... at least, not officially."

"Not an admiral," Anna Mae exclaimed. "How can that be? What happened?"

"He said it just happened," Zach answered. "Vice President Hayworth burst into his office unannounced and told him to submit his retirement papers by the end of the day. The admiral said when he asked her for a reason, she exploded and yelled at him. Then she threatened him. She said if his retirement papers weren't on the CNO's desk by four o'clock, he would be brought up on charges."

"Brought up on charges? You've got to be kidding. Admiral Hadley is one of the most decent and honorable men I have ever known. Surely he's going to fight this?"

"No. He said he had had enough. He said he'd been thinking a lot about retirement anyway. Said he can't stand the new administration. All of the appointments from President Cantwell's administration have been forced to resign or have been fired. The admiral said he's never seen anything like it. He said Borden's administration is purging anyone who doesn't kowtow to their insane, radical ideology. He said *everyon*e is afraid of that evil, screaming witch Hayworth. His words—not mine."

"That sounds awful," Anna Mae sighed. "What's the admiral going to do?"

"He said he is selling the condo," Zach replied. "He said there's no reason to stay in Washington anymore and there are just too many memories. He sees Jean every where he looks. His son in Florida has been badgering him to move down there to be closer to him. Said he is at least going to look at some properties there."

"That would be good for him," Anna Mae offered. "He would be able to enjoy his grandchildren."

"True," Zach agreed. "but that's not the worst part. Do you remember Gene Croft?"

"Gene Croft?" Anna Mae muttered, a puzzled look on her face. "The name sounds familiar but I can't place it."

"He and I worked together on a large data warehouse project in Nashville a year ago. It housed huge amounts of clinical and medical research data."

"Now I remember. That was the project that had a lot of issues. The company suddenly cancelled the whole project and let sixty consultants go with no notice or explanation."

"Yep, that's the one," Zach agreed, nodding his head. "Gene was killed yesterday when his car exploded, sitting right in his driveway. The bomb blast flattened his house and blew out windows two blocks away. His wife is five months pregnant. The doctors don't think she will survive."

"A bomb?" Anna Mae gasped. "What about the baby?"

Zach exhaled noisily, shook his head, and said, "She's only five months along. The baby is just too small."

"How dreadful," Anna Mae moaned as she sat on the couch beside Zach, leaning her head on his shoulder.

Zach and Anna Mae sat silently for several minutes. Zach picked at his trousers, debating whether he should tell Anna Mae the rest of what Admiral Hadley had told him and about the short phone call warning him. Zach stared at the same spot on the carpet for a long time. Anna Mae stirred. She got up from the couch and grabbed Zach's hand.

"Come on, let's go to bed. It's late," Anna Mae urged.

"There's more," Zach blurted out, knowing he would not be able to keep the frightening news from Anna Mae.

"Okay, out with it," she said, settling down on her knees in front of Zach.

"Bill Huffman, another consultant that works at the same firm as Gene, also died in a suicide bomb blast in Washington, D.C. James Wirth was found murdered in front of his townhouse. Jeffery Wagner and his wife, Jennifer, were found murder in their home, execution style. Hadley said the police think it was a robbery gone wrong, but the Admiral doesn't believe it and I don't believe that either. Wirth worked for Mitchell Sciences on the same project as Gene Croft. Jeffery Wagner was an FBI agent who was going to turn whistleblower. The morning Gene's car exploded, he was leaving for the airport. Gene had a meeting scheduled with Paul Hunt and *now*, Paul Hunt is missing."

"Paul Hunt!" Anna Mae exclaimed. "I heard you mention his name just last week. Zach I'm frightened. All these people…," Anna Mae's voice trailed off as a worried look clouded her face.

Zach did not know what to say. He just shrugged.

"Zach, you know or have worked with all those men. What is going on?" Anna Mae fretted.

"Something terrible," Zach answered. "Something has the Admiral really spooked, but he wouldn't tell me. Anna Mae, the Admiral is really scared. I could hear it in his voice. He warned me. Told me to be very careful. He was about to say something else but we got disconnected. I called him back twice, but it went straight to voicemail."

"Why did he warn you?" Anna Mae asked.

"I don't know. Maybe that was what the Admiral was going to say when we got disconnected. I know he wouldn't warn me without a good reason. I'll call him again tomorrow.

"Zach, how did Admiral Hadley know Gene Croft and the other men?" Anna Mae probed. "Were they in the Navy?"

"No. He told me he found out they were all involved in something terrifying. Something related to a virus, but that's as much as he would say." Zach answered.

"Let's go to bed. We can talk more about this tomorrow."

"There's more," Zach said. "I learned about Bill Huffman, James Wirth, and Paul Hunt from a different phone call. The caller tried to disguise his voice, but I recognized it. It was Dad."

"Your Dad?" Anna Mae questioned. "Why would he disguise his voice."

"I don't know. He didn't explain," Zach explained. "He was very short. He only told me about the men and then he said, 'You may be next. Watch your back.',"

"You may be next," Anna Mae blurted out. "What did he mean by that?"

"I don't know," Zach shrugged. "That's all he said. Then he hung up. I'm certain I heard a small plane's engine in the background just before he hung up."

"Zach what is going on?" Anna Mae asked, a look of fear clouding her face.

"I don't know," Zach said. "I didn't recognize the number. I tried calling the number back, but it immediately went to a voice mailbox that had not been setup. There's nothing more we can do tonight. Let's go to bed."

As Zach got up from the couch, he nearly fell over Tripp who had been lying at his feet with his chin on Zach's feet.

"Come on, Tripp. Let's go to bed," Zach said as he reached down and patted the hound's head.

Anna Mae waited at the bottom of the stairs while Zach checked all the doors to be certain they were locked. He turned off the living room light and together they started up the stairs to their bedroom. Tripp squeezed past them and waited at the top of the stairs, tail wagging furiously.

"Rug. Now," Zach ordered as he reached the top of the stairs, pointing at the rug beside the bed.

Tripp's ears drooped. The hound scampered over to the rug, circled twice, and laid down, keeping his eyes fixed on Zach.

Zach crossed the bedroom, opened the closet door, and knelt down on one knee. He thumbed a five digit code into the gun safe anchored to the floor. He pulled open the door and lifted out his custom-grade, STI

Lawman 45 ACP semi-automatic pistol. As his fingers slid across the diamond-checkered walnut grips, he shuddered as he remembered the last time he had held the STI Lawman in his hands. The confrontation he had had with the ruthless criminal, *al-Ta'abin* had nearly cost him his life.

Zach grabbed a magazine, loaded it with nine .45 caliber cartridges, then shoved the magazine into the pistol. Sporting a five-inch barrel, the pistol was not an easy weapon to conceal, but Zach preferred it for its superior accuracy and its enormous stopping power. If you put a round from the STI Lawman anywhere on your target, the target would not be getting up, period.

Zach chose not to pull the slide back and load a cartridge into the chamber. He carried the weapon over to his side of the bed and gently laid the pistol in the top drawer of the nightstand.

"Do you really need that?" Anna Mae questioned. "What about Mazie?"

"Don't worry," Zach asserted. "I will keep it with me at all times. I'll make certain she can't get near it."

"You really think it is necessary to have it at all times?" Anna Mae probed, a worried look on her face.

"Yes, I do, actually," Zach affirmed. "I've never heard Admiral Hadley trip over his tongue so much. The tone in the Admiral's warning also has me spooked. I could tell he is worried *and* frightened. I have a very uneasy feeling and I am not going to take any chances."

Monday, Feb. 9th – 9:31 p.m. EST
Abandoned Barn
North of Manassas, Virginia

The drivers-side window of Edger Cordell's Cadillac XT5 SUV exploded into thousands of tiny fragments. A shower of small chunks of glass cascaded onto Edger's shoulders and fell to the ground.

"The next one goes through your brain if you don't tell me where it is," Special Agent Williamson roared.

"I told you I don't have it," Edger wailed.

Do you not understand me? I *will* kill you if you do not tell me where it is?"

"You're going to kill me anyway," Edger bleated. "You'll just have to find it."

"If that's the way you want it," the man hissed, pointing the 9mm semi-automatic directly at Edger's head.

Williamson's finger tightened. The trigger released, striking the firing pin. A few milliseconds later the back of Edger's head exploded. Hair, fragments of skull, and blood splattered the interior of the car. Edger's death was instantaneous. His body relaxed and crumpled to the ground.

"He's dead. What are we going to do now?" Field Agent Tiner asked.

"Doesn't matter. He wasn't going to tell us anyway. You go through the car. I'll check his pockets."

Tiner removed a pair of rubber gloves from his pocket and pulled them on. He ran around the rear of the Cadillac and opened the passenger door. Being careful to avoid the blood splatters, he opened the glove compartment and pulled out its contents. After searching through the contents and finding nothing of interest, he threw the contents on the floor. Noticing a briefcase lying on the backseat, Tiner slammed the front door and opened the rear door. He rifled through the briefcase's contents, again finding nothing of interest. Tiner swore and slammed the briefcase against the opposite door.

"There's nothing inside the car or in his briefcase," Tiner informed Special Agent Williamson as he rounded the rear of the Cadillac. "Is there anything in his pockets?"

"Just some change, a chapstick, a handkerchief in his jacket, and a wallet in his hip pocket," Williamson replied, stuffing a wad of bills from the wallet in his trouser pocket and throwing the empty wallet through the shattered and missing window.

"It has to be here somewhere. He told the person on the phone he had it with him."

Williamson opened the front door, carefully reached in with his gloved hand, and pulled the keys out of the ignition."Here, look inside the trunk," he said, tossing Tiner the keys.

"There's absolutely nothing in here and I mean nothing," Tiner yelled after a quick search.

"It has to be here somewhere," Williamson complained. "It must be on him somewhere. Strip him and go through his clothes."

Tiner stripped off Edger's jacket, dug through all the pockets, then ripped out the lining and squeezed every inch of the material. He repeated the process with Edger's shirt. Williamson had stripped off Edger's trousers, also coming up empty.

"What now?" Tiner shrugged.

"We'll have to go through the car again," Williamson answered. "Let's drag him out of the way. You grab his feet."

"Huh, what's this?" Tiner exclaimed as he began to tug at Edger's feet. "The heel of one of his shoes is coming off."

"Let me see that," Williamson barked, kneeling down to get a closer look. "Well, what do you know. This is old-school, cold war stuff."

Williamson stood up holding a computer flash drive in his hand and quickly stuffed it in his trouser pocket. The two men picked up Edger's limp body, put his clothes back on, and dumped it in the front seat of the Cadillac. Williamson leaned in, shoved the keys into the ignition, and started the engine.

"Take the Lexus and shove it in the river," Williamson ordered.

Williamson watched while Tiner eased the Lexus up against the back bumper of the Cadillac.

Leaning inside the Cadillac, Williamson pulled the gear lever into Drive and pushed the door closed.

"Okay, push it into the river," Williamson shouted.

Tiner began pushing the Cadillac. Slowly the car rolled forward toward the river, picking up speed as it began rolling down a grassy embankment. The Cadillac hit the water with enough momentum to cause it to float twenty feet out into Little Bull Run River. The two men watched as the Cadillac sank and disappeared from sight.

"Let's get out of here," Williamson shouted.

Tiner slid over to the passenger seat. Williamson jumped into the driver's seat, shifted into reverse, turned the Lexus around, and headed for the highway. He slowed the car down and turned off the headlights as they approached the highway. Seeing no traffic coming from either direction, Williamson turned on the headlights and roared out onto the highway, tires squealing as he accelerated back toward the interstate. Ten minutes later the two men were speeding down Interstate Sixty-Six back toward the city.

"Job well done," Tiner laughed as he turned and looked over at Williamson.

Chapter Eight

Tuesday, Feb. 10th – 7:12 a.m. EST
Zach Templeton Residence
Big House Plantation Road
Bluffton, South Carolina

Zach Templeton stirred under the covers, reached his hand out, and rubbed his nose. He pulled his hand back under the covers and drew them up under his chin. Something hot blew across his face. Zach slowly opened one eye. A pair of soft brown eyes stared back at him. Zach closed his eye and sighed heavily. Again, something hot blew across his face, followed by a sloppy wet tongue sliding across his face.

"Okay. Okay," Zach moaned. "I'll take you out."

Zach rolled back the covers, slid his legs off the bed, and put his bare feet on the floor. Tripp, the redbone coon hound, danced in circles, eager to get outside. Zach eased off the bed, trying not to wake his wife, Anna Mae.

"Zach, you don't have to be careful. I'm awake," Anna Mae announced. "He was over here a minute ago. You take him out and I'll go start the coffee."

Zach leaned over and kissed Anna Mae on the cheek. He straightened up, grabbed the clothes he had draped over the bedpost, quickly got dressed, and shoved his feet into a pair of old boots sitting at the end of the bed. Zach sat on the edge of the bed, still worried by the disturbing phone call from Admiral Hadley as he laced up the boots. He stood up, walked around to the nightstand, and lifted out the pistol. Zach shoved the pistol into a leather belt holster and slipped it behind his trousers, making certain the metal clip hooked over his belt.

"Come on, Tripp, let's go," he called out to the impatient hound.

Tripp raced down the stairs, ran to the back door, and stood waiting for Zach to catch up. At the bottom of the stairs, Zach snatched a jacket from the closet. He unlocked the back door and pulled the door open. Frantic to get outside, Tripp nosed the screen door open and flew out into the yard. Zach stepped out into the uncommonly cold morning air and quickly pulled the door shut. He shivered, reaching for the zipper of his jacket.

"Brrrr," he exclaimed as he zipped up the jacket and stuffed his hands into the pockets. He opened his mouth and breathed out, watching the warm vapor form a wispy cloud that swirled away and dissipated in the crisp, cold air.

Zach watched as Tripp ran from one side of the yard to the other, looking for that special spot. About to sit down, Zach stopped when he noticed the porch chairs were covered with beads of moisture from a heavy, overnight dew. Rather than bother to get something to wipe the chair off, he leaned against the porch railing, staring at the shafts of light filtering through the trees as the sun began its rise above the eastern horizon. The bright rays of sunlight cast an unearthly golden luminescence as they lit up the heavy mist hugging the base of the trees.

"Hey Tripp," Zach yelled, suddenly realizing the rambunctious hound was no longer in the yard. "Tripp, where are you?" he yelled more loudly.

Zach stepped off the porch and headed for the line of trees at the end on the property. Halfway across the yard, he stopped and bent over and rubbed his stiff, aching knee, a permanent reminder of his nearly life-ending encounter with a vicious terrorist. Lying in bed or sitting for long periods of time caused his knee to stiffen up. The discomfort was worst in the mornings after getting out of bed. Even on one of his good days, the injury caused Zach to walk with a significant limp.

As Zach looked up, his gaze took in the old arched, wooden bridge that crossed the small stream flowing along the back of the property. It was on the very spot where he now stood that his eyes had first beheld the beautiful woman standing on that bridge that later had become his wife. He smiled, remembering the sense of amazement that had filled his heart that unforgettable day when he had first touched her delicate hand.

Zach's daydream was broken by raucous squawking and fluttering of wings as dozens of birds suddenly took flight from the trees at the end of the property. Thinking the birds must have been startled by Tripp chasing some animal through the thick undergrowth, Zach returned to his search for the boisterous hound.

"Tripp, where are you?" Zach yelled again as he approached the edge of the property. There was sudden movement in the dense undergrowth beyond the stream. A reddish-brown flash flew out of the tall weeds, bounded across the small stream, and raced toward Zach.

"Hey, watch out!" Zach shrieked, twisting sideways trying to avoid a collision. Too late, Zach grabbed for his leg when Tripp slammed into Zach's injured knee. In pain, Zach lost his balance and toppled over, landing forcefully on the wet, muddy ground.

"What's the matter with you?" Zach yelled, massaging his aching knee.

Tripp ran a few feet away, laid down on the ground, flattened his ears, and put his chin between his paws. Zach rolled over and struggled to his feet. Standing upright, he looked down at the mud covering his trousers.

Zach took a step toward Tripp and without saying a word raised his arm and pointed at the house.

Tripp rose up from the ground and made a beeline for the house. He leaped up onto the porch and laid down by the door. Zach limped back to the house, stopping several times to rub his throbbing knee. He stopped at the edge of the porch and glared at the apprehensive hound. Tripp, sensing he was in big trouble, laid his chin on the floor and looked the other way.

Zach just stood there glaring at the dog. Every few seconds Tripp's eyebrows would twitch as his eyes glanced in Zach's direction. Working desperately to suppress a smile, Zach stepped up on the porch.

"Don't move," Zach ordered as he reached for the doorknob. He pulled the door open a crack and hollered, "Anna Mae get me an old towel please."

Anna Mae slid the baking pan she was holding into the oven, turned, and rushed off toward the linen closet in the hallway. She returned, stepped part-way through the back door, and held out an old, tattered beach towel.

"I saw the whole thing from the kitchen window," she grinned, trying hard not to laugh. "Looks like both of you might need a bath."

"Ha, ha. *Very* funny," Zach grumbled. "That blasted hound nearly broke my leg."

"He's so excitable. You know how he loves to run."

"Yeah, tell me about it."

Both Zach and Anna Mae looked down at the sad hound and quickly turned away.

"Don't you dare laugh at him," Zach urged.

"Wipe his feet and take him into the bathroom. I just put a coffee cake in the oven. It should be ready by the time you two guys get cleaned up."

Anna Mae turned, smiled broadly, and disappeared in the direction of the kitchen

"You have earned yourself a bath, my friend," Zach grumbled as he leaned down on his good knee and began wiping the mud from Tripp's feet.

With the worst of the mud cleaned off, Zach grabbed Tripp's collar and led him through the house and straight into the bathroom.

Twenty-five minutes later, a wet and fuzzy Tripp bounded into the living room and threw himself on the floor, pushing himself along the carpet as he rubbed one side and then the other. He jumped up and shook ferociously, slapping his long floppy ears. He dove onto the floor and repeated the process.

"Tripp, stop that," Zach hollered as he walked into the living room, dressed in clean clothes.

Awakened by all the racket, Mazie walked out of her bedroom clutching Raffee, her favorite stuffed animal.

"Daddy," she cried out, tottering toward Zach and rubbing her eyes with her free hand.

Zach leaned over, scooped Mazie up, and patted her back. "How's Raffee this morning?" he asked, referring to the stuffed giraffe tucked under Mazie's left arm. Now four years old, Mazie had learned how to say 'giraffe', but the mispronounced name she had used for the stuffed toy as a two year-old had stuck. Poor Raffee was a bit soiled and had lost an ear and one of his eyes. Anna Mae had repaired numerous split seams and tears over the past two years. In spite of that, Mazie refused to give him up. Zach and Anna Mae did not know what they were going to do when Raffee's repairs finally gave out.

"Let's go see what Mommy has for breakfast," Zach said as he turned and headed for the kitchen. "Mmmm, smells delicious."

With Mazie balanced on his left hip, Zach grabbed a sippy cup from the cabinet, picked up the milk carton sitting on the counter, and poured the cup full of milk. He set the sippy cup on the table, put Mazie in her booster chair, and pushed her up to the table. Mazie reached out and grabbed the cup.

"Yea, cake," Mazie chattered when she saw Anna Mae heading toward the table with three plates loaded with coffee cake fresh from the oven.

Eighteen minutes later, Zach drained the last swallow of his coffee, pushed back from the table, and said, "I'd love to sit longer, but I really need to get some work done. Mister Hollins expects a solution for the data transmissions issues I told you about last night."

Zach picked up his and Mazie's dirty plates and carried them to the sink. He poured the remaining coffee from the pot into a travel mug, kissed Anna Mae and Mazie, and headed for the stairs. Before Zach had reached the stairs, Tripp jumped up from his rug, raced up the stairs, and laid down in his usual spot beside Zach's desk.

Zach punched the monitor's On button, sat down in his chair, and waited for the computer to complete its boot-up sequence. While he waited, he browsed through the previous day's mail.

"Junk. Junk. More junk," Zach complained, ripping the useless advertisements in half and tossing them into the trash can. "Good grief," he whined at the computer, annoyed that it was taking so long to complete an operating system update.

The computer finally having completed the update, Zach laid his hand on the mouse and guided the mouse pointer to the email icon located on the left side of the status bar. He hovered the pointer over the icon and clicked the right mouse button. The email program opened, advising that it was sending and receiving data. Once the process was complete, Zach expanded the folder tree and clicked on the inbox. Seventeen new emails filled in the Inbox pane. Zach's eyes immediately fell on the subject line of one particular email halfway down the list of new, unread emails.

ᒣᑦ⅃ⵙᑐ ᒣᑎᒥᕮ ᐯᒥᒣᑎ ᐸᑌᑦⵙ ᐸᒥᑕᗝ.

Shocked to see a second email coded with the same odd symbols, Zach clicked on the email's subject line and watched as multiple lines of similar gibberish filled the document pane on the right side of the application.

"What on earth is that?" Zach remarked, staring at the bizarre jumble of meaningless characters. "Who sent that?" he asked as his eyes glanced up at the "From:" block.

"Diveman@mail.com," Zach exclaimed out loud, recognizing the sender of the email. "I know who that is!"

Already knowing the key to decrypting the odd characters, he copied and pasted the subject line into a blank document then translated it to a readable font. Zach stared at the translated text: "Guard This With Your Life". The cursor blinked at the end of the line like a lighthouse beacon.

Tuesday, Feb. 10th – 10:15 a.m. VST
Tepuy Boardroom
Cayena-Caracas Hotel
Caracas, Venezuela

Situated along the Cordillera de la Costa Central Mountain range of northern Venezuela, the elegant, five star Cayena-Caracas Hotel, offered its guests the most breathtaking views in the entire city of Caracas. Each one of the hotel's luxury suites had been meticulously designed using a different décor. Each of the suites also included a stunning private terrace. Guests overwhelmingly described the hotel's rooftop terrace and its private garden as simply majestic. Every small detail of the hotel had been designed with top-of-the-line luxury in mind. The hotel's legendary La Sibilla Restaurant was said to serve the best Italian food anywhere outside of Italy. An impeccably well-trained staff, instructed to pamper every guest to insure that their guests felt like royalty, rounded out the hotel's five-star services.

Equipped with state of the art technology and luxurious executive furniture, the hotel's exclusive Tepuy boardroom offered a level of sophistication and absolute privacy that *only* the Cayena-Caracas Hotel could offer. The Tepuy boardroom also offered direct access to a fabulous private restaurant area able to seat twenty people, giving meeting attendees the opportunity to end their meetings with a sumptuous meal, served in an exclusive and *exceptionally* private setting.

One of the immaculately dressed members of the hotel's kitchen staff backed out of the boardroom and carefully pulled the gleaming mahogany double doors closed. As he pushed a now-empty serving cart toward the elevator, two men dressed in black suits stepped in front of the doors, the telltale bulge under their jackets quite unmistakable.

Gerard Schechter, seated at the head of the long, highly-polished conference table, had arrived at Simón Bolivar International Airport in a Bombardier Global 7000 private jet just over three hours earlier. The aircraft's standard sixteen-seat interior had been refitted to include a full dining room, multi-media entertainment theatre, and a private bedroom. Schechter's list of modifications had pushed the aircraft's normal $73 Million dollar price tag to well over $90 Million.

A black stretch limousine, waiting in the baggage area, had whisked Gerard Schechter to a private VIP entrance at the rear of the hotel. The hotel's day manager, arriving two hours early, had personally escorted Schechter to a spectacular suite on the top floor of the hotel. A new suit, tailored to Schechter's exact specifications, and a full array of his favorite toiletries sat waiting on an exquisite antique vanity's marble countertop. With two crisp one hundred dollar bills safely tucked in his jacket pocket, the day manager wished Herr Schechter a good day and departed.

In the boardroom, a mouth-watering assortment of breakfast items had been set up on a long table along the north wall: parfait glasses filled with cereal or yogurt and fruit; three flat woven baskets filled to overflowing with various fruits, croissants, and bagels; dessert breads; toast; butter, jams, and jellies; coffee and tea; and a large ice-filled silver bowl containing carafes of milk.

From his position at the head of the table, Schechter motioned toward the array of food and watched as the meeting attendees rose from their seats and began filling plates with the various goodies. Having already eaten in his private suite, Schechter filled a fine-china cup with coffee, stirred in a half-teaspoon of sugar, and returned to his seat.

The ten men attending the hastily called meeting had all arrived throughout the previous day in their luxurious, private jets. Due to their highly recognizable faces, four of the men had arrived under the cover of darkness. As the ten attendees had arrived, each one was picked up at the terminal by a stretch limo with darkened windows. Ushered in through the hotel's private VIP entrance, each man was then escorted through a cleared and guarded hallway to a private elevator. Once all attendees had arrived, the private elevator was locked and armed security guards took up positions at stairwell exits and elevator doors on each floor. Absolutely no one was allowed access to the top two floors of the hotel, except for carefully vetted staff members. All meals, business materials, or any required personal items had already been delivered to their suites. Once the meeting began, only the members were allowed into the boardroom. Any valets, personal assistants, or body guards were required to remain in their assigned suites. The two door guards were the only others allowed on the upper floor.

Of the ten men at the meeting, five came from the ultra, top-secret, invitation-only Bilderberg Group. Three came from a shadowy and evil group called The Skull and Bones Society. The last two men, the only Americans, were high-degree Freemasons. The inconceivable, combined wealth of the ten men seated at the conference table, while hard to quantify accurately, rose to somewhere beyond half a trillion dollars.

Two years earlier, the ten men, deeply alarmed by world events, had formed a new and extremely secretive order named L'Ordre de la Lumière, known only to a tiny and select handful of individuals. The order, representing the elite of the world's elite, had been formed with the intention of governing the world by controlling governments, manipulating global politics, and dictating the world's economy, specifically by reducing the world's population.

The world's ten most powerful individuals, a small but extremely powerful subset of the "Committee of 300", were meeting in the emergency conclave now taking place, arranged under a strict and absolute media blackout. Editors of local newspapers and television news outlets had been personally warned of the dire consequences they would suffer if *any* news of the gathering were to leak out. In no uncertain terms, they were told to report that the men were *never* here and the meeting did *not* take place.

Nine months earlier, following the order's annual meeting in Montreux, Switzerland, one nosey journalist snooping for a story had learned of the order's existence from the loose lips of an order member that had over indulged on martinis at a dinner party. Another order member had overheard the conversation and had distracted the journalist so he could read the note the journalist had written on the pad he carried: "a group of king-makers seeking to impose a one-world government." Mysteriously, the nosey journalist and the loose-lipped order member both had unfortunate and fatal accidents soon after leaving the party.

Gerard Schechter, the order's current leader, had assumed his position as Eminent Grand Commander one month before the previous annual meeting after the order's founding member, fifty-two year-old Philippe Marcel Leroux, suffered a massive heart attack and died on the way to the hospital.

While the other nine order members finished their breakfast Schechter reviewed a short half-page of notes lying on the table in front of him. Ready to begin the meeting, Schechter picked up a spoon and clinked it against his water glass. "Gentlemen, please finish with your breakfast and deposit your plates and silverware in the tub at the end of the serving table. Grab a juice or coffee if you wish, but be quick. We need to get started."

The noise level in the boardroom rose as the meeting attendees rose from their seats, cleared away their dishes, and returned to the table. Schechter waited until all attendees were again seated.

"Are you ready to record?" Schechter asked, turning toward the man seated on his left.

"Yes, Herr Schechter, I am ready," Király Zoltán, a Commercial Banking and Oil tycoon from Budapest Hungary, the order's Royal Scribe, answered. Zoltan, a heavy-set, man with a swarthy complexion and thinning gray hair, opened a leather notebook and slipped a pen out of a loop beside a pad of ruled paper.

Turning toward the man seated on his right, Schechter looked at the order's Grand Secretary General and said, "I know there were two items of business left open from the annual meeting. However, we have much more pressing matters to discuss. Therefore, we shall table those items until the next annual meeting."

"Agreed," Stefanos Zerviades, a shipping tycoon and petroleum baron, from Patras Greece, the third-largest city and commercial hub for all of Western Greece, acknowledged. "Those items are routine and can certainly wait until the next meeting."

"Moving on then," Schechter announced. "For the rest of the meeting you are free to express your views and ideas in a relaxed atmosphere. However, I must warn you that absolutely nothing discussed here today may be mentioned outside this room, and I mean *nothing*. Is that clear?"

Schechter began at his left and went around the table getting verbal agreement from each one of the attendees. Satisfied everyone understood and agreed, he opened the meeting for discussion.

Király Zoltán scribbled a quick note on the pad, replaced the pen in its storage loop, and closed the notebook as no written record of the remainder of the meeting would be allowed.

Not waiting to be recognized, Konrad Sivert from Gothenburg Sweden, fashion industry tycoon and President of the World Economic Forum, pushed his chair back and stood. Sivert, six foot five inches tall with light blond hair and icy blue, close-set eyes, waited for everyone's attention.

"Herr Schechter, esteemed members," Sivert began, glancing around the table. "It does not matter how much money we have. We *must* use it to access and control the organizations that create the policies that control governments and the people who serve in them. If we do not, the real power of our great wealth will never be realized. We..."

"It's never about the money," Kangjon Jong-Soo from Daegu, South Korea, chairman of the world's largest technology manufacturer, seated diagonally across from Sivert, interrupted. "It's about power *and* control!"

"That's what I said," Sivert shot back, glaring at Jong-Soo. "If you would be quiet and let me finish, I would..."

"Gentlemen, we are not here to argue," Schechter admonished both men.

It was well known among the other members that Sivert and Jong-Soo had an immense dislike for each other. A similar incident at the annual meeting had deteriorated into shouting and name calling. Two other members had had to step in between them to prevent a physical altercation.

Schechter continued, "We will not have a repeat of what happened in Montreux, gentlemen. Rather than rehash old arguments, let's get on with the crisis that brings us here today. Király, will you see if our guest is ready?"

Király Zoltán lifted a cellphone out of his jacket pocket, tapped in a number, and waited. After several seconds, Ambrus Németh, Zoltán's personal assistant, answered. Zoltán spoke into the cellphone, "Ambrus, is our guest ready?"

Zoltán held the cellphone away from his ear, looked over at Schechter, and nodded his head, "Our guest is ready, Herr Schechter."

"Good," Schechter replied. "Have him escorted to the boardroom. Tell your assistant to wait with him at the entrance. We will summon him when we are ready."

Zoltán spoke softly into the cellphone, ended the call, and stuffed the cellphone back into his jacket pocket.

Schechter turned away from Zoltán and looked at the man seated at the far end of the table. "Before we let our guest in, I and the other members are quite distressed. We have recently learned there has been a leak of the projects details. Worst of all, I have been informed that the leaked knowledge may now be beyond our control. This failure is extremely concerning as it would likely alert the authorities and give them reason to investigate before we can implement the final phase. Chander, when we devised our plan, you informed us the university in Ch'angsha gave us assurances this could not happen. You told us they had such elaborate security a leak was impossible. We wish to know what happened."

All eyes turned and stared at the man seated at the far end of the long, gleaming table.

Chander Sumeet Vemulakonda, from Chennai, India, CEO of the largest telecom conglomerate in all of Asia, swallowed hard and stood up. "I am as distressed as you are, Herr Schechter," Vemulakonda offered in his defense. "I was assured by the head of their viral research department that such leaks were simply not possible. I travelled to their facility in Ch'angsha and I spent an entire week with their Director of Clinical Operations. Every scenario met our requirements exactly as we defined them."

"Promises are not good enough," Schechter snapped. "The damage from this is enormous. We will be fortunate if we are able to contain it.

Chander, this was *your* responsibility. We are going to determine what caused this and you will make certain it cannot happen again."

"Yes, Herr Schechter," Vemulakonda choked as he sat down, vowing in his mind that whoever was responsible for the leak was going to pay a very heavy price for the embarrassment he had just suffered.

"Király, go see if our guest has arrived," Schechter instructed, nodding toward the door.

Király Zoltán pushed his chair back, stood up, and walked over to the double doors. He pulled one of the doors open and stuck his head out. His assistant was standing there with a fiftyish man dressed in a dark gray, three-piece business suit. Zoltán motioned for them to come over to the door. He leaned toward his assistant and whispered something in his ear.

"Come with me," Zoltán said, grabbing their guest's arm and pulling him through the door. "Stand here."

The man's pasty white skin glistened as he stood in the beam of sunlight shining in through the boardroom's east window. He nervously shifted his weight from one foot to the other. A bead of sweat formed in front of his right ear and rolled down his neck.

A look of deep apprehension spread over the face of Chander Vemulakonda when he recognized the man that had just been ushered into the boardroom.

Zoltán laid his hand on the back of an extra chair that had been pushed out of the way and rolled it toward the man.

Pointing at the chair, Zoltán said, "Sit. We have some questions for you."

The four men sitting on the north side of the table swiveled their chairs around and stared directly at the man.

"Identify yourself for the group," Schechter ordered.

"I am Zhen Ping Zhou," the man answered, his hands visibly trembling in his lap. "I am Director of Clinical Operations for Hunan Medical University in Ch'angsha, China

"Then you are responsible for security and control of all the data related to the project. Is that correct?"

"Yes, Herr Schechter, that is correct."

"Are you aware of the recent failure in your security systems that has allowed information related to the project to leak out?"

"Yes, the system alerted me of that failure, but I immediately called the Ch'angsha police," Director Zhou said, quavering as he spoke. "All the airports, train, and bus terminal were notified. The police informed me that units were dispatched immediately to the apartment where the thief lived. They caught the thief's accomplice as he was exiting the apartment building. In the confusion, the thief and his wife must have escaped into the thick woods behind the apartments. A search began immediately. However, earlier this morning the police chief informed us that as yet they have not been found, but the search is continuing."

"Did the thief share the information with anyone?"

"I do not believe so. The accomplice said they had not ."

"Are you certain of that?" Schechter questioned.

"Yes, of course. There was not enough time. I revoked the internet access of the researcher even before he returned to his lab station. The police caught the accomplice quickly and turned a flash drive over to us. The flash drive has been destroyed," Zhou stammered, avoiding eye contact with Schechter as another bead of sweat rolled down his neck, soaking into the collar of his shirt.

"Director Zhou, I believe you are lying to us," Schechter stated.

"No, Herr Schechter," Zhou whimpered. "I would have no reason to lie to you."

"Oh, really," Schechter snapped as he leaned over and tapped Király Zoltán on the shoulder. "Play the tape for our friend here."

Zoltán grabbed the cellphone lying in front of him, selected a file, and tapped play. He rose, walked over to Zhou and held the phone close to his ear. Zhou's shoulders drooped and began to shake, his eyes frozen on the cellphone. He opened his mouth to talk but nothing came out.

"Nothing to say, Director Zhou," Schechter taunted, waiting for an answer. Receiving no reply, he asked, "How much did they pay you to allow this leak?"

Zhen Ping Zhou shook his head, breathing in short gasps.

"How much did they pay you?" Schechter bellowed.

"No, Herr Schechter, I did no such thing," Zhou wailed, trembling and turning pale.

Schechter glared at the trembling man for a long time. Finally, he looked at Király Zoltán and said, "Get him out of here."

Zoltán rose, grabbed Zhou by the jacket and dragged him to the door. He pulled the door open and spoke to his assistant. Zhou, quivering and terrified, stared at the floor as Ambrus Németh lead him toward the elevator.

Schechter motioned for Zoltán to come over to the table. Upon reaching the table, Zoltán bent over and Schechter whispered in his ear. Zoltán walked to the far corner of the room, pulled a cellphone from his jacket pocket, and tapped in a number. Turning away from the group to mask his conversation, he spoke softly into the cellphone, "Kill him. Remove all his identification. Make certain he is not recognizable then dump him in the river."

Waiting until Zoltán returned to his seat, Schechter then addressed the group, "Whether we can depend on Hunan Medical University to complete this project is a discussion for a later time. The two critical issues that concern us here today are: Number one, how big is the leak; and Number two, can we contain the leak before it threatens our intended outcome? Can you answer those two questions, Mister Oates?" Schechter asked as he turned and stared at the man seated at the far, right end of the table.

Seated on the north side of the conference table, adjacent to Chander Vemulakonda, Bahram Oates represented the lightweight in the group in terms of wealth. Worth only a paltry half billion dollars, the Order had recruited Oates's membership not for his wealth, but for his deep connections into America's political apparatus. As a former president, he could move freely among Washington's political establishment.

Oates rubbed his tired, dark-brown eyes and rose from his chair. At six foot four inches, his hands rested comfortably on the table. His once dark, black hair had turned to salt-and-pepper gray. Deep lines creased his skin at the corners of his eyes and across his forehead, creating a worn, tired appearance to his face. His physical characteristics gave testament to the tremendous stress that came with serving as President of the Unites States.

Unlike the rest of the members who were impeccably dressed, Oates's loosened red silk tie hung askew from his unbuttoned collar. The pompous scowl on Oates's narrow face as he turned and faced Herr Schechter did not go unnoticed. Originating in the Persian language, Oates's first name roughly translated to "winning over resisting people". During his two terms as president, just as that name indicated, he had been a master manipulator and often resorted to outright intimidation. Oates was not used to being summoned. He did not like it and his face showed it.

Oates glared at Herr Schechter. He pulled his shoulders back and said, "Our special FBI unit intercepted a phone call from a Ning Bo Chia, the accomplice in China, to a Rear Admiral Charles Hadley. We sent agents to Hadley's place of residence, but it appears he was not home. According to neighbors he is in the process of selling his condominium. The agents returned later that night and gained access to the condominium. There were many boxes in various states of being packed, but Hadley was nowhere to be found. Most of the closets had been packed into large wardrobe boxes, so it is impossible to know if he packed a suitcase and has fled."

"Did the accomplice send any files to Admiral Hadley?" Schechter asked.

"We think so, but we cannot be certain of that because Hadley uses a one hundred twenty-eight bit encrypted email service. We have techs working on getting access to his email, but so far they have been unsuccessful. If he did receive an email with directions to something like a file sharing server and has already read and deleted it, we will have no way of knowing that."

Schechter rubbed his temples and glared at Oates. "What is being done to prevent this blunder from interfering with our plan?" he asked. "This must be kept quiet at all costs."

"I directed that FBI agents we can trust be sent to Florida where Hadley is suppose to be moving. If they locate him, he will be questioned and then he will disappear."

"Has Hadley talked to anyone else?"

"So far only one. Agents are monitoring his cellphone service twenty-four-seven. There have been no other calls in or out. That makes us think he has now obtained a burner phone. If that is the case, we will have no way of knowing where he is or who else he may be talking to."

Schechter shook his head, and opened his mouth to speak but before he could say anything, Oates continued, "Admiral Hadley is very close friends with former President Paul Cantwell. We expect that if Admiral Hadley contacted anyone, it would be him. The most likely way he would try to get information to Cantwell would be through his rat lawyer, Edger Cordell. We were correct. Two agents overheard part of a conversation Cordell had at a restaurant in Arlington, Virginia. He did have a copy of the information."

"Has that been taken care of?" Schechter queried.

"He refused to give it up, but the agents found it. Hidden in the heel of his shoe no less."

"And what about Cordell?"

"Cordell is now at the bottom of a river."

"If Hadley has already talked to Cordell, wouldn't it be safe to assume he has talked to others as well?"

"We don't know that. I haven't heard from Director Conroy as yet."

"Well, find out," Schechter demanded, anger tingeing his voice. "Gentlemen, take a short break while we wait for Mister Oates to elaborate."

The other order members scrambled out of their chairs, picking through the pastries that remained and refilling coffee cups. Gathering in small groups, they engaged in quiet conversations. Oates reached into his jacket pocket, pulled out an untraceable burner phone, and tapped in a number.

"Yes, sir," Jerome Conroy, Director of the FBI answered on the fourth ring.

"Have you learned if Hadley is talking to anyone else?" Oates asked.

"There may be one other individual by the name of James Templeton. He and Hadley go way back. Templeton is another story. He's former CIA and knows how to cover his tracks. The two men I contracted to eliminate him and recover anything he might have had were attacked by an unknown assailant. When those idiots awakened, Templeton, his wife, and Templeton's computer were gone. Pfitzner has no idea who attacked them or where they may have gone."

"That is unacceptable," Oates spoke softly, turning away from Herr Schechter. "You know what to do with those two idiots. We must retrieve that information."

"I am aware of that, sir," Conroy conceded. "We are tracking everyone associated with Templeton. We will find him *and* the information, sir."

"Instruct all the agents you can trust to keep their ears open. Have them talk to anyone that might have knowledge of any leaks, but make certain they do it quietly. If they do hear of anything, notify me immediately, then silence anyone that is a threat. When you have the information, verify it and then destroy it."

"Yes, sir. Will do," Conroy acknowledged.

Oates ended the call and dropped the burner phone back into his jacket pocket.

"Gentlemen, Mister Oates is now ready to update us," Schechter announced. "Please return to the table."

The order members finished their conversations and returned to the table.

"Well, Mister Oates, enlighten us," Schechter challenged.

"The fat pig, Cordell, has been silenced," Oates responded. "We have the flash drive containing the project information he possessed. It will be verified and destroyed."

"Is that all Mister Oates?"

"There was one other leak but the stupid fool ran his car into a gasoline tanker," Oater answered, choosing not to inform Herr Schechter that there was another leak and the assassins hired to retrieve the information had failed and the individual associated with the leak along with his wife and computer were missing.

"I am not certain I believe you, Mister Oates," Schechter threatened, fixing an icy stare directly at Mister Oates. "You were promised a lot of money to make certain this kind of thing did not happen. There have been at least three leaks already. If there are any others, you *will* find them quickly and you *will* eliminate them and any information they might have. I don't care how many there are. I don't care who they are. I don't care how important they are. *Silence them all.* We will not allow years of work to be destroyed by a stupid security flaw. It is past time that we eliminate all those that are unenlightened and pose a threat to the New World Order."

Turning away from Mister Oates and starting at his left, Schechter went around the table asking each order member if they had any urgent business that could not wait until their next scheduled meeting. Nobody had any urgent business, or, more likely true, none that they cared to mention, considering Herr Schechter's sudden foul mood.

Schechter stood to his feet, raised his arm, and shouted, "Saluer. À l'unisson nous levons les bras."

The order members jumped to their feet, raised their arms in unison, and shouted, "*Annonçant le début du Nouveau Monde des Âges.*" Their shout roughly translating to, "Announcing the Beginning of the New World of the Ages."

The ten order members bowed at the waist, straightened up, and crossed their arms, forming an "X" across their chest. With the meeting concluded, all but Herr Schechter and Mister Oates exited the boardroom, gathering in the adjacent dining area, eager to partake of a sumptuous brunch buffet.

Herr Schechter grabbed Oates's arm and pushed him to the opposite side of the room. With a quick nod of his head, Schechter signaled the Order's scribe, Király Zoltán. Zoltan bowed slightly and pulled the door to the boardroom closed.

"Mister Oates, you *must* do something about these leaks," Schechter threatened. "It is not just the money. If information about the new virus leaks out too soon, it will jeopardize our entire plan."

"We believe the leak is small and can be quickly contained," Oates asserted. "It is not as bad as you think it is."

"That is not what I have been told," Schechter challenged. "and I warn you Mister Oates do not try to lie your way out of it. We have eyes and ears everywhere. Surely you must know this."

"Well then, you must also know they are being silenced," Oates countered.

"Be careful, Mister Oates. You promised this... this Eagle, as you call him, would be easily controlled. Well, it seems he cannot keep his mouth shut. See to it that he is silenced as well."

"But he is... You can't expect me to...,"

"You will do exactly as I order you to do!" Schechter snapped. "Is that understood?"

Oates bit his tongue and nodded agreement.

"One other thing, Mister Oates. Considering these leaks, we will have to move up the timetable. Contact *Prince Marduk*. Have him inform the lab in China that they absolutely must complete their portion of the project within three days. I am unconvinced that the leaks can be silenced before the final portion of our plan is implemented.

"I don't think that is....,"

"Mister Oates, I am warning you for the last time," Schechter shouted. "You were paid a very large sum of money to do *exactly* as you have been instructed. You assured the Order that you had people that could perform the tasks we required *and* could keep their mouths shut. I believe you have failed miserably. If you do not want to suffer the same fate as the leakers, I suggest you return to America and do as you have promised. Did I make myself clear?"

"Yes, sir, Herr Schechter."

"You are a very smart man," Schechter taunted as he patted Oates on the shoulder. "Let us go join the others.

Chapter Nine

Tuesday, Feb. 10th – 1:26 p.m. EST
Zach Templeton Residence
Big House Plantation Road
Bluffton, South Carolina

Leaning on one elbow, Zach's eyelids drooped heavily as he stared blankly at the computer monitor. Having hurried back upstairs to his office after consuming a delicious lunch of meatloaf, fried potatoes, and green beans followed by chocolate pie, his favorite, Zach was having great difficulty staying awake.

His elbow slid off the edge of the desk, jarring him awake. Rolling his shoulders, he leaned back in his chair, and returned his attention to the email open on the monitor. Furrowing his brow, he stared at the second bizarre email in just eight days now displayed on the screen. Just like the first email, it had been encrypted using the Masonic Code, but there the similarity ended. Zach tried decrypting the interior code with the trifid cipher like he had with the first email, but it failed to decrypt. Unlike the first email, the entire message had been encrypted, leaving Zach with no key to determine how to decrypt the message.

About to try another decryption cipher, Zach turned his head sideways and listened intently when he heard the doorbell ring.

"Zach, Sheriff Fortunato is here," Anna Mae hollered up the stairwell a few seconds later. "He needs to talk to you. He said it's important."

"I'll be right down," Zach answered.

He guided the mouse pointer over the open email, copied the encrypted message, pasted it into a document, and saved it. He closed the email, signed out, and closed the email application. He rolled his chair back, pushed himself up, and headed for the stairs. Upon reaching the bottom of the stairs, he saw Sheriff Fortunato standing there waiting. As his name suggested, Sheriff Fortunato was clearly Italian, with thick, close-cropped, dark hair and equally dark eyes and olive skin. He was of medium height with a narrow, angular face. Zach guessed him to be in his late thirties. His uniform was crisp, perfectly ironed, with razor sharp creases. He carried himself very straight with an air of authority, leaving little doubt that this man was a professional. The only flaw was a shirt stretched a little too tightly, perhaps suggesting too much pasta.

"Good morning, Mister Templeton. I'm Antonio Fortunato, Sheriff of Beaufort County," the man said, offering his hand.

"Good afternoon, Sheriff Fortunato," Zach responded, shaking the sheriff's hand. "What can I do for you? My wife said it was important."

"Is there somewhere private we can talk?"

"Ah… sure. We can talk in the living room."

"Would you like some coffee, Sheriff?" Anna Mae asked, having heard the sheriff's introduction.

"Yes. That would be great. Black please."

"You gentlemen go on into the living room. I'll be right in with the coffee."

"Follow me, Sheriff," Zach said, pointing toward the living room.

Sheriff Fortunato waited, then followed Zach into the living room, and took a seat on the couch. Zach took a seat in the matching loveseat sitting opposite the couch.

"I meant to drop by sooner and introduce myself, but it always seemed like I was busy."

"Well, I'm glad you did drop by, Sheriff. What is it you needed to talk to me about in private? Anna Mae said it was important."

"Have you …," Sheriff Fortunato stopped when he saw Anna Mae enter the living room carrying a tray loaded with a carafe, two coffee cups, two plates, each loaded with a warm-from-the-oven cinnamon roll, and a stack of napkins.

Anna Mae set the tray on the coffee table, poured two cups of coffee, and handed one to each of the men.

"Enjoy. The rolls just came out of the oven," Anna Mae said as she turned and walked to the doorway. She slid the living room's pocket door closed and returned to the kitchen.

"This smells delicious," the sheriff commented as he held the plate up to his nose and sniffed in the delicious aroma. "Mmm, it's fantastic," Sheriff Fortunato exclaimed, finishing his first bite. "I will definitely have my wife call your wife for the recipe."

For the next few minutes, the two men made small talk alternating between bites of cinnamon roll and slurps of coffee. The sheriff stuffed the last bite of roll into his mouth and wiped his mouth with a napkin.

"Tell your wife thank you," he said as he wiped his fingers. Sheriff Fortunato refilled his coffee cup, took a swallow, and continued, "Now the reason for my visit. Have you spoken to your parents recently? Say, within the last week."

"No," Zach lied, deciding not to mention the bizarre email he had received and the stern warning his father had given him over the phone. "I spoke to my dad on the phone maybe three weeks ago. Why? Did something happen?"

"Victor Tejada, the Tulsa County Sherriff, called me an hour ago and asked that I get in touch with you. It seems your parents are missing."

"Missing," Zach blurted out. "When? How do you know there're missing?"

"Sheriff Tejada told me one of your parents' neighbors became concerned when they didn't show up this morning for a surprise breakfast gathering for a close friend. A neighbor, the…," Sheriff Fortunato hesitated, opened a small notepad, and flipped through several pages. He continued, "…the Perkins said your parents organized the event and would not have missed it. The Perkins drove back to your parent's house, peeked in the garage window, and saw their car. When no one answered repeated knocks at their door, they called the local police. When the police arrived and could not get an answer at the door, they broke a window and forced their way in."

"What did they find?" Zach asked, edging forward on the loveseat.

"Sheriff Tejada told me they found evidence of a struggle. Several kitchen chairs knocked over. A few broken dishes. In the bedroom, they found bloodstains on the carpet and it appears a computer is missing. There were a bunch of loose cables hanging out from a compartment in the desk. As far as the police could tell, there were no clothes or anything else missing. The really odd thing is that all the doors and windows were locked. It had to be someone they knew or someone knocked on the door and forced their way in."

"How long have they been missing?"

"Hard to tell exactly, but no more than a day. The Perkins talked to them early yesterday. The police canvassed the neighborhood, but nobody heard or saw anything. Did your parents get along? Is there any reason they would go out of town without telling you?"

"They get along great," Zach snapped. "And no, they would *not* go out of town without telling me."

"I'm sorry, Mister Templeton, it is not my intention to upset you," Sheriff Fortunato asserted. "I researched you so I know your background. You know these are routine questions. We are trying to find out what happened to your parents."

"Sorry," Zach apologized. "This is a bit of a shock. You said there were bloodstains."

"Yes, but I was told they were small and the police do not believe they would indicate any major injuries. Do you know why anyone would want to kidnap your parents? Enemies? Ransom demands? Anything like that?"

"No, none that I can think of. Dad worked for a government intelligence agency, but that was a long time ago. My parents have social security and a small pension. Certainly not enough money to consider them to be a target of kidnapping and I have not received any ransom demands."

As Zach sat there, he reran in his mind the bizarre email he had been gazing at when the sheriff arrived. It was definitely from his father, dated just yesterday. It would have to have been very close to or at the exact time they had disappeared or had been kidnapped. Ominous thoughts flashed through Zach's mind. Could his dad have been typing the message when they were kidnapped? Did the message have a hidden meaning. If so, what? Was he being drawn into yet another conflict with evil? What was…

"Mister Templeton," Sheriff Fortunato prompted, tapping Zach on the knee. "Are you still with me?"

"Sorry, Sheriff. I guess my mind was elsewhere. I tried to think of anything that would help you, but I'm coming up blank."

"Is your father involved in any subversive groups that would like to overthrow the government?"

"Absolutely not," Zach scowled, looking directly at Sheriff Fortunato. "Like I said, my dad worked for the CIA and he nearly lost his life helping me track down a terrorist. Why would you ask a question like that?"

"Sheriff Tejada informed me that the FBI is pursuing a group that has some stolen information and they believe your father may be involved"

"What kind of information?"

"They wouldn't say. I'm going to ask you again. Have you had any contact with your dad recently?"

"No I have not," Zach declared. "I already told you I haven't spoken with him in three weeks and I don't know anything about any missing or stolen information. Are we done? I have some work I need to finish."

"Sorry to have bothered you," Sheriff Fortunato said as he pushed himself up off the couch.

Zach stood, walked over to the living room door, slid it open, and followed the sheriff as he exited the living room and headed for the front door.

Reaching for the door knob, Sheriff Fortunato turned his head toward and kitchen and called out, "Thank you for the coffee and cinnamon roll Misses Templeton. It was delicious."

Zach stood waiting for the sheriff to leave. Stopping halfway through the door, the sheriff pulled out a business card and handed it to Zach. "Mister Templeton, something tells me you know more than you're saying. Call me if you hear from your father."

"I will. Good day, Sheriff," Zach said.

Zach pushed the door shut, turned, and walked into the living room. He gathered up the cups and dishes and carried them into the kitchen.

"Where do you want these?"

"Just set them on the counter beside the coffee maker," Anna Mae answered. "I'll take care of them later. What did the sheriff want?"

"Mom and Dad are missing," Zach answered "The sheriff thinks they were kidnapped."

"What?" Anna Mae gasped, dropping the plate she had been drying. "Kidnapped? When?" She grabbed a broom and swept the broken shards into a pile as Zach began to explain.

"The police in Tulsa think it could have been no more than a day ago. The Perkins, their neighbors to the south, got suspicious when they didn't show up for a surprise event they had organized. The Perkins said there was no way they would have missed it. Mister Perkins peeked in the garage and saw Dad's car. Nobody answered when they knocked on the door so they called the police. When the police could not get anyone to answer, they forced their way in."

"Zach, come over to the table and sit down," Anna Mae said as she grabbed a new coffee cup from a cabinet, filled it, carried it over to the table, and set it in front of Zach. "What did the police say they found?"

Zach blew across the steaming surface of the coffee, staring at the swirling steam rising from the cup. He took a sip and answered, "They didn't find much. Some overturned furniture and some blood stains in the bedroom Dad used as an office, but…."

"Oh, Zach, no!"

"No. It's not that bad. They said the blood stains were small and would not indicate any major injuries."

"Do the police have any idea why someone would kidnap them?"

"No. The police don't have any clues as yet. They canvassed the entire neighborhood, but nobody heard or saw anything. The only thing that seemed to be missing was Dad's computer. The sheriff asked me if Dad belonged to any subversive groups. He said something about some kind of information being missing. The FBI thinks Dad may be involved and the sheriff basically accused me of lying. He thinks I know more than I told him."

"Zach?" Anna Mae questioned, a look of concern clouding her face. "Does this have anything to do with Agent McClain's disappearance and the odd mail you received a week ago? Oh, and Admiral Hadley being forced to retire and Gene Croft being killed by a car bomb. And now the FBI thinks your Dad is involved in stealing information."

"Anna Mae, I don't know what is going on," Zach answered. "I received another encrypted email just this morning, but I have not been able to decrypt anything except the subject line. I tried to decrypt the body of the email with the same cipher as the first one but it didn't work. The internal message has to be based on a different cipher than the first one."

"What did the subject line say?" Anna Mae asked.

Zach hesitated, wondering if maybe he should have withheld the information about the second email. He didn't want to frighten Anna Mae any more than she already was. Picking at his fingernails, he answered, "It… ah… said something about… ah… protecting the email."

"Zach, tell me *exactly* what it said," Anna Mae urged, knowing there was something Zach did not want to say. His body language always gave him away. "Zach, stop picking at your fingernails and tell me what it said."

Knowing he could not lie to Anna Mae, he just blurted it out, "The subject line said 'Guard this with your life'."

"Zach, why?" Anna Mae asked, her voice trembling as she imagined Zach being sucked into another encounter with dangerous criminals.

"I don't know why," Zach shrugged. "If I can decrypt the email, then maybe I will know why it is so important."

"How are you going to be able to do that if you don't know what the cipher is?"

"There has to be something in the email," Zach said, sighing deeply, speaking to himself as much as to Anna Mae. "I have to look at that email again."

Before Anna Mae could answer, Zach grabbed the cup of coffee and headed upstairs. Anna Mae watched as Zach disappeared up the stairway, wondering what new and unknown threat the odd email carried with it.

Anna Mae returned to the kitchen sink. She stood there staring at the dishes she had been washing. "Why is this happening again?" she groaned

Anna Mae leaned against the kitchen sink, worried and uneasy, as she looked up and stared out the window. Internally, she battled with a mixture of anger and dread. Angry that Zach seemingly was being drawn into yet another battle with something evil. Twice he had answered his country's call and had volunteered without hesitation, the last time nearly costing him his life. "*Hasn't he already given enough*?" she thought. Anna Mae could not shake the sense of dread building in her heart because she knew from personal experience that evil men will stop at nothing to carry out their evil plan.

Knowing that she was also in this danger with Zach, no matter what, she laid the dish cloth on the edge of the kitchen sink, picked up Mazie, and headed upstairs to see if she could help Zach decrypt the odd email.

Anna Mae set Mazie in the corner in front of her play kitchen, walked over to where Zach sat staring at the computer monitor, and laid her hand on his shoulder. Zach reached up and laid his hand on hers.

"Zach, whatever is going on we are in this together. I came up to see if I could help you decipher that email."

"Thanks. I could use some fresh ideas," Zach said as he scooted sideways to make room for her to sit beside him. Anna Mae grabbed a chair and sat down next to Zach.

"What does the email say?" Anna Mae queried.

"Nothing really," Zach answered as he opened the document he had pasted the email into. "Just the subject line and then a bunch of gibberish. There is no clue whatsoever as to what cipher my dad used to encrypt this."

"He wouldn't have sent this to you with no way to decipher it."

"I agree, but only the subject line decoded and it has no reference to any key."

"What do we do?"

"I haven't a clue," Zach huffed.

Tuesday, Feb. 10th – 2:08 p.m. EST
Warner & Lewis Realtors
4800 Block Bethesda Avenue
Bethesda, Maryland

Admiral Hadley sped into the parking lot of the Warner & Lewis Realtors office and screeched to a stop, already fifteen minutes late for the appointment he had rescheduled. Anxious to get the meeting over with and return home to continue with his packing, he didn't have time to worry about the feeling he was being followed.

He turned off the engine and rushed inside to meet with his agent, Darryl Finley, regarding an offer someone had made on his condo. He pushed the door open and saw Mister Finley sitting on a chair in the lobby waiting. Wearing a dark winter-weight suit, a light blue shirt with white collar, French cuffs with dazzling black onyx cuff links, a red silk tie with diagonal stripes, and a pair of expensive, black wingtip shoes, he stylishly portrayed the image of the office's top performing agent.

"Admiral Hadley," Mister Finley beamed, offering his hand. "I was beginning to wonder if you were going to make it."

"Sorry I'm late," Admiral Hadley apologized. "I had a bit of a distraction. You said you have received an offer on the condo."

"Yes I did and I think you are going to like it. A lot. Come into the conference room. I have the offer right here," Mister Findley said, patting the folder under his arm.

Admiral Hadley followed Mister Finley into the glass-enclosed conference room, pulled out one of the chairs, and sat down at the end of the long conference table. Mister Finley pulled out a chair, sat beside the admiral, and laid the folder on the table. He flopped the folder open and pushed it over in front of the admiral.

"Let's get right down to business," Mister Finley said, smiling broadly. "The buyers absolutely loved the view and the top-end upgrades you have made to the condo. To show their interest, they made a $65K over-list offer of $1,915,000 with no contingencies whatsoever."

Admiral Hadley's jaw dropped for a few seconds as he gazed at the offer. Then he nearly shouted, "Are you kidding me? Give me a pen!"

"Gladly," Mister Finley said as he lifted the Meisterstück Classic Rose Gold-Coated Montblanc pen out of his shirt pocket and handed it to the admiral.

The admiral grabbed the pen and hurriedly signed two copies of the contract. "Nice pen," he said as he leaned back in the chair, admiring the exquisite pen. "What happens next?"

"The buyers would like a quick close in three weeks. Can you do that?"

"Ah… I think so. Most of the packing is done. I haven't found a place in Florida yet. I guess I can put my stuff in storage for a while."

"Great. I'll get the signed contract over to the buyers and a copy to the settlement company. Things should go really quickly as there is no inspection and no appraisal because the offer is all cash. The close can happen as soon as you are ready."

"Wow," Admiral Hadley grinned. "I had no idea the sale would go so quickly and for that much over asking. I guess I had better get home and finish packing. Thank you, Darryl."

The two men shook hands and exited the conference room. Admiral Hadley headed for the door and Mister Finley headed for his office. Being both the seller's and buyer's agent for the Hadley property, his one-hundred thirty-four thousand dollar commission would assure him a place as the top producer of monthly sales for the tenth month in a row.

Elated with the quick sale and the huge amount over the asking price, Admiral Hadley's mind was on finalizing his move. He failed to notice the same dark gray sedan that had been following him earlier had parked six spaces down in the same row. He backed out of the parking space and exited the parking lot onto Bethesda Avenue. His mind filled with the necessary tasks he would have to complete to meet the quick close, he did not notice the dark gray sedan exit the parking lot and follow four car lengths behind him.

Halfway home, he glanced up and made a routine check of the rearview mirror and noticed a dark gray sedan that looked like the one he had seen earlier. Glancing at the mirror every few seconds he confirmed that it was the same sedan following him. He moved over into the far-right lane and exited the freeway, turning onto Willard Avenue. After passing through two traffic lights, he turned into the parking lot of an ethnic grocery store and parked.

The dark gray sedan followed him into the parking lot and parked three spaces to his left. Admiral Hadley reached under the seat and grabbed his Glock. He racked the slide back to put a round in the chamber, took a deep breath, and waited.

Chapter Ten

Tuesday, Feb. 10th – 2:33 p.m. EST
Zach Templeton Residence
Big House Plantation Road
Bluffton, South Carolina

Both Anna Mae and Zach had been staring at the computer monitor without any success. Unable to discover the slightest clue as to what cipher had been used to encrypt the email, Zach pushed back from the desk and shrugged.

"I don't know what else to do," Zach grumbled, banging his fist on the desk. "There just isn't any way to decipher this thing unless we have the key."

"But Zach, there has to be a way," Anna Mae coaxed. "Your dad wouldn't send this to you without some way of deciphering it. We have to be missing something."

"I don't know where else to look," Zach snapped, turning back toward the monitor.

Anna Mae grabbed the arm of Zach's chair and turned him back toward her. "Zach, don't snap at me. I know you're frustrated. So am I. We just have to keep working at this. I love you. We're in this together."

"I'm sorry. I know that. I'm just worried," Zach said as he leaned over and kissed Anna Mae. "There are only five words we know for certain. We have picked them apart every way we know how. We have rearranged them in every combination possible. What else is left?"

"Well, let's forget everything we have tried," Anna Mae suggested. "Let's look at them again."

Fifteen minutes passed as Zach and Anna Mae tried every new permutation they could think of. The results were the same as before. Nothing.

"This just isn't possible," Zach growled as he pushed himself back from the desk. "I've had it. There's no point in looking for something that's not there. We don't have a key and we don't even know what cipher Dad used."

"I'm afraid I have to agree with you," Anna Mae conceded. "But why would your dad do that?"

"You've got me," Zach sighed. "It doesn't make any sense. That's not like Dad."

"We need a break," Anna Mae suggested. "Let's go downstairs. There's still some cinnamon rolls left."

Halfway to the stairs, Zach flinched when a text notification chimed from his cellphone. Zach grabbed the cellphone from the desk, swiped the screen, and tapped the Text app icon. A new text from a phone number he did not recognize sat at the top of the list of texts. He turned the cellphone toward Anna Mae. "Do you recognize this number?"

Anna Mae leaned forward and stared at the number. "No. I don't know that number. Open it and see what it says."

Zach tapped the text message and gawked at the odd message displayed on the cellphone.

Zachman DCT MTOY – Read & Delete

"That's from Dad," Zach exclaimed. "Nobody else ever calls me Zachman! Anna Mae, write these letters down. D - C – T then M – T – O – Y."

Zach watched as Anna Mae snatched a notepad from his desk and wrote the letters down. He verified that she had written down all the letters. Satisfied, he closed and deleted the text. To be certain the message was permanently deleted, he tapped the three vertical dots at the top of the screen and selected the Trash entry. Then he clicked the Empty Trash selection, exited the Text app, and rebooted his phone.

"What on Earth do these letters mean?" Anna Mae asked.

"It must be the cipher and the necessary key to decipher the email. It has to be."

"But it's just random letters. How will you know what the cipher is?"

Zach rummaged around in the deep corners of his mind trying to match the letters to a cipher from his days in the SEALs. Slowly, one by one, he ticked off the list of all the ciphers he had ever heard of, but he came up blank. None of the ciphers he knew could possibly match the first three letters. He closed his eyes and slowly went through the list again. Still nothing.

"I'm getting nowhere," Zach complained.

He sat down in his chair and jiggled the mouse to awaken the computer. He opened an internet search tool, typed in the word *cipher*, and pressed enter. Scrolling down through the pages of results, he clicked on entry after entry without any success. Finally on the fourth page of results, he clicked a result that claimed to contain 'A virtually uncrackable cipher that relied heavily upon a random source for an encryption key.'

The first page listed fifteen Code and Substitution type ciphers, none of which would match the letters his dad had sent. Looking further down on the second page, he came to an alphabetically arranged group simply titled Ciphers.

"There it is!" Zach shouted, staring at the fifth cipher in the list. "It must be a double column transposition cipher. That matches the letters DCT. Look, right here the website says: 'To make the message even more difficult to decipher, the double column cipher takes the text produced by the first algorithm and runs it through the encryption a second time using a different keyword. This transposes the columns twice and makes the message nearly impossible to decipher.'"

Zach that's great," Anna Mae said. "Now all we have to do is find out what key your Dad used."

Zach clicked on the double column transposition cipher link and waited for the screen to fill. Switching to the email application, he copied the body of the encrypted email, switched back to the website, and pasted the email text into the CIPHERTEXT block. He typed in the letters MTOY in the KEYWORD block and clicked the Decipher button. The PLAINTEXT block filled with useless gibberish.

"Well, that's not it," Zach groaned. "The last four letters must be another clue of some kind."

Zach typed the letters in reverse order and every other combination he could think of, but the result was always the same; a screen full of gibberish.

"It's obvious that these letters aren't the key. They have to stand for something else. Your Dad would have used something we would understand. Say the letters slowly. Maybe it will trigger something in our brains."

"M – T – O – Y."

Both Anna Mae and Zach racked their brains for a meaning of the four letters. In exasperation, Zach threw his arms in the air and said, "We're getting nowhere. I need a break. Let's take a break and come back to it later."

Frustrated at not being able to decipher the message, Zach lifted his foot and shoved the office chair back toward his desk."

"Zach," Anna Mae scolded. "That won't do any good."

"Sorry," Zach mumbled. "I know, but this is important. I need to find out what that email says."

He walked over and picked up Mazie who had been busily playing in the corner, stacking and restacking a pile of blocks. He set her on his hip and together they made their way down the stairs and into the kitchen.

Zach poked the power button on the coffee brewer and set Mazie in her highchair. After filling her sippy cup with juice, he grabbed two cookies from the cookie jar, and set them in front of Mazie. While Mazie attacked the cookies, Zach stood beside the coffee brewer waiting for it to complete it's warm up cycle. Thirty seconds later the coffee brewer chimed and the selection buttons lit up.

"What kind of brew would you like?" Zach called out as he slid open the drawer containing assorted coffee pods.

"Anything's fine," Anna Mae answered, staring off into space.

Zach selected two French Roast pods, brewed two cups of coffee, and carried them over to the table. He set one in front of Anna Mae and sat down at the table holding the other. They sipped their coffee in silence wondering what new danger might be hidden in the strange email.

Tuesday, Feb. 10th – 3:02 p.m. EST
Friendship Heights Shopping Center
4400 Block Willard Avenue
Bethesda, Maryland

Admiral Hadley raised his Glock and held it against his chest as the driver's door of the dark gray sedan began to open. Holding his breath, he waited. The admiral exhaled and laughed as he watched a late, middle-age woman climb out of the dark gray sedan and rush off toward the supermarket. He released the magazine, racked out the bullet in the chamber, reinserted the magazine, and slipped it back under the seat.

Shaking his head, he looked over his shoulder, backed out of the parking space, drove through the shopping center's parking lot, and turned right onto Willard Avenue, continuing the drive back to his condo.

Arriving at his condo fifteen minutes later, he could not believe his good fortune when he noticed an empty space in the first row next to the building. He steered his vehicle into the empty space and turned off the engine. Focused on the fantastic offer he had received on the condo and in a hurry to return to packing up the last few items, he completely forgot about the Glock nestled under the seat. Admiral Hadley grabbed his copy of the signed sales contract from the passenger seat, climbed out of the car, and headed for the building's west entrance. After a quick ride up the elevator to the eleventh floor, he was about to slide his key into the deadbolt when he noticed the door was slightly ajar.

Easing the door open with his foot, he stepped inside. Glancing from side to side, he surveyed the interior of the condo. Nothing seemed to be amiss. Everything appeared to be exactly as he had left it. He thought perhaps in his haste to make the appointment with his real estate agent, he had failed to completely latch the door. He pushed the door closed, plopped the sales contract on the hall table, and hurried up the stairs two at a time.

As he stepped into his office, it became instantly apparent he had not failed to latch the front door. The computer was lying on the floor with the cover off, the internal components smashed, and pieces of the motherboard strewn across the floor. About to reach for his cellphone to call the police, someone slipped up behind him and pushed the cold muzzle of a gun against his neck.

"Do not move," a deep, husky voice advised. "Not even a twitch or you're dead."

"How did you get in?" Admiral Hadley demanded, but as soon as the words escaped his mouth, he remembered he had terminated the security monitoring contract due to the pending sale of the condo. Otherwise, the police would have already arrived.

"You do not need to know," the voice answered. "We are going to leave. Do not make a sound."

The man shoved Admiral Hadley toward the stairway. With the muzzle of the gun jammed against his neck again, the admiral and the man made their way down the stairs.

At the bottom of the stairs, the man pushed Admiral Hadley toward the front door and said, "We are going to take the elevator. Do not be stupid."

Believing he would not get another opportunity, Admiral Hadley reached for his weapon as they stepped through the door but found his holster empty. The man slapped the side of Admiral Hadley's head with his weapon and snarled, "I told you not to be stupid. Do as I said or I will kill you right here! I still have the gun pointed at your back." The man slipped the gun behind the open flap of his coat and pushed the admiral toward the elevator. "I will not hesitate to shoot you. Now go!"

Together, the two men got on the elevator and rode it in silence to the ground floor. The elevator door slid open and the two men exited the elevator and walked slowly down the hallway toward the building's west entrance.

"Good morning, Admiral Hadley," Misses Judith Markley, the owner of the condo on the eight floor, greeted as she passed them.

"Good morning, Judith," Admiral Hadley responded, tipping his head as he continued walking toward the exit, not saying another word, to keep from getting the woman involved.

Admiral Hadley pushed the exit door open and the two men walked out into the bright afternoon sun. Squinting against the brightness, Admiral Hadley headed for the parking lot. "*If only I had remembered my Glock*," he derided himself silently as he stepped up over the curb and started down the row of parked cars.

"The black suburban halfway down the second row," the man instructed.

Upon reaching the suburban, the assailant pulled the rear door open and said, "Stand right here, behind the door." He pulled a set of handcuffs from behind his back. "Hands behind your back," he ordered as he prepared to put the handcuffs on Admiral Hadley's wrists. Occupied with the handcuffs, the assailant did not see the hooded man creeping around the back of the suburban with a weapon in his left hand and a ballistic baton in his right hand. Stepping lightly in gum-soled shoes, not making a sound, he slipped up behind the assailant.

A muffled *whack* was the only sound heard as the hooded man struck the assailant at the base of his skull. The assailant lurched forward, landing against Admiral Hadley as he slid to the ground.

Shock filled Admiral Hadley's face when he turned around and saw the face of the hooded man standing at the rear of the vehicle. "But you're supposed to be missing. What is…"

"Never mind," the hooded man said. "Get him in the vehicle and out of sight. Dump him in the back and get his cellphone. Quick! I'll explain later," the hooded man ordered. "Admiral, hurry! We need to get out of here. My car is in the next row. Light green Chevy Lumina."

Admiral Hadley grabbed the man by his shoulders and hoisted him up onto the back seat of the suburban. Grabbing his legs, he pushed him the rest of the way into the suburban. He patted the man down until he located his cellphone. He stuffed the cellphone in his pocket, slammed the door, and sprinted between the cars parked in the next row. The hooded man, already climbing in the driver's side of the Chevy Lumina, motioned for the admiral to get in the passenger side. The hooded man started the engine and as soon as the admiral jumped into the passenger seat. He slipped the car into reverse, backed out of the parking space, and shifted the car into Drive. He sped out of the parking lot, turning right onto Somerset Terrace. After winding his way through the Friendship Village neighborhood, he turned right onto River Road, joining the early pre-rush hour traffic. Just shy of two miles later, he turned right onto the ramp for west bound Interstate Four-Ninety-Five and crossed over the Potomac River into Virginia.

Satisfied no one was following them, he pulled his hood down and turned toward the admiral. "Hello, Admiral Hadley. It's great to see you again."

"I don't understand," Admiral Hadley said.

"I know about the virus, Admiral" Secret Service Agent David McClain answered.

"How?" Admiral Hadley asked. "I just found out myself from a friend in China whose nephew is involved in the research."

"Being assigned to the White House, I hear things. They think they're being quiet, but when tempers flare and they shout at each other, if you listen carefully, you would be surprised what you can pick up. They think I didn't hear, but I did."

"Who is they, if I may ask?"

"I'm not certain I should tell you, but it goes high. Really high," David McClain answered.

"May I ask where we are headed?"

"A safe house in the country. It's not far. Out near Marshall, Virginia. Your old friend James Templeton is there."

With a very puzzled look on his face, the admiral asked, "Why is James there?"

"Because James Templeton also knows. I sent a warning email to him with some documents attached. Only after I had already sent the email did I realize I sent it using my personal email provider. The new *rogue* FBI listens to everything. So, I knew it would be intercepted. That's why I had to disappear. That's also why I had to snatch up James and his wife. And it's a good thing I did. Two of Conroy's hired goons were already there."

"Conroy?" Hadley asked, a look of utter shock on his face. You mean as in Director of the FBI Conroy?"

"Oops, I didn't mean to let that out," McClain grinned. "And yes, that is the Conroy I meant."

"Okay, but why were you here at my condo today," Hadley asked.

"I have a friend in the Secret Service that is feeding me information. He said he overheard your name mentioned. So, I have been watching you."

"So, who was the guy in the suburban?"

"A highly-placed secret service agent that answers directly to Conroy who answers directly to Eagle."

"You have got to be kidding!"

"I wish I were, Admiral. I told you this mess went *really* high. How much do you know about the virus?"

"I read enough of the information my friend sent me, to be absolutely terrified. If it is even half as lethal as the documents suggest, the world could be facing an epidemic of Biblical proportion."

"I don't understand some of the science, but I can assure you it is as lethal as you fear it is. Maybe even more."

"But why?"

"Have you ever heard of the L'Ordre de la Lumière, Admiral."

"The what?"

"That's what I thought," David McClain remarked. "I would have been very surprised if you had heard of it. It's French. It means 'The Order of Light'. It is a group of ten of the world's most evil and powerful men. They represent anything but light."

"How do they figure in this?"

"I imagine you have heard of the New World Order."

"Oh yes," the admiral answered. "They want to crash the world economy and then initiate a great reset to form some kind of utopia."

"That's true, Admiral. But to reach their utopian dream they believe they must eliminate three hundred fifty thousand people per day until they reach a population goal of one to one and one half billion."

"You're kidding!"

"I wish I were kidding. That group of ten men have the money, power, and resources to accomplish anything they want. This new virus is designed to do just that. People will die on a scale not to be believed."

"Who is in that group of ten?"

"Good question. It is so secretive, I doubt if outside the group itself there are more than three of four individuals in the entire world that know even one of the members, let alone all of them."

"If this Order of Light is so secretive, how did you come by this information?" Admiral Hadley asked.

"The story is, there was one group member that got a little drunk at some function and bragged about his membership to a reporter. That reporter and the loose-lipped order member never made it home, but not before the reporter sent a short text to an associate. The associate talked to a friend. And now both the associate and his friend are also dead."

"If they're both dead, wouldn't that be the end of it?"

"It seems the friend had a friend. He told me the story. He only had one name. Now, he has disappeared and I can no longer reach him."

"So, you have one name?"

"Yep."

"Well, who is it?"

"Bahram Oates."

Admiral Hadley turned and looked at his old friend in utter shock. "The former President of the United States?"

"Yep, that's the one."

"But he's not that rich," Admiral Hadley noted.

"I believe he was recruited for his ties to the underbelly of Washington politics. He knows a lot of very important and powerful people."

"Do these people know that you know?"

"I don't think so. Not yet anyway."

"David, you know they will find out. What happens then?"

"They will do everything in their power to find me and silence me. That's why we have to act fast. We have to get this information to the right people before it's too late."

"Agreed," Admiral Hadley acknowledged. "I sent a copy to Edgar Cordell but I haven't been able to reach him."

David McClain turned off Interstate Four-Ninety-Five onto Interstate Sixty-Six. The two men remained silent for the rest of the trip.

Admiral Hadley stared out the window, deep in thought, wondering if he was asleep and in the middle of some horrible nightmare.

Tuesday, Feb. 10th – 4:10 p.m. EST
FBI Headquarters
900 Block Pennsylvania Avenue, NW
Washington, D.C.

Special Agent Williamson knocked on the door to FBI Director Conroy's office and waited, impatiently shifting his weight from one foot to the other. Not receiving an answer, Agent Williamson raised his arm and knocked a little harder.

"Enter," an agitated voice from the other side of the door announced.

Agent Williamson opened the door, entered the office, and waited for Agent Tiner to follow. Agent Williamson pushed the door closed and together the two agents walked over and stood in front of Director Conroy's desk. The Director had a phone cradled against his left ear. He pointed at the two chairs sitting in front of the desk.

"I'll have to call you back," Director Conroy said into the phone. He laid the handset back on the phone and glared at Agent Williamson. Director Conroy stood up, shoved his chair backwards, and leaned forward with his hands on the desk shaking his head. Fire burned in his eyes.

In all his years with the FBI, Agent Williamson had never seen the Director in such a state. His eyes were red. His shirt collar was unbuttoned and his tie hung askew. He looked like he had slept in his suit and it was only late afternoon.

"I can't believe that imbecile Foster let Hadley give him the slip," Director Conroy seethed.

"Foster?" Agent Williamson questioned, knowing that Foster was purported to be the best agent in the Secret Service.

"Yes, Foster," the Director snapped. "The idiot let someone sneak up on him and slug him from behind. When he woke up, Hadley and whoever helped him were long gone."

"We have the information Hadley sent to Cordell," Agent Williamson stammered as he laid a small USB flash drive on the desk and pushed it toward the Director. "I assure you Cordell won't be talking to anyone."

Director Conroy picked up the USB flash drive and dropped it in his inside jacket pocket.

"Well, have you located Hadley's friends yet?"

Agent Williamson swallowed hard, trying to keep his emotions in check and answered, "Pfitzner and his stooge met a similar fate. Someone hit them from behind. Disappeared just like Hadley. When they woke up, the Templetons were long gone. And the computer was gone also. We have to assume it had some or all of the information on it."

The smoldering rage in Director Conroy's mind blazed from red to white hot. He balled his hands into tight fists and slammed then on the desk, upsetting a pen holder and several other items. "Are you guys FBI agents or are you circus clowns?" he roared. "Templeton has a son. What about him?

"His son's name is Zachariah. He lives in South Carolina. I have agents on their way to grab him and his family as we speak."

"We have to find out who else Hadley may have talked to and silence them. These leaks *must* be eliminated! You idiots need to do your jobs. If you can't, speak up and I will find some agents that *can* do their jobs."

Agent Williamson's temper flared, getting the best of him. He rose from his chair and took a step toward Conroy, about to challenge him. Agent Tiner jumped up from his chair and grabbed Williamson's arms, and pulled him to the corner of the room.

Director Conroy stared directly at Williamson and said, "Your partner is a wise man. You should thank him. One more second and you would have found yourself fired or worse. I want you to round up Hadley, his friends, his associates. I don't care who they are or how many there are. Find them! Now get out!"

Agent Tiner dragged his partner out of the Director's office and into the hallway.

"Are you out of your mind, Martin?" Agent Tiner sputtered. "Nobody, and I mean nobody, challenges the Director. You do know he carries a weapon at all times don't you. I have never seen him so upset. You are lucky he let you walk out of his office alive."

"Someday, that pompous jerk is going to get what's coming to him," Agent Williamson ranted. "I'd like to jam that gun he carries down his throat.

"Well, not today," Agent Tiner remarked, "Let's go see if we can find a lead as to where Hadley has gone."

Tuesday, Feb. 10th – 4:42 p.m. EST
United States Botanic Garden
Independence Avenue SW & Third Street SW
Washington, D. C.

A black Lincoln Towncar limousine with blacked out windows rolled slowly down Independence Avenue SW and stopped at the traffic signal at Third Street SW. The driver checked for cross traffic to his left then turned right. Two hundred feet later, he turned right onto Maryland Avenue SW and began looking for an empty parking space. Halfway down the block, he pulled into the lone empty space and left the engine idling.

Underneath his overcoat, dressed in a charcoal-gray suit and white shirt, unbuttoned at the collar, Bahram Oates, former President of the United States, hauled his six foot four frame out of the back seat of the limousine, stepped up onto the sidewalk, and started walking southwest. He walked past thirteen parked cars then turned left and headed down the pathway leading into the United States Botanic Garden. Upon reaching the First Ladies Water Garden, he stopped for two minutes, pretending to admire the fountain. Turning to his right, he followed the path leading toward the Rose Garden.

Oates ambled along the path, now missing the beautiful plants and brightly colored flowers that had filled the flower beds until the killing freeze last fall. Stopping short of the Rose Garden, he walked over to a concrete bench positioned next to a row of trees and sat down. He crossed his legs, pulled the collar of his overcoat up to his chin, and waited.

Becoming impatient, he rotated his wrist and looked at his watch. "He was already supposed to be here," Oates muttered softly, his breath making a wispy cloud in the frigid air. He looked back in the direction from which he had come and saw the other man that had slipped out of the limousine standing thirty feet away, also pretending to be admiring the picturesque scenery. Feeling vulnerable sitting out in the open, Oates would wait only five more minutes and then he would leave.

Oates fidgeted and stamped his feet in the cold as the five minutes passed. About to stand up to leave, he saw the pudgy, five foot ten inch form of Adam West hurrying down the path from the Independence Avenue side of the park. West walked past Oates and sat on the other end of the bench. Slightly out of breath, West apologized, "Sorry, I had trouble getting out of a meeting. Is it safe to talk here in the open?"

Oates reached under his overcoat and into his jacket and pulled a small rectangular box from his left jacket pocket. He pushed a slide switch to the On position and set the little box on his lap. "It's okay now. This sound jammer will mask our conversation and block any listening devices."

"Okay. What is so important that it couldn't wait until tomorrow?"

"Herr Schechter has ordered that the timetable be moved up. You must contact the lab in China and inform them that they have only three days to complete the mutation."

"Three days," West sputtered. "That is not possible. You cannot just flip a switch and make those complex processes go faster."

"I will give you Schechter's number and you can call him and tell him that. Do you have something to write his number on?"

Oates stared at West, waiting for him to respond "Well? I'm waiting."

"I will call them as soon as I get back to a secure telephone line."

"I thought that would be your answer," Oates mocked.

"Why the shortened timeline?"

"He is afraid..." Oates stopped mid-sentence and tapped West on the leg. "Someone is coming." Oates pulled the Herringbone Pattern Newsboy Cap he was wearing low on his forehead, hoping the approaching couple would not recognize him.

Oates and West watched as a young couple hurried down the pathway. Hand in hand, they walked past, giving no indication whatsoever that either one had recognized the former President of the United Sates.

"As I was about to say, Schechter is afraid the information that has leaked out could interfere with our plan if certain individuals were to find out. We must have the virus sooner to make certain no one can stop it."

"I know what the people in the lab are going to say, but I'll go make the call right now," West said as he started to push himself up from the bench.

"Wait. There's one more thing," Oates said as he turned and looked directly at West. "Schechter is absolutely livid that Eagle can't seem to keep his mouth shut. He wants him silenced. *For good.*"

"What?" West gasped, his mouth hanging open. "You cannot possibly be serious."

"Yes, I am absolutely serious. He *must* be silenced and soon."

"But we can't... I don't..."

"Stop and think about it, Adam. Once that stupid imbecile is out of the way, you know who will move up to take his place, right?"

A look of understanding flashed across Adam West's face as he realized who it was that would take Eagle's place.

"I think you're starting to get it," Oates chuckled. "She is going to be so much easier to control. She will believe anything we tell her. That will give us access to *all* the agencies."

"Yes, it does make sense when you think about it," West conceded. "But how?"

Oates slipped his left hand into his inside, right jacket pocket and pulled out a red velvet box. He removed the glove from his right hand. Holding the box in his left hand, he flipped the lid open, revealing an ornate looking gold ring. "This right here," Oates said, pointing at the tip of a leaf-like embellishment. "The tip of the leaf pulls off." He pulled the tip part way off, revealing a tiny needle then pushed it back on.

"Be very, *very* careful," Oates advised as he closed the box and handed it to West and slipped his glove back on. "That tiny needle is covered with an extremely potent biotoxin called maitotoxin. It comes from some kind of marine organism. The exact one is not important. There is enough toxin on that needle to kill an elephant. Just remember, one tiny poke and you will be dead within a few minutes. There is absolutely no treatment or cure. It causes heart failure. Almost certainly the medical examiner will rule his death as heart failure."

"But what if the medical examiner doesn't rule heart failure and suspects foul play?" West questioned.

"I think that is highly unlikely, but to be safe, you are going to order Director Conroy to do it."

"Conroy? I didn't know he took orders from the Order."

"He was approached a few months ago. Money is his idol. He likes expensive clothes and fast cars. It really didn't take much coaxing for him to agree to do our bidding."

"How do I get the box to him?"

"Come on. You're the assistant to the President of the United States," Oates said sarcastically. "Invite him to dinner at a fancy five-star restaurant. He'll jump at the chance. Tell him what we want and then promise him any car he desires. No limit whatsoever on the cost. Anything he wants. Tell him this must be done as soon as possible."

West rolled his wrist over and glanced at his watch. " I've got time. I will do it tonight, as soon as I call the lab and explain to them the requirement to deliver the virus in no more than three days."

"Well then, get to it," Oates said.

"Yes, sir," West acknowledged. He pushed himself up from the bench, turned to this left, and hurried down the pathway toward Independence Avenue.

Oates switched the sound generator off and slipped it back into his jacket pocket. He turned and watched as West disappeared from sight. He nodded at the man standing thirty yards away. The man turned and hurried down the pathway. Oates stood up and started back toward the warmth of the waiting Lincoln Towncar.

Across Independence Avenue in the Humphrey Building in an office on the northeast corner of the sixth floor, a hand reached up and switched off the camera that was pointed downward toward the United States Botanic Garden. The man removed the camera from the tripod it was attached to and placed the tripod in a closet. After removing the SD card, he placed the camera on the shelf. He stuffed the SD card in his pocket and closed the closet door. After waiting for the sound of voices in the hallway to fade, he eased the door open, pulled it closed as quietly as he could, and headed for the White House.

Tuesday, Feb. 10th – 5:42 p.m. EST
Zach Templeton Residence
Big House Plantation Road
Bluffton, South Carolina

Frustrated at not having been able to decipher the encrypted email, Zach and Anna Mae had taken a quick break to grab some supper. Zach pushed away from the table and stretched, anxious to get back to the puzzling email. He took one last swallow of water and headed for the upstairs. He stopped in the doorway, turned back, and looked back at Anna Mae.

"You go work at deciphering that email while I clean the table and stack the dishes," Anna Mae said. "I'll get Mazie into her pajamas and then I'll join you."

Zach nodded his head, turned, and hurried up the stairs to his office. He dropped into his chair and tried several more keywords he had thought of during their quick break for supper. Every single attempt had the same frustrating result. A PLAINTEXT block full of gibberish.

Having finished getting Mazie into her pajamas, Anna Mae reached the top of the stairs and walked into the office. She pointed Mazie toward the pile of blocks in the corner, pulled an extra chair over beside Zach, and looked over his shoulder.

"Try putting the letters together in different orders," Anna Mae suggested.

"I already tried that and nothing," Zach muttered, shaking his head, having rearranged the letters in every possible combination he could think of.

"Try breaking the letters into groups. Like M space TOY," Anna Mae suggested.

Before Zach could type the letters and press Enter, Anna Mae blurted out, "Zach, wait. I know what it means. M dash TOY. It's Mazie's toy."

"That sounds good," Zach said as he typed the word *Giraffe* into the KEYWORD block and clicked the Decipher button. "So much for that," Zach complained as the PLAINTEXT block once again filled with gibberish. "What else could it be?"

"Remember when Dad was here last? How he and Mazie played hide-and-seek with that old giraffe. What did Mazie and Dad call that beat up old thing?"

"That's right. I'll try RAFFEE."

Zach typed the giraffe's nickname into the KEYWORD block and clicked the Decipher button.

"WOW, that's it," Zach exclaimed.

Zach quickly copied the deciphered text and pasted it into a word processing document. He inserted spaces between words where the cipher had removed them during the encryption process. Zach and Anna Mae stared in disbelief at the words that filled the screen.

> J SENDS LOVE TRUSTED SOURCE HAS DISCOVERED PLAN TO RELEASE NEW DEADLY MUTATED VIRUS HUNDREDS OF MILLIONS WILL DIE HAVE PROOF SOMEONE HIGH IN WH ELIMINATING ANY ONE WHO KNOWS YOU ARE IN EXTREME DANGER
> CONTACT J SOON SATP CH

Zach and Anna Mae read the short message, turned, and looked at each other with a look of shock, the color draining from their faces.

"This is not from Dad," Zach said. "It says 'J sends love' and look how it is signed. *CH* could only be one person. That has to be Charles Hadley."

"No, not again," Anna Mae quavered as she grabbed Zach and held him tight. "Zach, I'm scared. I can't go through that again. And what about Mazie?"

"From the tone of the Admiral's message, I don't think we're going to have a choice. I'm going to save this to a flash drive for safe keeping." Zach fished around in the top drawer of his desk for a flash drive. He located one, shoved it into an empty USB slot, and saved the document. "The last line says to contact J soon, but how do we do that? Dad's cellphone goes straight to voice mail. What on Earth does S-A-T-P mean?"

They both stared at the four letters. Zach shrugged his shoulders and shook his head, "If it's another code, it makes no sense."

Anna Mae leaned in close to Zach and sounded out the letters, "S A T P. Maybe SAT something?"

"It must mean the old SAT phone!" Zach exclaimed. "What else could it be." Zach spun around in his chair and took off for the closet. He threw open the closet door and began shoving boxes and plastic containers aside. Finding the box he wanted at the very back of the top shelf, he lifted it down and carried it to his desk. He flipped the lid off and pulled out some of the contents, dumping them in disarray. He grabbed the SAT phone and tried to turn it on, but the phone displayed a blank screen. As he had expected, the battery was completely dead. Back to the box, he searched for the charging unit. With the charger in hand, he bent over beside the desk and plugged the charger into the wall outlet and the other end of the wire into the phone.

"We'll have to wait for a few minutes while the battery charges up. How about a...?" Zach said, holding up his travel cup. "Never mind," he said when he realized the cup was nearly half full.

"I'm going downstairs to clean up the kitchen," Anna Mae said as she headed down the stairs.

Zach raised up out of his chair and walked over to the corner where Mazie was playing with her favorite blocks. He eased himself down on the floor. Helping Mazie stack blocks, he waited for Anna Mae to return from the kitchen.

"Zach, I'm back," Anna Mae called out ten minutes later as she reached the top of the stairs. She walked over to where Zach and Mazie were playing. "How much longer do we need to wait for the phone to charge?"

"Maybe another fifteen minutes," Zach answered.

Anna Mae sat down on the floor and joined Zach and Mazie in the game of stacking blocks. Zach and Anna Mae would stack the blocks and Mazie would knock them down, giggling in delight as the blocks crashed down in a pile around her. After many rounds of stacking the blocks and knocking them down, Zach glanced at the clock. "Close enough," he said as he pushed himself up from the floor and walked over to the desk. He picked up the phone and pressed and held the power button.

"It's on," he announced. "I'll call the old SAT number and see if Dad answers."

Zach yanked the center drawer of his desk open and pulled out his old day planner that would have his Dad's old SAT phone number recorded. He flipped through the pages to the contacts section. Running his finder down the page, he stopped at the next to last entry. Holding his finger under the SAT phone entry, he punched the number into the SAT phone. He disconnected the charging cable and walked over to the south facing window and waited for the SAT phone to register on the satellite system. The searching indicator flashed on and off for ninety seconds and then the connection indicator appeared in the lower right corner of the display. Zach pressed the Call button and waited.

Zach waited while the signal made its way several hundred miles up to the receiving satellite and then back down to the called SAT phone. Faint crackles and low-level buzzing filled Zach's ear as he waited for an answer.

"Hello, Zach, I've been waiting for your call," James Templeton answered.

"Dad, I got the Admiral's email. What is…,"

"Sorry, there's no time," Zach's Dad interrupted, "Just listen and do as I say."

As instructed, Zach sat quietly and just listened, a look of foreboding growing on his face. Two minutes later, he ended the call without a word and laid the SAT phone on the desk. He turned and looked at Anna Mae with a worried look on his face, knowing this was going to frighten Anna Mae even more.

Zach hesitated for a few seconds not wanting to tell Anna Mae what his Dad had instructed them to do, but there was no time to waste. He said, "Listen carefully. You must do *exactly* as I say. Pack a bag for you and Mazie for a few days, but *only* what is absolutely necessary. You must do it quickly. We have only a few minutes."

"Pack a bag," Anna Mae gasped. "Zach, what are you talking about?"

"Anna Mae, please," Zach begged. "Just do as I say. Dad said we are in grave danger. We have to get out of here *now*!"

Zach, I need to know what is going on," Anna Mae insisted.

Zach looked at his watch, made a quick calculation in his head, and said, "Please. No questions," Zach pleaded. "We have less than twenty minutes to get a few things together and make it through the woods to White House Plantation Road."

"Through the woods? Zach, you can't be serious? It's already dark."

"Dad has arranged for someone to pick us up there. It is too dangerous for them to come straight to the house. There isn't time to explain right now. Get a bag packed. Quickly."

The look of fear on Zach's face persuaded Anna Mae that she needed to do what Zach said. Zach raced back to the closet and pulled out a soft-sided travel bag and tossed it toward Anna Mae. For himself, he grabbed a small tote bag. As he started to stuff some clothes into the bag, he yelled to Anna Mae, "Remember just enough for a couple of days."

Anna Mae picked up Mazie and the travel bag and hurried down the stairs to get some clothes and a toy or two for Mazie. While Anna Mae was busy packing her and Mazie's bag, Zach finished stuffing clothes into his bag. He rushed over to his desk and grabbed the small USB drive and stuffed it into his pocket. He powered down the computer, disconnected his large external, backup drive from the computer, and threw it into the bag. A quick survey of the room did not reveal anything he absolutely had to have. Hoping everything would still be there when they returned, he turned and hurried down the stairs.

"Anna Mae, are you about ready?" Zach called out upon reaching the bottom of the stairs.

Anna Mae came running out of Mazie's room with the travel bag in her left hand and holding Mazie's hand in her right hand. "We're ready, I guess," she said. "Except for our coats."

Zach dropped his bag and fumbled around in the coat closet, searching for coats for everyone. He handed two coats to Anna Mae and slipped his coat on.

"What about Tripp?" Anna Mae asked.

"He's coming with us," Zach answered. "He knows the way through the woods better than we do. We need to leave the lights on in the house to make them think we're home."

"Who is *them*?"

"I don't know. Dad didn't say. Well, I guess we're ready. Let's go out the back door as quietly as we can."

The three Templetons went to the back door. Anna Mae picked up Mazie and they slipped outside into the dark. The light spilling out through the house's windows, provided enough light for them to make it to the end of their property. On his way out and before locking the door, Zach had grabbed the flashlight that always sat by the back door.

"Tripp, stay close," Zach ordered.

Together they made their way to the back of the property and over the wooden bridge that crossed the small stream that ran along the northern edge of the property. They all stopped while Zach watched the house for a few seconds to see if anyone had followed them.

Zach held his finger to his lips and told Mazie she needed to be very quiet. He put his hand down near his knee and patted his leg. "Tripp. Come here, Tripp." Zach snapped a leash to his collar and said, "Go, Tripp".

The old redbone, coon hound took off, straining against the leash as he began making his way through the woods. The hound's ability to pass under the low-hanging branches and shrubs, made it tough going for Zach and Anna Mae. In the darkness with Zach using the flashlight infrequently and keeping it low and pointed toward the ground, it was nearly impossible to see low-hanging branches coming. Slapped and scratched often by the dense undergrowth, the Templetons kept slogging their way toward White House Plantation Road.

"Zach, slow down," Anna Mae urged. "Those branches hurt and my legs are getting cut on the brambles."

"Sorry, but we're almost out of time," Zach urged. "We've got to keep going. We should be getting close."

"Mommie, it hurts," Mazie complained after getting smacked by a thick branch.

"I'm sorry, sweetie," Anna Mae soothed. "We'll be out of the woods soon." Anna Mae adjusted the travel bag's strap on her shoulder and put her arm in front of Mazie to shield her.

A few minutes later, they intersected an open path that led to White House Plantation Road. Anna Mae reached up and tapped Zach on the shoulder and whispered, "Zach, I know where we are. It's only thirty or forty yards to the road now."

The hair stood up on Tripp's back. He stiffened and growled low in his throat. Zach kneeled down on one knee, pulled Tripp close to him, and commanded him to sit. "Quiet, Tripp," Zach urged as he pointed the flash-light toward the road and flashed the light three times. Tripp would not be quieted, a deep growl still coming from his throat.

Immediately the distinctive *pffft pffft* of a sound-suppressed weapon echoed through the dark woods. Bark and splinters of wood ripped from a nearby tree stung the side of Zach's face.

"Down! Now!," Zach yelled as he dropped onto the dirt and pulled his STI Lawman semi-automatic from its holster.

Chapter Eleven

Tuesday, Feb. 10th – 3:20 p.m. PST
BioGen Pharmaceuticals
Minto Road, Watsonville, CA

Doctor Robert Mueller snatched the handset off the phone sitting on the corner of his gleaming mahogany desk and punched in a four digit number. As soon as he heard someone answer, he bellowed, "Doctor Chaudhari, Come to my office, now!"

"What is it that has you so upset?" Doctor Mueller asked, turning toward Doctor Kenneth Thompson.

"Wait till Doctor Chaudhari gets here. I don't want to have to explain it twice," Doctor Thompson snapped.

Doctor Mueller drummed his fingers on the desk as they waited for Doctor Chaudhari to show up. About to pick up the phone and call again, he looked up as the door swung open and Doctor Chaudhari rushed into the room.

"What took you so long?" Doctor Mueller asked.

"Never mind," Doctor Thompson roared. "Just sit down and listen."

Doctor Chaudhari quickly grabbed one of the chairs sitting in front of Doctor Mueller's desk, turned it toward Doctor Thompson, and sat down.

Doctor Thompson glared at both men and continued, "Eagle is not happy. This process is taking too long. Phase one is already complete and phase two was supposed to start in a few days. What is taking so long?"

"The last report we had was that there was an issue with the introduction of the linker enzyme that triggers the mutation process. It is a very tedious and complex process. We are…"

"We have heard these excuses before," Doctor Thompson exploded. "You were given an extension of one week with the promise the final virus would be ready for dissemination by the end of this week. That is only three days away, Doctor. Eagle told me to pass along a warning. If it is not ready as you promised, you will suffer the consequences. Both your careers will be over and you will be lucky to escape with your lives. Is that clear?"

"Yes, Doctor Thompson. I understand," Doctor Mueller gulped.

Doctor Thompson turned and looked at Doctor Chaudhari, "Well?"

Unable to speak, Doctor Chaudhari just nodded his head up and down.

"I'm glad for your sakes. Call Doctor Yu right now. I want an update on the current progress," Doctor Thompson ordered, turning toward Doctor Mueller.

"But it is only seven in China."

"I don't care. Call him!" Doctor Thompson roared. "Use the conference phone."

Doctor Mueller rolled his chair over to the conference table, punched the conference phone's on button, and tapped in Doctor Yu's number from memory. He pulled a handkerchief out of his pocket and wiped his face as he waited for the connection to be made. Everyone listened as the phone in China began to ring.

On the sixth ring a sleepy voice answered, "*nǐ hǎo*"

"Doctor Yu, it's Doctor Mueller and Doctors Thompson and Chaudhari. You are on the conference phone."

"Doctor Mueller, it is very early. What is it you want?"

Doctor Thompson pushed Doctor Mueller aside and leaned toward the phone. "This is Doctor Thompson. We wish to know when the final virus will be ready. You have been given an extension and it appears you may not make the date you promised."

"I was going to call you later this morning," Doctor Yu replied. "Mister West called not an hour ago. He is demanding we complete the mutation in no more than three days. Fortunately late yesterday Doctor Tang had a breakthrough. He devised a method of simplifying the DNA-binding, seed sequence before the introduction of the synthetic Cas9 nuclease enzyme. That simplified the process and effectively eliminated the off-target cleavage at the target gene. He then had one successful run of beginning the mutation of the virus. Doctor Tang will arrive at the laboratory early this morning to verify he can repeat the process. Once he has verified that the steps can be repeated, the process can be moved to the pilot process lab and then a day or two after that it can be put into full production. I am confident we can have enough mutated virus to begin the dissemination phase in three or four days. It is simply not possible to do this in three days."

"You had better be correct with your estimate, Doctor Yu," Doctor Thompson warned. "I want detailed updates twice a day on your progress. Communicate directly with Doctor Mueller."

"Yes, Doctor. I will provide two updates every day."

"See that you do," Doctor Thompson said as he poked the End Call button on the conference phone. "Doctor Mueller see that Doctor Yu's updates are forwarded to my assistant as they arrive. And you, Doctor Chaudhari, I want you to review each update as soon as it arrives and verify that their progress is on track for the promised date."

"Yes, sir," Doctor Chaudhari answered, breathing a sigh of relief that the meeting was over.

Doctor Thompson turned and left the office without saying another word.

"Doctor Chaudhari you may go now, but make certain you are reachable. Your assistant is to know where you are every minute of the day. Is that clear?"

"Yes, Doctor Mueller."

Doctor Mueller waved Doctor Chaudhari out of his office and went back to the report he had been working on when Doctor Thompson had barged into his office unannounced.

Tuesday, Feb. 10th – 6:41 p.m. EST
Palmetto Bluff Woods
Bluffton, South Carolina

Lying as flat as he could on the soggy, wet ground, Zach reached up and pulled a jagged sliver of tree bark from the side of his face. As he rubbed the side of his face, he felt his fingers becoming sticky. Raising his right shoulder, he did his best to wipe the blood running down his face. The gunman in front of them presented a far greater threat than a trickle of blood. He needed to do something to eliminate the threat and quickly.

"Anna Mae, are you there?" Zach whispered, reaching his hand backwards.

Anna Mae tapped the bottom of Zach's foot and whispered, "We're here. Zach, what are we going to do? Mazie's scared to death."

"I'll think of something," he answered, his attention returning to the immediate threat in front of them.

Unable to come up with any other options, Zach let go of Tripp's leash and slipped his ST1 Lawman into his left hand. No longer restrained, Tripp raced off in the direction of the shooters. Zach grabbed a pine cone that was lying nearby and tossed it to his left. Grabbing his weapon from his left hand and taking aim at the origin of the muzzle flash, he squeezed the trigger of his pistol twice. He heard a gasp and the sound of someone falling to the ground. Almost immediately, another shot rang out from the same general area. More splinters erupted as the slug buried itself into the tree Zach was hiding behind.

Two more shots rang out, but from fifty feet to the left of the original shooters. Zach heard rustling, a thump, and another groan from the area of the original shooters. As the echo of the gunshots faded away, the woods became deathly silent.

A voice from the area of the last two gunshots called out, "Zach Templeton, is that you? Come out and show yourself."

"Be quiet. Don't say anything," Zach ordered, "We don't know who that is."

"Zach Templeton, is that you?" the voice called out again. "Lay down your weapon and come out."

Wednesday Feb. 11th – 7:50 a.m. ChST
Zhongnan University Xiangya Medical College
Tongzipo Road, Yuelu District
Ch'angsha, Hunan Province, China

Doctor Huang Yan Tang, Assistant Director of Virology Research, who had replaced the missing Doctor Li as project researcher, sat sipping his mid-morning tea with his feet up on his desk. Arriving before dawn, he had already completed two test runs in the level 4 biolab of a new method for synchronizing the nucleotide enzyme insertion. He was completely exhausted.

Doctor Tang sputtered, coughed, and nearly fell out of his chair when he saw Politboro Committee Secretary Chen Kun Ma walk into his office accompanied by Tao An Lee, Party Secretary of all of Hunan Province. Secretary Ma, one of the seven most powerful politicians in all of China, was ruthless and greatly feared. The political decisions he and the six other Politboro secretaries made affected every facet of life in China. Few people ever saw the Secretary from a distance let alone stood face to face with him in the same room.

Intimidated and more than a little frightened, Doctor Tang leaped up from his chair and stood before his desk. He bowed deeply as Secretary Ma approached and stood in front of him.

"Doctor Tang, I am told the mutated virus project has not been going well and will not be completed on time as promised," Secretary Ma challenged.

"Secretary Ma, I have only recently been assigned to this project because Doctor Li is missing," Doctor Tang replied, his voice trembling slightly. "Only yesterday was I able to complete my review of what we currently know of Doctor Li's research. I believe I have found the mistake in his methodology. I have revised the approach to the mutation of the base virus by first simplifying then synchronizing the addition of the final enzyme. If we are able to initiate the process, we may then be able to finalize the process and move it to the pilot process lab in a few days. If that is successful, we could expect to …"

"It must be completed quicker," Secretary Ma demanded, interrupting Doctor Tang's explanation. "The Chairman is *very* unhappy. He directed me to come here and inform you personally that the project is most important and must be completed soon. Effective immediately, you are now the Director Of Clinical Operations. Your first duty is to fire Doctor Yu. Since replacing the missing Doctor Zhou, Yu has made excuse after excuse. You will see to it that he is severely punished for his failure to complete this most important work. Doctor Tang, you will identify whatever resources are needed to complete this project as soon as possible. There will be no more excuses. Do you understand?"

"Yes, Secretary Ma, I understand."

"Sit down, then. Let us talk," Secretary Ma said, pointing at the chair beside the desk. Secretary Ma sat in Doctor Tang's office chair and continued, "I bring new instructions from the Chairman himself. The mutated virus is to be reengineered to be lethal to everyone but those of Asian descent. I have been told you can do this, yes?"

"Ah… Yes, of course," Doctor Tang exaggerated, deciding it would be better to lie now and hope he could find a way to do as the Secretary asked. "If my understanding of Doctor Li's underlying design is correct, it should be a simple matter of identifying a different base pair on the genome and then applying the nucleotide enzyme. But I must tell you the human genome is quite complex. The process of identifying the marker for Asian descent and altering the targeting of the mutation process could add several days to the process."

"I do not understand," Secretary Ma protested. "I was told you already have the human genome mapped. "Why should the Chairman's request add more time to the process?"

Doctor Tang spent the next few minutes trying to explain to Secretary Ma the human genome's complexity and why altering the target gene this late in the process could be extremely difficult and time consuming. He could see by the glazed look in Secretary Ma's eyes that his attempt to explain had failed. About to attempt a less complicated explanation, he was startled when Secretary Ma suddenly leaped up from his chair.

"You have three days to produce the mutated virus as has been promised or you will stand before the Party Chairman and explain why you have failed," Secretary Ma snarled, stepping to within inches of Doctor Tang. "I can promise you it will be a most unpleasant day. A further word of warning. If the slightest word of the altered target leaks out you will die a miserable death. Do you understand?"

Terrified and unable to speak, Doctor Tang nodded his understanding and watched as the two men turned and left the room. He slumped into his chair and reached for his now cold cup of tea. Shaking badly he could not hold the cup of tea without sloshing it upon the desk. He set the cup back down and stared at the same spot on the desk for a long time.

Rousing from his trance-like stare, he realized he could not afford to just sit. Inaction would cost him his life. He leaped to his feet, snatched the project design manuals, and rushed out the door, heading for Doctor Yu's office.

Chapter Twelve

Tuesday, Feb. 10th – 6:56 p.m. EST
White House Plantation Road
Bluffton, South Carolina

Zach heard low voices but he could not make out what they were saying. Risking getting shot, Zach raised his head up slightly, trying to pinpoint the location of the voices. Unable to see anything in the pitch black night, he settled back onto the wet, leaf-carpeted ground. The earthy scent of rotting vegetation drifted up from the wet ground, filling his nostrils. He reached backward, located Anna Mae's hand, and gave it a squeeze.

"We have to do something," Zach whispered. "We can't just lay here. Be ready to run for the road. I'm going to shoot in the direction where I heard the voices"

Zach planted his left elbow on the soft, squishy soil, and raised up, aiming his weapon in the general direction the second set of shots had come from. He took a deep calming breath readying himself to fire, his finger tightening on the trigger of his weapon.

A familiar voice called out in the darkness, "Zachman, are you there?"

There was only one person in the world that had ever called him by that nickname. Zach grabbed Anna Mae's arm and said, "Come on. There's only one person that knows that nickname. Grab your suitcase. It's safe."

Zach, eased the hammer of his pistol to the safe position, jumped up, and holstered his weapon. In the darkness, he grabbed Anna Mae's hand and helped her up. He took the frightened Mazie and soothed her. Together they scrambled down the path toward White House Plantation Road.

Zach switched on the flashlight, illuminating the path that led toward the road. As they reached the clearing at the end of the path, he pointed the flashlight to his left. A dark gray van with blacked out windows sat parked at the edge of the road. Upon reaching the van, Zach hesitated. "I don't know you," Zach challenged. "Who are you and how did you know my nickname?"

"I'm Agent Carl Rodgers. David McClain sent me," the man answered.

"How do I…,"

"There's no time to explain. We have to get out of here. Get in the van, NOW!" Agent Rogers yelled.

"It's okay," Zach told Anna Mae. "David sent him. Get in the van." Zach held Anna Mae's hand and helped her up into the van. He handed Mazie up to her and called out to Tripp.

"Come on. We've got to go!" Agent Rodgers pleaded.

"We can't leave him," Zach objected. Zach yelled, "Tripp." Then he whistled.

There was movement in the undergrowth beyond the road. "Come on, Tripp. Come now," Zach called out again.

The coonhound came bounding through the Bottlebrush Buckeye shrubs and Virginia Creeper vines lining the edge of the road and slammed into Zach's legs.

"Come on. Get in the van you silly dog," Zach said as he reached down and grabbed the loose end of Tripp's leash. "You're lucky you didn't get strangled."

Tripp leaped up into the van and up onto the seat beside Anna Mae and Mazie. Zach, unhooked the leash, stepped up into the van, slammed the side door closed, and slid onto the rear seat behind Anna Mae and Mazie. Agent Rodgers ran around to the other side of the van, jumped into the driver's seat, and started the engine. He jammed the van into reverse and roared backward down the road to a small turnaround. He backed into the turnaround, made a quick u-turn, and sped off toward the southwest.

One-quarter of a mile down White House Plantation Road, Agent Rodgers turned right onto Rephraim Cemetery Road and increased his speed, continually checking the rearview mirror for any signs they were being followed. Satisfied no one was following them, he turned left onto Myrtle Ford Road for a short half-mile, then left onto New Riverside Road. Passing through the edge of the small community of New Riverside, they entered the western edge of Pritchardville. The van slid to a stop at the intersection with State Highway Forty-Six and turned left onto the highway.

Rather than turning right and staying on Highway Forty-Six to Interstate Ninety-Five, the normally expected route, Agent Rodgers continued straight onto State Highway One-Seventy, appropriately named Alligator Alley. The van passed through the Savannah National Wildlife Refuge Area, crossed over the Savannah River, and entered Georgia.

After, crossing over the western fork of the Savannah River, they entered the city of Savannah, Georgia. Nearing the end of their journey, Agent Rodgers slowed down, turned left off of Gulfstream Road and onto Patrick S Graham Road, and entered the Savannah/Hilton Head International Airport. Following the general aviation signs, the van pulled up and parked in front of the Southeast General Aviation service center on the southwest corner of the airport.

Zach stepped down out of the van and hooked the leash to Tripp's collar. Anna Mae followed, holding Mazie tightly. Carrying one small travel bag each, they followed Agent Rodgers into the general aviation service center. As Agent Rodgers stepped up to the service counter, he pulled out his credentials and held them out for the gate agent.

"I believe these folks have been pre-cleared to the ramp area," Agent Rodgers advised.

"Yes, sir," the gate agent replied. "I have been notified to expect them. Go through the door to your right."

Agent Rodgers turned, pointed toward the door, and guided Zach and his family through the door marked RAMP.

Standing in the doorway he said, "I hope you have a safe trip. Agent McClain is waiting for you."

Zach stopped, transferred Tripp's leash to his left hand, and shook Agent Rodgers's hand. "I can't thank you enough. You saved our lives back there."

"Mister Templeton, it was my honor," Agent Rodgers responded, smiling widely. "Agent McClain told me what you did for our country. I wish I had time to get to know you, but Agent McClain is waiting."

Agent Rodgers patted Tripp's head then watched as the Templetons turned and headed for the aircraft parking area. He let go of the door, turned quickly, and headed for the exit.

Zach grabbed Tripp's leash close to his collar and led Anna Mae and Mazie out to the gleaming white Gulfstream 550 sitting on the ramp. Zach looked up at the beautiful Gulfstream jet, tail number N462ML, November-four-six-two-Mike-Lima. Looking at the sleek aircraft, he remembered the last time they had flown on the aircraft to Washington, D.C., for the presidential awards ceremony.

Kip Johnson, the pilot, had been notified by the gate agent that his passengers had arrived. He hurried down the stairs and met Zach as they walked up to the aircraft.

"Zach, it's great to see you again," he said as he grabbed Zach's hand and pumped it vigorously.

"Curry," Mazie squealed, still having trouble pronouncing the letter L. She held out her arms when she saw David McClain coming down the stairs toward them. Mazie had become quite attached to David when he had been assigned to the Templetons for the duration of their stay in Washington.

Anna Mae handed Mazie to David. Mazie immediately hugged David's neck, nearly choking him. With one free hand, David reached out to shake Zach's hand. "Sorry to rush you, Zach, but we do need to get going. We've been sitting on the ground here quite awhile. The longer we sit here, the greater the possibility we'll be discovered."

"I'll take those," Kip Johnson said as he grabbed the two bags and headed for the cargo hold.

"I'll hold her until you get settled," David said, motioning toward the aircraft's open cabin door.

Anna Mae walked up the stairs and disappeared into the cabin. Zach started to follow but stopped when Tripp's leash became taught.

"There's nothing to be afraid off," Zach soothed, getting down on one knee and rubbing the hound's ears. Zach raised up and started up the stairs again, but Tripp refused to budge.

"Looks like it's a No Go," David snickered.

"Okay, we'll do this the hard way." Zach grunted as he picked up the hound and tottered up the steps.

David McClain walked up the stairs behind Zach. Once in the cabin, he handed Mazie over to Anna Mae. Kip Johnson loaded the bags into the cargo hold and secured and latched the cargo hold door. He hurried up the stairs and closed and secured the forward cabin door.

"Everybody get settled and fasten your seatbelts," Kip advised. "We're ready to go as soon as I get the engines started and obtain final clearance from the tower. Hey, Zach, you want to ride right seat?"

"You bet I do," Zach exclaimed with a big grin spreading across his face.

Kip waited for Zach to enter the cockpit and slide into the right-hand seat. Kip eased his six foot two inch frame into the left-hand seat and began double checking the pre-flight check list. Satisfied, he slid the clipboard into its storage compartment.

"Are you buckled up?" he asked, looking over at Zach.

"Yes sir, captain," Zach beamed.

"Well then, let's roll," Kip announced. He turned forward, tuned the radio to the SAV Clearance Delivery frequency, and pressed the transmit button on the yoke, "Savannah Clearance, November-four-six-two-Mike-Lima is a Gulfstream G-five-five-zero, Request VFR flight to Manassas Regional at flight level two-niner-zero."

"November-four-six-two-Mike-Lima, Savannah Clearance, Cleared out of Savannah class Bravo airspace. On departure fly runway heading. Maintain VFR at two-thousand five-hundred. Departure frequency one-two-five-point-two. Squawk five-six-three-one."

"Cleared out of Savannah class Bravo. On departure fly runway heading. Maintain two-thousand five-hundred. Departure is on one-two-five-point-two. Squawk five-six-three-one. November-four-six-two-Mike-Lima."

"November-four-six-two-Mike-Lima. Readback correct."

Kip reached over and dialed the four-digit code into the transponder and tuned the radio to the Savannah Ground frequency.

"Savannah Ground, Gulfstream November-four-six-two-Mike-Lima, at general aviation, request taxi for VFR departure, with information foxtrot."

"Gulfstream four-six-two-Mike-Lima, Savannah Ground, hold there is cross-traffic on the taxiway behind you."

"Roger Savannah Ground."

Two minutes later the radio crackled to life, "Gulfstream four-six-two-Mike-Lima, Savannah Ground, Traffic behind you has cleared. You are clear to taxi, taxi runway one-zero via Alpha and hold."

"Runway one-zero via Alpha, hold short, Gulfstream four-six-two-Mike-Lima."

Kip Johnson pushed the throttles forward, twisted the steering yoke to the right, and slowly eased the Gulfstream 550 toward the taxiway. He straightened out the steering yoke and increased the throttles slightly. The Gulfstream bounced slightly as it rolled down taxiway Alpha. Kip taxied the plane to the south end of the airport and stopped short of the active runway.

"Savannah Tower, Gulfstream four-six-two-Mike-Lima, holding short runway one-zero."

"Four-six-two-Mike-Lima, Savannah Ground, continue hold short for traffic inbound on final two and one-half miles."

"Savannah Ground, Four-six-two-Mike-Lima, continue hold short."

Kip keyed the cabin intercom, "One plane inbound on final and we are next. Make certain your seatbelts are buckled."

Anna Mae leaned forward in her seat and peered out the window to watch the inbound plane as it landed. An American Airlines Airbus A319 jet flared over the threshold of the runway and flashed by the small private jet. Tires screeched and puffs of smoke rose into the air as the jet settled onto the runway.

"Four-six-two-Mike-Lima, Savannah Tower, you are cleared for takeoff. Fly runway heading and report to departure control at two-thousand five-hundred."

"Gulfstream four-six-two-Mike-Lima, cleared for takeoff, fly runway heading, report at two-thousand five-hundred roger."

Kip eased the throttles forward, steering the Gulfstream onto runway one-zero. Lined up on the centerline, he set the brake and pushed the throttles all the way forward, waiting for the twin Rolls-Royce BR710 engines to spool up. When the engines reached seventy percent thrust, he released the brake and the sleek Gulfstream began its take-off roll. Kip's eyes scanned the gauges and indicators as the Gulfstream accelerated toward V1, the decision speed where a pilot can still abort a takeoff . All gauges reported normal and no warning indicators. At VR, rotation speed, he pulled back on the control yoke and the nose wheel lifted off the ground. A few seconds later, the Gulfstream reached V2, safe take-off speed. With over two thousand feet of runway remaining, the rear wheels lifted off the runway and the jet began its climb-out into the inky black sky. At two hundred feet, Kip pointed at the landing gear, lever. Zach reached out and pushed the lever to the full retract position.

At precisely two thousand five hundred feet, Kip, dialed the radio to the departure control frequency, thumbed the transmit button, and contacted departure control, "Savannah Departure, Gulfstream four-six-two-Mike-Lima, two-thousand five-hundred runway heading, two-five miles southeast of Savannah VORTAC."

"Gulfstream four-six-two-Mike-Lima, climb and maintain one-eight-thousand, turn left, heading zero-three-zero. Contact Jacksonville Center on one-two-four-point-niner."

"Leaving two-thousand five-hundred for one-eight-thousand, heading zero-three-zero, contact Jacksonville Center, one-two-four-point-niner, four-six-two-Mike-Lima."

Kip pointed to the radio and watched as Zach tuned the radio to the Jacksonville Center frequency. "Jacksonville Center, Gulfstream four-six-two-Mike-Lima, climbing through four thousand five hundred approximately three-zero miles southeast of the Savannah VORTAC."

"Jacksonville Center, four-six-two-Mike-Lima, you're radar contact thirty southwest of Savannah VORTAC. Traffic eleven o'clock, five miles, southeast bound, altitude indicates four thousand five-hundred, climbing VFR type unknown."

Kip looked slightly to his left, scanning the skies for crossing traffic. After spotting the aircraft at approximately six miles, he acknowledged, "Four-six-two-Mike-Lima has traffic in sight, will maintain visual separation."

"Jacksonville Center, four-six-two-Mike-Lima, roger, thanks, good day."

Kip continued his climb out, leveling off at twenty-nine thousand feet. He keyed the intercom, "It is safe to move around the cabin. It will be a beautiful night for flying. Aircraft ahead of us all report smooth air. There are assorted soft drinks and snacks in the galley at the rear of the cabin. Enjoy the ride."

Anna Mae unbuckled her seat belt and checked on Mazie who was fast asleep. She reached across the aisle and tapped David on the shoulder. "Can you stay with Mazie while I go to the galley and grab a soda? Do you want anything?"

"Be glad to," David responded. "Grab me a ginger ale and a bag of nuts, if there are any."

In the cockpit, Zach looked over at Kip and asked, "Who arranged for the aircraft?"

"Your friend, Admiral Hadley," Kip answered.

"But he's not an admiral anymore. How did he swing it?"

"He still has several pretty important friends. Let's just say it's kind of a loan."

"A *kind* of a loan. What exactly does that mean?" Zach questioned.

"The aircraft wasn't scheduled to go anywhere. As long as no one misses it, we're okay."

"And if someone does miss it?"

"Those *close* friends of Admiral Hadley will say they did not authorize it and they know nothing about the aircraft being missing. *And* then it's off to jail for me and the end of my flying career."

"Kip you should not have gotten involved in this."

"Oh, no, my friend. The admiral told me enough about what is going on to convince me that losing my career or going to jail is nothing compared to what might happen."

Zach really could not argue with what Kip had just said. He turned back toward the instrument panel, enjoying his time in the cockpit.

Wednesday Feb. 11th – 8:38 a.m. ChST
Zhongnan University Xiangya Medical College
Tongzipo Road, Yuelu District
Ch'angsha, Hunan Province, China

Arriving red-faced and slightly out of breath, Doctor Huang Yan Tang threw open the door to Doctor Yu's outer office and blew right past his administrative assistant. Doctor Tang slammed open the inner office door and barged in with no regard to the meeting taking place.

Doctor Tang turned toward the man seated in front of Doctor Yu's desk and yelled, "Get out!"

Frightened by the sudden outburst, the university's budget director scrambled out of his chair, gathered up the budget reports he had been discussing, and rushed out of the office. Doctor Tang walked over to the open door, slammed it closed, and locked it.

"What is the meaning of this?" Doctor Yu sputtered as he stood up, banging his chair against the credenza behind him.

"Come around the desk and sit here," Doctor Tang ordered, pointing at the chair the budget director had just vacated.

"You cannot come in here and shout orders at me."

"You *will* sit here or I will drag you from behind that desk and shove you into the chair," Doctor Tang roared, taking a step toward Doctor Yu.

Doctor Tang towered over Doctor Yu by a full six inches and outweighed him by forty pounds. Deciding a physical confrontation would be unwise, Doctor Yu headed for the chair as ordered, his fists balled up in anger.

Doctor Tang walked past him and stood behind the desk. Slowly he sat down and stared directly at Doctor Yu. "You have been replaced. As of this instant, I will be taking over responsibility for all gain-of-function development here at Hunan University. I have been made Director of Clinical Operations. I will be…"

"You have no right. You cannot do this," Doctor Yu interrupted. "I am…"

"Shut up you pompous pig!" Doctor Tang snarled. "Secretary Chen Kun Ma of the Central Committee just left my office. These orders came directly from him. I am now your superior. I suggest you address me as such."

"*So, the report that someone had seen Secretary Ma leaving the university was true*," Doctor Yu thought. Before he could object, Doctor Tang continued.

"What methods did Doctor Li use to test the theory that is described in the project design book? He must have had some kind of success or he would not have deleted all his work before he went missing."

"I do not know," Doctor Yu shrugged. "The technology department has not had any success in restoring the missing files. They tell me the backup system has been malfunctioning for several weeks. They are waiting on a part they need to make repairs."

"You idiot," Doctor Tang exploded. "Backup systems are critical. They must run every day. What kind of department are you running?"

"But, Chang Hu is responsible for…"

"No, Doctor. You are responsible for everything that happens in this department. Without a record of Doctor Li's work, I will have to start at the beginning and I do not have time for that. Secretary Ma gave me only three days to complete the process and have the final mutated virus ready for delivery. In addition, he requested that I alter the virus so that it is lethal to everyone but those of Asian descent. I agreed and told him that was possible."

"You should not have agreed to that modification, Doctor Tang. It will greatly complicate the mutation process. You will have to reanalyze the genome to locate the proper target."

"I know that, but I had little choice. Secretary Ma said the Chairman himself requested this change. Where should I begin?"

"I do not know. I am not a researcher. I simply manage the department."

"So, you are nothing more than a useless bureaucrat," Doctor Tang mocked. "Get out of my sight! Report immediately to the Party Secretary of Hunan Province. He will inform you of your reassignment and whatever punishment Secretary Ma feels is appropriate."

Doctor Yu started to say something but Doctor Tang bolted around the side of the desk and grabbed Doctor Yu by the front of his shirt and screamed, "YOU failed to make this process work. I should drag you out into the street and execute you myself for your failure you disgusting pig. Now, get out!"

He let go of Doctor Yu's shirt and pointed toward the door. Doctor Yu turned, grabbed his briefcase and coat, unlocked the door, and raced out of the office.

Shaken and worried, Doctor Tang sat down at the desk. After pouring over the design notes and project sequencing diagrams for several minutes, he suddenly sat up straight. He closed the project notebook, gathered up his personal notes and rushed off toward the level-4 biolab.

After two more failed attempts to mutate the virus, Doctor Tang stretched inside the bulky and uncomfortable bio-suit, as best he could, trying to relieve his tense muscles. Expecting another failure, his eyes opened wide and a smile crept across his face when the amount of off-target cleavage that occurred at the chromosome's targeted gene location was well below the defined limit. All that was left was to introduce the DNA-cutting, nucleotide enzyme. Carefully he opened the port and introduced the enzyme. "One little change. Just one little change was all that was required," he muttered to himself, confident success was finally within his grasp. If he was correct, the double-stranded DNA enzyme molecule would cut the DNA strand at the target point within the crossover region and the strand exchange would take place.

The next test would be an enzymatic assay to verify the on-target gene edits. He prepared the sample and waited for it to complete.

"No, this can't be," he groaned inside the bio-suit.

Doctor Tang's elation quickly turned to dismay as he realized his latest attempt had advanced further, but still it had failed like all the others.

Tuesday, Feb. 10th – 7:50 p.m. EST
FBI Headquarters
900 Block Pennsylvania Avenue, NW
Washington, D.C.

FBI Director Jerome Conroy leaned back in his chair, yawning deeply as he rubbed his tired, gritty eyes. He had returned thirty minutes earlier from an unexpected dinner engagement with Adam West, Assistant to the President of the United States. At first, he had asked West to reschedule because of his workload, but West had been adamant and when a high ranking member of the Order of Light demanded your presence, you simply did not refuse.

Director Conroy was now even further behind on his budget task. Before the interruption, he had been struggling with the monumental task of trimming one-hundred million dollars from the FBI's budget for the remainder of the year. Every pass he had made at cutting the budget had come up short by at least ten million dollars. If he cut the budget any deeper, the agency simply would not be able to properly complete its mission, but that did not matter because the number he had been given was a hard number. Left with no other options, the field agents would simply have to make do with their old vehicles. There would also have to be fewer trips to the gun range for practice as well as deep cuts to travel and overtime.

Unable to keep his mind on the budget, he planted an elbow on the desk, leaned his chin on his hand, and stared off into space. Still reeling from the order he had been given, he replayed the meeting in his mind. "*I must be dreaming?*" he told himself. With his free hand, he fingered the little red box West had given him and told himself, "*No. It was not a dream.*" He had been given an order and he was going to carry it out, but how was he going to get Eagle alone. He couldn't just call him up and say, "*Hey, let's talk.*" He would have to think of a believable excuse, but first he had to complete the budget cuts.

Director Conroy stretched, leaned back over his desk, and picked up the yellow highlighter lying beside the large binder containing the current year's budget, determined to find the additional ten million dollars he needed. About to highlight another budget line item for potential reduction or elimination, he jerked when the phone rang, making a jagged yellow line halfway down the page.

Expecting the phone call to be his wife wondering when he would be home, he picked up the handset and said, "I told you I…,"

"I need to see you. NOW!" an angry voice shouted and hung up.

"Absolutely amazing," Director Conroy smiled, unable to believe his ears. Another interruption would cause him to be less than fully prepared for tomorrow's session with the Senate Finance and Appropriations Committee. He would have to come in early in the morning and get as much done as he could and simply hope for the best.

Director Conroy dropped the highlighter on the desk, closed the budget binder, and pushed his chair back. Still smiling, he stood up and headed for his private bathroom. Standing in front of the sink, he assessed his appearance. Dark bags colored his cheeks below his eyes and he could really use a shave, but he dare not keep the *man* waiting. Recognizing the angry tone the man had used, the Director knew it would be a very unpleasant meeting, but it would allow him to complete the task he had been given.

Leaning over the sink, he splashed cold water on his face and reached for a towel. After drying his face, he straightened up, buttoned the top button of his shirt, pulled his blue and gray silk tie up tight, adjusting the knot so that it was exactly centered. He grabbed a comb from the medicine cabinet and quickly ran it through his thinning gray hair. He flipped the light off and walked back into his private office.

It was too late to call for a driver as the only people left in the building would be the security and janitorial staff. Left with no other choice, he would have to drive himself. He lifted his jacket off the hall tree in the corner and slipped it on. Rather than putting the budget binder away, he decided to just leave it lying on the desk. He twisted the lock on the door knob and pulled the door closed as he exited the office.

Standing in front of the elevator, he slid his access card into the security reader and waited. Lighted numbers above the elevator door indicated the elevator's progress as it rose from the ground floor. The numeral 'eight' lit up and the door slid open. A quick ride down the elevator deposited Director Conroy at the basement parking garage level. He exited the elevator and walked half way down the second row of empty parking spaces. Nearing his car, he punched the Unlock button on his key fob. The headlights on his black BMW Series 7 sedan flashed twice and the driver's door popped open.

Director Conroy pulled the door open all the way and slid into the contoured driver's seat, upholstered in the finest, glove-soft leather. He reached out, punched the Start button and waited for the curved display to awaken and complete its startup tests. The interior of the BMW Series 7 sedan went beyond luxurious to the point of being called opulent. The cabin was strikingly modern, using only the highest quality materials and finishes. While costing well beyond one-hundred thousand dollars, Director Conroy could not care less because the vehicle, purchased as a symbol of his position and power, would soon be replaced with something much better.

Watching the rear display on the center of the dash, he backed out of his assigned parking space and squealed the tires as he roared out of the parking garage.

Meeting little traffic in downtown Washington, D.C., at the late hour, he sped out of the parking garage onto Ninth Street, heading south. One block later, he turned right on Constitution Avenue NW. Five blocks later, after passing the Ellipse on the south side of President's Park, Director Conroy turned right onto Seventeenth Street NW.

Skirting the east side of the White House grounds, he turned onto West Executive Avenue NW and stopped at the security gate. Holding out his credentials, he waited for the security guard to verify his identity. A second security guard walked completely around the vehicle holding a long pole with a mirror at the end as he examined the undercarriage of the vehicle for any potential threats. The outside security guard nodded the all clear signal toward the guard station. The inside security guard punched a button, raising the safety barrier.

Director Conroy returned his credentials wallet to the inside pocket of his jacket and drove past the guard station. He continued south and parked in the staff parking area adjacent to the West Wing of the White House.

"Good evening, Director," the security guard at the lobby entrance said, holding the door open.

Director Conroy simply nodded and walked past the security guard. He turned right past the lobby and then turned left, passing miscellaneous offices and the Roosevelt Room. The hard leather heels of his expensive, Italian shoes clicked softly as he walked down the dimly lighted hallway. At the end of the hallway, he turned right and entered the darkened Press Briefing Room. Choosing a seat in the row closest to the door, he sat down, and waited. About to nod off, he heard hurried footsteps coming down the West Colonnade hallway.

A man in a dark, pinstripe business suit with his tie loosened at the neck and hanging askew walked into the Press Briefing Room and gestured for the Director to follow him. The two men made their way through the Press Corps offices and entered the Palm Room. The man pushed the doors shut and locked them.

"I want an update on the search for Admiral Hadley and his associates," the man demanded.

"I had an agent trailing him," Director Conroy answered. "He had Hadley in custody and was about to put him in his vehicle when somebody slugged him from behind. When the agent woke up, Hadley and whoever had helped him were gone."

"Any idea who it was?"

"No, not for certain, but we suspect it could have been McClain."

"You mean David McClain the Secret Service Agent?" the man exploded.

"Yes, we think so."

"If you haven't already, I want an all-out search begun for Hadley and McClain."

"Already done," Directory Conroy advised. "I have every agent I can trust working on this."

"What about Hadley's friends? Has he talked to anyone?"

"We intercepted an email Hadley sent to Edgar Cordell, Cantwell's former communications director."

"And?"

"We retrieved the information and let's just say Cordell will not be talking to anyone."

"Anyone else?"

"Hadley and a now retired CIA spook by the name of James Templeton were really close. I hired two contractors to grab Templeton and his wife, but the same thing happened as with Hadley. Somebody interrupted the kidnapping. We think it was McClain that time as well."

"When you find McClain, kill him," the man raged. "Please tell me there is no one else."

"The only other possibility is Zach Templeton, James Templeton's son. James and his son were instrumental in stopping the virus fiasco a couple of years ago."

"Yeah, I remember that do-gooder," the man sneered. "Cantwell awarded him the Presidential Medal of Freedom. How does he figure in this?"

"As a civilian, he's a senior data analyst, but he's also a retired US Navy SEAL. That's how he knows Hadley. Pretty tough individual I'm told."

"Is there anything else I should know?"

"No, sir," Director Conroy lied. "We are closing in on Hadley. We don't know exactly where he is, but we do know he is somewhere in the Northeast. Likely somewhere around the DC area."

Director Conroy thought it best not to reveal the fact that at this point in time he really had no idea where Hadley or McClain were. Such an admission would certainly be the end of his career and maybe even his life. That is, if the man in front of him would be alive tomorrow. Director Conroy bent down and pretended to tie his shoelace. He carefully slipped the protective cover off the leaf-like embellishment of the ring on his right hand and stood up. Holding the protective cover between his fingers, he waited for his opportunity.

"I don't care who or what this Templeton is or anyone else for that matter," the man barked. "I want this catastrophe put to bed, now! Kill them all if you have to. Knowledge of this absolutely *must not* leak out."

"Sir, that many more deaths are going to be very hard to explain."

The man turned and stared at Director Conroy with a look that could bore through steel and snarled, "Are you deaf? I said kill them all! Is that clear?"

"But, Sir," Director Conroy protested, edging closer to the man. Pretending to lose his balance as he stepped around one of the seats, he brushed against the man.

"Hey, watch out," the man blurted out as he grabbed his arm. "What was that?"

"I'm sorry. I broke a button on my sleeve earlier. I forgot all about it."

"You should be more careful, you stupid idiot. I repeat. Find the leaks and kill them. I repeat. Kill them all! Am I clear?"

"Yes, sir. I will contact my agents as soon as I get back to my car."

"Good. Sit and wait five minutes," the man said. He rose, unlocked the doors, and left the way he had come.

Director Conroy carefully slipped the cover back on the ring and smiled. With his eyes fixed on his watch, he waited only three minutes. He exited the Palm Room and hurried through the West Wing and out to his car.

Shaking inside, he sat for several minutes, trying to get his emotions under control. He slipped out his cellphone and punched a speed dial number.

"Any success locating Hadley or McClain?" he asked as soon as the agent on the other end answered.

"No sir, nothing," the agent answered. "We have every agent available watching, but so far they have not turned up?"

"Not acceptable," Director Conroy exploded. "We have to locate them. Call in more agents."

"We have already called in everyone we can trust."

"Well then, use informants. Whatever you have to do. Find them!"

"Yes Sir. We will notify you the instant they are located."

"Arrgh," Director Conroy bellowed as he hurled the cellphone across the car in a fit of rage. The cellphone struck the window control on the opposite side of the car and shattered into several pieces. The Director watched as two large pieces of silver trim fell off the door and landed on the floor.

He dug in the pocket of his jacket for his travel pack of antacid tablets. He flipped open the lid, shook two out into the palm of his hand, and tossed them into his mouth. Grimacing, he quickly chewed the chalky, unpleasant tasting tablets.

One thing that provided Director Conroy some relief was the fact that he knew Eagle would soon suffer what would look like a sudden and fatal heart attack.

Rather than drive all the way home and have to drive back to the office if Hadley or McClain were located, he decided to just go back to the office. He started the engine, backed out of the parking space, and headed back toward FBI headquarters.

Wednesday, Feb. 10th – 8:28 p.m. EST
White House, Oval Office
1600 Pennsylvania Avenue, Washington D.C.

Immediately upon entering the Executive Residence, President James Borden told his wife he wasn't feeling well and that he was going to go lie down. Overcome by a wave of dizziness as he entered the bathroom, he grabbed for something to steady himself. Missing the doorjamb and catching only the corner of a towel, the towel bar ripped loose from the wall when his full weight hit the towel. Hearing the crash, his wife leaped up from the couch and rushed into the bathroom. A panic-stricken flurry of activity erupted when the President's wife discovered him lying unconscious on the floor of the bathroom. She immediately raced into the living room, dialed the White House switchboard, and requested that they alert the on-duty emergency medical response team.

Within two seconds, the duty operator punched the extension for the emergency medical response team and notified them of a medical emergency in the Executive Residence. The paramedics on duty grabbed their gear and made a mad dash for the Executive Residence. When they arrived in the Executive Residence bathroom, one paramedic began opening the various equipment cases and drug box while the other paramedic checked the President for a pulse and breath sounds.

"No pulse!" he shouted. "Grab the defibrillator. I'm starting CPR."

He ripped the President's shirt open, interlocked his fingers, placed his hands on the President's chest, and began pumping.

"Is he going to be alright?" the President's wife stammered, edging closer to her fallen husband.

"I'm sorry ma'am," the paramedic barked, out of breath. "You have to back up and give us room to work."

The paramedic continued pumping while the other paramedic prepped the defibrillator's leads, connected them to sticky pads, and placed them on the President's chest. "Hold compressions," he said as the last pad was placed. He looked at the trace on the defibrillator's monitor display and saw a flat line."

"Continue compressions."

The first paramedic resumed pumping on the President's chest while the other paramedic charged the defibrillator. "Clear," he yelled when the "Ready" lamp illuminated. The paramedic doing compressions raised his hands in the air while the other paramedic punched the "Shock" button. The President's body convulsed as the pulse of electricity coursed through his chest.

"No conversion. Continue CPR."

After ten minutes of trading duties, the two paramedics were exhausted. Four more attempts to shock the President's heart and an intracardiac injection of adrenalin to get it to start beating had all been unsuccessful. The paramedic that had been doing chest compressions sat back on his heels and wiped his forehead on his sleeve and asked, "Anything?"

"Nothing. It's still a flat line," the other paramedic answered. "Any objection to calling it?"

The paramedic that had been doing chest compressions just shook his head.

"Time of death, Eight-forty-seven PM."

By that time a small crowd of senior officials, Capitol Police, and on-duty members of the White House Medical Unit had gathered at the bathroom door. The President's chief of staff who happened to be working late poked his head into the bathroom as one of the paramedics turned the defibrillator off and began gathering their gear. "What is going on?" he asked.

The President's dead," one of the paramedics answered. "It looks like a massive heart attack. We did everything we could. It's been a flat line for twenty minutes."

A military physician assigned to the White House Medical Unit pushed his way past the President's chief of staff and consulted with the paramedics. He dropped to his knees, laid his stethoscope on the President chest, and listened carefully for a long while. He leaned back, removed the stethoscope, and shook his head.

"I'll call the coroner," the military physician announced. "Everyone out. I need to seal the room."

The President's chief of staff backed quickly out of the room, snatched his cellphone out of his jacket pocket, and called the White House duty operator.

"White House Communications Center. Staff Sergeant Williams."

"Sergeant, this is Leonard Morgan, the President's Chief of Staff. The President is dead. Call the Vice-President, then call Chief Justice Tyler. Call the state patrol and instruct them to provide an emergency escort for Justice Tyler. Have them bring the Chief Justice to the Executive Residence as quickly as possible."

"Yes, Sir," Staff Sergeant Williams exclaimed. "Right away, Sir."

The maitotoxin that had overwhelmed the calcium channels of President James Borden's heart had already begun to metabolize. By the time anyone would think to look for the presence of toxins, any detectable level of the toxin would be long gone. With no other known cause, the Presidents death would be ruled to be the result of a massive heart attack.

Wednesday Feb. 11th – 9:50 a.m. ChST
Zhongnan University Xiangya Medical College
Tongzipo Road, Yuelu District
Ch'angsha, Hunan Province, China

Doctor Huang Yan Tang sat on a hard stool, hunched over with his arms inside the biosafety cabinet which was equipped with the highest efficiency particulate, HEPA filters available in both the exhaust and supply air systems to prevent exposure to the extremely dangerous pathogens stored in the level four biolab. Working with thick rubber gloves, Doctor Tang struggled to complete his fourth attempt to create the mutant virus, each labored breath he took fogging up the front of the clear plastic hood of his protective suit.

Upon completing the introduction of the nucleotide cutter enzyme, he subjected the resultant test sample to the same validation test as the three previous attempts. He groaned and slapped the surface of the work countertop when he learned his fourth attempt had failed like all the others.

"What did I do different than Doctor Li did?" Doctor Tang fumed, frustrated and angry over yet another failure. "He *must* have had some kind of success or he would not have deleted his work. What did he do that was different?"

The panic he had felt when he had rushed out of his office on his way to the biolab returned with a vengeance. He had been certain he had the solution to overcome the synchronization problem and produce the mutated virus that Secretary Ma demanded. As he sat there staring at the result of his fourth failed attempt, an intensely painful gnawing began to boil in his stomach. Each minute seemed to fly by faster than the previous one. Time, which he had precious little of, was slipping through his fingers like water. If he did not produce a successful run soon, he would feel Secretary Ma's wrath for certain.

Everybody had heard the stories about those who had failed to obey Ma's orders or had displeased him in some way. Not just demanding and mean, Secretary Ma was downright cruel and sadistic. It was rumored that he had had someone executed right in his office because he publicly defied and humiliated the Secretary. Doctor Tang knew that for something as important as the virus, if he failed, the punishment would be severe.

Determined to not meet such a horrible fate, he grabbed the material from the failed attempt with his heavily gloved hand and headed for the incinerator. After the material had been dropped down the chute, he slammed the lid closed and pushed the button to ignite the incinerator. Once the flame reached a temperature of twenty-five hundred degrees, the material dropped into the first combustion chamber. From there any gaseous components were fed to a secondary combustion chamber and finally to an air pollution device. All materials from the incineration process would be tested by a decontamination specialist before being discarded.

Needing to study the process design notebook again, Doctor Tang would have to leave the containment area because all outside materials were expressly forbidden to be brought inside the containment area. He disconnected his air feed hose, entered the decontamination chamber, and closed and sealed the access door. He punched a large button on the wall and waited while the decontamination liquid sprayed the outside of his moon suit. When the spray stopped, he exited the decontamination chamber and clambered out of the protective suit.

The process design manuals and lab notes were piled on the researcher workspace just as he had left them. Digging through the binders and papers, he located the notebook explaining the design of the nucleotide cutter enzyme. An early, handwritten note at the bottom of the page written by Doctor Li mentioned the problem of complexity. The note said there were just too many items to synchronize which resulted in the enzyme creating excess off-target cleavage? The note also mentioned the target positioning?

With the vague information contained in Doctor Li's note in mind, Doctor Tang poured over the design sequences again looking for any clue as to why all his attempts had failed. He read and reread all the design criteria and lab notes.

"What did I do wrong?" Doctor Tang yelled, banging his fist on the open notebook. "I followed all the steps meticulously. It should have worked."

He read through the process design sequences one more time and determined he needed to realign the target positioning. Dreading having to climb back into the moon suit again, he trudged back to the biolab and went through the process of climbing into the pressurized suit. After closing and verifying all the seals were fully engaged, he entered the biolab again.

The dejection on Doctor Tang's face was obvious to see when the fifth attempt to create the mutated virus failed yet again.

"What am I missing?" he sputtered inside his positive pressure, biohazard suit.

Becoming more and more desperate, he realigned the target a second time and repeated the process. Another failure.

"I can't believe it," he screamed inside the suit. Sweat beaded up on his forehead and ran down into his eyes. He shook his head trying to clear his eyes. A vision of himself standing before a firing squad suddenly filled his mind. "I've got to be missing a critical step. I must make this work."

Swearing and grumbling to himself, he repeated the laborious process of exiting the containment area. Leaning his chin on his hands, he studied the entire design process for a fourth time.

"What did I do differently than Doctor Li did?" he asked himself for the second time. "I followed his steps exactly. I aligned the… Wait. What's this?"

Chapter Thirteen

Wednesday, Feb. 10th – 9:50 p.m. EST
White House
Office of President's Chief of Staff
1600 Pennsylvania Avenue, Washington D.C

Newly sworn in President Karen Hayworth and Adam West hurried down a dimly illuminated hallway and entered West's office. West pushed the door closed and crossed the office pointing at the chair in front of his desk. "Sit down and listen to what I have to tell you," he said as he removed his jacket and threw it at the table sitting in the corner of the office. He pulled open the middle drawer of his desk, removed a small square box, and pushed the slide switch.

"You can't order me around!" President Hayworth exploded, standing beside the chair with her hand on her hips.

West placed his hands on the desk and leaned forward with a menacing look on his face. "Listen up, simpleton," he snarled. "People in this administration have had enough of your screeching and constant opposition."

"You can't talk to me like that," she roared.

West straightened up, stepped around the desk, and rested his right leg on the corner of the desk. "Shut up!" he countered. "I suggest you remember who put you in office. Borden said he couldn't stand you and didn't want you. The party apparatus didn't want you either. The Order threatened to expose Borden if he didn't accept you on the ticket. The party couldn't afford to have him exposed so they went along. The Order put you in place and now the Order owns you and you know it."

President Hayworth started to interrupt, but West held up his hand and continued, "Without the Order you would still be a nobody. How do you think you got to where you are right now, at this very moment. Do you think tonight was an accident?"

"You murdered the President. I will expose you. I will...."

"No you won't. Because if you do, your crimes will also be exposed and you will go to prison. I will make it my mission. Now, are you going to shut up and listen."

President Hayworth glared at West but did not say anything.

"Good. Now listen," West said. "We thought we had all the data regarding the previous election secured. However, it seems a data analyst stumbled across that data. He made a copy and passed it to an investigative journalist. Both he and the journalist are dead, but we have learned that someone else has knowledge of that data and has also obtained a copy. It has also come to our knowledge that Rear Admiral Charles Hadley has learned of the virus China is working on. So, we now have two problems. We need more assets to find and silence those that intend to expose the election data and to stop knowledge of the virus from getting out to the public. Borden always refused to authorize legal action. That is part of the reason why you are now the President."

"What is it you need from me?" President Hayworth asked warily.

"We need you to authorize whatever assets are necessary to apprehend and eliminate those involved."

"If Hadley is involved, I'll give you anything you want. I will authorize a shoot on sight order if that will help."

"Yes it would, very much. I just happen to have the paperwork right here."

Mister West pulled some papers out of the top drawer of his desk and handed them to President Hayworth. She quickly read through the order. She stood, laid the papers on West's desk and signed them.

"A word of warning," West advised. "If the Order ever perceives that you become a threat, you know what will happen! With that in mind, it would be very unwise for you to mention what went on here tonight. To anyone!"

"I understand. Anything else?" President Hayworth asked.

"Not tonight," West replied. "Go to the Executive Residence and take care of any remaining details regarding the transition of power. You will need to take possession of the nuclear codes. I will contact you soon with more details of what is coming in the future."

West watched as the new president, Karen Hayworth, turned and exited the office. As a parting shot, she slammed the door harder than necessary. West laughed, knowing that President Hayworth would *not* be on the list to receive the vaccine to protect her against the coming virus. Neither were the majority of Congress. Only those that had pledged their loyalty to the Order would survive the coming plague.

West picked up his cellphone from the desk, scrolled through his contacts list, selected one, and pressed the "Call" icon.

Tuesday, Feb. 10th – 10:05 p.m. EST
FBI Headquarters
900 Block Pennsylvania Avenue, NW
Washington, D.C.

FBI Director Jerome Conroy, a yellow highlighter in his hand, continued marking items to be cut from the upcoming year's budget. He laid the highlighter down, cleared his calculator, and went through the entire budget, totaling the items he had highlighted. Exhausted and barely able to keep his eyes open. Completely out of character, his tie was loosened and his jacket was hanging over the back of his chair. He swore and threw the highlighter against the wall when he saw that the total cuts he proposed were still seven million dollars short of the necessary one-hundred million dollars the senate finance and appropriations committee was demanding. After hunting through the top drawer of his desk for a new highlighter, he flipped the budget binder back to page one, ready to search for more items to be cut. The phone sitting on the corner of the desk rang, interrupting the silence in the room.

"Director Conroy."

"This is Adam West. President Borden was pronounced dead at eight forty-seven tonight. Hayworth has already received the oath of office and is now officially President of the United States."

"What are they saying is the cause of death??" Director Conroy asked.

"The on-call medical personnel said it appeared to have been a massive heart attack."

"I know she is first on the order of presidential succession list, but Hayworth?"

"Hayworth will work to our advantage. She was selected as Vice President not by Borden but at the Order's insistence. She will do our bidding or she goes to prison."

"So, how does that help with our current situation?"

"Hayworth signed a shoot-to-kill order for Rear Admiral Hadley not even five minutes ago. The way the order is worded it can be made to apply to anyone that is involved with Hadley. Inform your agents of the order and see to it they follow it. There are to be no attempts to capture Hadley or his associates. Kill them on sight. Is that clear?"

"Yes sir. I'll spread the word to my agents immediately."

"One more thing. Make the bodies disappear."

"Absolutely," Director Conroy answered, but the line had already gone dead.

He laid the phone in its cradle and leaned back, a look of shock spreading across his face. Never in his entire career had he received a shoot-to-kill order for anyone, let alone for an American citizen. There was no time to debate the ethics of the order. He reached out to pick up the phone when it started ringing.

"Talk to me," Director Conroy barked into the phone, angry because he had expected to have heard from his field agents several hours ago. A tension headache was building in the back of his head, adding to his anger and frustration.

On the other end of the phone call, FBI Special Agent Martin Williamson moaned in pain as he tenderly repositioned his arm in the temporary sling he had fashioned around his neck. "Agent Williamson, Sir, we were about to grab Templeton's son, but he got away," Agent Williamson stammered, trying to talk through the intense pain shooting up his arm.

"What?" Director Conroy bellowed. "And why are you whimpering?"

"We were ambushed. I took a hit in the arm and I must have hit my head when I fell."

"Tell me you didn't go to a hospital. There would be records."

"No, I didn't go to a hospital. I bandaged my arm myself as best I could. I'll get care from our doctor when I get back to DC."

"Grabbing Templeton up should have been easy. It's only one man and his family."

"The Templetons had help. We didn't expect any trouble. Somebody must have warned them. They went out the back door of their house and disappeared into the woods."

"What kind of help?"

"It was dark. I don't know for certain, but it had to be professional help. Whoever it was had heavy firepower. They had to have been hidden and waiting on the road north of the Templeton residence. The caliber of the shell casings I found indicate military type weapons. Agent Tiner's dead. When I came to, they were gone. I don't know where or what direction they went."

"What about Tiner's body?"

"Don't worry. I assure you nobody will find it."

"I suppose you have no news about Hadley either?"

"No, Sir. Since he disappeared there have been no sightings."

Director Conroy rose from his chair, leaned against his desk, stripped off his tie, and threw it at the credenza behind him. The tie landed half on and half off the credenza. Slithering like a shiny red snake, the tie slid slowly off onto the floor. Shaking his head, the Director yelled into the receiver, "President Borden is dead and Vice-President Hayworth has already been sworn in. She issued a shoot-to-kill for Hadley and anyone that is helping him. Hadley and the Templetons must be found. Once they're dead make the bodies disappear. I don't care how many agents you have to assign to get this done. You have a job to do. Go do it!"

"Yes sir," Agent Williamson answered. He ended the call and leaned against the driver's side door, dropped the cellphone on the seat beside him, and rubbed his injured left arm. A dark purple ring was beginning to develop around the large goose egg on his forehead.

Director Conroy looked at the open budget and other papers spread out on his desk and shrugged. Having been notified of the President's death a few minutes ago, there would certainly not be a budget meeting tomorrow. He grabbed his jacket from the back of the chair and headed for the parking garage.

"Wow," Agent Williamson blurted out. He picked up the cellphone and laid it on his right leg. Searching through his contacts list with his one usable hand, he called every agent he knew he could trust between South Carolina and Washington D.C.

Agent Williamson dropped his cellphone into his jacket pocket, started the engine, and pulled the gear lever down to reverse. Being careful, able to use only his right hand, he turned his car around and headed for the Hilton Head Airport. Having already notified the pilot of the bureau's private plane, he wanted the plane ready to take off the instant he arrived.

Cradling his painful injured arm in his lap, the forty minute drive to the airport in Hilton Head was going to be agony. The throbbing pain in his arm and his boiling anger grew more intense with every passing mile.

"Ow," he shrieked when the car hit a large chug hole in the road, causing his arm to bang against the door. After pulling over to the side of the road, he adjusted the position of his arm in the sling, trying to relieve the discomfort.

"Somebody is going to pay and pay dearly," Agent Williamson seethed as he pulled the vehicle back onto the roadway and sped off toward the airport.

Tuesday, Feb. 10th – 10:42 p.m. EST
29,000 feet above rural Virginia

Kip Johnson, piloting the sleek Gulfstream G550 now on a heading of zero-five-eight after several course changes ordered by the Washington Air Route Traffic Control Center, keyed the passenger cabin intercom, "Good evening, folks, we are approaching the DC area. We are currently passing over Harrisonburg, Virginia. Once Air Traffic Control gives us a vector, we will start our descent into the Manassas area and should be on the ground ten minutes after that."

"Would you like to give me a hand?" Kip asked, looking over at Zach, sitting in the right seat.

"Absolutely," Zach responded, eager to put his aircraft knowledge to use.

"How much do you know about flying?" Kip asked.

"I know quite a bit, but it goes way back to my days in the Navy when I was in aviation electronics before I joined the SEALs."

"That's great," Kip said. He pointed at various instruments and asked Zach if he could identify them. Kip was surprised there were only a few Zach could not identify. Although, in Zach's defense, the ones he missed were rather new and had only been added in the last several years.

"I have some frequencies written on the notepad here," Kip said, pointing at the notepad affixed to the center of the control yoke. "When I point at one, just punch it into the radio here."

Zach, excited to have been asked to participate, sat up a little straighter, ready to do as Kip ordered.

"Are you able to decipher the radio traffic?" Kip asked.

"Only a little," Zach responded. "They talk so fast. A lot of it is just a jumble."

"You've got to remember, most of these guys do this for a living. Some have repeated this information hundreds of times. The more you listen, the easier it will become. Okay, be ready. We should get our vector soon."

Five minutes later the radio in the cockpit crackled to life, "Four-six-two-Mike-Lima, Washington Center, turn left, heading zero-four-four, descend and maintain four thousand five hundred, contact Potomac Approach on one-two-eight-point-five-two-five."

"Washington Center, four-six-two-Mike-Lima, heading zero-four-four, descend and maintain four thousand five hundred, contact Potomac Approach on one-two-eight-point-five-two-five."

Kip pointed at the Manassas Regional ATIS frequency he had written on his notepad, then pointed at the radio. Zach tuned the radio to the Manassas ATIS (Automatic Terminal Information Service) frequency and they listened to the continuously transmitted information. The airport's ATIS system provided various weather information, wind speed and direction, temperature, altimeter settings, and the active arriving and departing runways.

Kip then pointed at the Potomac Approach frequency and waited for Zach to make the change.

"Potomac Approach, Gulfstream four-six-two-Mike-Lima three-five miles southeast of Manassas. Inbound, full stop landing at Harry Davis with Oscar."

"Gulfstream four-six-two-Mike-Lima, Potomac Approach, Squawk three-three-seven-one and ident."

Kip dialed the requested code into the transponder and keyed the ident button.

"Four-six-two-Mike-Lima, radar contact three-three miles southeast of Manassas. Manassas altimeter two-niner-point-niner-five, Make straight in approach runway three-four right, contact Manassas Tower on one-three-three-point-one."

"Make straight in approach runway three-four right, contact Manassas Tower on one-three-three-point-one, four-six-two-Mike-Lima."

Kip corrected the aircraft's heading to line up with the active arriving runway and pointed at the flaps lever and called out, "First notch, five degrees."

Zach reached out and pushed the lever to its first notch. As the flaps extended, Kip dropped the landing gear. His eyes flashed back and forth across cockpit displays and the Flight Management System, looking for anything that would signify a problem. Satisfied everything was okay, one last time Kip pointed at a frequency on the notepad and waited for Zach to tune the radio.

"Manassas Tower, four-six-two-Mike-Lima, five mile final runway three-four right."

"Manassas Tower, four-six-two-Mike-Lima, Runway three-four right cleared to land."

"Runway three-four right cleared to land, four-six-two-Mike-Lima."

"Third notch, fifteen degrees," Kip instructed, pointing at the flaps lever. "From this point on don't touch anything. Just enjoy the ride."

As the Gulfstream flared over the threshold of the runway, Kip eased back on the throttles, reducing the aircraft's airspeed to one-hundred fifty knots. He applied a bit of right rudder to compensate for the fifteen knot wind blowing from zero-one-zero. When the end of the runway and the horizon line converged, Kip pulled back on the control yoke, allowing the aircraft to settle smoothly onto the runway. He taxied the aircraft to the end of runway three-four right and turned onto taxiway Bravo. At the intersection with taxiway Charlie, he turned right and followed the taxiway to the general aviation area. An airport ramp service worker guided the aircraft to an open spot on the parking ramp. Kip set the parking brake and shut down the engines. While the airport ramp worker placed chocks in front of and behind the wheels, Kip waited for Zach to lift himself up out of the co-pilot's seat and exit the flight deck.

Kip lifted himself up out of the pilot's seat, followed Zach into the passenger cabin, and opened the forward hatch. The pungent smell of burned jet fuel wafted in through the open hatch.

"Great landing," Anna Mae complimented as Kip extended the stairs.

"Thanks, I aim to please," he replied with a big smile on his face. "How long do you think we'll be here?" he asked the man standing on the ramp waiting for the passengers to deplane.

"Depends on the Admiral," the man answered. "No more than a few hours, hopefully."

"Okay, I'll have the aircraft fueled as soon as I finish the paperwork. I won't file the provisional flight plan until I hear from the Admiral."

"That's good," the man said. "We may need to depart in a hurry. The authorities do not know we are here. The Admiral doesn't want the aircraft on the ground any longer than is absolutely necessary."

"The aircraft will be ready," Kip assured the man.

"Folks, hurry up the Admiral is waiting," the man called up the stairs.

Anna Mae leaned over to pick up Mazie but she held out her arms to Agent McClain. He picked Mazie up and positioned her on his hip while Zach hooked the leash onto Tripp's collar. Anna Mae and Agent McClain made their way down the stairs. Zach stopped on the first step when the leash became tight. Tripp had his head part way out of the doorway but would not go any further.

"Come on, Tripp," Zach urged, tugging on the leash.

Despite Zach's urging, Tripp would not budge and pulled back into the aircraft. Zach stepped back into the aircraft and tried to calm the nervous dog. No amount of soothing, stroking, or sweet talking seemed to matter. The frightened dog simply would not budge. Zach considered shoving the dog out the door, but, in the end, decided it would be easier to just pick him up and carry him down the stairs.

"Okay, we'll do this the hard way. Again," Zach sputtered as he picked the dog up.

Wobbling from side to side, Zach stumbled down the stairs and set Tripp on the black asphalt.

They waited while Kip unlatched the cargo hold and retrieved their bags.

Zach reached out his free hand and gave Kip a firm handshake. "I *really* appreciate the opportunity to fly the right seat. I *loved* it."

"Glad to have you with me," Kip answered. "Maybe we can do it again sometime. Maybe I'll even make you a pilot."

"*Real* soon," Zach added as he let go of Kip's hand.

Anna Mae, Agent McClain carrying Mazie, and Zach with Tripp in tow walked into the general aviation terminal, carrying their small bags, packed with the few items they had had time to gather. Happy to be on the ground, Tripp strained against the leash, tail wagging furiously. Seeing the three adults and one small child that had been described to him entering the terminal, a man rushed over and introduced himself.

"Mister McClain, Mister Templeton, I'm Martin O'Dell," the man said. "Admiral Hadley arranged for me to meet you and drive you to the safe house. The Admiral sends his regrets. He would have met you himself, but he had pressing matters that required his attention."

Zack took a step toward Mister O'Dell, straining to hold Tripp back. The hair on Tripp's back stood up and a low growl emanated from deep in his chest. "It's okay, Tripp," Zach urged. "He's a friend."

Zach let the leash slide through his hand slightly as Tripp walked over and sniffed Mister O'Dell's leg. He lowered his hand down and let the dog sniff it. Tripp's tail began to wag and he licked the man's hand. "He approves," Zach quipped.

"Mister O'Dell, I know we're in Manassas, Virginia, but where are we headed now?" Zach asked

"A safe house." Mister O'Dell answered.

"A safe house where?"

"It's not far."

"That doesn't tell me much."

"It's better if you don't know in case we get caught before we get there."

"Get caught?" Zach queried, a look of concern clouding his face.

"By whom?"

"The FBI for one," Mister O'Dell replied.

"But we haven't done anything," Zach protested. "Why would the FBI want us? Does it have something to do with the strange emails I have received?"

"Mister Templeton, I can't tell you anymore," Mister O'Dell said. "The Admiral will be able to explain everything when we get to the safe house. I have a van parked out front. The longer we stand here talking the more at risk we are. We have to get going. Follow me"

Mister O'Dell led Agent McClain, and the Templetons thru the general aviation terminal's exit doors and to a dark blue van parked in the waiting area. With all his passengers loaded into the van, Mister O'Dell started the engine and sped out of the waiting area onto the airport access road.

"How far?" Zach asked, leaning over the front seat.

"Not far," Mister O'Dell answered. "Shouldn't take more than forty or forty-five minutes."

Zach sat back against the seat. Anna Mae leaned her head on Zach's shoulder. Zach sighed deeply, left with no choice but to sit there and watch the scenery pass by. Agent McClain was busy playing patty-cake with Mazie.

Chapter Fourteen

Tuesday, Feb. 10th – 11:02 p.m. EST
Tyler Residence
Walker Glen Court
Great Falls, Virginia

Admiral Hadley slipped out of a white van and looked at the large house sitting fifty yards back from the driveway. He started up the walkway, guided by the soft glow from accent lights that defined the edges of the immaculately manicured walkway. Awestruck, the Admiral approached the front door of the enormous ten thousand plus square foot, three-story house. Beautiful flower beds full of plants Admiral Hadley couldn't name framed both sides of the entranceway. Given the late hour, he hesitated as he reached out, about to press the doorbell. Having noticing several cars parked along the curved driveway and bright light shining from all the windows, he assumed there must be some kind of party or gathering within the house.

About to punch the doorbell, Admiral Hadley was interrupted by the sound of a car racing down the driveway. The car passed the other cars lining the driveway and parked at the end of the driveway. A lone passenger stepped out of the car, hurried to the house, and disappeared through a side entrance. Admiral Hadley reached out his index finger and pushed the doorbell.

Thirty seconds passed before he heard footsteps approaching. A hazy figure passed by one of the leaded-glass, floor-to-ceiling, side windows. The large door swung inward and an elegantly dressed young man stood in the doorway.

"May I help you?" the man asked.

"I am Rear Admiral Charles Hadley," the Admiral replied, holding out his government ID. "I need to see Chief Justice Tyler on a very pressing matter."

"I'm sorry but Justice Tyler is entertaining guests. I do not believe he would want to be disturbed."

"Tell Justice Tyler I am the former Director of Naval Intelligence. It is critically important I speak with him. Just five minutes. If I can't convince him it's important, I will leave."

"Very well," the man said, holding the door open. "Come inside. I will see if Justice Tyler will see you."

Admiral Hadley stepped inside to a two-story grand foyer. The man closed the door and said, "Wait here."

Admiral Hadley's eyes were drawn to the right side of the foyer where a magnificent curved staircase rose to a second floor mezzanine. Looking straight ahead, Admiral Hadley could see through the open floor plan to the largest kitchen he had ever seen. Several people leaned against a large island in animated conversations. Beyond and to the right of the island a large dining table, sitting in front of a huge window, was loaded with a wide array of chafing dishes, dinner ware, and various serving items. Three individuals, all dressed alike in black trousers and white shirts, appeared to be in the process of dismantling what must have been the service for a very large dinner party.

The man that had answered the door disappeared into the crowd of people to the right of the table. Thirty seconds later, someone peered around the edge of the living room wall and stared at him for several seconds. The person disappeared from view and the Admiral continued to wait. A full minute passed. Finally, two men walked around the wall and approached the Admiral.

"Admiral Hadley, this is Chief Justice Matthew Tyler" the man that had answered the door announced. The man turned and returned the way he had come.

"I'm sorry to bother you sir, but the matter I have to discuss with you is quite urgent," Admiral Hadley said.

"Patrick said you needed five minutes, but I am inclined to give you only two minutes," Justice Tyler declared, a look of annoyance clouding his face. "I just this minute returned from a very distressing situation and need to speak with my guests before they leave. I only came as a courtesy because of your rank. It is late and my guests are ready to leave. Why should I listen to you?"

"This matter is very serious and should be discussed in private," Admiral Hadley appealed.

"If I responded to every request that someone said was serious, I would never get anything done. I think you should be on your way, Admiral."

"I have uncovered a plot that could threaten the lives of hundreds of thousands of people. Maybe even millions. You must at least look at what I have."

"Come now, Admiral. Millions? Really?" Justice Tyler mocked, reaching for the door.

"Please, sir," Admiral Hadley begged. "I have proof. You must look at this. Just a few minutes in private, please."

Justice Tyler stared at Admiral Hadley for a few seconds, deliberating whether he should call for help to have the admiral escorted out.

"Someone in the White House is involved and I can prove it," Admiral Hadley asserted, holding up the papers in his hand.

Hearing the word *White House* and having had a very unsettled feeling as he administered the oath of office to a new president, Justice Tyler decided he would listen to what Admiral Hadley had to say but would withhold the news of President Borden's death. "Against my better judgment I will give you two minutes. In my office," Justice Tyler said, pointing to an open door on the left side of the foyer.

Admiral Hadley followed Justice Tyler into a room to his left. The room was dark, but moonlight spilled in through the west window. The north wall was lined with bookshelves. A large desk stood on a rectangular rug in the middle of the room. Justice Tyler pushed the door almost closed, leaving it open an inch. After walking behind the desk, he switched on a brass desk lamp and motioned toward a leather chair in front of the desk.

Admiral Hadley gazed around the impressive room, covered in exquisite ash paneling. In the light from the desk lamp, he could see the book shelves, lined with impressive leather-bound books, filling the entire wall behind the large mahogany desk. The Admiral sat in the leather chair, embellished with gleaming brass nail heads trimming the outline shapes of the arms. Scooting the chair closer to the large desk, he waited for Justice Tyler to take a seat behind the desk.

"You have two minutes to convince me that I should listen to you," Justice Tyler said, glancing at the large gold watch on his wrist. "Let's have it."

"Before I start, you need to know I am taking a huge risk in coming here. A secret service agent broke into my condo and tried to kidnap me. I only…"

"A secret service agent tried to kidnap you," Justice Tyler interrupted. "Come now, Admiral Hadley." Justice Tyler scoffed as he began to rise.

"Please, Sir. You said two minutes. You must hear this."

"Very well. Continue." Justice Tyler settled back onto his chair.

"I only escaped because another secret service agent intervened and slugged the other agent from behind. Several people have already died trying to protect this information."

"You can't be serious."

"Yes, I am. According to the agent that helped me, the orders came directly from FBI Director Conroy."

"Who is this agent that helped you?"

"I think he would rather his name not be revealed. At least not yet. Do you know Edgar Cordell?"

"Yes, of course. He was former President Cantwell's communications director."

"I sent a copy of the information to him. He missed a meeting and now no one can reach him. We fear the worst."

"You said other people were dead. Who exactly?"

"Yes. An independent virology researcher died from a car bomb in his own driveway and two more researchers from a related research firm, one killed by a car bomb, the other one murdered right in front of his condo. All three involved in virology research. All murdered within a few days. Doesn't that seem more than a little suspicious?"

"Yes, I would agree that is somewhat suspicious. You have my attention, for now. Continue."

"Those are the only ones I know about at this time, but what ties these deaths together is that a biolab in China is on the verge of creating a new mutated, deadly virus. More deadly than you could ever imagine."

"And how do you know this?"

"From another virology researcher, a Doctor Chin Zheng Li, that is, I mean was, directly involved in the development of the virus."

"You used the word *was*. Does that mean Doctor Li is dead also?"

"I don't know that. I certainly hope not. It just so happens that Doctor Li is a nephew of the nurse that was assigned to my case when I had my carotid bypass. I recently learned that nurse, Ning Bo Chia, is vacationing in Ch'angsha, China. The information I have came directly from Doctor Li. As I understand it, he decided he could not be involved in something so hideous. He made a copy of his work then deleted that work from the lab's computer system and went to his uncle for help. Ning Bo sent me a copy of the information Doctor Li took with him when he left the lab for the last time. I'm guessing Ning Bo sent me a copy just before they attempted to leave Ch'angsha. I tried to call him as soon as I realized who had left the message on my voicemail. A heavily accented voice claiming to be from the Ch'angsha police answered and demanded that I tell them who I was. I hung up immediately. I have not heard anymore from either Ning Bo or Doctor Li."

"That's quite a story, Admiral Hadley," Justice Tyler said, shaking his head in amazement. "Just for argument's sake let's say I believe you. Why would this Ning Bo send the information to you?"

"During my extended convalescence due to an unexpected complication, Ning Bo and I became good friends. I remember he was quite amazed to learn I was a rear admiral. Over the course of four weeks, I think I may have mentioned that I had been Director of Naval Intelligence. I can only assume he felt I was the best person he knew to receive the information. I am afraid to call his number again. So, that is the best assumption I can make."

"Is that all or is there more?"

"Oh, yes, there's more and it's worse," Admiral Hadley asserted. "Much worse."

"How much longer will it take for you to finish this fantastic tale?" Justice Tyler asked, glancing at his watch again. "You have used up the two minutes I promised you."

"No more than a couple of minutes more. Please, you must hear the rest."

"Go on and finish then."

"Doctor Li's notes said that a routine visitor to the lab's clinical director in Ch'angsha was a Doctor Kenneth Thompson. Li said he always came in early and mostly stayed out of sight. I did some research on Doctor Thompson. He's an MD, Ph.D., and is Director of Microbiology, Immunology, and Genomics at Beckman Institute for Cell Engineering. A real genius in the field of virology according to the articles I read. It seems a little more than coincidental that an American virology expert would be in China at the very lab where this dangerous gain-of-function virus engineering is occurring. Wouldn't you say?"

"Yes, I would have to agree. It does seem highly suspicious. Anything else?"

Admiral Hadley hesitated momentarily, not wanting to violate the promise he had made to David McClain to keep his name confidential, but he felt like he had no choice, knowing Justice Tyler would never believe what he was about to tell him unless he provided a corroborating source. He hoped David would understand.

"Yes, but before I continue can you agree to keep the identity of my source confidential?" Admiral Hadley asked.

"Yes, but only on the condition it doesn't require me to break any laws."

"Fair enough," Admiral Hadley conceded. "The secret service agent that prevented my kidnapping works in the White House. Because of his proximity to very important people he hears things."

"Is that Agent David McClain, the one that has recently been reported missing?"

"Yes, he's the one. David told me he finally reached a breaking point. He's fed up. Couldn't stand all the lies. He said FBI Director Conroy has been a frequent visitor to the White House. I know that would not be out of the ordinary except that he comes in late in the evening and not through a normal entrance to avoid the visitor logs. He meets with someone in the darkened press room when no one else is there. David had suspicions about those meetings. So, one night he hid in the press room, hoping it was just routine. That night Director Conroy and two other individuals met in the room. What David heard shocked and outraged him. Several days later he decided he had to disappear."

"Who were the two other individuals?" Justice Tyler asked.

"President James Borden and his personal assistant and director of communications, Adam West."

"This is dangerous ground Admiral Hadley. Are you certain you wish to continue?"

"Yes. You need to hear what went on in that meeting."

"I need to stop you right there Admiral Hadley," Justice Tyler advised. "Before you continue, I would like to have Justices Clark and Kennedy joins us. They just so happen to be here attending a dinner party with us."

"As long as they agree to keep Agent McClain's name confidential, I would have no problem with that," Admiral Hadley responded.

Justice Tyler pulled his cellphone from his pocket and tapped a short text message. A short time later there was a soft tapping on the office door. Patrick, the young man that had answered the front door, poked his head into the office and said, "You needed to see me, sir."

"Yes, Patrick. Please ask Justices Clark and Kennedy to join us right away."

"I will tell them, sir," Patrick answered as he backed out of the door and disappeared.

The two men sat in silence as they waited for the two justices to arrive. Several minutes later there was again a soft tapping on the office door.

"Come in," Justice Tyler called out.

Associate justices Walter Clark and Dwight Kennedy entered the office, looking somewhat puzzled to have been called away as they were saying their goodbyes and were preparing to leave. Chief Justice Tyler introduced the two associate justices to Admiral Hadley. After the introductions were completed, he asked Justice Clark to close the office door. Once everyone was seated, Justice Tyler gave them a condensed version of what the Admiral had already shared without revealing Agent McClain's name.

"Gentlemen, Admiral Hadley has asked that you keep the name of the source and the information he is about to share strictly confidential," Justice Tyler said. "As you know I was called away earlier. I just returned from swearing in Karen Hayworth as the new President of the United States. President Borden is dead."

There was dead silence in the room as the other men digested what Justice Tyler had just said.

Justice Dwight Kennedy was the first to speak, "He was supposedly in good health. What happened?"

"The on-duty medical personnel said it appeared to be a massive heart attack."

"This is not going to be well accepted," Justice Kennedy said, shaking his head. "The people don't much care for Hayworth."

"Agreed. We are well aware of her, let's say, frequent outbursts," Justice Tyler acknowledged. "But that is not why I called you into my office. "What Admiral Hadley has uncovered appears to be a very troubling and serious matter. Even more so considering tonight's events. I believe it is imperative we hear the rest of what Admiral Hadley has to say. However, I need your assent of confidentiality before we continue. If you cannot give that assent, the meeting is over."

Chief Justice Tyler looked at each justice in turn and received verbal assent to keep what they were about to hear strictly confidential.

"Good. Gentlemen, Admiral Hadley just informed me that a Secret Service Agent by the name of David McClain has obtained alarming information that is related to what I have just told you. He obtained this information because of his close proximity to certain people as part of his duties being assigned to the White House. Agent McClain became increasingly concerned by some of the things he overheard and because of after-hours meetings that occurred when certain individuals entered the White House surreptitiously to avoid signing the visitors log book. The names of the individuals attending those meetings is the reason I requested your presence."

"Who are the individuals?" Justice Kennedy asked.

"President Borden, his personal assistant, Adam West, and FBI Director Conroy."

"The President," Justice Kennedy exclaimed with a look of concern. "This secret service agent spied on the President? That is likely privileged communication. Should we continue with this conversation?"

"Yes, I believe we should," Justice Tyler responded. "When you hear what was said in that meeting, I think you will agree."

"Okay, I will listen," Justice Kennedy said. "But if I hear anything that goes to executive privilege, I will call a halt to this meeting."

"Justice Clark, do you agree?" Justice Tyler asked.

"I would have to agree with Justice Kennedy," Justice Clark acknowledged. "We must be very careful."

The strained look and posture Justice Clark exhibited did not go unnoticed. Justice Tyler assumed it was likely due to the President's untimely death and the sensitivity of the subject about to be revealed. He turned toward Admiral Hadley and said, "Continue with your information, Admiral, but be as brief as you can be."

"Gentlemen, first I want to elaborate slightly on what Justice Tyler just told you," Admiral Hadley began. "Information has come into my possession that exposes ongoing efforts to develop a mutated virus that would be more lethal than anything you could imagine. This information came directly from the researcher that was tasked with developing the process. For the sake of time, I will not go into the technical details of how this process works. In his notes, the researcher indicated he had success in cutting the

DNA strand of one virus and inserting material from a totally different virus. The result, a new, wholly unknown virus, engineered to have a lethality rate in the eighty to ninety percent range."

"What?" Justice Kennedy exclaimed. "Why would someone do that?"

"That's what the meeting in the White House was about," Admiral Hadley replied. "There is a group of very important and very rich people that want to reduce the world's population. They want…"

"Oh, come now, Admiral," Justice Kennedy interrupted. "We've heard about these shadowy groups for years. You don't really expect us to believe that do you?"

"Yes, Sir, I do," Admiral Hadley shot back. "In that meeting Agent David McClain overheard, the President…"

"I'm not listening to this," Justice Kennedy blurted out as he began to rise.

"Please sit down," Justice Tyler ordered. "Let Admiral Hadley finish."

"Thank you," Admiral Hadley mouthed. "During that meeting Agent McClain personally heard FBI Director Conroy confirm that the three virology researchers, Edgar Cordell, former President Cantwell's Communications Director, and a newspaper reporter that had evidence of massive election fraud during the previous election had been taken care of. Then the President ordered Director Conroy to do *whatever* was necessary to retrieve any remaining copies of this information and silence anyone that knew of its existence. Gentlemen, that would include me and several of my friends. After Director Conroy left, the President and Mister West mentioned a biomedical engineering firm in California has prepared a method to spread the new virus when it has been completed. The President was arrogant and believes he was above the law. He let it slip that he was taking orders from former President Bahram Oates who is a member of a highly secret order of some kind. The President bragged that the members are the world's ten richest men. They can…"

"This has gone on long enough," Justice Clark exploded. "This is nothing more than hearsay."

"It is not hearsay, Sir," Admiral Hadley snapped. "Agent McClain confided to me that he has the entire meeting on tape."

"Matthew, recording the President is unacceptable!" Justice Clark objected.

"Not when the President is, or was, engaged in committing felonies. If you…"

"Gentlemen, that is enough," Justice Tyler barked, interrupting Admiral Hadley. "Lower your voices and remain civil or this meeting is over."

"Sorry, Sir," Admiral Hadley apologized, returning to a sitting position.

"I am deeply concerned by what you have told us tonight," Justice Tyler said. "However, I am somewhat inclined to agree with Justice Clark about this all being hearsay. What exactly did you expect to come out of this meeting?"

"My best hope would be emergency application of the twenty-fifth amendment and arrest warrants for now President Karen Hayworth, an arrest warrant for FBI Director Conroy, and appointment of new acting FBI Director. It would also include arrest warrants for others involved that we know about at this time; FBI Special Agent Williamson, Assistant to the President, Adam West, and Andrew Holt, Director of the Unites States Secret Service."

"Do you have any idea what you are asking?" Justice Kennedy asked. "You have no proof."

"I do have proof, Justice Kennedy," Admiral Hadley asserted. "I just did not feel safe bringing it with me."

"I don't believe you have proof," Justice Clark challenged. "This is ridiculous and it must stop."

"If it's proof you want, it's proof you'll get," Admiral Hadley fired back in frustration. "Justice Tyler, if I deliver proof of everything I have told you, Can I expect you to do anything?"

"Like I said earlier, I am inclined to believe you. Certainly you must agree that to do as you ask would require undeniable evidence and plenty of it. Can you produce that?"

"Yes, Sir, I can. I can have it here tomorrow."

"Do not forget you have agreed to keep all this in strict confidence," Justice Tyler reiterated, looking directly at Justices Kennedy and Clark. "If you violate that promise, I will see to it you pay a heavy price. You may go."

Admiral Hadley watched as the two justices stood up, pushed their chairs back, and left the office. "Thank you for hearing me out Justice Tyler and I hope I didn't put you in a difficult spot."

"Well, you certainly did, but if you can prove what you shared here tonight, something must be done. Immediately."

Chief Justice Tyler ripped a sheet of paper off a pad lying on his desk and wrote something on it. He spun the sheet of paper around and pushed it across the desk toward Admiral Hadley. "Can you be there with your proof tomorrow at nine o'clock?"

"Yes, I can be there with my evidence." Admiral Hadley rose, walked over beside the desk, and held out his hand, "I sincerely appreciate your taking the time to hear me out. I assure you it will have been worth your time."

"Be very careful, Admiral Hadley," Justice Tyler said as he grasped the Admiral's hand. "If these evil men know you have the information they want, they will stop at nothing to get it back. You and anyone around you are in extreme danger. Come, I will show you out"

Justice Tyler pulled the office door open and escorted Admiral Hadley to the front door. "Be safe," he said as he watched the Admiral walk out the door and start down the walkway.

In the house, Justice Clark quickly excused himself from the festivities. In a secluded spot, he took out a cellphone and tapped a speed dial number.

Secret Service agent Waterhouse, waiting for the Admiral's return, saw the Admiral's signal to follow him. He followed two steps behind the Admiral, watching for anything out of the ordinary. At the end of the walkway, Admiral Hadley pointed to the end of the lane. While the Admiral walked around the waiting van and climbed in, Agent Waterhouse trotted down to the end of the lane. After a careful check of the surrounding area, he signaled back to the driver of the van that everything was all clear.

The van's driver started the engine and drove to the end of the lane. He slowed slightly and turned left. Admiral Hadley waved at Agent Waterhouse as the van disappeared into the darkness. Deep in thought, Admiral Hadley hoped he had not over promised. If he failed to deliver the proof needed, millions were going to die.

Tuesday, Feb. 10th – 11:34 p.m. EST
Collins Horse Farm
Old Carters Mill Road
Marshall, Virginia

In a pitch black, moonless night, a dark-colored sedan drove slowly down Atoka Road. The drizzle that had been falling from a heavily overcast sky turned to a steady light rain. The only sound inside the sedan was the rhythmic whump-whump of the windshield wipers as they scraped back and forth across the rain-streaked windshield. The driver slowed as he approached an intersection. Well past eleven o'clock at night, no other traffic approached from either direction. The driver stopped briefly at the stop sign, turned left onto Old Carters Mill Road, and continued northwest.

One mile down the narrow country road the dark-colored sedan turned off of Old Carters Mill Road, drove down a short gravel lane, following the left side of a large circle drive. Driving between two large horse barns and the main house, the sedan parked behind a dense grove of shortleaf pine trees.

Several minutes later a dark blue van drove down the same lane, followed the right side of the circle lane, and pulled up beside a large, log-cabin style house. The driver turned off the engine. The right door slid open and the occupants began climbing out. Zach stepped out onto the gravel drive and stretched. Anna Mae handed the sleeping Mazie to Zach and also stepped out onto the drive.

Light from a small lamp in the house's living room spilled out through the window, partially illuminating the wooden deck that wrapped around the house. One lone figure with his ball cap pulled down to cover most of his face climbed out of the sedan and walked through the trees. Startled, Zach turned, about to climb back into the van to protect his family.

"It's okay. He's with us," the van's driver, Martin O'Dell, advised.

The lone figured jumped up onto the deck, opened the door, and waved at the van's occupants, motioning for them to enter the house. Once everyone entered the house, the doors were locked and double-checked, and the drapes pulled tight, the man from the sedan turned toward Zach and pulled off his ball cap. Zach cocked his head, looking intently at the man. A quick flash of recognition registered deep somewhere in Zach's brain, but something was off. It simply could not be who his mind told him was standing there in front of him.

The man blinked out his colored contact lenses and pulled the cotton packing out of his cheeks.

"President Cantwell?" Zack exclaimed with a bewildered look. "Is that you?"

"Paul Cantwell at your service," he answered, a huge grin spreading across his face.

Zach rushed across the room and the two old friends gave each other a bear hug.

"Sir, what are you doing here?" Zach asked, backing away.

"Let's just say I called in a favor. A very *big* favor," former President Paul Cantwell answered. "Hi, Anna Mae and you too Mazie," he beamed, waving at the two standing across the room.

Mazie, awakened by all the activity, stood beside Anna Mae holding Raffee, her favorite toy, in one hand and rubbing her eyes with the other. Fully awake, Mazie recognized Paul Cantwell, ran over, and hugged his leg.

Paul dropped down on one knee and said, "My, you've grown into such a big girl and you still have ah… What is his name?"

"Raffee," Mazie chimed as she grabbed President Cantwell around the neck.

Paul gathered up the little girl and stood up. "I'll save the explanation for later once we're all settled. Zach, I think there are some folks in the kitchen you would like to see." Paul started toward the kitchen, beckoning for everyone to follow him.

The instant Paul stepped into the kitchen, Mazie let out a squeal. "Pa Pa," she burst out, holding her arms out toward James Templeton, her grandfather, as poor Raffee fell to the floor.

Paul hurried over to where the dining table stood and transferred Mazie to James Templeton's waiting arms. Mazie hugged her grandfather's neck, nearly choking him.

"Mom, Dad?" Zach sputtered as he stepped into the kitchen. "I thought you were… I don't understand. What are you doing here?"

"It's going to take a lot of explaining, Son," James Templeton answered. "But I think maybe it should wait until President Cantwell has given us his explanation."

Anna Mae, now standing beside Zach, reached out and hugged her mother-in-law, Margaret Templeton. Zach hugged his dad and then his mother, tears glistening in his eyes, having learned they were both safe and sound.

"Before I begin my explanation, how about joining me at the table," President Cantwell said. "I believe you all know my lovely wife, Christine. Christine, honey, could you get coffee for anyone who wants some?"

Poor little Mazie was already asleep in her grandfather's arms. "Go ahead and pour me a cup. I'll be right back," Anna Mae said as she eased the sleeping Mazie from James's arms. "What room should we use?"

"Back into the living room, down the hallway to your left, then take the second room on the left," President Cantwell answered."

As Anna Mae left the room, Christine Cantwell loaded a tray with coffee cups and set it on the table. She grabbed a full pot of coffee from the brewer on the counter and filled the cup of everyone that had taken a cup from the tray. No one spoke, enjoying the fresh, hot coffee, as they waited for Anna Mae to return.

As soon as Anna Mae returned and took a seat at the table, President Cantwell began, "I will try to be brief considering the late hour. This entire debacle really began back during the last election. Well, probably before that, but that's a tale for a different time. As you all know, many of us are convinced there was rampant cheating and fraud that occurred during the previous election which resulted in what we feel is an unelected president taking control of the White House. We were laughed off as conspiracy theorists, election deniers, lunatics, and crackpots. A few of us *and* a group, unknown to the current administration, that had access to the underlying data refused to simply go away."

President Cantwell stopped, gulped a swallow of coffee, took a deep breath, and continued, "Those individuals, whom I will not name at this time, have worked tirelessly, digging, gathering, and collating whatever data they could find while staying under the radar. A few weeks ago a data analyst uncovered a gold mine quite by accident. Before access to that gold mine disappeared, the data was copied and along with some other evidence it was being prepped for submission to the Supreme Court. However, the identity of the lead analyst responsible for the final documentation was compromised. We still do not know how or who. The result—that analyst was found murdered. Two bullets in the back of his head. It was most assuredly a professional hit. We decided to pull back and tighten our security before continuing. We absolutely could not risk losing what we had gained."

After taking another gulp of coffee, he continued, "Another deep concern surfaced a few days ago. I received an alarming phone call from Edgar Cordell, my communications director when I was still in the White House. He informed me he had received a phone call from Rear Admiral Charles Hadley. He…"

"I received a phone call from the Admiral just yesterday," Zach interrupted. "He told me he was forced to retire. Had a nasty run in of some kind with the Vice President. After that I received several encrypted emails. Then a phone call from Dad telling me we had to get out of the house immediately. We sneaked out of the back of the house and through the woods where we got shot at. If it had not been for Agent Carl Rodgers, we would be dead. After a quick ride to the Savannah airport, we met Agent David McClain. We boarded the Gulfstream the Admiral had used when he was on active duty. Now here we are. Mister President, what on Earth is going on?"

"Zach, I'm sorry you and your family got caught up in this," Paul Cantwell responded. "Somebody in the White House is scared and is trying to silence *anyone* that may have information related to their evil plot."

"But I don't know anything, or, at least, I didn't until just now."

"Well, your Dad does and by implication they assume you do also because you and your Dad worked together in the past."

Zach turned and looked at his Dad with a look that was an odd mixture of annoyance and questioning.

"Sorry, Zach" James Templeton sighed. "I didn't want to get you involved."

"Let's get back on track," Paul Cantwell urged. "Mister Cordell informed me that Admiral Hadley had received some frightening information describing an even more concerning issue than a stolen election. He has information concerning a plot to release a new and unknown virus. A mutation of some kind that would be far more deadly than the one you helped prevent, Zach. The Admiral transferred a copy of the information to Mister Cordell as a backup. Now, no one can reach Mister Cordell. He is missing and his car is also missing. We fear the worst. I must warn you. The people behind this will stop at nothing to achieve their evil goal."

"Who exactly is behind this?" Zach asked.

"To answer that question, I will ask Agent David McClain to elaborate. David, be brief please."

Agent McClain, who had been leaning against the kitchen counter listening, walked over beside the table and began his explanation. "As you all know, I am, or was, assigned to the White House. That allowed me to overhear things. I became very concerned when I learned of after-hours, secret meetings with visitors that entered through nonstandard entrances to avoid having to sign a visitor log. One night I hid in the press briefing room where these meetings took place. The attendees at that meeting were: President James Borden, Adam West, Assistant to the President and White House Communications Director, and FBI Director Jerome Conroy. A meeting between these individuals under normal circumstances would not be unusual. However, this meeting was late at night and off the books. What I heard will make your blood run cold. I doubt you would believe me even if I told you. So, I have it all on tape. You can listen for yourselves."

Agent McClain took a mini recorder out of his pocket, set it on the table, and switched it on. As the tape played, Agent McClain identified individuals as they spoke. After several minutes of listening, Zach interrupted, "David, stop the tape and replay the last twenty or so seconds again." Zach turned his ear toward the tape player and listened carefully. "Again, please," Zach said.

After the second time, Agent McClain stopped the tape and looked at Zach, "Do you understand what the Director called him? I have listened many times and I just can't understand it."

"Oh, yeah. I understand it alright!," Zach snarled as a cold shudder ran down his back. "He called him '*Marduk*'. That's the name of one of the members of that depraved, secret order that tried to release a deadly virus two years ago. We were told they were all dead. From what we learned, that order was pure evil. I can't believe this. If one of them survived and is now assistant to the President and the President knows about it, our country is in far more trouble than you can imagine."

"It gets worse," Agent McClain said. "Listen to the rest of the tape."

Agent McClain punched the play button as everyone seated at the table leaned in a little closer to be certain they could hear everything that was being said. Anna Mae grabbed Zach's hand and squeezed it tight, frightened by the mention of the Order of The Illumined Elite.

When the taped meeting ended, the people seated around the table looked at each in horror, not wanting to believe what they had just heard.

Anna Mae, the first one to speak, looked up at Agent McClain and asked, "Can they really do that?"

"We have no reason to believe they can't." he answered. "I have just recently learned of the plot to spread the new mutated virus that is currently being created. Admiral Hadley has a lot of information about the virus. If he were here he could share in more detail what he has learned about the virus."

About to say more, Agent McClain reached in his pocket and retrieved his cellphone. He swiped the screen, tapped the text message icon, and quickly read the short text that had just arrived. He looked up at Zach and said, "Admiral Hadley just turned onto Old Carters Mill Road. He'll be here in two minutes. Zach, go unlock the front door."

Zach pushed his chair back, stood up, and hurried into the living room to unlock the front door. He opened the door and stepped out onto the deck, waiting for the Admiral to arrive. A white van turned off of Old Carters Mill Road and drove slowly down the gravel drive toward the house. The tires crunching on the loose gravel as it came to a stop behind the dark blue van.

"Zach, my boy" Admiral Hadley burst out as he slid out of the passenger side of the van and hustled up on the porch. As Zach greeted the Admiral, the driver of the white van, backed up, pulled past the dark blue van, and parked out of sight. As soon as Zach and the Admiral stepped inside the house, Agent McClain pushed the door closed, locked the door knob lock, and twisted the dead bolt.

"Admiral, I think there are some people in the kitchen that would like to be brought up to date on what you know," Agent McClain said as he took hold of the Admiral's arm and ushered him toward the kitchen.

"Hi, folks," the Admiral greeted. "I had hoped to be here when you arrived but my meeting with Chief Justice Tyler took longer than I expected."

"How did it go, Admiral?" James Templeton asked. "Did he agree with you?"

"President Borden is dead," Admiral Hadley blurted out.

Filled with unbelief, all eyes turned and looked at Admiral Hadley. When no one spoke, the Admiral continued, "The medical personnel that attended him said they believed it was a massive heart attack. Chief Justice Tyler informed us. He had just returned from swearing in Karen Hayworth as President."

"Hayworth is President!" James Templeton cringed, a sour look on his face as if he had just swallowed a spoonful of vinegar.

"Hard to believe," Admiral Hadley agreed, shaking his head. "But true. It just so happened that Justices Kennedy and Clark were at Justice Tyler's residence attending a dinner party. Chief Justice Tyler called them in to join us after I mentioned that Agent McClain had secretly taped a meeting then President Borden was in. I think Justice Tyler believes what I had to say, but the other two justices seemed pretty doubtful, especially Justice Clark. There is just not enough hard evidence. They want more proof."

"So, now what?" James Templeton asked.

"I told him I would get more evidence."

"How are you going to get the proof Justice Tyler wants?" Zach asked.

"I have an idea but I can't tell you yet. I'm not certain it will happen." Admiral Hadley answered. "Tomorrow will tell. Hopefully." Admiral Hadley rolled his arm over and glanced at his watch. "I think for now we should all get some sleep. Tomorrow is going to be a very busy day."

Zach laid his hand on Agent McClain's shoulder. "Thank you, David, for getting us out of South Carolina alive." He tapped Admiral Hadley on the arm. "When you see Kip, tell him thank you and that I really appreciated him letting me sit in the right seat."

"I will. I want you to know he volunteered, without hesitation, to help us out even though it will likely cost him his job. And it might land him in prison along with the rest of us if my plan fails."

Anna Mae took Zach's hand and guided him toward the bedroom where Mazie was sleeping soundly. Margaret Templeton and Christine Cantwell gathered up the few dishes sitting on the table and carried them to the kitchen. Standing in the doorway, James Templeton flipped the light switch off as the ladies exited the kitchen.

"Good night everyone," he called out as he and Margaret headed down the hallway to their bedroom. The Cantwells and Admiral Hadley said their good nights as they slipped into their bedrooms and closed the doors.

Exhausted from the day's activities Admiral Hadley undressed quickly and slid under the billowy comforter covering the bed. In spite of the evening's events, within a few minutes, he was asleep and already dreaming of being dragged off in chains headed for a very, very long prison sentence.

A short eighteen minutes later, Admiral Hadley was roused from a fitful sleep by the ringing of his cellphone. He reached out and snatched the cellphone off the end table, pulled it under the covers, and nestled it against his ear.

"Huh, hello, who is this?" a half-asleep Admiral Hadley croaked.

"Sorry, I call late," came the broken English answer. "Ning Bo say call you. Is Chin Li."

"Doctor Chin Li!" Admiral Hadley sputtered, shocked fully awake by the name he had just heard. "Where are you?"

"Airport. Charlotte," Doctor Li answered.

Admiral Hadley reached for his watch and groaned when he saw the time. He did a quick calculation in his head and then asked, "Doctor Li, do you have any money?"

"Yes, have little."

"Is there anywhere close to you where you can get something to eat?"

"I see some kind burger place across aisle."

"Great. Get something to eat and then find a place where you won't be noticed. Get some sleep if you can."

"Yes, get eat. Find place sleep."

"I'll be there as soon as I can," Admiral Hadley advised. "Probably take around two hours. I'll text this number as soon as we arrive in Charlotte."

"Two hours. We wait. You text."

"Doctor Li, I am so glad you made it."

"Yes, we glad. You saved life."

"Don't worry. I'll be there in two hours."

"Not worry. We Wait. Sleep somewhere."

Admiral Hadley ended the call, threw the comforter back, and clambered out of the bed. Searching in the dark for the light switch, he tripped over his shoes he had left lying in the middle of the floor and went down onto his knees.

"Yeow," Admiral Hadley cried out, as he rolled onto his side, clutching his left knee. After rubbing his knee for a few seconds, he pushed himself up and limped over to the wall, found the light switch, and flipped it on. Grabbing his clothes from the chair where he had tossed them not even twenty minutes ago, he limped back to the bed and sat down. He dressed as quickly as he could while favoring his sore knee. Standing up with all his weight on his right leg, he tested his left knee by adding a little weight to this left side. He groaned. "This is not a good time for this," he grumbled. Knowing he had to get moving before his knee stiffened up even more, he limped over to the door and hobbled out into the hallway.

After limping part way down the hallway, he eased the door open to the bedroom where Zach and Anna Mae were sleeping. Enough light spilled in from the hallway so he could make his way over to the bed.

"Zach, Zach," Admiral Hadley whispered as he nudged Zach awake. "Quick. I just heard from Doctor Li. I need to go get him. Do you want to go with me?"

"Yeah, sure," Zach mumbled. "Where are we going?"

"Charlotte."

"Charlotte? As in Virginia?"

"Yes, I'll explain on the way. Doctor Li is the proof I need. We have to go get him. Now!"

"What's going on?" Anna Mae mumbled, raising her head off the pillow.

"I have to help Admiral Hadley pick up Doctor Li," Go back to sleep."

"I'll call Kip while you get dressed," Admiral Hadley said. "I'll meet you in the living room. Hurry. We need to be out of here in five minutes."

"I'm hurrying," Zach answered as he swung his legs out of bed.

Admiral Hadley punched a speed dial number on his cellphone and limped out of the bedroom.

On the fifth ring a sleepy voice answered, "This is Kip, Admiral. What do you need?"

"Get the aircraft warmed up and be ready to go the instant we get there. We'll be leaving here in five minutes."

"Okay, Admiral. Where are we going?"

"Charlotte. We need to do a pickup ASAP and return here."

"The plane is already fueled and serviced. Text me when you are ten minutes out and I'll have the engines running."

"Will do," Admiral Hadley acknowledged. "See you in about forty minutes."

"I'm ready," Zach said as he rushed into the living room.

"Okay, let's go," Admiral Hadley said as he grabbed the door knob and opened the front door. "We'll take the van. "You drive. I tripped over my shoes and fell. My knee is killing me."

Admiral Hadley waved at the white van's driver to bring the van up to the house. The van's driver started the engine, backed away from the trees, and drove up beside the porch.

"Are we going somewhere, Admiral?" the driver asked through the open window.

"Not we," Admiral Hadley answered. "Zach here is going to drive. You stay here and watch the house. Make certain no one gets in. Come on, Zach, get in. Let's go."

Zach climbed into the driver's seat of the van while Admiral Hadley hobbled around the front of the van and climbed up into the passenger seat. Zach buckled his seat belt and dropped the van into gear. "Which way, Admiral?" Zach asked as they approached the end of the lane.

"Turn left, then right at the first intersection onto Atoka Road," Admiral Hadley advised. "We are reasonably certain no one knows where the safe house is or that we are here, but Conroy has a lot of contacts. So, be on the lookout."

Zach did as the Admiral had instructed. The van disappeared down the road, Zach's eyes flashing from side to side, looking for anything unusual.

Wednesday, Feb. 11th – 12:50 a.m. EST
Charlotte International Airport
Charlotte, North Carolina

Tired and exhausted, Chin Zheng Li and Min Ju Jiang exited the gate area where their flight had unloaded its passengers. Chin carefully watched for anyone that looked as if they were watching them as he and Min Ju made their way across the center aisle of the concourse, dragging one roller-bag each. The mostly deserted concourse filled with a flurry of activity whenever an international flight landed and the passengers made their way through customs. The two bags Chin and Min Ju dragged behind them contained everything they owned, the few things they had been able to gather before fleeing Ch'angsha, China.

Two gates down the aisle Chin noticed a fast food restaurant on the left side of the aisle. He directed Min Ju into the restaurant and located an empty table in the back corner of the restaurant next to a large window overlooking the ramp. The two weary travelers sat down on the tall, stool-like chairs sitting next to the table.

Chin reached in his pocket and pulled out what little money the man in Hong Kong had been able to give them. Chin laid the money on the table and looked at the bills and a few scattered coins. He looked at the menu board hanging over the restaurant's counter, trying to compare the cost of the various items listed there to the money lying on the table.

"The Admiral said probably two hours before he arrives. He said we should get something to eat then find a place to sleep, but I do not know what we can afford," Chin shrugged. "I do not understand how American money works."

"I came here to America once with my parents before we were married," Min Ju said. "I think I can remember how this money works."

Min Ju looked back and forth between the menu board and the money lying on the table several times.

"We can only afford one small sandwich and a drink," she said, pushing the money into two piles, one for what the food would cost and the other for what was left over. The left over pile only contained a single one dollar bill and seventeen cents in change.

"Here," Min Ju said, handing the needed money to Chin. "This should be enough. The only items we can afford are the third one from the bottom of the list on the big board and the smallest drink size they have."

Chin took the money and walked over to the counter and waited for the on-duty attendant to notice him. "Small turkey and little drink," Chin said pointing at the small size cup in the dispenser.

"Is that all," the attendant asked.

"Yes, is all," Chin answered, nodding his head up and down.

The attendant turned to his left, grabbed a turkey sandwich from the cooler, and pulled a small drink cup from the dispenser. "What kind of drink do you want?"

"Would like water."

The attendant turned around and filled the cup with water then set it beside the sandwich. Chin held out the money. The attendant took the money and counted out the amount he needed. "The water is free," he said as he handed two one dollar bills and a few coins back to Chin.

"Is free?" Chin marveled, a puzzled look on his face.

"Yes, the water is free."

"Thank you. Thank you," Chin said, bowing slightly at the waist.

Chin picked up the sandwich, the water, and the change and hurried back to the table where Min Ju waited. He set the items on the table and said, "Odd man say water is free. Should I buy something else?"

"No, maybe we should keep it in case we might need it later. Why did you say the man is odd?" Min Ju asked.

"Look at him," Chin replied. "He has metal ring in his nose and wooden spools in his ears."

"America has many strange ways. It will take much getting used to."

Min Ju unwrapped the sandwich, took the first bite, then handed it to Chin. Chin took a bite. As he chewed, he tapped Min Ju's arm and pointed at the large jumbo jet that had just been pushed back from the gate. They could hear and feel the rumble when the pilot pushed the throttles forward and the huge aircraft began to slowly roll down the alleyway between concourses. They watched the aircraft until it turned and disappeared down a taxiway. Several minutes later, Chin saw the aircraft roar past the window and disappear into the dark sky.

The turkey sandwich went back and forth several more times as they quickly devoured it. After they emptied the cup of water, Chin took the sandwich's wrapper and the empty cup and dropped them into a trash container. He came back with a napkin for Min Ju and one for himself.

Sitting at the table staring out the window, his chin resting on his palm, Chin's eyelids slowly drifted closed. They were both exhausted from the horribly long travel day, having had only short catnaps since departing Hong Kong over twenty-four hours ago. It all started with an over-sold flight from Hong Kong to Seoul, South Korea, then a long flight to Atlanta, Georgia, nearly two hours to pass through customs, and finally, the short flight to Charlotte, North Carolina.

Only after boarding the flight in Seoul and feeling the wheels of the aircraft leave the ground, did Chin Li begin to feel as if they had escaped. The fake IDs and passports provided them in Hong Kong had worked without any questions. Chin relaxed some as he leaned back in the seat, but he was still apprehensive of what laid ahead for him and his precious Min Ju.

Min Ju smiled as she looked at the sleeping Chin. She was very proud of him for refusing to be involved in the development of such a horrible thing as the virus. She was glad they had escaped but she had no idea what had happened to Chin's uncle. "*Perhaps the Navy Admiral would know*," she thought. She would let Chin doze a few more minutes before they went to find a more isolated place to sleep.

Chapter Fifteen

Wednesday, Feb. 11th – 12:55 a.m. EST
Williamson Residence
Murray Lane
Annandale, Virginia

It had taken FBI Special Agent Matthew Williamson a little over twenty minutes in light traffic to drive the fourteen miles from FBI Headquarters to his home on Murray Lane. He walked straight to the refrigerator and dropped a handful of ice cubes in a glass and then filled it with water from the kitchen sink. Working with one hand because of his injured arm suspended in a haphazard sling crafted from a kitchen tea towel, he then spent the next twenty-five minutes calling every agent he could trust to see if anyone had spotted Admiral Hadley.

With all the calls made and still no sign of Admiral Hadley, Agent Williamson refilled the glass with water, pushed aside a heap of dirty clothes, and slumped down on the ratty, threadbare couch in the living room, taking care to not bump his throbbing arm. Having taken only one small sip from the glass, he rolled the cold glass back and forth across his forehead. A massive headache was building that ran from one temple across his forehead and all the way around to the other temple. It felt as if a metal band was slowly being tightened around his head. He shook out three aspirins from a half-full bottle that had been sitting on the end table, popped them into his mouth, and took a swallow from his glass of water. He tilted his head back and swallowed the pills.

Agent Williamson sat alone in the dimly lit living room as he did every night, he and his wife having parted two years earlier. She had moved out while he was involved in one of his cases, saying she could no longer tolerate the long hours he was away from home or his caustic, disagreeable personality when he was home.

Hardly ever home, exhausted and miserable when he was, cleaning house fell to the bottom of his list of priorities. A fine layer of dust covered every surface. The room's odor was stale and sour, literally from two years of neglect. Papers and clothes were strewn on chairs and on the floor. Dirty dishes piled high on the kitchen counter only added to the air's unpleasant aroma. He had become even more sullen and ill-tempered over the past year.

Further adding to the house's abandoned, unkempt, couldn't-care-less atmosphere was the potted plant his wife had left sitting on the library table. Sitting untouched between the two bedrooms since she had left, all the leaves had fallen off the dry, brittle plant, littering both the table and the floor. One single dead stem rose from the dirt, a glaring testament to her absence and a striking symbol of his dead personal life.

"*So, this is what my life has come to,*" he thought with a forlorn sigh as he glanced around the room. When he was at home, he sat alone staring at the condo's blank walls. Other than his work, he had nothing to do and nobody to do it with. Driven to the point of obsession to succeed at his job, he had completely given his life over to lies and deception. He would do *anything* to succeed, exactly as his boss expected. It had become a way of life, eating away at the relationships in his life. Rather than admit what had driven away all the people in his life, he became more sullen, enraged over the slightest disagreements. Even his family avoided him. He had become depressed and unlovable.

Suffering miserably, Agent Williamson shoved a stack of papers off the end table and set the glass of water down. Leaning forward with his elbows resting on his knees he rubbed his temples, trying to massage away the vicious headache raging away inside his head.

Thinking the headache might ease up if he lay down, he rose from the couch, intending to crawl into bed. Halfway across the living room, his cellphone rang. He rushed back to the end of the couch and grabbed the ringing cellphone from the end table.

After a quick glance at the display, he swiped the screen and barked, "Purnell, what is it? Have you found Hadley?"

"One of the other agents just called me," FBI Field Agent John Purnell stammered, knowing his boss was not going to like what he had to tell him. "He thought he saw the van that was seen leaving Hadley's place."

"How long ago?" Williamson demanded.

"He thinks about thirty to forty minutes ago. He……"

"What?" Williamson bellowed. "Thirty to forty minutes! Why did he wait so long to let you know?"

"He said he lost them around Marshall when they got off I-Sixty-Six. He tried to relocate them before calling."

"Well, did he?"

"No. He said the van just vanished. He's backtracking his route and is still looking."

"I'm headed that way. Call him and tell him to keep looking, then you head that way as well. The President issued a shoot-to-kill warrant. It also applies to anyone aiding him. Do not try to apprehend them. Just kill them! I should be there in about thirty minutes."

Agent Williamson's hair-trigger temper flared like gasoline poured on a fire. He ended the call and kicked the end table. He shouted a string of obscenities as the table upset and the glass and table lamp that had been sitting on the table crashed onto the floor.

"Idiots! Idiots! Idiots!" he raged. "When this is over, I'm going to fire every last one of them."

He tore through the clutter lying on the hall table looking for his car keys, shoving various items aside. More papers swirled in the air and fell to the floor, adding to the clutter. "Where are they?" he bellowed. He dashed into the kitchen and searched the counter. They were not there either. He rushed back into the living room. Spinning in a full circle, he tried to remember where he could have laid the keys as his eyes fell on various surfaces.

"Where could they be?" he asked himself over and over.

His blood pressure rising dangerously high, he raced around the house trying to find the missing keys. Finally, he remembered the one place he had not looked. "The freezer," he shouted.

He raced back into the kitchen, ripped open the freezer door, and saw the keys lying on the shelf right below the ice cube bin. "Stupid idiot," he growled, remembering that he had laid them down when he put ice cubes in his glass.

He scooped up the keys and ran out the door without shutting the freezer door. Realization dawned on him as he started the engine. He shrugged, backed out into the street, and squealed down the street, heading toward Marshall, Virginia.

Wednesday, Feb. 11th – 1:01 a.m. EST
Atoka Road
North of Rectortown, Virginia

Following Admiral Hadley's instructions, Zach stopped at the first intersection and turned right off Old Carters Mill Road onto Atoka Road.

"Where now?" Zach asked.

"Follow this road into Rectortown," Admiral Hadley replied. "It's a small town, nothing more than a wide spot in the road. In the middle of town, you will turn left onto Rectortown Road. Follow that all the way through Marshall. Not long after that it connects with Interstate Sixty-Six. We'll take that all the way to the exit for Manassas Regional Airport. Exit forty-four I think. I'll bring it up on GPS once we get on the interstate."

Two and one-quarter miles down Atoka Road Zach slowed down as they approached the small village of Rectortown. They entered the tiny village, which did not consist of more than a half dozen houses. All the houses were dark. A few streetlights illuminated the three gravel streets that intersected the main paved road.

They passed a small white church sitting close to the road. At the end of the first block, Zach saw a dilapidated service station. The pumps were long gone and tall weeds had grown up around the building. All the windows were broken out, the likely target of young boys with nothing else to do.

A light flashed off something shiny just past the old station as Zach drove by. Barley visible in the dim light cast by the streetlight on the opposite side of the street, a black suburban sat parked close to the building.

"Admiral, black suburban parked by that old building," Zach shouted as he speeded up, squealing around the intersection onto Rectortown Road.

Admiral Hadley twisted around in his seat and watched the suburban's headlights come on as it roared away from the old building.

"Step on it, Zach. We can't afford to let them stop us."

Zach stomped the accelerator clear to the floor and clutched the steering wheel tightly as the van began to pick up speed.

The lone man in the suburban grabbed his cellphone from the center console. With one eye on the road and the other on the cellphone, he tried to punch a speed dial number. Reaching the intersection going too fast, he stomped on the brake pedal. The cellphone slipped out of his hand and fell down between the seat and the center console. Making a grab for the cellphone, he took his eyes off the road and missed the intersection. The passenger side front wheel slid off into the ditch.

"It looks like they slid off the road coming around the corner," Admiral Hadley advised, staring out the back window. "Maybe we can gain some distance and lose them. It's less than five miles to Marshall. If we can get there first and pass under the interstate, maybe they'll think we took it."

The man in the suburban slammed the gear shift into Reverse and jammed his foot on the accelerator. The rear wheels spun wildly, sending up a thick cloud of blue-white smoke. He shifted into Drive, rocked forward, and then shifted back into Reverse. The extra backward momentum was just enough to allow the rear wheels to grab the road's surface. The suburban roared back up onto the roadway.

Realizing the cellphone was unreachable without getting out of the vehicle, the man decided the best course of action was to resume the chase and kill Admiral Hadley and his accomplice then worry about the cellphone. He slammed the suburban into Drive and roared off down Rectortown Road in pursuit of his quarry.

Zach watched the speedometer move past seventy. He eased up on the accelerator, fearing they would crash on one of the tight curves. The road curved to the right and they were now heading in a southerly direction.

"Admiral, do you see them?"

"Not yet. Maybe they got stuck in the… No, wait. I see headlights. Faster Zach!"

"I'm driving as fast as I dare. This road is really narrow. If I miss a curve and drive off the road, we're done."

"Zach, they're gaining on us. We're never going to lose them."

Zach pushed down harder on the accelerator, but had to ease off a few seconds later when he saw a curve sign coming up. Still driving dangerously fast, Zach nearly drove off the road as he rounded the curve, the driver's side tires kicking up gravel before he could steer the van back into the center of the road.

"What are we going to do Admiral?" Zach yelled. "We need a plan."

"It's obvious we can't outrun them," Admiral Hadley fretted. "We'll just have to find a spot and confront them."

"Great. Just great," Zach grumbled.

"When you get into Marshall, don't take the interstate," Admiral Hadley grunted as he unbuckled his seat belt and scrambled into the back of the van. "Just drive through town. I'm glad McClain had the forethought to bring some weapons with him. Find a good spot with some cover. I'll bring the weapons and some ammo up front."

Zach slowed the van down to fifty as he entered the outskirts of the city of Marshall. He barreled past a library, a convenience store, and a donut shop.

"God is watching over us," Zach praised as he saw the traffic signal at the intersection with Main Street was green. He blew through the intersection and continued past more businesses, a multi-story apartment building, and a fast food joint.

Admiral Hadley set extra ammo between the driver seat and the passenger seat. He laid two rifles and two handguns beside the ammo, then hopped up into the passenger seat. "An SR twenty-five sniper rifle for you, an H&K submachine gun for me, and a Glock Gen5 pistol for me and your ST1 Lawman for you if you need it," Admiral Hadley exclaimed.

Looking for a spot to make a stand, Zach sped through the last block of the city and passed underneath the Interstate Sixty-Six overpass. Not more than a thousand yards ahead on the left was exactly what they needed, a short, ornamental brick wall at the entrance leading into a housing development. Zach jammed on the brakes. Admiral Hadley flew up against the dash, having failed to rebuckle his seat belt after returning from the back with the weapons.

Zach whipped the steering wheel to the left, sliding sideway off the highway, nearly tipping over. The van came to rest on Piney Branch Lane partway behind the short brick wall.

The two men looked at each other and grabbed a rifle and a hand gun each.

Wednesday, Feb. 11th – 1:10 a.m. EST
Charlotte International Airport
Charlotte, North Carolina

Min Ju poked Chin's arm and said, "You told me the Navy Admiral said we should find a safe place to get some sleep. We should go now and find such a place."

"You are correct, Min Ju," Chin agreed, yawning deeply. "Let's go."

Chin slid down off the tall chair and waited for Min Ju to follow him. As he started to walk away from the table, he patted his pocket to reassure himself the burner phone he had been given in Hong Kong was still there. Twenty minutes after they had entered, they left the fast food restaurant and strolled down the concourse hoping to look like any other tourist as they searched for an out of the way place where they could sleep and feel safe.

They passed many shops that were closed due to the late hour. Chin spotted a news stand several yards down the concourse that was still open. "Min Ju, come help me check prices. I want to buy something with our remaining money."

They entered the store, being careful that their bags did not bang into any of the displays. Chin and Min Ju walked past displays full of key rings, refrigerator magnets, coffee mugs and various other souvenir items. Passing shelves full of tee shirts and other clothing items, they reached the end of the store. Turning down the other aisle, they started back toward the front of the store.

"There it is," Chin chimed. "Come on."

Chin led Min Ju down the aisle to a display full of various candies and other snack items. "Here, this one," Chin said, pointing at a bag of lemon drops. "Do we have enough money?" he asked.

Min Ju looked at the price tag stuck on the edge of the package. "Let me see the money."

Chin dug in his pocket, pulled out all the money they had left, and held his hand out toward Min Ju.

Min Ju counted the money and then subtracted the price of the candy. "Yes, but it will take nearly all the money we have. Are you sure we should spend it on candy?"

"Please," Chin insisted. "It is your favorite candy. The Admiral should be here in two hours. After that, we will not need any money."

"But what if he doesn't come?"

"Then it will not matter. This little bit of money will not help us."

Min Ju nodded her head in agreement. Chin grabbed the package of candy and made his way to the cash register. He held out the package of candy and all the money toward the cashier. "Take money needed," Chin said

The cashier picked through the money, leaving only four coins. Chin bowed and thanked the woman. Chin and Min Ju left the store and started back down the concourse toward the main terminal. As they walked, Chin tore open the package and shook out one lemon drop for Min Ju and one for himself. The open bag of candy went in the pocket of his jacket.

Nearing the end of the concourse, Chin spotted a deserted gate on his right. The sign above the Gate C4 agent's station announced the next flight would depart at six fifteen the next morning. He tugged at Min Ju's arm.

"We can sit here and sleep," Chin said. "The next flight is not for many hours."

Inside the Gate C4 seating area, they selected the two seats closest to the window overlooking the mostly deserted taxiway and sat down, positioning the roller bags in front of their feet. Chin pulled the burner phone out of his trouser pocket and placed it in his shirt pocket to be certain he would not miss the Admiral's call. He leaned against the wall and Min Ju put her head on Chin's shoulder. Both were asleep in less than two minutes.

Wednesday, Feb. 11th – 1:15 a.m. EST
Piney Branch Lane
South of Marshall, Virginia

Zach shoved the driver's side door open and jumped out, armed with an SR-25/MK11 Semi-automatic Sniper Rifle. The sniper rifle was fully loaded with 7.62x51mm NATO rounds, carried in a thirty round detachable box magazine. A spare magazine lay on the ground beside Zach's right foot. Zach's ST1 Lawman semi-automatic was tucked behind the waistband of his trousers. Admiral Hadley jumped out of the other side of the van, armed with the 9mm Heckler & Koch MP5 submachine gun with a fully loaded fifty round magazine. A spare magazine fully loaded with ballistic ammo laid beside the Admiral's foot.

The two men did not have long to wait for their pursuer. As Zach's knee hit the ground, the black suburban passed under the interstate overpass and slid partly off the highway, coming to a stop directly across from them. The driver's side door flew open.

"Lite em up!" Zach screamed. "Aim for the doors."

Before Zach could pull the trigger of his sniper rifle, the driver's side window of the van exploded into hundreds of tiny, razor-sharp fragments of glass. He flinched as several of the jagged chunks rolled down the collar of his jacket, slicing stinging cuts on the side of his neck. To give Zach some covering fire, Admiral Hadley quickly leaned around the passenger door and fired a short burst of rounds from the H&K submachine gun.

Having a shoot-to-kill authorization, the man in the suburban immediately began firing at his quarry upon arriving. He ducked back behind the rear of the vehicle. Taking advantage of the lull, Zach stood up and fired five rounds at the front of the suburban. The rounds tore through the sheet metal fenders, ripping large holes in the soft metal of the radiator. Bright green fluid began to pour out onto the highway. Knowing the van's door would provide him very little protection if the man aimed for the door, Zach raced around the back of the van, scampered across the road, and rolled up against the brick wall.

"Admiral, over here," Zach shouted as he stood up and fired another burst of rounds.

Just as Admiral Hadley stepped from behind the door, the man in the suburban leaned around the side of the vehicle and emptied the magazine of his Glock. Admiral Hadley scurried across the road and leaped over Zach, and landed with a whump, knocking the air out of him. Gasping for air, he pointed at the spare magazine lying beside the van. Still wheezing, he held the submachine gun above the brick wall and fired a burst from the H&K. Zach dropped the sniper rifle, raced across the road, and grabbed the H&K's spare magazine.

"It's loaded with G2 RIP ammo," Admiral Hadley sputtered, still sucking in air. "We've got to end this before more law enforcement shows up."

Zach ejected the empty magazine from his rifle and shoved in the spare. "Okay, get the other magazine loaded," Zach said as he stood up and fired another five rounds.

The man behind the suburban released the empty magazine in his Glock and reached his hand backward, feeling for the spare magazine carrier attached to his belt. The carrier held only one magazine. He grabbed the magazine and shoved it into his Glock. With the radiator punctured, both front tires flat, his cellphone out of reach, and very little ammo, he knew he needed to end this quickly. He was about to make one last attempt to put down the two men firing at him.

Zach poked his head around the edge of the wall and yelled out, "Lay down your weapon. NOW! If you don't, the next magazine has G2 RIP ammo. It will cut you in half. Show him Admiral."

Admiral Hadley struggled to push himself up, aimed for the open door, and fired a short five-round burst, literally ripping the door to shreds."

"Well, what will it be?" Zach shouted. Zach ducked down behind the wall and waited for an answer.

Knowing he was trapped and seriously outgunned, the man behind the suburban looked at the Glock in his right hand, trying to decide what to do.

Zach shouted again, "Don't waste your life on a fight you can't win." Receiving no answer, he shouted as loud as he could to the Admiral, "Take him out!"

The man behind the suburban tossed his weapon out to the middle of the highway. "I'm coming out. Don't shoot," the man yelled, knowing the battle was lost.

"Come on out," Zach shouted as he stood up and started toward the suburban. "Is there anyone else in the vehicle?"

"No," the man answered. "I'm alone."

"If you're lying, you're dead." Zach warned.

Zach approached the man cautiously, keeping the rifle pointed directly at the man's chest. Zach pushed the man up against the hood of the suburban, turned him around, and quickly patted him down. Finding no weapons, Zach grabbed the man's handcuffs from the pouch on his belt. He snapped the man's own handcuffs around his wrists while Admiral Hadley pointed the menacing MP5 at him.

"Keep him covered, Admiral."

Zach walked around the suburban to make certain no one else was hiding in the vehicle. Finding no one, Zach walked back to the front of the suburban and leaned his rifle against the left fender.

"What do we do with him?" Zach asked as he walked up beside the man.

"We can't leave him here," Admiral Hadley wheezed.

"Let's find out who you are?" Zach said as he spun the man around and lifted the man's credentials wallet from his jacket pocket. "Well, FBI Field Agent Kevin L. Stokes, why were you chasing us?"

Agent Stokes stood silent, refusing to answer.

"Admiral, it seems that Agent Stokes has nothing to say. He's seen us and our vehicle. We'll have to take him with us. Admiral, tape his mouth with duct tape and throw him in the back of the van."

"You'll never get away with this," Agent Stokes stammered. "There's a shoot-to-kill authorization on the Admiral and anyone that is helping him."

"Who authorized that?" Zach demanded, poking his .45 caliber pistol's muzzle against Agent Stokes's chest.

"The President. You're as good as dead," Agent Stokes sneered.

Zach looked at Admiral Hadley, realizing the stakes had increased dramatically. "Get him out of here."

Admiral Hadley reached for Agent Stokes's arm but went down on one knee, clutching his right side.

"Admiral what's wrong," Zach shouted.

"I guess I... I was a little too slow," Admiral Hadley gasped as he pulled his hand away from his side, revealing a large and growing red stain.

"Can you make it over to the van?" Zach questioned.

"I'll try."

Zach turned and looked at Agent Stokes with a threatening gaze of white-hot anger. He jammed the muzzle of his menacing .45 caliber pistol against Agent Stokes's forehead.

"If I so much as *think* you are going to try something, I will blow the top of your head off," Zach snarled. "Do you understand me?"

"Yes," Agent Stokes gulped.

Zach grabbed Agent Stokes's arm and dragged him over to the back of the van, taped his mouth, and pointed inside the van. Agent Stokes sat down on the end of the van and swung his legs up. Zach taped his ankles together and shoved him further inside.

"Don't do anything stupid and you won't end up dead," Zach advised.

Zach ran back over to the suburban, and with a herculean effort, managed to get it off to the side of the road. He hoped no one would notice the bullet holes until they were long gone.

Zach rushed back over to the van and found Admiral Hadley leaning against the van, looking pale. He helped the Admiral up into the passenger seat. Zach ran around the front of the van and as he climbed into the driver's seat, he looked over at Admiral Hadley. "How are you doing, Admiral?"

"Hurt's like the Devil," Admiral Hadley grunted.

"How about the bleeding? Is it slowing any?"

"I don't think so."

"We need to get you help. I'll call McClain and tell him to meet us in Rectortown at the old gas station."

Zach started the engine, jammed the van into gear, turned the van back onto the highway, and drove back the way they had come while he made the call to Agent McClain, hoping no law enforcement would notice the bullet holes in the front fenders and doors of the van or the missing driver's side window.

"Zach," Admiral Hadley sputtered. "You've got to go get Doctor Li."

"No. I can't leave until I know you're alright."

"No, Zach. You must go. It is critical that Justice Tyler hears his evidence. Doctor Li is the key to stopping this disaster. Without him we are doomed. You must promise me."

"Okay, I promise. How will I know him?"

"He's waiting at the Charlotte Airport," Admiral Hadley moaned as he dug in his pocket. "Here, his burner phone number is the last call in my phone. Kip is waiting at the airport in Manassas. You've got to go quickly before someone realizes the plane is missing."

Admiral Hadley groaned and slumped back in his seat. Zach pocketed the Admiral's phone and pressed a little harder on the accelerator. When they reached Rectortown, Zach parked the van beside the same old gas station where the suburban had been parked.

Several minutes later, Zach saw headlights coming down Atoka Road from the North. A dark colored sedan turned down the street to the east of the old station and circled around the block. When Agent David McClain was satisfied the vehicle parked beside the station was the van Admiral Hadley and Zach Templeton had left the safe house in earlier, he pulled in beside the van and turned off his lights.

"What happened to you guys?" Agent McClain asked through the open window when he saw the bullet holes in the passenger door and right front fender.

"Hurry, the Admiral is in bad shape," Zach hollered. "We need to get him to a doctor."

Agent McClain tore around the van and yanked the passenger door open. Together they pulled the Admiral out of the van and dragged him to the back. Zach threw the rear doors open. "Slide forward," he shouted at Agent Stokes."

As gently as they could they laid the Admiral down in the back of the van. Agent McClain pressed his fingers against the Admiral's neck. He moved his fingers to the other side of his neck. He stood up and shook his head. "I'm sorry Zach. He's gone."

"No!" Zach shouted. "No."

Zach pulled his pistol from behind his waistband and pointed it at Agent Stokes's head. "You filthy scum. I'm going to kill you right here. Right now."

"Zach don't," Agent McClain pleaded as he grabbed Zach's arm. "It won't bring the Admiral back and you'll be charged with murder."

Zach's finger tightened on the trigger. Desperately, he wanted to make Stokes pay for what he had done, but deep down inside he knew David was right. His finger eased off the trigger and his arm fell to his side.

"What happened?"

"We got made by one of Conroy's stooges," Zach growled. "He was parked here by the station. Chased us all the way through Marshall. We couldn't outrun him. So, we had a gun battle just south of the Interstate. He knew he was outgunned. So, he gave up. We couldn't just leave him or he would blab to Conroy."

"What do you want me to do?"

"Let's trade vehicles. The bullet holes in the van are too obvious. You take Agent Stokes and the Admiral back to the ranch. Take care of the Admiral then dump Stokes in one of the empty horse stalls. We'll figure out what to do with him when we get back from Charlotte."

"Charlotte? What's in Charlotte?"

"The proof needed to convince Justice Tyler about the conspiracy," Zach answered. "I don't have time to explain any further. I'm already running late. I'll explain it all in the morning."

"Okay, Zach. I'll take your word for it. What do I do if our friend there makes trouble?"

"Shoot him," Zach barked, looking directly at Agent Stokes.

Zach jumped out of the van and climbed into the sedan. Agent McClain climbed into the van and left first, turning left, heading north on Atoka Road.

Zach turned right onto Atoka Road and then left onto Rectortown Road, heading back toward Marshall.

"I sure hope this Doctor Li is worth the Admiral's life," Zach said out loud.

To avoid the scene of the earlier gun battle and to take a route no one would expect, Zach turned left and headed east on Highway Fifty-five. To make up some of the lost time, Zach kept the sedan's speed five miles per hour over the posted limit, hoping his speeding would not attract the attention of a state trooper.

Chapter Sixteen

Wednesday, Feb. 11th – 1:30 a.m. EST
Charlotte International Airport
Charlotte, North Carolina

A man in dirty gray coveralls strolled slowly down the walkway of the nearly deserted Concourse C. As he approached Gate C4, he noticed two people sleeping near the window that overlooked the ramp. He turned into Gate C4 and approached the two people.

Startled awake, Chin Li jerked when the man tapped him on the shoulder. Chin shook Min Ju awake. They grabbed their bags, and were ready to run for their lives. The man stepped sideways, blocking their escape.

"I'm sorry," he said. "Don't run. You're not in trouble. I just need to clean this area. I didn't mean to frighten you."

Chin stopped and looked at the man, not certain he could believe him. "You not have cleaning things."

"Look out there in the walkway," the man said pointing behind him. "See. My cleaning supplies are in the gray barrel."

Chin looked where the man pointed and saw a gray barrel with wooden handles sticking up out of it and two white bottles hanging on the rim.

"Okay. Where we go for quiet? Get sleep?" Chin asked, his heart rate and breathing beginning to slow.

"Go toward the main terminal," the man said, pointing to his right. "Just before the main terminal there's a seating area on the left. It should be quiet and the chairs are much more comfortable."

"No bother anymore?"

"No. You shouldn't be bothered there. I have already cleaned that area."

"Yes. We move," Chin acknowledged. "Come Min Ju we must go to other place."

Chin and Min Ju grabbed the handles of their roller bags and exited Gate C4. They turned right as the man had instructed and began to look for the seating area as they walked toward the main terminal.

"I see it," Chin announced. "Ahead. Just before the big doors."

"I see it too," Min Ju said.

They walked the last one hundred feet of the concourse walkway and turned left into the seating area. They walked past two sleeping couples and found two seats toward the rear of the seating area. As they had done in Gate C4, they sat down and positioned their bags in front of them. Chin lifted the burner phone out of his shirt pocket, tapped the power button to wake it up, and looked at the time. He grimaced when he saw that they had only been asleep for a little over thirty minutes. That meant the Admiral would not arrive for another hour and twenty minutes.

"You sleep. I watch," Chin said to Min Ju.

"How much longer?"

"Over one hour yet."

"That's a long time. You need sleep too," Min Ju protested.

"Too frightened. Sleep later."

"The Admiral will come. We are in America now. We are safe."

Min Ju honored her husband and would not argue with him. She leaned her head on his shoulder and was quickly asleep. Chin propped his feet up on his roller bag and watched as an occasional passenger or airport worker came down the walkway. Not as certain of their safety as Min Ju had said they were, Chin checked his cellphone often as the minutes slowly ticked by. Whenever his eyes would get heavy, Chin changed position or pinched his arm. He vowed he would not allow anyone to sneak up on them again.

Wednesday, Feb. 11th – 1:52 a.m. EST
Manassas Regional Airport
Manassas, Virginia

Having made the trip from Rectortown to the Manassas airport without incident, Zach drove past the JPC JetCenter and turned into the general aviation parking area. Expecting to be gone for only a few hours, Zach picked a spot in the short term parking section and parked.

As he climbed out of the car he waved to Kip, seeing him standing in the aircraft's doorway waiting."

Using Admiral Hadley's cellphone, Zach had called Kip Johnson when he was ten minutes away from the airport and told him to get ready for a quick departure. Zach slammed the door. He punched the lock button on the key fob and hurried into the JetCenter. Kip had exited the plane and was waiting for Zach, holding the door to the ramp area open.

"Where's the Admiral?" Kip asked.

"We had a run in with one of Conroy's agents. Admiral Hadley got hit. He's dead."

"What?" Kip blurted out. "Admiral Hadley's dead?"

"I'm really sorry, Kip. I know you two were really close. He was my friend too."

Kip just stood there as if he were frozen.

"I'm sorry, but we have to go. Now. The Admiral was adamant. He made me promise to get Doctor Li. He said it was critical that I get him to Chief Justice Tyler."

Zach reached out and pushed Kip toward the stairway. The two men hurried up the stairway into the Gulfstream. As soon as Zach stepped into the cabin, Kip pulled the stairway up and sealed the forward hatch.

"Want to fly in the right seat again?" Kip asked, a look of sadness obvious on his face.

"Thanks, Kip, but not this time," Zach answered. "I don't much feel like it. Maybe on the way back from Charlotte."

"I understand. Get buckled up. The preflight is done. All that is left is to start the engines and we'll be on our way."

"Oh, Kip, I learned that there is a shoot-to-kill authorization for anyone assisting Admiral Hadley. We need to do this quickly and quietly."

"Understood."

Kip disappeared into the flight deck and settled down into the pilot's seat. He buckled his safety harness, stuffed the radio system earphone into his left ear, and started the engines. The tower at Manassas Regional had ceased operations at midnight. So, there was no need to get clearance to taxi. A quick scan of the instruments indicated no problems with the aircraft. He released the parking brake, eased the throttles forward, and the aircraft began to roll toward taxiway bravo.

As he taxied, Kip tuned to the AWOS frequency and listened, "Manassas Regional. Automatic weather observation. Zero-seven-zero-two Zulu. Weather: wind two-five-zero at six. Visibility ten. Six thousand five-hundred scattered. Temperature twenty-five Celsius. Dew Point twenty-three. Altimeter two-niner-point-niner-seven. Density Altitude one thousand two-hundred."

Satisfied with the weather report, Kip tuned to the CTAF (Common Traffic Advisory) frequency and keyed the transmit button to announce his intentions, "Manassas Regional Traffic, Gulfstream G-five-five-zero, Taxing to runway Sixteen Left and hold short via taxiway Bravo, Manassas Regional."

Receiving no response, he continued taxiing toward the active runway. He turned left at the end of the taxiway and stopped just short of the runway apron and listened again to the CTAF frequency. About to proceed onto the runway, the radio sputtered to life.

"Manassas Regional traffic, Cessna three-six-four-eight-Whiskey ten miles North, at two thousand, landing Sixteen Left, Manassas."

Kip removed his hand from the throttles and waited for the inbound traffic to clear. The Cessna landed, rolled down the runway, and turned off the runway onto a taxiway. With the runway clear of traffic, Kip taxied out onto the runway and set the brake.

Kip keyed the passenger cabin intercom, "Zach, this runway is only three hundred feet longer than the specified takeoff distance for this aircraft. We're loaded pretty light so we should be okay. I am going to spool the engines up to full power before releasing the brake and then do a steep climb out."

Kip shoved the throttles forward and waited for the engines to spool up to max. He released the brake and the aircraft began its takeoff roll. Kip watched the airspeed indicator as the aircraft raced down the runway. The instant the airspeed reached V2, he pulled back on the yoke more than usual, but not so much that the tail cone would contact the runway. From a bystander's perspective it would have looked as if the aircraft had leaped into the air. The Gulfstream lifted off the runway with just two hundred feet to spare.

In the passenger cabin, Zach gripped the arm rests of his seat tightly as the Gulfstream ascended into the sky.

"Wow. I wouldn't want to do that every day," Zach yelled to Kip through the open cockpit door. Feeling better that the aircraft was well into the sky and heading for its cruising altitude, Zach relaxed and began to replay the events of the day.

Kip eased the yoke forward slightly to reduce the climb angle and make his passenger feel more comfortable. The aircraft continued its climb out as it disappeared into the moonless night.

Wednesday, Feb. 11th – 2:27 a.m. EST
Piney Branch Lane
South of Marshall, Virginia

Special Agent Williamson had arrived in the Marshall, Virginia, area twenty minutes earlier. He had driven north to Rectortown looking for the van Admiral Hadley and his accomplices had been reported to be driving. Not finding Hadley's van or the black suburban FBI Agent Stokes was driving, he continued north on Atoka Road. After making a u-turn at Old Carters Mill Road, he returned to Rectortown and stopped at the old abandoned gas station.

He tapped in Agent Stokes's cellphone number for the fourth time, pressed the call button, and waited. After five rings the call went to voicemail. "Why is he not answering?" Agent Williamson exploded. He tapped in a different number and waited.

"Purnell, have you heard from Stokes?" Agent Williamson asked as soon as the agent answered.

"No. Nothing. I have tried calling him four times, but he is not answering."

"Where exactly did he say he saw Hadley's van?"

"He said he saw the van get off the interstate at the Marshall exit, but he lost it after that."

"No direction? Just that the van got off the interstate?"

"That's all he told me."

"Great. Just Great. I've driven through Marshall and clear up to Rectortown. I can't find Stokes anywhere. If you hear from Stokes call me immediately."

Agent Williamson ended the call before Agent Purnell could answer. Angry and frustrated, Agent Williamson dropped the cellphone in his jacket pocket and squealed out of the old gas station's parking lot, heading south on Rectortown Road. Determined to find Agent Stokes, he drove around the town of Marshall, looking for Stokes's black suburban. Even driving slowly down the streets, it only took Agent Williamson fifteen minutes to cover all the streets in the small town. Agent Stokes or his black suburban were nowhere to be found.

"He can't have just disappeared," Agent Williamson fumed, sitting in the parking lot of a closed fast food restaurant near the south end of town, tapping on the steering wheel trying to decide what to do next. He turned and looked north up Winchester Road, the town's main street, and exhaled noisily. About to pull out of the parking lot, he turned the steering wheel to the right, but stopped suddenly.

"South. I haven't gone south," he said as he squealed out of the parking lot. Heading south on Winchester Road, he roared under the interstate overpass. As he cleared the overpass, he saw a black suburban sitting on the side of the road. He stomped on the brakes and skidded to a stop in the middle of the highway. He threw the door open, jumped out, and rushed over to the suburban.

"What is this?" he bellowed when he saw the puddle of fluid on the highway and the bullet holes in the front fenders and passenger door. He yanked the driver's side door open and did a quick search of the interior. Not finding a body or any blood, he had to assume Hadley or one of his accomplices had kidnapped Agent Stokes. He lifted his foot and shoved the door shut so hard a shoe print was clearly visible in the skin of the door. Shouting obscenities, he stomped back to his vehicle, jumped in, and pulled off the highway in front of the suburban.

"The Director is going to love this," he muttered as he dug his cellphone out of his jacket pocket and tapped the Director's speed dial number.

"Tell me you found Hadley," FBI Director Conroy said, answering on the third ring.

"No Sir," Agent Williamson answered. "There's no sign of Hadley. I found the suburban Agent Stokes was driving just south of Marshall but he is nowhere to be found. The front tires are flat and there are bullet holes in the front fenders. The passenger door is ripped to shreds. Somebody had some really heavy firepower."

Agent Williamson waited for the Director to say something but there was silence. "Director? Are you still there?"

"Yes, I'm here. I'm trying to decide what to tell West. I am *not* going to tell him we are unable to find one man. That would be the end of my career and your career." Agent Williamson listened to another long period of silence. "We need to meet," Director Conroy said. "Somewhere halfway. How about Mary's Diner? Do you know where that is?"

"No. Never heard of it," Agent Williamson answered.

"It's in Annandale on Columbia Pike. Just east of Sleepy Hollow Road

"That will take me nearly an hour,"

"Make it sooner," Director Conroy snapped as he ended the call.

"Why couldn't he just have told me on the phone," Agent Williamson moaned, not looking forward to a long drive back into the city and then what would likely be a very unpleasant meeting with the Director.

He slipped his vehicle into gear, made a wide, sweeping u-turn and headed back toward the interstate.

Thursday Feb. 12th – 3:30 p.m. ChST
Zhongnan University Xiangya Medical College
Tongzipo Road, Yuelu District
Ch'angsha, Hunan Province, China

"I don't understand what I am doing wrong," Doctor Huang Yan Tang agonized inside his positive pressure, biohazard suit. His sixth, seventh, and eighth attempts to create the mutated virus Secretary Ma had demanded had all failed. None of the attempts had even come close to producing the result he had been tasked to create. No matter what approach he tried, he simply could not control the complex process. The off-target cleavage became uncontrollable and the process failed to target the proper chromosome position. Knowing he was quickly running out of time, sweat beaded up and ran down his face despite the filtered air flowing into the biohazard suit.

"What did Doctor Li do differently?" Doctor Tang whined for the third time as he dumped the result of the eighth failed attempt into the incinerator. "Perhaps if I increase the amount of the linker enzyme, the process will target the correct chromosome position before the off-target cleavage reaches a critical level," he muttered to himself as he returned to the workbench to begin the ninth attempt to create the virus.

Doctor Tang repeated all the steps he had used in the previous attempt except that he increased the amount of the linker enzyme.

"No! No!" he shrieked when he looked down and realized in his rush he had picked up the wrong nucleotide linker enzyme.

Expecting to see yet another failure, he half-heartedly began to verify the process before dumping it into the incinerator like all the other failed attempts.

"What? This cannot be!" he gasped, not believing his eyes. The off-target cleavage was well below the critical level and the preliminary verification appeared to show that the process had targeted the correct position on the chromosome.

He sat back and mentally went over the steps he had gone through. According to the project design plan, the process should not have worked, but it did. Elated, he captured the result and stored it in a safety vessel for further testing. Repeating the steps in his mind so he would not forget, he headed for the decontamination room.

After eight failed attempts and ready to give up, a simple mistake had resulted in success. Doctor Tang stepped out of the level-four, high-containment area, excited and in a hurry to record the steps and the incorrect nucleotide linker that had caused the process to work. Once outside the high-containment area, he reattached an air feed line and then rotated the high-containment area's door handle to the locked position. The inflatable gaskets of the shower room's double interlocking doors hissed as they sealed the shower room completely. He punched a large button on the wall and waited while his positive-pressure breathing suit was sprayed with decontamination liquids. After a final rinse, he unhooked the air feed line from his suit. Doctor Tang released the clear helmet's seal and pulled the gas tight zipper all the way down. He quickly extricated himself from the bulky suit and hung the suit on a hook near the shower room's exit.

Determined to not forget anything, he ran down the hallway toward his office. A group of students on their way to class had to dodge out of the way to avoid being knocked over. He shoved the door to his office open, rushed over to his desk, and tore through the clutter on his desk looking for a pad of paper or notebook.

Writing furiously, he included the data confirming the four-fold reduction in off-target cleavage at the targeted chromosome position he had obtained by simplifying the CRISPR Cas9 System. He noted that he had selected a GAAA linker enzyme by mistake. When the mistaken enzyme, the GAAA linker, was added to the process, it acted as a spacer sequence and the two nucleotide chains linked into a single chain. As a result, when the artificial Cas9-sgRNA enzyme was introduced into the target cell, the modified Cas9-sgRNA complex successfully cut the cell's DNA, inducing the desired genomic mutation.

Doctor Tang laid his pen down and balled his right hand into a fist and flexed his fingers after feverishly writing two pages of notes thoroughly describing the successful mutation process. After reading through his notes twice to verify their accuracy, he picked up the phone to call Committee Secretary Ma and inform him of his success

"I must speak with Secretary Ma," Doctor Tang shouted as soon as someone answered.

"The Secretary is a very busy man," Secretary Ma's lieutenant protested.

"But this is important. I must speak with him."

"He is in a meeting. He wishes not to be disturbed."

"This is Doctor Tang. I am Director of Clinical Operations at Hunan Medical University. I have successfully created the virus the Secretary has requested. I assure you he will want to speak with me."

"Very well," the lieutenant answered. "I will see if the Secretary wishes to be disturbed."

Doctor Tang paced back and forth as far as the telephone cord would allow. "How long can it take to ask the Secretary a simple question?" he grumbled as he continued to pace back and forth.

After three more trips back and forth in front of his desk, someone picked up the phone. "The Secretary will talk with you in a few minutes. He has very important party members in his office. As soon as he concludes the meeting and they have left, he will talk with you."

Before Doctor Tang could protest, he heard the telltale click of being put on hold. He went back to pacing as he waited yet again.

Growing angrier with each trip in front of his desk, Doctor Tang waited a full twelve minutes before he heard a click and the voice of the Lieutenant, "Committee Secretary Ma will speak with you now." He heard another click before he could say anything.

Two more minutes passed. Finally he heard the annoyed voice of the Secretary, "What is so important that you should attempt to interrupt my important meeting?"

Despite the anger raging inside him, Doctor Tang knew better than to snap at the Secretary. To do so would bring swift retribution. He took a deep breath to calm his nerves. "Secretary Ma! Secretary Ma!" Doctor Tang babbled. "I have solved the synchronization issue. I have been able to create the mutant virus as you requested."

"That is good," Secretary Ma replied.

"Because of a simple mistake I selected an incorrect nucleotide linker enzyme. That mistake allowed me to…"

"Doctor Tang, I do not care about the details," Secretary Ma interrupted. "I only care that you were able to create the virus. How soon can this new development be moved into the pilot process and then into full production?"

"Perhaps two or three days. Then, if all is successful, major production can begin a day or two after that."

"As you are aware, we are already behind schedule. You must decrease the time to full production."

"But Secretary Ma, this process cannot be rushed. To do so could cause…"

"Are you defying me, Doctor Tang?"

"No Secretary, I would never do that."

"Very well. I expect full production in two days. Is that understood?"

"Yes, Secretary. I understand"

Doctor Tang pulled the handset away from his ear when he heard Secretary Ma hang up. "Stupid buffoon," Doctor Tang fumed, staring at the handset in his hand. "Stupid! Stupid! Stupid!" he shouted as he slammed the handset back on the cradle and stood there shaking. If he hurried the process and it failed, he would be blamed. He would certainly lose his position at the university and he would likely end up in prison. Left with no other options, Doctor Tang turned and raced out of his office. He sprinted down the hallway, headed for the biolab. Left with no options, he would simply have to find a way to shorten the process. Filled with increasing fear, he scrambled into his positive-pressure suit, worried that if he became careless and made a mistake in the biolab, it would likely be fatal.

Secretary Ma had hung up the phone and immediately picked it back up. He needed to call Doctor Thomson to inform him they would be in production in two days. About to dial the number, he realized it was not yet three o'clock in the morning in Washington, D.C. He would have to wait at least three hours before he could tell Doctor Thompson of his great success.

Chapter Seventeen

Wednesday, Feb. 11th – 3:12 a.m. EST
Mary's Beltway Diner
Columbia Pike
Arlington, Virginia

Forty-five minutes after discovering the bullet riddled suburban, FBI Special Agent Williamson squealed into the parking lot of Mary's Beltway Diner. He skidded to a stop in an empty parking space and bumped up against the curb. Two spaces away sat the Director's black BMW 7i. Agent Williamson had driven well over the speed limit, hoping to arrive before the Director because the Director hated to be kept waiting. Adding to the Director's growing anger would be the fact that Agent Williamson had been unable to track down Admiral Hadley or any of his accomplices.

Agent Williamson turned off the engine, climbed out, and trotted toward the diner's entrance. Slightly out of breath, he pushed the door open and stepped inside. The air in the diner was stale and saturated with the smell of fried bacon and coffee. The clanking of dishes and silverware and lively conversations filled the air despite the early hour. Scanning the booths, he saw the Director to his left, sitting in a booth along the side window, hunched over a cup of coffee. The Director looked up and their eyes met.

Director Conroy, his jaw clenched and his face drawn into a menacing scowl, motioned for Agent Williamson to join him. Agent Williamson had never seen the Director in such a disheveled state. No suit jacket, no tie, a rumpled shirt, and he looked as if he had not shaved for two days. No one would have guessed he was the top man in the country's premier law enforcement agency.

Agent Williamson walked over to the booth where the Director was seated and slid in across the table from him. About to speak, Agent Williamson, mouth open, stopped when the Director held his hand up. The Director looked down at the half-empty cup of coffee sitting in front of him. Shaking his head, he reached out, picked up the cup, and took a swallow of the black, lukewarm brew. He grimaced and set the cup back on the table.

"Okay, give me the latest," Director Conroy said.

"With Agent Stokes now missing, I only have Agents Purnell and Mendez left that I can trust," Agent Williamson answered. "I contacted each one while driving here. Neither one has anything new to report. There haven't been any sightings of Hadley or his accomplices since Stokes reported spotting Hadley's vehicle earlier tonight."

"Doesn't it seem a little odd for Hadley or one of his accomplices to be out so late at night? Where did Agent Stokes say the vehicle was headed?"

"I can't be certain. I have not heard from Stokes since that earlier report."

"What?" Director Conroy blurted out. "What kind of morons do you have working for you? Why didn't Stokes call you when he made this latest contact?"

"I don't know that. He should have contacted me as soon as he made contact. The last time I spoke with Stokes I told him to find a place to park in the vicinity of where he thought the vehicle might have been headed and wait for me to arrive in the area."

"That's not good enough. Call Purnell and Mendez and tell them to meet you in the Marshall area. Do it *now*! I will wait."

Agent Williamson lifted his cellphone out of his jacket pocket and called the two agents and instructed each agent to proceed immediately to the Marshall area and wait for him to arrive in the area. He passed on the description he had of the vehicle Stokes had spotted exiting the interstate and informed the agents he would contact them with additional instructions when he arrived.

When Agent Williamson finished the last conversation, Director Conroy continued, "As soon as this meeting is over you will return to the Marshall area and you *will* find Hadley. This nightmare has to end within the next twenty-four hours. West is livid that information regarding this operation has leaked out and even more so that we have been unable to find Hadley. Do I need to tell you what will happen if we fail to retrieve the information and silence the leaks?"

"No, Sir. I am quite aware what will happen."

"No, Agent Williamson. I don't think you are. If West goes down, we all go down. You will be charged with treason and, at best, you will spend the rest of your life in prison."

"But I…."

"Just shut up and go!" Director Conroy snarled, his voice rising enough to get the attention of a young couple sitting two booths away. He lowered his voice and added, "This ends tonight! I don't care what it takes!"

"Yes, Sir," Agent Williamson responded, fighting hard to suppress the words threatening to come out of his mouth. He quickly slid out of the booth and headed for the exit.

Agent Williamson shoved the diner's door open so hard he nearly knocked the man entering off the sidewalk. Without an apology or even an acknowledgement, Agent Williamson stomped down the sidewalk to his car. He yanked the driver's door open, slid inside, and slammed the door. Swearing to himself, he jammed the key into the ignition and started the engine. Gripping the steering wheel so hard his knuckles turned white, he took several deep breaths, waiting for his anger to subside.

With his anger somewhat under control, he backed out of the parking space and squealed out of the parking lot, turning right onto Columbia Pike.

"Someday he's going to push me too far and I'm going to tell him what I think of him," Agent Williamson sneered, knowing deep down inside he would do no such thing.

Slamming his hand on the steering wheel, he roared through the early morning traffic, blaring his horn at anyone too slow in getting out of his way. A plan of what he intended to do to Admiral Hadley and his friends for causing him to suffer the Director's rage began building in his mind. "They are going to pay and pay dearly," Agent Williamson ranted as he sped down the street.

Wednesday, Feb. 11th – 4:22 a.m. EST
Collins Horse Farm
Old Carters Mill Road
Marshall Virginia

Exhausted and bleary eyed, Zach turned off Old Carters Mill Road, drove down the gravel lane, and stopped behind the bullet-riddled van, parked beside the porch. He turned, reached over the seat, and tapped Chin Li on the knee.

"Chin, wake up. We're at the safe house. I'll get your bags out of the trunk. Then you and Min Ju follow me into the house."

Chin Li stirred and opened his eyes. "Yes, we follow," Chin answered as he patted Min Ju on the leg.

Zach saw the curtains part in the window beside the front door. He opened the car door, raised his hand above the car's roof, and signaled David McClain who was peering out the window of the house.

Chin pushed the rear door open and climbed out of the car. Reaching back into the car, he took Min Ju's hand to help her out of the car. Zack slammed the trunk lid and waited for Chin and Min Ju to follow him up onto the porch. As they approached the front door, David McClain pulled it open and quickly ushered them inside. As soon as they were inside, he pushed the door closed and locked it.

"Any trouble?" he asked.

"None. It was a quick flight down and back," Zach answered, suppressing a yawn. "Where is the Admiral?"

"We put him in an empty stall next to Agent Stokes," David answered. "We decided not to contact the authorities until you returned. What do you think we should do?"

"We know we can't trust the FBI," Zach answered. "It's very possible they have contacted the local authorities. We will just have to wait until I can get to Justice Tyler first thing in the morning."

"I think you're right," David Agreed. "It's only a few more hours. Who are your friends?"

"I'm sorry. This is Chin Zheng Li and his wife Min Ju Jiang."

"Nice to meet you," David said as he reached his hand out.

"I glad meet you," Chin responded, taking David's hand and bowing at the waist.

"Everybody's exhausted," Zach said. "Where are we going to put Chin and Min Ju?"

"We're out of bedrooms," David answered. "I can move my stuff to the den and put them in the bedroom I'm using."

"No, not want be trouble," Chin said. "We just glad be here. Can sleep anywhere."

"I don't mind, really," David stressed.

"Please, we take den," Chin insisted.

"Okay, if you're sure."

"Yes, I sure. House beautiful. We fine."

"David, you go back to bed" Zach said. "I'll get them situated. I'm beat. It's been a really long night."

"Okay, I'll see you in a couple of hours," David answered. He turned and headed back to his bedroom.

"Chin, Min Ju, follow me."

Zach ushered his new acquaintances into the den. He grabbed pillows, sheets, and blankets from the closet, opened the hide-a-bed, and quickly made up a bed for Chin and Min Ju.

"The bathroom is just down the hall on the left. I'll be in the bedroom two doors down on the right," Zach said, holding up two fingers on his right hand and pointing at the bedroom door. "If you need anything, just knock on the door, okay?"

Chin walked up to Zach and grabbed his hand. "We so glad your help," Chin beamed, pumping Zach's hand vigorously. "I know much. Have proof. Will show who you say."

"That's great," Zach answered. "We'll have to be up in just a few hours. Get some sleep"

Chin bowed as Zach grabbed the door knob and pulled the door to the den closed. Zach hurried down the hall and eased his bedroom door open. Undressing quickly and dropping his clothes in a pile at the end of the bed, he eased under the covers.

"Did the trip go okay?" Anna Mae yawned, raising her head off the pillow.

"No problems. I got our new friends settled in the den. Go back to sleep. We have to be up no later than seven."

Anna Mae mumbled something unintelligible and dropped her head back on the pillow. Zach plumped up his pillow, laid his head down, and was sound asleep in less than two minutes.

Barely an hour later Admiral Hadley's cellphone, laying on the nightstand, rang five times and went to voicemail. Two minutes later the cellphone rang again. Zach roused by the repeated buzzing and ringing reached for it, but it went to voicemail before he could answer it. Immediately the cellphone rang again. Determined to silence the annoying ringing, Zach grabbed the cellphone and swiped the answer icon.

"Hello, who is this?"

"Admiral Hadley?" a deep husky voice answered in a questioning tone.

"No, this is Zach Templeton" Zach answered. "Who is this?"

"Why do you have Admiral Hadley's cellphone?"

"Hang on a minute," Zach said as he slid out of bed and went into the living room to avoid disturbing Anna Mae. "Okay. I'm not going to tell you anything until I know who this is and why you are calling."

"I would rather not say," the husky voice answered. "Were you involved in a shootout with the FBI earlier this morning?"

"I repeat, before I talk to you, you're going to have to tell me who you are."

"It's not safe. I can't."

"No name – no talk," Zach insisted.

Silence…

"Well then, I'm hanging up."

Silence...

"If you decide to tell me your name, call me back," Zach said as he tapped the End icon.

Zach stared at the silent cellphone. Assuming the man was not going to call back, he turned and headed for the bedroom. As he put his hand on the doorknob the cellphone rang again.

Zach swiped the cellphone and said, "I'm warning you. This is the last time. Tell me your name or I will hang up and block your number."

"You must promise you will tell no one," the same husky voice said. "If you do, we'll both end up dead."

"If I like what I hear, I will promise," Zach agreed. "Now, tell me your name and why you called."

"My name is Michael Draper. I'm the..."

"I know who you are, if you really *are* Michael Draper," Zach interrupted. "How do I know you are who you say you are?"

"Did you just take a trip to Charlotte to pick up a man named Chin Zheng Li?"

"How could you know that?"

"The Admiral called me earlier tonight and alerted me in case there was any trouble."

"Okay, say I believe you. Why are you calling?"

"I would rather talk to Admiral Hadley. Where is he?"

"Admiral Hadley is dead," Zach answered.

"What? When?"

"The government just murdered my friend!" Zach snapped. "From what I'm hearing, it seems the government has been flooded with evil, murderous men. Why should I trust you?"

"I assure you I am not part of the conspiracy that is overtaking Washington," Mister Draper asserted. "I am taking a huge risk in calling you, Mister Templeton. If anyone finds out, I will end up dead also."

"I'm not convinced. I think I will hang up."

"No! Please don't," Mister Draper begged. "This treason must be stopped. It goes all the way to the top. The President's death was not a heart attack."

Zach heard Mister Draper's affirmation of what he already suspected. He considered what had been said, unsure if it was not just a ruse to gain his trust.

"Mister Templeton, did you hear me?"

"Yes, I heard you," Zach responded. "Can you prove that?"

"Yes I can. I knew my suspicions would never be believed. So, I hid a small camera in the room where these meetings were taking place. I have FBI Director Conroy on video deliberately jabbing the President with a large ring on his left hand. Then less than thirty minutes later he is dead. They did this to remove him and replace him with Hayworth. They will have no trouble controlling her which will give them access to all the agencies. If we don't stop them soon, it will be too late."

"Say I believe you. Who is them?"

"Adam West, FBI Director Jerome Conroy, former President Bahram Oates, and some other very rich men."

"Former President Oates? You're kidding," Zach exclaimed.

"No, not in the least. He is the tie to a very secret organization. Way more secret and powerful than the Order of The Illumined Elite you battled several years ago."

"If it's so secret, how do you know about it?"

"There is a defector. That is all I can tell you. I won't say any more."

"Why did he come to you?"

"Unknown to me, his grandfather and my grandfather were good friends. He had to go to someone. He chose me. Beyond that I do not know."

"Who is this defector?"

"I will not tell you. I made a solemn promise to never reveal his name."

"Okay. Who is in this *secret* order?"

"The defector would give me only one name. A very evil man by the name of Gerard Schechter. He is the Eminent Grand Commander of the L'Ordre de la Lumière. It's French and translates to The Order of Light."

"Why is he risking his life to tell you that?"

"The men that rule the order are the world's richest men. They control hundreds of billions of dollars of wealth. Because of that the tendrils of their financial control reach everywhere. Oates is the access to the powerful politicians in Washington they need to make their plan succeed."

"Can you prove any of that?"

"Not unless the defector is willing to come out of hiding."

"What will encourage him to do that?"

"We have to expose West, Conroy, and their associates. If he sees them locked up, he may feel safe enough to come forward."

"That is a lot to swallow, Mister Draper. For now, I'm going to believe you."

"That's great. What happened to Admiral Hadley?"

"He got hit during a shootout with the FBI. I didn't know he had been hit until we traded vehicles with someone. By that time he was already dead."

"I'm sorry," Mister Draper said. "I know you were friends. How much did the Admiral tell you about what is going on?"

"He told me about a virus the Chinese are working on and that if it were to be released, millions of people will die. He said he knew some of the people involved. That is why he met with Chief Justice Tyler, but Tyler said he needed more proof. That was the reason he was going to Charlotte to pick up Doctor Li."

"That's all he told you?"

"Yes, Zach lied, still somewhat uncertain he could fully commit to believing the man on the other end of the conversation. "He was going to fill me in on the flight to Charlotte, but, obviously, that did not happen. How do you figure into this mess?"

"The Admiral and I were friends for a long time. He confided in me that he had stumbled upon a serious threat. Knowledge of this virus came from a nurse that was part of his care team when he was in the hospital. That nurse stumbled upon this plot while visiting relatives in China. Doctor

Li was directly involved in the creation of a mutated virus. When he realized the horrible death and misery the virus would cause, he started communicating back and forth with someone named Tu Jin Lam, an epidemiologist here in the U.S, who happens to be his wife, Min Ju's cousin. It was Min Ju's uncle, Ning Bo, that helped them escape out of China. Sorry, that is the condensed version. If needed, I can fill in the holes at a different time."

"Okay, Mister Draper, that helps explain a few things," Zach said even though Admiral Hadley had already explained how he had learned of the virus. "Doctor Li's English is pretty limited. He couldn't tell me much. Admiral Hadley told me it was imperative that he get Doctor Li and his documents to Chief Justice Tyler. What I don't understand is why the Admiral went to a Supreme Court justice and not someone in the scientific community."

"It's because of who is behind this plot," Mister Draper answered. "I know you remember the attempt the Order of the Illumined Elite made to spread a deadly virus."

"You bet I do," Zach grimaced. "Their plot was to spread a deadly airborne virus a couple of years ago. Anna Mae and I were able to stop a crazed maniac that called himself the *Snake*. I nearly died in the process. After the ordeal was over, I was told everyone in the order was dead."

"Everyone thought so, but it turns out that is not true," Mister Draper declared.

"Not all dead?" Zach lied again. "How do you know that?"

"In my position in the White House I hear a lot of things. I have learned that one of the newest initiates to the Order's supreme council survived because no one but the other council members knew of his existence. The initiation was ultra secret, attended only by the other supreme council members. They're all dead so absolutely no one knew about him. After the other Order members died, he went deep and ceased all mention of the Order. That is, until recently."

"Yes, I know that," Zach revealed. "They call him *Marduk,* Prince of the Golden Serpent, and his real name is Adam West, Assistant to the President of the United States."

"Mister Templeton, How did you learn of this?"

"You first," Zach challenged. "I need to see if what you say lines up with what I was told."

"You must give me your absolute assurance that you will tell no one. That man and his new associates are extremely powerful and are also extremely dangerous. Those men are evil and they would stop at nothing to silence any that oppose them."

"I give you my word. I will tell no one," Zach agreed. "Now, continue."

"As you know Adam West is my boss. I overheard a conversation one night, totally by accident, but it goes much higher than West. West has had late night, and very secret meetings with the President and FBI Director Conroy. There are also several other high-ranking individuals in some pharmaceutical company that are involved in this as well, but I do not know their names. From what I overheard, they are somehow involved with China in developing a deadly, mutated virus. This *Marduk* has now joined forces with the new evil secret order I mentioned earlier. This new order wants to drastically reduce the world's population and usher in their vision of a new world order."

"I have already been told the President of the United States was involved in this and now he's dead and Hayworth is President," Zach said. "I know Hayworth is a radical liberal and I have heard rumors that she also believes in a liberal utopia, but I never believed it would actually happen and certainly not in my lifetime."

"You can believe it," Mister Draper affirmed. "If we don't do something soon, there will be no way to stop it. Hayworth went on national television to announce the death of President Borden and that she had been sworn in as President. Hayworth is just a puppet. The Order of Light is using her to spread their lies. She told the American people that the initial virus that is currently spreading is just a strain of the flu. That is not true. It is the host for the new mutant virus. If the mutant virus is released, many millions will die. There will be nothing anybody can do. It will burn through the world's population like a wildfire."

"I had no idea," Zach cringed.

"What did Admiral Hadley tell you?" Mister Draper asked.

"He only told us about the new virus. If he knew anything about the secret meetings he didn't tell us. Secret Service Agent David McClain is here. He is the one that told us about the secret meetings. He even has one of the meetings on tape."

"Agent McClain is there? I assumed he was dead."

"Yes, he is here. President Cantwell is here also. Admiral Hadley had been confiding in him as well. President Cantwell has gone into hiding because he has undeniable proof Adam West and a number of his cronies are also guilty of election fraud. Cantwell's former communications director had a copy of that proof, but now he is missing. The data analyst that uncovered that verifiable proof of the fraud is dead along with two of his associates."

"Does President Cantwell have that proof with him?"

"I believe he does."

"We have got to get that proof along with the information Doctor Li has about the virus to Chief Justice Tyler as soon as possible. With my video and Agent McClain's audio we should be able to sway the Chief Justice.

If West manages to get his hands on that proof and destroys it, we will have nothing and then it's over."

"I agree totally. The Admiral had a meeting set with Justice Tyler for later this morning. Can you meet us there in a couple of hours. Say around eight or a little after?"

"Where?"

"At Justice Tyler's residence in Great Falls, Virginia. Do you know where that is?"

"No, but I'll find it. I will be there. Mister Templeton, be very careful. West and his criminal associates are desperate. They will not hesitate to kill you and everyone around you if they have to."

"Yes, I know that quite well. I will see you in a couple of hours."

"I am really sorry about Admiral Hadley. I know you two were close. He mentioned you in the call earlier this evening. He must have had great respect for you to involve you in this. Be safe."

Zach heard a click as Draper ended the call. Zach dropped the cellphone in his pocket and started toward the bedroom. After glancing at his watch, he realized there was only thirty minutes left before the alarm on his cellphone was scheduled to go off. Rather than risk waking Anna Mae, he decided to sit in the recliner and rest his eyes. Zach plopped down in the recliner, raised the foot rest, and was fast asleep almost instantly.

Wednesday Feb. 11th – 6:02 a.m. EST
Adam West Residence
Fulton Street NW
Washington, D.C.

Adam West, Director of Communications for the President of the United States, made the final loop of his red silk tie. He pulled the knot up tight to his collar and centered the knot over the top button of his white shirt. Stepping back from the mirror, he double checked his appearance. Satisfied, he exited the bathroom, grabbed his suit jacket from the bed, and walked through the master bedroom he shared with his wife Debra. In the hallway, he turned left and headed for the stairs.

Stopping momentarily at the bottom of the stairs, he hollered in the direction of the kitchen, "Sorry Deb, but I won't have time for coffee. I have a million things to get done. I'll call you this afternoon and we can decide on a restaurant for dinner tonight."

"That'll be great," his wife called out from the kitchen.

West grabbed the doorknob. About to open the door, his cellphone buzzed in his pocket. He slipped the cellphone out and glanced at the display. Recognizing the international number, he set his briefcase on the floor and swiped the Answer icon.

"Adam West."

"Mister West, is Doctor Huang Tang. Have important news."

"I always speak with Doctor Yu. Connect me with Doctor Yu."

"Doctor Yu is incompetent pig. He fired by Party Secretary Ma. I must speak with you. Is very important."

"Very well," West answered, annoyed by the delay in getting his day started. "Hold on while I go somewhere private."

Leaving his briefcase sitting by the front door, West turned around and headed back for the stairs. Taking the stairs two at a time, he hurried to the top of the stairs, turned right, rushed into his study, and pushed the double doors closed.

Leaning against his desk, he spoke into the cellphone, "Go ahead, Doctor Tang. What is so important?"

"Is much great news," Doctor Tang gushed. "I have make breakthrough. Find way overcome complexity. Off target cleavage near zero and virus mutation successful."

"It's about time. When can we expect full-scale production?"

"Must go in pilot plant first, then to final production. Two days. Maybe three."

"Three days is too long," West shouted. Lowering his voice, he continued, "You have no more than two days to have the final product ready to deliver or you will suffer the consequences."

"Will try, but cannot promise," Doctor Tang answered.

"I said no more than two days. You *will* have it in two days!"

"Yes, two days."

"I will pick it up personally. Be certain it is ready." West ended the call before Doctor Tang could answer.

Despite the time being only three AM in California, he scrolled through his contacts list, selected Doctor Thompson's number, and tapped the Call icon.

On the fifth ring, a sleepy Doctor Thompson answered, "Hello, who is this?"

"This is West. We need to talk, now."

"Okay, hold on," a suddenly wide awake Doctor Thompson answered as he slid his legs out from under the covers.

In the dark, he fumbled his way to the bathroom, flipped on the light, and eased the door closed.

"Go ahead."

"China called. I told them they had no more than two days to have the product ready. Are you ready for the final step?"

"Yes, we are ready. There has been more than ample time since dispersal of the host pathogen. Is the vaccine ready?"

"Yes. As you know, the number of people that will receive the vaccine is quite limited. Enough for only two doses will be delivered to you by special courier."

"Only two?"

"Yes, Doctor. Only two. Choose wisely," West advised, then ended the call.

A stunned Doctor Thompson stared at the silent cellphone. He had known protection against the coming plague would be limited, but the news that he would receive only two doses was staggering. Who, besides himself, would receive the one remaining dose?

Still in his study, West walked around to the other side of his desk and pulled out a small booklet from a secret compartment. Holding his finger under an entry written on the last page, he tapped in a thirteen digit number, pressed Call, and waited.

"Yes, *Marduk*. What do you have to tell me?" a metallic sounding voice asked.

"Greetings, Eminent Grand Commander," West answered. "I have been notified that the final step of our plan is nearly ready. I am to pick up the final product in no more than two days. The equipment for dispersal is ready."

"That is good news, *Marduk*. What about that blabbermouth Borden?"

"He's dead and Hayworth has already been sworn in."

"More good news, but what about the leaked information? Has it been retrieved and have those involved been silenced?"

"I believe all but one copy," West replied, knowing it would not be wise to lie to the Grand Commander who had eyes and ears everywhere.

"What are you doing to retrieve it?"

"The first thing Hayworth did was to issue a shoot-to-kill order for Hadley and any of his associates. We are closing in. An FBI agent spotted the van Hadley is using. I will call FBI Director Conroy as soon as I hang up and advise him to eliminate all of them. Once that is done a clean-up team will be sent to the location to eliminate any and all evidence."

"Very well. What about the vaccine. How many doses have you distributed?"

"Two doses will be delivered to the moron in California, but they only contain water. I have two real doses. One for me and one for my wife."

"Even better news, *Prince Marduk*," the Eminent Grand Commander laughed. "You will be greatly rewarded by the .L'Ordre de la Lumière for your extraordinary service."

"It is but my humble honor to serve the Order, Oh, Eminent Grand Commander," Adam West answered.

West ended the call and immediately tapped a speed dial number.

"Yes, sir," Director Conroy answered.

"I have just spoken with the Grand Commander. What is the situation with Hadley and his associates?"

"Two agents are on their way to the location where Hadley's van was spotted. I am about forty minutes away."

"Eliminate everyone you find and I mean everyone. Notify me when it is completed. I will send a team to clean up."

"Understood," Director Conroy acknowledged.

West ended the call, rushed out of his study, down the stairs, and hollered 'Bye' to his wife as he flew out the door.

Wednesday, Feb. 11th – 6:30 a.m. EST
Collins Horse Farm
Old Carters Mill Road
Marshall Virginia

Zach lay in the recliner with his head tilted sideways at an odd angle. Snoring softly, he was jolted awake by the sound of his cellphone alarm. Despite being groggy from lack of sleep, he pushed out of the recliner, grabbed his cellphone from the coffee table, and silenced the alarm. He shuffled into the kitchen. Yawning widely, he reached up into the cabinet, lifted out the container of coffee, and loaded the coffee maker with grounds. He grabbed the pot and headed for the sink to fill it with water. Passing by the window over the sink, he noticed a flash of light out by the horse barn.

Zach quickly set the coffee pot down and switched off the light. Pushing the curtains aside slightly and staying low, he peered out the window. Enough light from the half moon allowed him to make out movement beside the larger horse barn. He watched for ten seconds for more movement. Two figures sprinted between the horse barn and the hay barn. They had been found. Zach rushed to the bedroom where Anna Mae was sleeping.

"Quick, get up. We've got company," he shouted as he shook her arm. "Get dressed, take Mazie, and head for the safe room. I'll alert Chin and Min Ju and the others. As soon as they get there, pull the door shut and lock it."

"Okay," Anna Mae answered as she squeezed his arm. "Zach, be careful."

"Don't forget Tripp," Zach added as he kissed Anna Mae and rushed to the den where Chin and Min Ju were sleeping.

"Chin, wake up," Zach urged, tapping Chin's shoulder.

"What?" Chin yelped, not remembering where he was.

"There are bad men here who want to hurt you. Get dressed quickly. Go to the safe room. This way." Zach pointed toward the side door in the den. "My wife, Anna Mae is waiting for you. Now! Quickly!"

Unable to wait to see if Chin Li followed his orders, Zach turned and ran to the bedroom where Agent McClain was sleeping.

He shook McClain awake and cautioned, "We've got company. Two men out by the horse barns. Throw some clothes on. Grab your weapon and meet me in the kitchen. No lights."

Zach raced down the hall and banged on the door to the other bedrooms. Continuing into the living room, he yanked open the front closet door, grabbed extra magazines for his weapon and headed for the kitchen. Agent McClain scrambled into his clothes, grabbed his service weapon and two extra, loaded magazines, and raced toward the kitchen. Roused by the banging, former President Cantwell and Zach's dad, James, poked their heads into the hallway.

"What's going on?" James Templeton called out.

"They found us," McClain hollered as he rushed past. "Two men out by the horse barns. Get Margaret and Christine to the safe room then come to the kitchen."

Stopping right behind Zach in the darkened kitchen McClain asked, "How did they find us?"

"They must have made the van," Zach sputtered.

"What can we do?" President Cantwell asked as he and James Templeton slid to a stop behind Agent McClain.

"In the van. Get whatever guns and ammo you can find and protect everyone in the safe room. The FBI must not get Doctor Li. He has to be protected at all cost."

"David, follow me. Let's go out the back door. I'll go around the house to the left and you go right. Maybe we can surprise them."

As Zach and David McClain raced to the back of the house, President Cantwell and Zach's dad ran out the front door, headed for the van.

Zach and David reached the back of the house. Zach took a deep breath, nodded to David, and yanked the back door open. Zach made a quick check and then the two men slipped out the back door. As soon as their feet hit the ground, they were welcomed with a hail of bullets as a raging gun battle erupted.

Zach dove to the left, seeking shelter behind a small shed next to the house. McClain grunted and fell to the ground. Zach poked his head around the shed and began firing to give McClain cover.

"Over here, quick!" Zach screamed.

Struggling, McClain began crawling toward the shed.

One of the attackers slipped out from behind a storage building and fired multiple shots at the prone McClain.

McClain groaned again and lay still. Filled with blinding rage, Zach stepped out from behind the shed and emptied his entire magazine at the shadowy form. Zach heard a yelp and a whump as the attacker fell to the ground. As Zach ducked back behind the shed, another hail of bullets slammed into the side of the shed, splinters and chunks of wood flying past his face.

Zach dropped down to one knee and ejected the empty magazine. Patting his left rear pocket, he felt for one of his spare magazines. The pocket was empty. They must have fallen out as he ran behind the shed. Switching the pistol to his left hand, he grabbed a magazine from his right rear pocket and slammed the only remaining spare magazine into his pistol. He released the slide lock, chambering a round. He glanced over his right shoulder hoping to see his dad or President Cantwell coming.

Zach edged his head around the corner of the shed. A barrage of bullets tore more large chunks of wood off the wall of the shed. Zach quickly ducked back to safety behind the shed. From the number of rounds that had hit the shed, there had to be multiple shooters. With only half a magazine left, he would not be able to hold off a concentrated attack. He needed help and soon.

Chapter Eighteen

Wednesday, Feb. 11th – 6:30 a.m. EST
Highway 50
East of Middleburg Virginia

Fumbling unsuccessfully to pull his ringing cellphone out of its holster, FBI Special Agent Williamson veered to the side of the highway and slid to a stop. He yanked the cellphone out of its holster, swiped the Answer icon, and hollered, "Yeah, go. Have you found them?"

"We're at a farm on Old Carters Mill Road," FBI Agent John Purnell screamed over the sound of gunshots. "It's on the north side of the road. I'm pinned down. I saw Kemp go down. I don't know where Mendez is. We need help!"

"Where on Old Carters Mill Road?" Williamson asked. He waited. No answer. "Where are you?" he shouted again.

Williamson adjusted the position of the cellphone. Pressing the cellphone harder against his ear, he listened carefully. The sound of gunshots blasted his ear. Then rustling and bumping sounds, and a loud thunk. The sound of the gun battle became distant and muffled.

"Purnell," Williamson shouted. "Purnell answer me! Purnell where are you? Purnell! Purnell!"

Williamson swore as he dropped the cellphone in the passenger seat. He tapped Old Carters Mill Road into the vehicle's GPS. The display indicated just over twenty-four miles. It would take him nearly thirty minutes to get there. He slammed his hand on the steering wheel, fearing the battle would be over by the time he got there.

After a quick check of traffic behind him, he jammed the accelerator to the floor and squealed away from the side of the road, blue-white clouds of smoke billowing up from the tires. The vehicle slid sideways into the oncoming lane of traffic. The driver of the large delivery truck bearing down on Williamson stomped on his brakes and attempted to swerve off the road to avoid being hit. The edge of the truck's bumper made contact with the rear of Williamson's vehicle, the force of the collision ripping the entire driver's side taillight assembly off. Clouds of dust billowed into the air and bits of glass and red plastic bounced across the highway.

Williamson whipped the steering wheel hard to the right, to correct the slide. Had Williamson's vehicle been going any faster the impact with the delivery truck would have rolled the vehicle over. As it was, he was able to correct the vehicle's path. He stomped on the accelerator and continued on his way. Williamson glanced in the rearview mirror and saw the driver of the truck jump out of the cab and wave his fist in the air. To avoid any more issues like that, he reached down and turned on the lights and siren.

Wednesday, Feb. 11th – 6:37 a.m. EST
Collins Horse Farm
Old Carters Mill Road
Marshall Virginia

President Cantwell and Zach's dad, James Templeton, had no more than stepped through the front door when they heard the gun battle erupt behind the house. As President Cantwell jumped off the porch, a shot rang out from somewhere near one of the horse barns. The bullet struck the wooden porch column, sending paint and wood chips flying.

"Get down," President Cantwell shouted. "There's more of them out by the horse barns."

James dived onto the floor, rolled off the porch, and took cover beside the van Admiral Hadley and Zach had driven earlier. He yanked open the side door and crawled inside, looking for the weapons Zach and the Admiral had used during the shootout earlier that night. Lying just behind the passenger seat James located the 9mm H&K submachine gun, still loaded with G2 RIP ammo.

"Cantwell," James shouted, tossing the SR-25/MK11 Sniper Rifle out the door of the van, followed by a fully loaded magazine. He slipped out of the door and moved to the front of the van. "Fire a wild shot to bring the shooter out into the open."

"One wild shot," Cantwell responded as he picked up the magazine and slid it behind the waistband of his trousers. He aimed wide of the barn and pulled the trigger.

"On the count of three," James advised, signaling with his hand. "One-two-three!"

Both men leaped out from their hiding places and laid down a barrage of non-stop fire at the spot where they had seen the muzzle flash until their magazines went empty. From beside the western-most horse barn they heard a shriek and a gasp. They quickly reloaded and ran toward the barn with their weapons at the ready.

One man lay on the ground, not moving. The man had been hit by two of the G2 RIP ammo rounds.

"Who is he?" James asked.

"He's not going to be telling us anything," Cantwell panted, seeing the lifeless look of death in the man's eyes. "Let's go help Zach."

Together they raced to the side of the house and peered around the edge of the building. Cantwell saw Zach crouched beside the shed. He picked up a small rock and tossed it at Zach. Startled, Zach glanced back over his right shoulder and saw Cantwell waving at him. Cantwell made a circular motion with his hand indicating he was going to go around the shed.

Zach pointed at the grip of his pistol and then made a slicing motion. James peeking around the edge of the house, made a thumbs-up signal, signaling that he understood Zach was low on ammo. Taking advantage of a lull in the gunfire, James rushed from behind the house and raced toward the shed. He slid up beside Zach and pulled him back from the edge of the shed. James pointed at one of the magazines laying a few feet away. Pointing his pistol around the edge of the shed, James fired in the direction of the shooter. Taking advantage of the covering fire, Zach rushed out and grabbed the magazine. Plumes of dirt flew into the air as bullets slammed into the ground around him. He dove back for the cover of the shed and grabbed his right leg.

"Are you okay?" James asked.

"I think so," Zach answered as he pulled a bloody hand away from his leg. "Doesn't feel like anything is broken."

"We need to end this before anybody else shows up," James barked as he turned and signaled Cantwell they were ready.

Zach ejected the half-empty magazine, stuffed it in his pocket, and jammed in a full one. "Now!" Zach yelled.

Together they stood up, left the cover of the shed, and began firing at the position of the shooter. Cantwell immediately sprinted around a stand of trees and circled around the north side of the storage building where the shooter was positioned. Inching along the backside of the building, he peered around the edge of the wall. The shooter's attention was fixed on the two men firing from the side of the shed.

Cantwell reached behind his back and felt for the Smith & Wesson collapsible baton he had picked up when it had rolled out of the van. His hand closed around the basketweave pattern of the thermoplastic grip. To avoid alerting the shooter, Cantwell carefully extended the baton to its full twenty-four inch length. He sucked in a deep breath and quietly stepped around the side of the building. One quick step and he cracked the shooter over the head with all the force he could muster.

The shooter fell to the ground, never knowing what hit him. "He's down," Cantwell yelled. "It's safe. Come on out."

Zach rushed over to check on McClain while his dad rushed over to the storage building. Zach kneeled beside McClain's still body and pressed his fingers against his neck, feeling for a pulse. Zach stood up shaking his head. Shivering in the cold morning air, an intense anger blossomed inside him. "Another brave man dead and for what," Zach snarled as he turned and headed for the storage building.

"Who is that rat? Zach snarled, looking at the prone body lying on the ground.

"Let's find out," Cantwell said as he used his foot to roll the man over. He patted the man's pocket, feeling a wallet in his left hip pocket. He pulled the wallet out and flipped it open. "Well, well, gentlemen. Meet FBI Field Agent Ramone Méndez. I'm afraid he can't return your greeting."

Zach knelt down and pressed the muzzle of his pistol against Agent Mendez's head. "McClain is dead. I'm going to send this man to Hell."

"Zach, don't," James shouted, pushing Zach's arm away.

"He killed my friend. He deserves to die."

"Yes he does, but murdering him will not bring your friend back. We'll take him with us and make him admit what the FBI is doing."

Zach pulled the pistol away, slid it behind the waistband of his trousers, and stood silent.

"Cuff him before he wakes up," James urged.

Cantwell lifted Mendez up enough to be able to slip a set of handcuffs from the pouch on his belt. He rolled Mendez over and handcuffed his arms behind his back.

Hearing a crunching sound when he took a step toward Cantwell to look at the credentials, James looked down and saw a cellphone lying in the dirt. "Look. He was on the phone," James blurted out. "We have to get everyone out of here!"

"Dad, you take Mom, Christine, Anna Mae, Mazie, and Min Ju and load them in the good van," Zach ordered. "Then head for Justice Tyler's house. Now! Quick! President Cantwell and I will take care of Agent Mendez. Then I'll make certain the shot-up van is out of commission."

James turned and ran back to the house to get everyone rounded up and loaded into the van while Zach and Cantwell dragged Mendez to the front of the house. Zach ran to the front of the van and put two rounds through the radiator. Then he walked around the van and shot each one of the tires. Cantwell watched as James hurried everyone out of the house and got them into the van.

Cantwell grabbed James's arm as he started toward the driver's door and advised, "I thought I saw a flash of headlights turning onto Atoka Road. To be safe, take the path behind the hay barn. Be careful you don't miss it. Follow it to the gravel road. Turn right. It connects with Atoka Road. Turn your lights off and wait for the car to pass. We'll be right behind you as soon as we get Chin Li."

James ran around the van and scrambled into the driver's seat. He started the engine, dropped it into gear, and roared off behind the hay barn. Slipping through the barely visible break in the line of trees, the van disappeared. Zach ran to the horse barn, drove the sedan from behind the barn, and stopped beside the house.

"Do you have the flash drive?" Zach asked as Doctor Li stepped down off the porch. Doctor Li affirmed that he did. "Great. Get in the back."

Doctor Li jumped into the back. Zach and Cantwell carried Agent Mendez around the sedan and loaded him into the back seat. Cantwell ran around to the passenger side of the sedan and yanked the front door open and had only slipped halfway into the passenger seat when Zach jammed his foot on the accelerator, spitting gravel out behind the sedan. Cantwell fell into the passenger seat as the passenger door slammed shut. The sedan roared off toward the hay barn.

"Make certain Agent Mendez stays quiet," Zach said, hearing a groan from the back seat.

Cantwell pointed his Glock 9 directly at Mendez and ordered, "Make a sound and you're dead. Understand?"

Agent Mendez blinked his eyes and stared as if unseeing.

"Do you understand me?" Cantwell asked again, moving the pistol closer to Agent Mendez's face.

Agent Mendez nodded his head, grimacing in pain.

"There," Cantwell shouted, seeing the hardly noticeable lean to the weeds where the van had slipped through the tree line. Zach steered the sedan through the narrow opening and followed the path the van made in the weeds. Two hundred yards through the field, both vehicles stopped behind a copse of Eastern White Pines and waited.

"Do you see anything," Zach asked.

"Not yet," Cantwell answered.

Three minutes later Cantwell pointed toward Atoka Road and announced, "There. Flying down the road. It must be whoever Agent Mendez was talking to."

As the speeding vehicle flew past, Zach drove around the van and waved at his dad to follow. Driving as fast as he dared with the lights off he followed a rutted path to the end of the pasture. He stopped briefly and looked at the closed gate. Deciding they could not afford the time to stop and open the gate, Zach pressed down on the accelerator and blew through the barbed wire gate. The sedan bottomed out as it crossed the ditch, bouncing the occupants up against the roof. Zach spun the steering wheel hard to the right and slid out onto Salem Oaks Road. A short eighth of a mile later the narrow dirt road intersected Atoka Road. Both vehicles turned left and sped off into the early morning darkness.

By the time whoever was in the vehicle they had seen speeding down Atoka Road arrived at the Collins Farm and found the agents, two dead, one handcuffed, and one missing, Zach and company would have already turned onto Highway 50. They would arrive at the Tyler residence earlier than planned, but given the circumstances, it was unavoidable.

Wednesday, Feb. 11th – 7:32 a.m. EST
Tyler Residence
Walker Glen Court
Great Falls, Virginia

Thirty five minutes later, the two vehicles turned left off Highway 50 onto Highway 60, then right onto Highway 267, bypassing Dulles International Airport on the west and north side. Ten minutes later they arrived at the Tyler residence and drove slowly down the lane. Zach had called ahead, alerting the security detail they were on the way. Zach pulled the sedan up to the end of the drive and stopped. James stopped the van behind the sedan. They all jumped out, stood on the sidewalk, and waited for the Secret Service agent to arrive.

"Where's Admiral Hadley?" Secret Service Agent Waterhouse asked. "We were expecting him to meet with Chief Justice Tyler later this morning."

"I'm Zach Templeton," Zach said, holding out his Secret Service credentials. "This is my Dad, James Templeton. Admiral Hadley is dead. We have got to see Chief Justice Tyler immediately!"

Agent Waterhouse reached out and grabbed the credentials, and examined them. "Hadley's dead? How?" Agent Waterhouse questioned as he handed the credentials back to Zach.

"A shootout with an FBI agent."

"A shootout with the FBI?" Agent Waterhouse exclaimed. "You had a shootout with the FBI and you come here demanding to see Justice Tyler. I can't...."

"My credentials say by authority of former President Paul Cantwell, correct?"

"Yes."

"That President Paul Cantwell, right there," Zach said pointing to his right.

"President... Ah, yes... Wow... Ah...," Agent Waterhouse sputtered, not having noticed the former president. "I'm sorry sir. I didn't recognize you in the dim light."

"That doesn't matter now. We need to see Justice Tyler now," Zach urged. "What we have to show him is time critical."

"Right now, Agent Waterhouse," President Cantwell stressed.

"Yes, Sir, Mister President" Agent Waterhouse agreed. He yanked out a cellphone and tapped in a number. After a brief conversation, the front door of the house opened. "The Justice was about to sit down to breakfast. He said to go on in. All of you. He'll meet you in the kitchen. Patrick will show you the way."

James Templeton noticed Agent Waterhouse's eyebrows go up when he saw the handcuffed Agent Mendez being dragged out of the sedan. "This is one of the FBI agents that ambushed us at the safe house where we were staying. He's going to explain to Chief Justice Tyler what has been going on in the FBI. Aren't you Agent Mendez?"

Agent Mendez glanced at James and nodded his head up and down in agreement. Placing his hand on Agent Mendez's shoulder, James guided him up the walkway behind Zach, President Cantwell, and the others. Christine Cantwell, Margaret Templeton, Anna Mae, and Mazie led the procession to the front door.

"Good morning ladies," Patrick greeted as he pulled the door open wider and motioned for them to come in. "Chief Justice Tyler is waiting for you in the kitchen."

Doctor Chin Li and Min Ju Jiang were awestruck by the enormity of the house, beyond anything they had ever seen in China. They had stopped and were admiring the immaculate, lighted flower beds along the front of the house. Zach stepped up behind Doctor Li, tapped him on the shoulder, and pointed at the open door.

"Am sorry. Is most beautiful," he grinned. "I beg pardon."

Zach urged Doctor Li along the walkway, limping along behind him. Doctor Li and Min Ju entered the house and stood beside those that had already entered. Zach held back, standing at the edge of the walkway, not wanting to track blood across the gleaming wood floor.

"Anna Mae, can you ask for a rag of some kind? I don't want to track up that beautiful floor."

Anna Mae waved at Patrick to get his attention. "My husband needs a rag of some kind. He has been wounded."

"Wounded?" Patrick blurted out. "I'll get something from the kitchen right away."

Patrick turned and raced off in the direction of the kitchen. Less than a minute later he came running with a kitchen towel in his hand. Stepping out the door, he handed Zach the towel. Zach scraped his shoe on the grass and wiped off as much of the blood as he could. He bent down and wrapped the towel around his leg and tied a knot in the loose ends. Together, he and Patrick entered the house.

"Come on into the kitchen," Patrick urged, pointing to his left. "I'll grab the first aid kit and we'll take care of the leg properly."

"I'll stay here and watch Agent Mendez," James said as he grabbed the agent's arm and pushed him toward one of the chairs sitting on either side of the front door. "Sit down and be quiet." James dragged the other chair over so that it faced Agent Mendez and laid his pistol in his lap.

The rest of the group made their way into the kitchen. Zach limped over beside the center island and leaned against it to take the weight off his injured leg. Patrick arrived carrying a large and well equipped first aid kit.

"Let me take that," Anna Mae said, taking the first aid kit out of Patrick's hand.

While Anna Mae tended to Zach's leg, he introduced everyone to Justice Tyler. "My Dad, James Templeton, is by the front door guarding Agent Mendez."

"Your Dad and President Cantwell I already know," Justice Tyler said. "Admiral Hadley was supposed to meet with me this morning. Where is he?"

"Admiral Hadley is dead," Zach replied.

"Dead?"

"He was killed in a shootout with an FBI agent."

"A shootout with the FBI?" Justice Tyler exclaimed, a look of shock spreading across his face.

"We had no choice. The FBI agent didn't give us any warning. He just jumped out of his vehicle and started shooting."

"What about the FBI Agent?"

"We left him handcuffed, lying in a horse barn at a farm not far from here. We were preparing to come here when we were ambushed by another group of FBI agents. As Secret Service Agent David McClain and I stepped out the back door, at least two FBI agents began firing at us. David went down. I scrambled behind a shed and tried to give some covering fire so David could crawl to safety. He was wounded and unarmed and one of the agents fired on him as he tried to crawl to the shed. McClain is dead."

"Agent McClain is dead also," Justice Tyler gasped. "I knew him. He was a highly decorated agent and a good man."

Zach nodded his head in agreement and continued, "Fortunately Dad and President Cantwell had gone out the front door. As they did, another shooter by the horse barn fired and nearly hit President Cantwell. They retrieved some weapons from the van. President Cantwell and Dad took out the shooter by the barn, then Dad made it over to the shed where I was. While Dad and I laid down some covering fire, President Cantwell snuck around the back of the storage building and whacked the remaining shooter on the head. That shooter, FBI Field Agent Ramone Mendez, is the one handcuffed sitting by the front door."

"That is a wild story," Justice Tyler said, shaking his head.

"That isn't the...," As Zach opened his mouth to say more, Mazie slipped out of Anna Mae's grip and ran over to Zach's side. "Daddy, I'm hungry."

Zach pulled one of the stools away from the island and eased himself onto the stool, being careful of his injured leg. He picked Mazie up and set her on his lap and kissed her on the forehead. "I know, Sweetie. We didn't have time for breakfast."

Zach switched his attention back to Justice Tyler and continued, "As I was saying. That isn't the half of it, but the rest of the details need to be shared in private. Before we do that, it has been a very stressful morning. Could I impose on your generosity to provide some breakfast for Mazie and the ladies?"

"Absolutely," Justice Tyler beamed. "It would be my privilege. Patrick, have Misses Fields prepare whatever this pretty little lady would like and the other ladies too. While she's doing that bring a carafe of coffee and some cups to my study please. Gentlemen, follow me."

Justice Tyler rose from the stool he was sitting on and headed for his study on the north side of the house. Zach and Doctor Li followed while President Cantwell signaled for James to escort Agent Mendez to the study as well. Justice Tyler pushed the study door open and waited for all the men to enter. James directed Agent Mendez to a chair in the corner of the room. James leaned against the wall while Zach, President Cantwell, and Doctor Li sat in the chairs sitting directly in front of the desk.

James bent over and spoke softly to Agent Mendez. "You had better tell the truth if you hope to escape a charge of treason and spend the rest of your life in prison, *or worse.*"

Waiting for the coffee to arrive, Justice Tyler walked between the desk and chairs, looked at Doctor Li, and said, "Doctor Chin Li, right?"

"Yes, name is Chin Li," he answered. "Please, not need doctor. Call me Chin."

"Okay, Chin, I am happy to meet you. Did you and your wife have a safe trip here to America?"

"Was much danger till leave Shanghai," Chin answered. "If not for Min Ju's uncle, Ning Bo, we be prison. Once on plane, we relax. Many, many hours later we arrive America. Mister Zach find us in Char... Char..."

"Charlotte, North Carolina," Zach explained.

"Yes, where he say," Chin said, pointing at Zach. "We only sleep few hours in last two days."

"And then this," Justice Tyler added.

A soft rap on the door.

"Come on in, Patrick."

Patrick rolled a serving cart loaded with a large carafe of coffee and a tray full of cups into the room.

"Thank you, Patrick," Justice Tyler said. "We are not to be disturbed for any reason. Oh, Patrick, tell the security detail to hide our guests' vehicles behind the garage. Have guards positioned at the end of the lane. No one, and I mean no one, is to enter this house!"

"Hold on a minute, Justice Tyler," Zach interrupted. "Michael Draper, Deputy Assistant to the President, is supposed to meet us here. He is a direct eye witness to much of the proof we have."

"Very well, Mister Templeton. Patrick, tell the guards to allow Mister Draper to enter, but absolutely no one else."

"Yes sir, I'll see to it," Patrick acknowledged as he backed out of the room and softly eased the door closed.

"Admiral Hadley told me you said you needed more proof," Zach began. "Well, here it is. For starters: the gun battle we had early this morning with the FBI Agents was on orders that came directly from FBI Director Conroy himself. Agent Mendez here will swear in court that Agent Williamson told him a shoot-to-kill order for Admiral Hadley and any of his associates was issued by new President Hayworth and passed to FBI Director Conroy."

Agent Mendez swallowed hard as all eyes in the room turned and looked at him.

"Well, Agent Mendez, is that true?" Justice Tyler asked.

"Yes, sir," Agent Mendez stammered. "Williamson ordered me and agents Kemp and Purnell to find Hadley and his accomplices. He said we were to kill everyone. When it was over, he would request a cleaning crew to remove any evidence."

"You can't be serious," Justice Tyler exclaimed. "Kill everyone?"

"Yes, sir. That is exactly what he said. I will swear to that in court. I was only ....."

Agent Mendez was interrupted by another soft rap on the door. Justice Tyler looked at President Cantwell then pointed at the door. Cantwell opened the door and Patrick poked his head in.

"Mister Michael Draper is here, sir."

"Come on in Mister Draper," Justice Tyler called out. "Patrick bring in another chair."

Overcrowded, the room had become stuffy. Justice Tyler rose from his chair, adjusted the thermostat, and returned to his chair. "Continue, Agent Mendez."

"Sir, I was just following orders," Agent Mendez whined. "I didn't know what I was getting into. Once you were recruited into Conroy's covert group, you had no choice. You followed orders or else."

"That's hardly an excuse and you know it," Justice Tyler scolded. "I want to know more about this *cleaning crew* I believe you called it. What exactly is that?"

"It's a group of Conroy's carefully selected agents. They come in after an event that needs to be covered up. You know, something like what happened at the farm this morning. They come in, clean up, and remove any bodies and evidence that could implicate the FBI."

"Unbelievable." Justice Tyler frowned and looked around the room. Shaking his head, he repeated, "Absolutely unbelievable."

"That isn't even close to the worst of it," Mister Draper spoke up. "Justice Tyler, please listen to the entire conspiracy we are about to lay out before you say anything."

"Okay, I'll listen," Justice Tyler agreed as he rose, walked to the serving cart, and filled a cup with coffee.

"I believe you have already heard the tape Agent McClain made of the meeting between President Borden and Director Conroy." Blowing across the steaming cup of coffee in his hand, Justice Tyler nodded his assent. Draper continued, "They were both taking orders from Adam West, the President's Communications Director. Have you ever heard of the L'Ordre de la Lumière?"

The blank look on Justice Tyler's face confirmed that he had not. "I would have been very surprised if you had. It translates to The Order of Light. It is an exceptionally secretive group of the world's ten richest men. If you remember, several years ago there was another fanatic group that tried to spread a deadly virus."

"Yes, I remember," Justice Tyler spoke up. "I was at the ceremony when Mister Templeton was awarded the Presidential Medal of Freedom for stopping the crazed assassin that was part of that group."

"Everybody was led to believe all members of The Illumined Elite were dead. Well, that is not true. One member survived and now takes orders from the much more powerful and evil Order of Light. That man is none other than Adam West, Assistant to the President of the United States. Working directly under West as his deputy, I overheard the end of a conversation. That and some other odd behavior made me suspicious. So, I listened and watched more carefully. I have a bit of a hearing problem. Because of that I have learned to read lips. One day I followed West to the US Botanic Garden. He met with a man and took a small box out of his pocket. I have to assume it was a jammer of some kind to mask their conversation. I couldn't understand everything that was said, but I did get that someone named Herr Schechter, or something like that, demanded the timetable be moved up. China is to have the mutated virus ready in a few days. Then the man told West that Herr Scheck wanted Eagle silenced for good." Draper stopped talking and waited for the name *Eagle* to sink in.

"Eagle as in the code name for the President?" Justice Tyler gasped.

"Yes, that is exactly who he meant," Draper answered. "The man told West to order Director Conroy to take care of it. The man then took a small box out of his pocket. After showing West something in the box, he told West to be extremely careful. Something about a toxin I think. West took the box and put it in his pocket. West got up and left. A minute later, the man got up and left. President Borden's death was not a heart attack."

"Do you know who the other man was?" Justice Tyler asked.

"Yes, Sir, I do," Draper replied. "The other man was former President Bahram Oates."

"You're telling me former President Bahram Oates ordered the assassination of the President of the United States?"

"Yes, Sir, that is *exactly* what I am saying and I will testify to that in court."

"If I hadn't heard it with my own ears, I would never believe such a wild story," Justice Tyler scowled. "You mentioned something about a mutated virus. How does that fit into this?"

"That's why Doctor Li is here," Zach spoke up. "He is the virology researcher that was assigned to create a deadly mutation of the Marburg virus. From what I understand, a target, host virus for the new mutation has already been released and is spreading. Network news has reported that a nasty flu virus is spreading across Europe and has recently reached the United States. While that flu is quite contagious and causes fairly serious symptoms, it is nothing like what will happen if the mutated virus is completed and released. It will..."

"What do you mean by host virus?" Justice Tyler interrupted.

"The host will combine with the mutated virus and become a chimera, meaning it will contain DNA from both viruses. It will be both but appear to be neither. To the human body, it will be a never before seen virus and it will spread like a wildfire. We have a little bit of a language issue with Doctor Li, but here is what I was able to understand. The new chimera virus will be ultra contagious because it was created as a sticky virus. It will be able to live outside a person in the air or on surfaces for up to nine days and its incubation period is six to twelve days. This is the key to its mobility because those infected will be contagious with absolutely no clinical signs. Doctor Li said the virus will have an eighty percent infection rate. If one hundred people are exposed, eighty will get sick. Ninety percent will get so sick they will need hospital care and at least half of those will die. Doing the math means that for every one hundred infected, thirty-six will die. Justice Tyler, that is catastrophic."

"Yes, is all true," Doctor Li interjected.

Zach saw the look of horror on Justice Tyler's face and continued, "Medical facilities will quickly become overwhelmed and then the percentage of deaths will explode. The result will be far beyond anything you could possibly imagine."

"Doctor Li why did you get involved in this and why are you here now?" Justice Tyler asked.

"In China not have choice," Doctor Li answered. "I ordered. Do what told. After many tries, I make virus."

"You mean the mutated virus is already out there?" Justice Tyler stammered.

"No. Not finish. When find out what Mister Zach say, I destroy product and... and...," Doctor Li stopped speaking and pulled a pen from his pocket and pretended to write.

"You mean written notes."

"Yes, yes. Destroy also notes. Have all on this," Doctor Li said, holding up a USB flash drive. "Ning Bo help escape. I here now."

"Will some other researcher be able to duplicate your work and, if so, how long?"

"Yes. Not take long, I think."

Justice Tyler looked at Michael Draper and asked, "Did you hear anything about this virus and when it might be ready from anything you overheard from Adam West?"

"He told me he would be traveling out of the country over the weekend," Draper answered. "So, I would think we only have two to three days, maybe less."

Justice Tyler sat there in silence, staring at the surface of his desk for what seemed like an eternity. Finally, he looked up, consulted a small notebook lying on his desk, grabbed the phone, and punched in a number.

"Albert, sorry to call you at home," Justice Tyler said the instant his good friend, Albert Goodridge, Chief Judge of the Superior Court of the District of Columbia, Criminal Division, answered. "How quickly can you get to your office?"

"Actually, I'm not at home. I'm already at the office. I came in early to prepare for a trial. What's up Matthew?"

"First, I need an emergency hearing with you and the US Marshall's office as soon as we can get there. Second, I need a State Patrol escort at my residence *immediately* for transport of federal witnesses. Get the escort started this way NOW!"

"Hang on I'll be right back," Judge Goodridge said as he laid his cellphone on the desk, grabbed the phone sitting on his desk, and punched in a number. After a quick conversation, he hung up the phone and picked up his cellphone. "Escort is on the way. The State Patrol watch commander said fifteen to twenty minutes. Anything else?"

"Yes. I want you to prepare of an arrest warrant for FBI Special Agent Martin Williamson and FBI Director Jerome Conroy. Have the US Marshall's office execute the warrant immediately."

"What?" Judge Goodridge exclaimed. "Matthew, you can't expect me to have the Director of the FBI arrested."

"They must be taken into custody!" Justice Tyler snarled into the phone. "Albert, we've known each other for many years. You must do this. President Borden was murdered. I have proof that those two men, and others, are involved in a conspiracy you will not believe. It will threaten the very existence of our country. There are only days to stop it. You must believe me."

"Matthew, you have got to be kidding."

"I wish I were. I have proof. As soon as the escort arrives and I get the witnesses to your office, I guarantee you will be as horrified as I am. Albert, please. You must do this."

"Very well. I'll prepare the warrant immediately and call the US Marshall's office to have it served. Where are Director Conroy and Williamson?"

"Director Conroy will probably be in his office. If Agent Williamson is not in the Rectortown or the Middleberg area, he may be on his way here to murder the witnesses."

"Okay. I'll alert the State Patrol to have units dispatched to those areas. Anything else?"

"No. Just pray that we arrive at your office safely."

"Okay, Matthew. I'll be waiting for you."

Chief Justice Tyler dropped the phone back in its cradle and looked up at Zach. "Zach, you, Mister Draper, Doctor Li, and Agent Mendez follow me. President Cantwell, you join us as well. I'm going to need your testimony to convince Judge Goodridge. Come on, follow me. We need to be ready to go as soon as the escort arrives."

Justice Tyler, stopped, picked up the phone again, and instructed the security detail to bring the van around to the side of the house. He rose from his chair, hurried to the door, pulled it open, and motioned for everyone to exit. About to step through the doorway he looked over at Zach's Dad and said, "James, I'll instruct Patrick to see that you and your family get whatever you need."

Everybody followed Justice Tyler out the door, through the kitchen, and to the house's side entrance.

"Gun! Gun!" someone screamed as the sounds of yelling and gunfire filtered through the door.

"Everybody, back into the kitchen!" Zach yelled as he and President Cantwell pulled their weapons out.

Zach raised his weapon and signaled for President Cantwell to open the door. As President Cantwell eased the door open bullets slammed into the door jam, sending dust, splinters, and chunks of drywall flying. Both men took cover on either side of the door. More gunfire rang out as the security detail engaged the shooter. Zach edged his head around the door jam. He could see the security detail firing at someone that had taken cover behind a dark gray sedan sitting sideways in the driveway.

"Cover me," Zach barked.

President Cantwell leaned partway into the doorway and began firing at the dark gray sedan. Zach crouched down and raced out the door and ran over to the van where the security detail had taken cover.

"Who is it?" Zach panted. "Nobody was supposed to get past the detail at the road."

"Agent Cruz radioed from the road that Justice Clark had urgent business with Justice Tyler," Agent Waterhouse shouted. "I thought it would be okay, so I told Cruz to let him pass. The next thing I heard was a gunshot and Cruz went down. Just then another car came sliding up to the end of the driveway. Someone leaped out and began firing at us."

"How many in your detail?" Zach asked.

"Just me, Cruz and one other agent. He and Cruz were out at the road. I haven't seen or heard him. I assume he is down as well."

"How much ammo do you have?"

"Only what's left in the clip," Agent Waterhouse answered.

"Do you have the keys to the van?"

Agent Waterhouse dug in his pocket and pulled out the keys for the van and handed them to Zach. Zach pressed the side door button on the key fob and waited for it to slide open.

"Okay. Cover me, but only fire if you have to."

Zach edged along the side of the van and jumped inside. He climbed between the seats and grabbed the sniper rifle and the H&K submachine gun he and Admiral Hadley had used in the earlier shootout.

"I'm coming out," Zach announced as he slipped out the side door.

Agent Waterhouse leaned around the van and fired two quick shots toward the sedan. Taking advantage of the lull, Zach raced to the back of the van and handed the H&K to Agent Waterhouse.

"Ever use one of these?"

"No."

"It has a full magazine and it's on full auto. Just point it and pull the trigger. Ready?" Agent Waterhouse nodded his head. "Go!" Zach yelled.

Together they stepped out from the cover of the van and began firing. As Zach and President Cantwell had raced out the side door, James pulled out his weapon and ran out the back of the house. Unseen by the shooters, he sprinted around the south end of the house and raced to the road. Using the ditch that paralleled the road, he advanced on the position of the shooters. He straightened up, fired at the shooters, and dove back in the ditch for cover.

Startled by the gunshots coming from a different direction, both the shooters stood up and fired at the new threat. Resting the sniper rifle against the van, Zach took careful aim and fired at the closest shooter. The shooter lurched and fell sideways. Agent Waterhouse fired a burst from the H&K, wounding the other shooter.

Silence.

With their weapons ready, Zach and Agent Waterhouse advanced on the position of the shooters.

"Zach, it's me," James shouted as he scrambled up out of the ditch.

"It's my Dad," Zach advised Agent Waterhouse.

Arriving first at the position where the shooters were lying, Zach kicked the weapons out of reach. Pointing their weapons at the men lying on the ground, Zach and James waited as Agent Waterhouse checked the last man that had arrived.

"He's dead," Agent Waterhouse advised.

"Look for his ID," Zach said.

Agent Waterhouse leaned down and patted the man's jacket. Feeling something hard on the left side, he reached inside the man's jacket and pulled out a black leather wallet. He stepped over beside Zach and handed him the wallet.

Zach flipped the wallet open and shook his head as he read the man's name, "Martin Williamson, FBI Special Agent."

"FBI Special Agent," Agent Waterhouse gasped. "We shot an FBI Agent?"

"Yes, and a Supreme Court Justice it seems," Zach answered. "Check him out."

As Agent Waterhouse pressed his fingers against the man's neck. The man groaned and opened his eyes.

"Justice Clark, can you hear me?" Agent Waterhouse asked, tapping the man on the shoulder.

Justice Clark opened his eyes and mumbled something unintelligible. He rolled his eyes and blinked twice and then his eyes drifted closed.

"I don't think his wound is life threatening, but he does need medical attention soon," Agent Waterhouse said. "Let's get him up to the house."

Zach handed the sniper rifle to Agent Waterhouse and James stuffed his pistol behind the waistband of his trousers. James grabbed Justice Clark's feet and Zach grabbed his arms. Together, they lugged him up to the house and laid him on the sidewalk leading to the side door.

James stepped into the doorway and hollered, "Someone call nine-one-one. We need an ambulance."

After hearing that someone needed an ambulance, Anna Mae came running out to see if Zach had been hurt.

"James, where's Zach?" Anna Mae squealed as she ran past James and flew out the door. "Is he hurt? Where is he?"

"I'm right here," Zach called out as he stood up beside Justice Clark. "I'm fine."

Anna Mae raced over to where Zach was standing and wrapped her arms around him, nearly suffocating him. After some time, she relaxed, released her grip on Zack, and stepped back. "What on Earth is going on? Who are these people?"

"The one lying over by the cars is an FBI Special Agent," Zach replied. "He's dead. This one here is US Supreme Court Justice Walter Clark."

"An FBI agent and a Supreme Court Justice tried to kill you?" Anna Mae blurted out. "That's crazy. These people are supposed to protect us not try to kill us."

"It certainly doesn't seem like that is true anymore," Zach responded. "First, Admiral Hadley and now this. It makes you believe the government has become the enemy?"

"What is wrong with our country? Why are these things happening?"

"It's exactly what God said we were to expect. In the Second Epistle of Timothy, somewhere in chapter three, I think, the Apostle Paul wrote, 'But evil men and seducers shall wax worse and worse, deceiving, and being deceived.' Anna Mae, the men behind this conspiracy are deceived by a great evil. They are consumed by it and they will not rest until those that believe in God have been eliminated."

"But, Zach, if the men that belong to that evil order release the virus Doctor Li has described, millions will die. What do we do?"

"I am going to follow through on what Admiral Hadley intended to do. I, Michael Draper, and Justice Tyler age going to take FBI Agent Mendez and we are going to go to Justice Tyler's friend at the highest court in DC. He will be..."

"What happened here?" Chief Justice Tyler sputtered as he exited the house, walked up beside Zach, and saw Justice Clark lying on the ground with a bright red stain on his stomach.

"Justice Clark here and an FBI agent started shooting at us as we were about to exit the house. I believe they intended to kill us, Michael Draper, and Doctor Li. Maybe even you now that you have learned about the conspiracy."

"I can't believe it. A supreme court justice is involved in this... this... anarchy?" Justice Tyler squatted down beside Justice Clark and shook him. "Walter. Walter. Wake up." Nothing. He shook him again. "Walter wake up! Tell me this isn't true."

He shook him harder, shouting in his face "Walter wake up! Talk to me."

Justice Clark's eyes fluttered several times and finally opened. "Matthew, you...,"

"Walter, what is it you want to say? Speak up."

"You... you... you...," Justice Clark wheezed. "You and all the self-righteous do-gooders like you are going to die. It's too late. You cannot stop it. Just a few days and you will suffer beyond your wildest nightmares."

"Walter, what is wrong with you? You are talking like a madman."

Justice Clark did not answer. He just glared at Justice Tyler with a deranged look on his face.

"Walter, tell me why you did this."

Justice Clark raised his head, grunted, and said, "*Annonçant le début du Nouveau Monde des Âges*." His eyes rolled back and his head thumped as it hit the sidewalk.

"What did he say?" Justice Tyler asked, looking up at Zach.

"It's French," Zach answered. "Something about a new world order, I think."

An ambulance screeched to a stop in the middle of the road, unable to get into the driveway. Two EMTs scrambled out of the cab, ran to the back of the ambulance, and unloaded a gurney. Bumping over the rough ground, they pushed the gurney up to where Justice Clark was lying.

"Get this piece of garbage out of here," Justice Tyler snarled.

Zach, James, Anna Mae, President Cantwell, and Justice Tyler watched the EMT's load Justice Clark's body onto the gurney. They lifted the gurney up, locked the wheels in place, and began pushing it back toward the ambulance. As the Ambulance sped away, two state Patrol cruisers screamed over the rise and slid to a stop at the entrance to the driveway.

"Dad, go see if you can move one of those cars out of the way," Zach hollered. "Tell the troopers we'll be ready to go in a minute or two. I'll go round everyone up. We need to get out of here."

James took off toward the cars blocking the driveway as Zach ran into the house to get Doctor Li and Michael Draper. James yanked open the door of the first car sitting sideways in the driveway. Finding no keys hanging in the ignition, he slammed the door and ran to the car sitting behind the first car. The keys were dangling from the ignition. He jumped in and started the engine. He put the car in gear, eased it up against the bumper of the first car, and pressed down hard on the accelerator. Blue-white smoke billowed out from behind the car. As he had hoped, he was able to push the first car off into the grass beyond the driveway. He shut the engine off, climbed out of the car, and raced off toward the house.

When he arrived at the house, the rest of the group was already loaded in the van waiting. He climbed into the passenger seat and slammed the door. Zach put the van in gear and drove to the end of the driveway. Justice Tyler stepped out of the van and had a short conversation with the trooper driving the lead cruiser.

"Let's go," Justice Tyler advised as he climbed back into the van. "One of the cruisers will take the lead. The other will follow behind us."

The lead cruiser roared around the van and hesitated, waiting for Zach to follow. Zach stomped on the accelerator. The three vehicles roared off into the early morning dawn.

Chapter Nineteen

Wednesday, Feb. 11th – 8:50 a.m. EST
Office of the Special Assistant to the President
1600 Pennsylvania Avenue
Washington D.C.

A hastily called meeting to discuss the necessary staffing changes, prompted by the sudden death of President Borden, had just concluded. Adam West, retaining his role as Special Assistant to the President, as expected, thanked the attendees, rose from his chair, and escorted them out of his office. He lifted his suit jacket off the hall tree standing in the corner, about to head off to another meeting on the other side of the White House complex. As he straightened the collar of his jacket, the cellphone in his pocket buzzed. He fished out the cellphone and checked the display. Surprised to see the same international number as earlier in the morning, he pushed the door to his office closed and locked it.

He swiped the Answer icon, pressed the cellphone against his ear, and said, "You are never to call me during the day unless specifically instructed to," he snapped. "What is the reason for this?"

"Sorry, is very important," an excited Doctor Huang Tang stammered. "Is much good news."

"Okay. Make it quick. I'm going to be late to a meeting."

"We have make good success with first test. We skip pilot plant. Go straight to final making of product."

"That is good news. When will the first run be ready for pickup?"

"Maybe twelve maybe fourteen hours. We have many people working."

"I will leave immediately. You must be certain it is ready when I arrive."

"I myself make certain, Mister West."

"You had better or you will suffer the consequences," West warned as he tapped the End icon.

Searching through the contacts list, he was about to make another phone call when the cellphone buzzed again. He swiped the Answer icon and said, "Hello." As he listened, his face contorted into a deep scowl. "When?" he demanded. He mashed the End Call icon and swore loudly.

He immediately opened the phone app again, searched through the contacts list, selected an entry, and tapped the Call icon.

"Yes," an irritated voice answered on the third ring.

"It's me again," West said. "I just got a call from China. They will have the first delivery ready in twelve to fourteen hours. We will have to move up the schedule. I'm going to leave immediately to make the pickup. Get the dispersal units ready for this weekend. That is when the crowds will be the largest. I will fly straight to your location. I will contact you when I am ready to return."

"We will be ready," Doctor Robert Mueller answered.

West ended the call and quickly made another call to the organizer of the meeting he was already late for. He explained that an emergency had come up and he would not be able to attend the meeting. Before the organizer could answer, he ended that call and made yet another call.

"EasyJet Air Service," a female voice answered.

"Adam West. I need to speak to Carl."

"One moment, please."

After several minutes of listening to soft jazz playing in his ear, West heard Carl's voice, "This is Carl. How can I help you?"

"This is Adam West. I need you to be ready to depart as soon as I get there. No more than forty minutes."

"Yes sir. What is the destination?"

"London," West answered, using the prearranged, coded city name.

"I will start the pre-flight on the overseas jet. It will be ready when you arrive."

"Good. I'm leaving now."

West ended the call and rushed to his desk. He pulled the bottom drawer open, unlocked a heavy metal box, and withdrew several large stacks of cash and a small vial of liquid. He stuffed the cash and vial in his jacket pocket and hurried out of his office. Stopping briefly at the desk of his administrative assistant, he advised her that he would be out of the office until further notice and would not be reachable. Half walking half running, he rushed to the parking area and climbed into his car. Panting from the exertion, he drew in several quick breaths to slow his breathing then started the engine, backed out of his assigned space, and roared out of the garage.

Rather than taking Interstate 695 which was plagued with construction, he headed east on New York Avenue Northwest. With the morning rush hour over, he could make better time once it connected with Highway Fifty. After glancing up at the rear view mirror several times, he became concerned when he kept seeing the same dark brown sedan several car lengths behind him. He was about to turn off onto a side street to see if the sedan kept following him. He checked the rear view mirror again and watched as the sedan turned left.

Remembering he had not called his wife, he dug out his cellphone and tapped a speed dial number. After a short conversation, he ended the call and followed the traffic merging onto the Baltimore-Washington Parkway.

Wednesday, Feb. 11th – 10:35 a.m. EST
Superior Court, District of Columbia, Criminal Division
Chief Judge's Chambers
500 Indiana Ave NW, Washington, D.C

Chief Judge Albert Goodridge looked up from the court docket he was scanning upon hearing a loud commotion outside the door to his office. His law clerk opened the door and poked his head in.

"Judge Goodridge, Chief Justice Tyler and a group of people are here to see you. He said it was most urgent."

"Yes, yes," Judge Goodridge acknowledged. "I have been expecting them. Show them in right away and find US Marshall Green and have him join us."

Judge Goodridge watched as Chief Justice Tyler and his group of five others hurried in through the door, followed by two state patrol troopers. Judge Goodridge instructed his law clerk to bring in some additional chairs. He waited while the chairs were carried in and everyone took a seat.

"See that we are not disturbed for any reason," Judge Goodridge ordered, looking at the two troopers. Once the troopers left the office and the door was closed, he looked at Justice Tyler and continued, "Okay, Matthew, I have the arrest warrants for FBI Special Agent Williamson and FBI Director Conroy prepared. I've climbed out on a very small limb here. Before I send a US Marshall to serve the warrants, I need an explanation that will justify their arrest."

"You won't need a warrant for Agent Williamson," Justice Tyler remarked. "He's dead."

"Dead? How?"

"We were about to leave my house and head here to your office when a car roared into the driveway. The driver jumped out and began firing at President Cantwell as he walked out of the house. It wasn't long before Agent Williamson drove in behind him and joined the fight. Fortunately, Secret Service Agent Waterhouse, Zach, and his Dad were able to outgun the two men. Williamson was wounded and died. The other man was wounded and should be at the hospital by now."

"Do you know who the other man is?"

"Oh, yes. I know," Justice Tyler snarled, anger boiling up inside his chest. "The other man is Supreme Court Justice Walter Clark."

"A Supreme Court justice is involved in this?" Judge Goodridge gasped. "Surely you must be mistaken."

"No, not a chance," Justice Tyler asserted. "Before the EMTs arrived and loaded him onto a gurney, I looked him in the eyes and asked him why he had done this. He was belligerent and said it was too late and that we would not be able to stop it. He threatened that we would suffer beyond our wildest nightmares."

"That sounds absolutely preposterous," Judge Goodridge protested. "Surely you don't believe that."

"Yes, Albert, I do believe it and you will believe it as well when you hear the rest of what we have to say."

"President Cantwell, did you hear what Justice Clark said?"

"Yes, Judge Goodridge, I heard every word," President Cantwell answered. "and I believe he meant exactly what he said. FBI Director Conroy is involved in an enormous conspiracy. But Conroy is only a tip of the iceberg, so to speak. He is being manipulated by people much higher than him."

"How do you know that?"

Zach motioned at President Cantwell. President Cantwell helped the still handcuffed Agent Mendez up out of his chair and directed him to stand in front of Judge Goodridge's desk.

"Who is this?" Judge Goodridge asked.

"This is FBI Agent Ramone Mendez," President Cantwell answered. "He is one of the men that attacked us at the safe house. He can tell you who ordered the attack. Go ahead, Agent Mendez. Tell the judge why you attacked us."

Trembling slightly, Agent Mendez swallowed hard and began. "Special Agent Williamson gave us... me and Agents Stokes and Purnell orders to find Admiral Hadley and kill him and anyone associated with him. He said we were to shoot on sight."

"Without any questions?" Judge Goodridge remarked.

"Yes, sir. He said Director Conroy had a shoot-to-kill order signed by the President. We were not to ask any questions. A clean up team would come as soon as we left and remove any evidence that would implicate the FBI."

"A shoot-to-kill order!" Judge Goodridge roared. "A clean up team removing evidence? The Director of the FBI ordering FBI agents to commit felonies? That's outrageous. Why would he do such a thing? This is just..."

"I believe Mister Michael Draper here can explain," Zach interrupted. "He can give eye witness testimony as to who is ordering all this."

Judge Goodridge shook his head, rested his chin on his hand, and motioned for Mister Draper to speak.

"I personally overheard Adam West, the President's communications director, on several occasions talking about a plan to release a deadly virus, mutated somehow to be extremely infectious and deadly. I don't understand a lot of the science behind it. Mister Templeton told me Doctor Li is one of the researchers that was involved. He fled from China and is here to explain how they intend to do this. West and Conroy also discussed silencing anyone that had obtained evidence that would prove the current administration had participated in massive election fraud during the previous election. Williamson and another FBI Agent by the name of Andrew Tiner murdered Edgar Cordell to recover the copy of the evidence he had in his possession. Cordell's body was found in a submerged car in the Little Bull Run River north of Manassas, Virginia. Gunshot wound to the head."

"Spreading a deadly virus, election fraud, and FBI agents murdering people," Judge Goodridge choked, looking from Zach to President Cantwell and back to Michael Draper. "I find it deeply disturbing that senior government officials could be involved in something so appalling."

"I have something even more shocking to tell you," Michael Draper added. "On several occasions West had meetings outside in the US Botanical Garden. I had confided in Speaker of the House Richard Kistler when I became aware of West's suspicious behavior. Speaker Kistler has an office on the top floor of the Rayburn House Office Building across the street from the Botanic Garden. Yesterday afternoon I followed West to a meeting he had there. He met a man sitting on a bench by the Rose Garden. I observed them with binoculars from Speaker Kistler's office. I had a significant hearing problem that was corrected several years ago. Because of that I had learned to read lips. The man sitting on the bench was Former President Bahram Oates. Oates ordered West to instruct Director Conroy to assassinate President Borden. He handed..."

"You can't be serious," Judge Goodridge interrupted. "You're telling me the Director of the FBI assassinated the President of the United States!"

"Yes, I am and I'm dead serious," Michael Draper responded. "Oates told West that someone named Schechter wanted *Eagle* silenced because he couldn't keep his mouth shut. *Eagle* is, or was, President Borden's code name. West looked stunned and asked Oates if Conroy belonged to the *Order*. Oates said he did not but that he would do anything for money. Then Oates handed West a small box and told him to be extremely careful. He told West the item inside contained some kind of toxin. I didn't catch the name. Then, just a few hours later President Borden is dead. I don't believe that is a coincidence."

"Who is this Schechter you mentioned?"

"I'm not really certain. The most I could find out for certain is that he is massively rich. There are rumors that he is part of an ultra secret organization of some kind. Just before the EMTs loaded Clark onto the gurney he swore some kind of oath or something. It was in French. Something about a new age or a new order. In view of what we have discovered about some *group* releasing a mutated virus, I believe we have to take his threat very seriously."

"What is your take?" Judge Goodridge asked, looking over at President Cantwell.

"I agree with Justice Tyler completely," President Cantwell answered. "We...,"

A soft tapping on the door interrupted President Cantwell's response. One of the state troopers eased the door open, allowing US Marshall Edward Green to enter. Marshall Green's eyes opened wide when he noticed the former president seated in front of Judge Goodridge's desk.

"Stand over here," Judge Goodridge ordered, pointing beside his desk. "Continue what you were saying President Cantwell."

"I was about to say we must act quickly. If the virus is half as deadly as Doctor Li has told me and it gets released, the death toll will be catastrophic. Doctor Li, tell Judge Goodrich why the virus will be so deadly."

Doing the best he could with his limited knowledge of English and Zach's assistance, Doctor Li explained how the mutated virus would combine with the host virus that had already been released and had spread worldwide. Judge Goodridge's face grew pale as he grasped the enormity of what would happen when the lab in China was successful and the mutated virus was released. Wringing his hands, Doctor Li apologized profusely for having had a part in the development of the virus. He pleaded with Judge Goodridge to grant him asylum.

"Of course I will approve your request for asylum, Doctor Li. I thank you for risking your life by coming to the United States to help expose this devilish plan." Judge Goodridge turned and looked at Zach. "What Doctor Li just described is sheer madness," Judge Goodridge gasped. "Why would anyone want to do such a thing?"

"A group of very evil individuals believe the world's population must be drastically reduced to save the planet," Zach answered. "We have to assume they have a vaccine to protect selected groups from the host virus so they would not be affected by the coming plague. Judge Goodridge, there may only be a few days left before the virus is completed. We must act immediately to stop this madness."

"After hearing Doctor Li's horrifying description of what the virus could do, I have to agree," Judge Goodridge remarked. He shuffled through some papers on his desk and handed one of the arrest warrants to Marshall Green and said, "I want you to go arrest FBI Director Jerome Conroy immediately. If he resists, shoot him!" Seeing the alarmed look on Marshall Green's face, Judge Goodridge added, "Marshall Green, I am not kidding! As you just heard, millions of lives are at stake! Go arrest Conroy now! When you have him in custody bring him here. Do not let him talk to anyone. We will hold him here until a new president can officially remove him and then he will be tried for treason. I will call Deputy Director of the FBI, Norman Bell and immediately promote him to be Acting Director of the FBI."

Marshall Green folded the warrant, stuffed it inside his jacket, and rushed out of the judge's chambers.

"Now we need to arrest Mister West and President Hayworth," Judge Goodridge announced. "Zach, you and James come here, stand in front of the desk, and raise your right hands. Chief Justice Tyler, join me please."

Together, Judge Goodridge and Chief Justice Tyler administered the oath, making Zach and James US Marshalls with full authority to arrest West and Hayworth. Judge Goodridge opened a drawer of his desk and pulled out two shiny gold badges and handed one to Zach and one to James.

"Now, go arrest those two criminals," Judge Goodridge snarled.

"There's one thing I need to do first," Zach said. "Give me just a minute."

Zach pulled out his cellphone, scrolled down through his list of contacts, selected one, and tapped the Call icon. Nervously tapping his foot, he waited for someone to answer.

"Naval Special Warfare. Petty Officer Olvera. May I help you?" Petty Officer First Class Glen Olvera answered on the third ring.

"Yes, Petty Officer Olvera, you can," Zach answered. "This is Senior Chief Zach Templeton, Retired. I need to talk to Rear Admiral Richard Jeffers immediately. It is critically important and time sensitive."

"Yes Sir, Senior Chief. Right away," Petty Officer First Class Olvera advised, recognizing Zach's name.

Less than a minute passed before Zach heard the Admiral's voice, "Zach Templeton, what a surprise. I didn't expect..."

"Sorry to cut you off, Admiral Jeffers" Zach interrupted, "but I have an urgent request." Zach turned and walked to the corner of the judge's chambers, lowered his voice and continued his conversation. After finishing his conversation, Zach joined James, Michael Draper, and Justice Tyler waiting by the door. President Cantwell stood off to the side of the group.

"Aren't you going with us?" Zach asked looking at President Cantwell.

"No," President Cantwell answered. "I think it would be best if I didn't enter the White House. It might look like I was behind this."

"I suppose you're right," Zach conceded. "We'll meet you later. I'll give you a call once we have West and Hayworth in custody."

Zach and James hurried out of the office on their way to arrest the President of the United States and his special assistant.

Wednesday, Feb. 11th – 11:20 a.m. EST
FBI Headquarters
900 Block Pennsylvania Avenue, NW
Washington, D.C.

US Marshall Edward Green stopped at the security desk next to the elevator and displayed his badge for the security guard on duty. Upon asking if the Director was in, the guard informed him that the Director had just concluded a meeting with two members of the Congressional Budget Committee.

"Would you like me to ask if the Director will see you?" the security guard asked.

"No," Marshall Green answered. "I will just slip in and announce myself. Give me a visitor's card that will access the top floor. After I go up, absolutely no one is to get on that elevator and no one is to know I was here. Do you understand me?"

"Yes, sir, I understand," the guard replied as he held out a plastic visitors card.

"That's good because if you were to let anyone on that elevator or tell anyone I was here, when I come back down I will arrest you for obstruction and haul you to jail," Marshall Green warned.

"Yes, sir," the guard answered. "I will see to it that no one gets on that elevator."

Marshall Green grabbed the card, turned, walked over to the elevator, and pressed the Up button. The elevator door slid open. He stepped inside, jammed the card into the access slot, and pressed the button for the ninth floor. The door slid closed and the elevator began its ascent. After a quick ascent, the elevator stopped and the door slid open. Marshall Green stepped out of the elevator, hurried to the Director's Office door, and entered. He flashed his badge at the administrative assistant and pushed the inner office door open without knocking.

Having just finished a budget meeting, Directory Conroy was bent over the budget report. He looked up, surprised by the unexpected interruption.

"What is the meaning of this," Director Conroy snapped. "You can't just walk in here unannounced. You have to..."

"Shut up and keep your hands on the desk," Marshall Greene shouted. "You are under arrest."

"You can't arrest me. I'm the Director of the FBI!"

"This warrant signed by Chief Judge Goodridge and Chief Justice Tyler says I can," Marshall Green yelled as he dropped the warrant on Director Conroy's desk.

Director Conroy snatched the sheet of paper off the desk and quickly read it. "I don't care what this lousy piece of paper says. You can't arrest me."

Director Conroy crumpled the warrant up and threw it at Marshall Greene. Reacting to the anger flaring inside him, Director Conroy yanked the top drawer of his desk open and grabbed for his weapon. Fully expecting the Director to do something desperate and stupid, Marshall Green already had his hand on the grip of his service weapon.

In a flash Marshall Green's weapon was out of the holster and pointing directly at Director Conroy's chest. "I wouldn't do that if I were you," Marshall Green shouted. "I will shoot you. Go ahead, give me an excuse."

Director Conroy's hand tightly gripped the semi-automatic lying in the desk drawer. "*Could he pull the pistol out and shoot the man standing two feet from his desk before he could get a shot off?*" he asked himself.

"I know what you're thinking and the answer is no. I already have several ounces of pressure on the trigger. I *will* shoot you before you even get your hand out of the drawer. I suggest you lift your hand out very slowly and place your hands flat on the desk."

Director Conroy vacillated with indecision, sweat beading up on his forehead. He desperately wanted to kill the man standing there threatening to arrest him, but he knew the man was right. Knowing he didn't stand a chance, his grip on the pistol relaxed. Very slowly he lifted his empty hand up out of the drawer and placed both hands flat on the desk.

"Wise move, Director," Marshall Green said. "Now, how would you like to do this? Do you want me to cuff your hands behind your back or would you like to have them cuffed in front of you so you can drape a coat over them? The choice is yours."

Marshal Green stared at Director Conroy, waiting for an answer. Receiving no answer, he said, "Well, I guess we'll do this the hard way."

As Marshall Green took a step forward, Director Conroy lifted his hands off the desk and held them in front of him. Marshall Green grabbed his pair of handcuffs and held them out. "Slip one side over your right wrist and interlace your fingers."

"You will pay for this," Director Conroy seethed as he did as instructed.

Marshall Green, still pointing his weapon at Conroy, used his left hand to slip the remaining cuff over Conroy's left wrist and snap it closed. He took a step backward and shoved his service weapon back into the holster.

"Where is your jacket?" Marshall Green asked.

"In the corner. On the hall tree."

Marshall Green, keeping his eyes on Conroy, stepped over and grabbed the jacket off the top peg. He draped it over the handcuffs and directed Conroy toward the office door. "Keep your mouth shut. Please, don't do anything stupid. It will only make matters worse."

Marshall Green opened the door and followed Director Conroy to the outer door. As he passed the administrative assistant's desk, Marshall Green handed her the visitor card and said, "See that the security guard downstairs gets this. Cancel all of Director Conroy's appointments. He will be out the rest of the day."

The two men exited the office and took the elevator to the basement parking level. Marshall Green loaded Director Conroy into the back seat, attached a second set of handcuffs to a metal ring on the floor, climbed into the driver's seat, and started the engine. He squealed out of the parking space and sped out of the parking garage, in a hurry to deliver his prisoner to Judge Goodridge.

Wednesday, Feb. 11th – 11:50 a.m. EST
Office of Special Assistant to the President
1600 Pennsylvania Avenue
Washington D.C.

After quickly passing through several security check points, Zach Templeton, Michael Draper, Chief Justice Tyler and two Capitol Police officers entered the Office of the Special Assistant to the President of the United States. Mister Draper led the group, stopping at the desk of Adam West's administrative assistant.

"Martha, is he in?" Draper questioned.

"No, Mister Draper he is not here," Martha answered. "He left just before nine-thirty. He said he would be out of the office until further notice and that he would not be reachable."

"Did he say where he was going?"

"No. He seemed stressed and very rushed. He literally ran out of the office."

"I'm going to check his office to see if there are any clues as to where he went."

Draper and Zach pushed the inner door open and entered West's private office. A quick scan of the desk revealed nothing but staffing reports spread out on his desk.

"It looks like he left in a hurry," Zach observed as he walked around behind the desk. "Look. One of the drawers is still open."

"Is there anything in it?" Draper asked.

"Just a metal box but it's empty. The key is still in the lock."

"He's been gone for an hour," Draper said, glancing at his wristwatch. "We'll have to track him down later. Let's hope Hayworth is in her office. Come on, let's go."

Zach and Draper exited West's private office and rejoined the group. Zach looked at one of the Capitol Police officers and said, "Notify the local police to put out a BOLO for West's vehicle."

"From the look of West's desk, it looks like he left in a big hurry," Zach informed the group. "There's nothing...."

"Zach, hold on. This might be important," Draper interrupted as he swiped the Answer icon on his cellphone.

"Are you certain?" Draper responded after listening for a few seconds. He listened again and said, "Okay. When?"

Draper ended the call, dropped the cellphone back in his pocket, turned, and looked at Zach with a worried look on his face.

"Well, what is it?" Zach asked.

"I had someone following West," Draper answered. "He drove to the College Park Airport and boarded a private jet. It took off no more than five minutes after he arrived."

"Did he see what kind of aircraft it was?"

"Yes, he watched West exit the flight center and walk over to one of the aircraft parked on the ramp. He said it was a Cessna Citation, tail number Nancy-two-three-six-Whiskey-Alpha. It took off and flew east for as long as he could follow it."

"Somebody, quick look up the number for the FAA," Zach shouted, holding his cellphone, ready to input the numbers.

Zach's dad yanked his cellphone out and tapped furiously. "I've got it," had said, then began to read off the numbers as Zach tapped them into his cellphone.

After explaining who he was and what he wanted and being transferred at least six times, Zach finally reached a department that could assist him. Zach told the man the departure airport, estimated time of departure, and aircraft type. The man put Zach on hold while he attempted to locate details of the aircraft and its flight plan. Zach waited nervously, listening to complete silence.

"Mister Templeton, are you still there?"

"Yes, I'm still here. What were you able to find out?"

"The flight log for College Park Airport in College Park, Maryland, shows a Cessna Citation departing at ten twenty-six a.m. According to the Flight Service Station, the only flight plan filed was for an eastbound VFR, no destination given."

"That's all?" Zach questioned. "There was no destination?"

"Sorry, that's all we have, Mister Templeton."

"Okay, thanks," Zach said as he ended the call.

"All the FAA could tell me is that a Cessna Citation departed at ten twenty-six a.m. eastbound with no destination given," Zach announced to the group.

"Where do you suppose he was going?" Zach's dad asked.

"China would be my guess," Michael Draper spoke up.

"If that's true, he's probably on his way to pick up the virus. That means we have only one day maybe two to stop this madness," Zach answered. "First, we have to go arrest Karen Hayworth and Leonard Morgan, her new Vice President. Who is going to fill the positions once we arrest them?"

"I have already called Richard Kistler, Speaker of the House of Representatives, and Christopher Post, President pro tempore of the Senate, to meet us," Chief Justice Tyler answered. "They will be waiting somewhere close to the Oval Office. Once the arrests have been completed, I will instruct them to join us. I will immediately swear in Kistler as President and Post as Vice President."

"This should be really interesting," Zach chuckled. "Let's go."

Fifteen minutes later Chief Justice Tyler, Zach, James, the Chief and Deputy Chief of the Capitol Police stopped at the desk of Muriel Carlton, the Secretary to the President. Justice Tyler quickly explained to Misses Carlton the reason for their presence. In no uncertain terms, he warned her to remain seated and to not interfere or she would be arrested as well. The deputy chief took a position outside the door as Zach and the team pushed the door to the Oval Office open and barged in.

"What is the meaning of this?" President Karen Hayworth sputtered. "I'm in the middle of..."

"Shut up and sit down," Justice Tyler shouted. Justice Tyler glared at the two people sitting in front of the President's desk with their mouths open. "Please stop whatever you are doing and leave. Go straight back to your offices and stay there until you are notified otherwise. Do you understand?"

The two men affirmed that they understood. Wasting no time, they closed their notebooks, grabbed their coats, and scurried out of the Oval Office.

"Zach, step out and have the secretary call the Vice President and tell him to come to the Oval Office immediately," Justice Tyler said.

Zach ducked out the door and ordered the secretary to tell the Vice President to come to the Oval Office immediately. Leonard Morgan, the newly appointed Vice President, made the short trip from his West Wing office in less than three minutes. Zach held out his US Marshall's credentials as the Vice President rushed into the secretary's office.

"Please join us in the Oval Office," Zach said, pointing toward the open door.

"What is going on here?" Vice President Morgan asked as he walked into the Oval Office and saw the crowd of people.

"Sit in this chair and be quiet," Chief Justice Tyler ordered. "We have some information to share with you and the President."

Vice President Morgan started to protest. The chief of the Capitol Police tapped his arm and suggested it would be wise if he sat and listened to what Justice Tyler had to say. Reluctantly, Vice President Morgan complied and sat down.

"President Hayworth, are you aware that Adam West is a member of a secret organization and is conspiring with a foreign government?" Justice Tyler asked.

"I know Adam is part of a group of some kind, but conspiring with a foreign government? I don't believe that." President Hayworth sputtered.

Justice Tyler directed Zach to share briefly what he had learned from Doctor Li about the virus and West's collaboration with the director of a virology lab in Ch'angsha, China. A look of shock and horror spread across the faces of the President and Vice President as Zach explained how deadly the mutated virus would be if it got released. The color drained from their faces when Zach described how hundreds of millions of people would die miserable deaths.

"Now, Mister Draper, will you share with the President and Vice President what you have learned," Justice Tyler directed as soon as Zach had finished.

"A little over a month ago I became concerned because of a conversation I overheard between Adam West and then Director of the FBI Jerome Conroy. To be brief, I personally witnessed and recorded several more conversations between them. I..."

"What do you mean by then Director of the FBI?" President Hayworth interrupted.

"Director Conroy has been arrested and is now in custody," Justice Tyler responded. "Now, be quiet and let Mister Draper finish."

"As I was saying, I also witnessed a meeting between West and former President Bahram Oates," Michael Draper continued. "During that meeting, Oates ordered West to have Director Conroy silence Eagle for good because he couldn't keep his mouth shut. Oates then handed West an object and told him to be very careful because it was coated with a toxin. We all know who Eagle is, don't we. Then, just a few short hours later President Borden is dead. And guess who's name was mentioned during the meeting to take his place."

"I had nothing to do with that," President Hayworth objected. "I had no idea what West was up to. He was..."

"Stop right there, Madam President. I warn you it will not go well if you continue to lie to us," Justice Tyler threatened. "Mister Draper show Madam President what we know."

Michael Draper slipped his cellphone out of his pocket, tapped the video player, and turned the screen toward President Hayworth. The color drained from the President's face as she watched the video of the meeting between Adam West and President Bahram Oates.

"See, Mister Draper has that and more. All on tape – times, places, and names. A certified lip reader will testify to what is being said. You will be charged as an accessory to the murder of President Borden."

"What?" President Hayworth gasped. "I don't know anything. I swear. I was only supposed to..." Shocked and horrified by what played out on the video, the President had slipped up and said too much.

"You were only supposed to what?" Justice Tyler challenged. Out with it or the handcuffs go on now and you go to prison for the rest of your life."

President Hayworth hesitated, not wanting to incriminate herself. She glanced to her right at Vice President Morgan. He shrugged his shoulders and looked away.

"Well, Madam President, I am still waiting. You have exactly one minute to tell me what you were supposed to do." Justice Tyler rolled his wrist over and stared at his wristwatch.

"You can't come here and try to threaten me. I will..."

"You *will* tell me what I want to know," Justice Tyler snapped.

President Hayworth stared at Justice Tyler but did not say anything.

"Time's up," Justice Tyler said. "Chief, put her in handcuffs."

"Wait... wait... You can't do this! You can't arrest me!"

"Oh, yes we can. You have committed a felony and you are going to prison unless you tell me what West ordered you to do. Start talking or go to prison. It's your choice."

President Hayworth again glanced over at Vice President Morgan who sat motionless, staring at the floor. Justice Tyler motioned at the chief to put the handcuffs on.

"I was supposed to help West get rid of Admiral Hadley," President Hayworth blurted out. "That's all he told me. I signed the arrest warrant."

"It wasn't an arrest warrant. It was a shoot-to-kill order."

"But he told me it was an arrest warrant. I wouldn't have signed a shoot-to-kill order for an American citizen."

"Oh, come now. Nobody is going to believe that. Your name is on the order. As a direct result of that order, Admiral Hadley is dead along with a highly decorated Secret Service agent and several FBI agents. You have committed a grave offense against American citizens."

"But I..."

"But nothing. When Conroy was arrested, he had the shoot-to-kill order bearing your signature in his possession. You are responsible for those deaths. You will be tried for murder and treason."

Vice President Morgan, looking deflated, sank in his chair and began shaking his head. Sitting behind the Resolute Desk, President Hayworth began to tremble and visibly wilt under the very real threat of being tried for murder and treason.

"To save the country the expense and embarrassment of a lengthy and most unpleasant impeachment trial and then a civil trial, I am going to make you a one-time offer that is good for the next five minutes. You and Vice President Morgan will be allowed to resign immediately and you both will agree to never enter politics again, ever. Not even to run for city dog catcher. Once you have resigned, you will be escorted out of Washington by the end of the day. Well, what do you say, Madam President?"

President Hayworth sat frozen for a long time. Realizing she had no other choice, she looked at Justice Tyler and said, "I accept." She turned and looked at Vice President Morgan. "How about you, Leonard?"

Vice President Morgan looked up from the floor. "I accept also," he affirmed without hesitation.

"President Hayworth, I want you to tell me everything you know about the mutated virus West and this secret order plan to release," Justice Tyler said.

"I don't know anything about a virus. I swear."

"You agreed to do West's bidding by helping him get rid of Admiral Hadley and you expect me to believe you didn't know what else he was doing."

"I didn't know anything about any kind of virus. I knew he had meetings with somebody from a big pharmaceutical firm in California. Bio... Bio... something. That's all I can remember. West knew I had several heated arguments with Hadley and had ordered him to resign. He used my dislike of Hadley to get me to sign the order. That's all I did. I swear."

"If we find out you are lying about any of this, we will hunt you down and see to it that you go to prison for the rest of your life. Do you understand?"

"Yes, I understand."

"Very well, let's get this done," Justice Tyler responded. He turned and looked at the Chief of the Capitol Police and said, "Chief, set up the video recording equipment. We need to get this on video."

While the chief got the video equipment ready, Justice Tyler instructed Zach to call Norman Bell, the newly appointed Director of the FBI, and have them locate a pharmaceutical firm with a name that started with Bio... and put them under surveillance.

The chief signaled that he was ready to record. Justice Tyler ripped a blank sheet of paper off a legal pad lying on the President's desk, thought for a few seconds, then quickly scribbled a few words on it and handed it to President Hayworth. She quickly read the few words written on the paper and looked up at Justice Tyler with a distraught look on her face.

"Lay it on the desk and read it verbatim," Justice Tyler ordered. "Okay, Chief, begin recording."

President Hayworth took a deep breath, swallowed hard, and began reading, "I, President Karen Hayworth, do herby voluntarily and immediately resign as President of the United States. To avoid prosecution for treason, I voluntarily agree and swear that I will never again seek political office of any kind. Should I do so, I understand that the charge of treason will immediately be reinstated and I will be arrested and tried for that crime."

"Vice President Morgan, it is now your turn."

Vice President Morgan stepped behind the Resolute Desk and repeated the same words as former President Hayworth.

"Chief, eject the memory card and hand it to me," Justice Tyler said. "Miss Hayworth and Mister Morgan stand by the door there and wait for your escort. Chief, call four of your most trustworthy officers and have them escort these two to their residences. Once they have gathered some basic items have them escorted to the safe house in Virginia. Arrangements will be made in the next two or three days to have them and their belongings relocated."

The Chief of the Capitol Police snatched his cellphone and called for a security escort. He ended the call and escorted the two disgraced politicians out of the Oval Office. Justice Tyler lifted his cellphone out of his pocket and instructed Richard Kistler and Christopher Post to come to the Oval Office immediately.

The two men, waiting in an unused office nearby, arrived in less than one minute. After quickly explaining what had just happened, Justice Tyler administered the oath of office to both men. Zach and Justice Tyler congratulated the two men and wished them well in their new offices.

Zach, James, and Justice Tyler exited the Oval Office and stopped in the secretary's office.

"What is going to happen when news of this political shakeup leaks out?" James asked.

"It's likely to be very, very bad," Justice Tyler replied.

"But what is more concerning is what will happen if we can't stop West and the virus gets released," Zach added.

The other two men grimaced and nodded their heads in agreement as they turned and hurried for the White House exit to attempt to locate

Adam West and prevent a catastrophe such as the world had never seen before.

Chapter Twenty

Wednesday, Feb. 11th – 1:15 p.m. EST
White House, Oval Office
1600 Pennsylvania Avenue
Washington D.C.

Sitting behind the Resolute Desk, Richard Kistler, the newly sworn-in President of the United States, knew he had to act quickly. When the press got wind of the political upheaval that had just occurred, the reaction would be swift and severe. To prepare for that eventuality, he called an emergency staff meeting to remove some of the current staff and appoint new people to fill critical staff positions. Muriel Carlton, the secretary to former President Hayworth, was genuinely relieved that Hayworth had been forced to resign and said she would be pleased to remain in her position as secretary to the President. Elated, President Kistler said he would be glad to have her on his staff.

Misses Carlton's first assigned task was to call former President Hayworth's and former Vice President Morgan's staff to the emergency meeting. President Kistler watched as those that had been summoned filed into the Oval Office. Bewildered looks flashed between the attendees when they saw who they thought was Speaker of The House seated in the President's chair. President Kistler motioned for quiet and waited for the buzz of puzzled conversations to cease.

"I can see that everyone is shocked to see me sitting here," President Kistler began. "Miss Hayworth and Mister Morgan have resigned their offices effective immediately. They have resigned to avoid prosecution for treason and to save the country from the embarrassment of an ugly and protracted trial. They both voluntarily agreed to never seek political office again and have been escorted to an undisclosed location. I and..."

Several of the attendees interrupted, attempting to speak at the same time.

"Silence!" President Kistler barked. "The event is over and done. There will be no discussion. I and Christopher Post have been sworn in by Chief Justice Matthew Tyler. It is imperative that we prepare for the public fallout that will most certainly come. I *must* have a staff that I can fully depend on. With that in mind, any of you that feel allegiance to Hayworth or Morgan and feel you cannot work with me or Vice President Post will be allowed to immediately resign and agree to never enter politics again, EV-

ER! Those that choose to resign now will sign a document stating those conditions. Once signed, you will receive a cash payment equal to six month's salary. Are there any who wish to resign?"

Donald Walsh, Hayworth's Chief of Staff, immediately lifted his hand in the air and made his way to the front of the crowd. Andrew Holt, Director of the US Secret Service, quickly followed.

"Very well, gentlemen," President Kistler acknowledged. "Step out into the secretary's office and wait. Are there any others?"

Two more attendees made their way to the front. They were also instructed to exit the Oval Office and wait. President Kistler looked from face to face, waiting for anyone else to accept the offer.

"The offer is still open for the next few minutes. Anyone that wants to still has the opportunity to resign. I assure you when the news hits the media, the reaction will be unsettling to say the least. There are things I cannot tell you at this time. Believe me when I say difficult times lie ahead. Be assured, those that choose to stay will be challenged immensely. Is there anyone else that wants to resign?"

President Kistler noticed someone in the back of the crowd lift her hand in the air. "Fine, please join the others in the secretary's office and wait." President Kistler waited, looking from face to face of those still remaining. "If you resign after this offer closes, you will get nothing except whatever vacation hours you may have accrued. Anyone else? Quickly, the offer is closing."

Seeing no one else desiring to resign, he thanked those remaining and advised them that there would be another meeting at four. They were instructed to bring ideas that would help formulate a plan to attempt to save the Republic. After instructing them to not divulge details of what happened until they were told it was okay to do so, he dismissed the group. President Kistler followed the last person out into the secretary's office and informed Misses Carlton of the details for those that desired to resign. An HR representative was summoned to accompany the group to Human Resources. Once agreements were signed, those resigning were to be escorted from the building.

President Kistler returned to the Oval Office. He and Vice President Post began the task of identifying individuals to fill the role of Chief of Staff and Director of the US Secret Service.

Two individuals were quickly identified. While Vice President Post walked to the other side of the Oval Office to make phone calls to those individuals, President Kistler grabbed the phone, intending to call the Chinese premier to see what he knew about the plot to create a mutated virus. About to tap in the number, he remembered there was a large time difference. A quick mental calculation told him it was only three AM in China.

The phone call to the Chinese Premier to expose what he knew about Hunan University and the biolab would have to wait.

Wednesday, Feb. 11th – 8:20 a.m. HST
Naval Special Warfare Command (WARCOM)
SEAL Group Three
Pearl Harbor, Hawaii

SEAL Team Three, having the geographic responsibility for the Middle East and SEAL Team One having responsibility for the Western Pacific, had received a priority one alert, within minutes of Zach's call to Rear Admiral Richard Jeffers, Commander Naval Special Warfare Forces, based in Pearl Harbor, Hawaii. Rear Admiral Jeffers had immediately notified Lieutenant Commander Thomas Watkins, Unit Commander, SEAL Team One. Their conversation was short and concise, outlining the special requirements of a high-priority, cross team response.

Lcdr. Watkins, Unit Commander SEAL Team One, scanned the brief notes he had scribbled during the phone call, quickly determining the three other individuals that would accompany him on the urgent mission. His selections were made based on each individual's unique combat skills. First would be James Wei, SCSWO, (Senior Chief Special Warfare Operator), because his mother was Chinese and he spoke fluent Chinese. Second would be Rudy Sanders, SWO1, (Special Warfare Operator First Class), because he was a demolitions expert. Rounding out the four man team would be Lieutenant Albert Chang, SEAL Team Three platoon leader, because of his skill with the RAD M91A2 sniper rifle. Like Senior Chief Wei, Lieutenant Chang was also fluent in Chinese.

Lcdr. Watkins instructed Boatswains Mate Second Class Chris Talley to locate the three individuals, have them pulled from their training sessions, and escort them to command headquarters on the double. While waiting for the men to arrive, Lieutenant Commander Watkins picked up the phone and made a call to the flight line. He hung up the phone and gathered the maps they would need and began developing a plan.

Slightly over fifteen minutes later, BM2 Talley and the three men rushed into the room, breathing heavily from their mad dash from the training facility.

"Have a seat gentlemen," Lcdr. Watkins said, pointing at the chairs sitting in front of his desk. "We have a priority one alert mission. Petty Officer Talley, I am waiting for a photograph to arrive. The instant it arrives make three copies and bring them to me.

"Yes, Sir," BM2 Talley acknowledged as he backed out and pulled the door shut.

Lcdr. Watkins continued, "Our task is to locate and return a certain individual by the name of Adam West. He is, ah.. was the Special Assistant to former President Hayworth. Yes, you heard correctly," he said holding up his hand to ward off any questions and continued, "She and Vice President Borden have both resigned effective immediately. They, Adam West, and others are involved in a conspiracy that involves an extremely deadly virus. West is believed to be on his way to a level four biolab in Ch'angsha, China, to pick up that virus. I believe we have the advantage because we are a good deal closer to China than he is. Once we intercept him, Petty Officer Sanders, Senior Chief Wei, and I will proceed to Ch'angsha and destroy the lab. Once that part of the mission has been accomplished, we will return West to the US and turn him over to the authorities."

Three raps on the door. "Enter," Lcdr. Watkins answered.

BM2 Talley pushed the door open, hurried over to the desk, and handed the photos to Lcdr. Watkins.

Lcdr. Watkins stood and handed a photo to each one of the men.

"This is a recent photo of Mister West. You can familiarize yourself with his face during the flight. Now, grab your GO bags and double time it to the flight line. We have an aircraft waiting."

The chairs noisily banged together as the men jumped up and followed Lcdr. Watkins out of the room to retrieve their GO bags. Running full speed, they arrived at the equipment room. Each man grabbed his specific GO bag, pivoted, and ran back out the door, headed for the flight line as fast as they could run. Arriving at flight operations, they ran through the hangar and out onto the flight line.

A two-tone, blue and white C-37B, an enhanced military version Cessna Gulfstream G550, sat on the ramp, engines already running. The four men ran up the stairs and into the aircraft. Waiting just inside the forward hatch, the copilot pulled the hatch shut and advised the men to be seated. Before the copilot could get into the cockpit and strap himself in, the aircraft began taxiing toward the duty runway.

The aircraft, having already been given priority clearance for takeoff, taxied directly to the active runway as traffic ahead of them moved out of the way. Without stopping at the threshold, the aircraft turned onto the runway. The pilot pushed the throttles all the way forward. The sleek jet roared down the runway and went wheels-up at eight fifty-six AM.

Wednesday, Feb. 11th – 11:48 p.m. EST
White House Plantation Road
Bluffton, South Carolina

An exhausted Zach Templeton turned onto the lane for his and Anna Mae's house and drove up beside the porch. He turned off the engine and leaned his forehead on the steering wheel, a deep sigh escaping from his lips. It had been a long, grueling, five hundred sixty-four mile drive from Washington, D.C. Stopping only long enough for bathroom breaks, refueling, quick walks to let Tripp stretch his legs, and time to grab some salty and sweet snacks, they had driven straight through, hoping to avoid the chaos that was already beginning to spread.

They all knew the news of the political upheaval would leak out eventually, but they had not expected the news to leak out within hours. Catching spotty news reports as they drove nonstop, they learned someone had almost immediately leaked the news. More than likely one of former President Hayworth's disgruntled staff members that had chosen to leave voluntarily had tipped off the press. Once the news had leaked out, it had spread like a wildfire in a hurricane. Riots and demonstrations were breaking out in many of the big cities. One news report they had tuned in to during the drive to South Carolina blamed newly-sworn-in President Kistler and other unnamed individuals for illegally forcing ex President Hayworth and ex Vice President Morgan out of office.

The "talking heads" in the main stream media, ardent supporters of the previous administration, were making the situation worse by non-stop attacks on the new administration, reporting that the forced resignations were nothing less than a political coup.

Zach climbed out of the car, opened the rear door, and let Tripp out. The redbone hound took off like a flash and disappeared into the darkness, happy to be home and in familiar surroundings. Zach reached in and picked up Mazie who was fast asleep.

"I'll go lay Mazie down on her bed then I'll come back out and help upload the luggage," Zach said. "Anna Mae, see if you can round up Tripp. I'm sure he would like something to eat."

Zach stepped up on the porch, pulled the screen door open, jammed his key into the lock, and unlocked the door. Stepping inside, he took a deep breath. The house smelled stale, having been shut up. He flipped the light switch on and made his way through the living room and into Mazie's bedroom. Gently, he laid her down and pulled a cover over her. He turned around and hurried back outside to assist with the luggage.

"Do we need to unload everything?" Zach asked, seeing his dad bent over, reaching into the trunk.

"Yes," James Templeton answered. "We'll need to make as much room for food as we can. I suggest only two suitcases for you, Anna Mae, and Mazie. Take warm clothes. Stuff them as tightly as you can. We'll have to conserve on heat. We don't know how long this madness will last. We left a few things at the cabin the last time we were there. I and your mother will just have to make do with what we have."

"Where is your cabin?"

"It's deep in the Pisgah National Forest, near the White Rock Trail-head."

"How long do you think it will take us to get there?"

"Probably a little over six hours. That is if we don't encounter any trouble along the way. With the riots breaking out we don't know what we might run into."

"What's our route?" Zach asked.

"The quickest way is the interstate through Columbia and up to Charlotte. Then Highway Three-twenty-one. The most likely places where we could run into trouble are the bigger cities."

"Can we afford to take time to catch a little sleep?"

"I don't think so. If the news reports are right about the growing unrest, the sooner we get to the cabin the better."

"We don't have much food in the house. Can we afford to take the time to go grab some?"

"It would have to be quick," James advised. "Is there anything close?"

"There's a twenty-four grocery store on the south side of Hardeeville. We could get there and back in a little over an hour."

"Okay. Let's get this stuff unloaded quickly. Margaret can help Anna Mae get packed."

Zach and James grabbed all they could carry and headed for the house. Zach carried his and Anna Mae's bags upstairs to their bedroom. While James went back to the car for the last of the luggage, Zach told Anna Mae to pack as much as she could into two suitcases. He told her they would be leaving for his Dad's cabin as soon as they returned from the grocery store.

"Zach, be careful," Anna Mae cautioned as Zach turned and started toward the door.

He stopped, turned around, and gave Anna Mae a hug and kissed her. "We'll be careful. We shouldn't have any trouble in a little town like Hardeeville. We'll be back in a little over an hour. Be ready to go."

"We'll be ready," Anna Mae said. "While you're there, grab a bag of dog food. I just gave the last we had to Tripp."

"Will do," Zach answered as he turned and hurried out the door.

Anna Mae whispered a quick prayer as she watched Zach disappear through the door.

"Mommy, where's Daddy going?" a sleepy Mazie asked.

"You should be sleeping," Anna Mae said as she reached down and picked Mazie up. "Daddy and Grandpa are going to get some food. Then we are going to go to Grandpa's cabin."

"Why?"

"It will be safer there."

"Can I take Raffee?"

"Of course you can, sweetie. Margaret, can you take Mazie while I go upstairs and get packed?"

Margaret took Mazie and carried her into the living room. Anna Mae rushed up the stairs with Tripp close behind. Fifteen minutes later Anna Mae dragged two overstuffed suitcases down the stairs and set them by the front door. Another ten minutes and she had all the food she thought they would have room for packed in boxes and sitting by the front door.

Sitting in the living waiting for Zach and his father, James, to return from their supply run, Anna Mae and Margaret had both drifted off to sleep. They both jumped, startled by the opening of the front door.

"Is everyone ready?" Zach asked as he stepped into the living room.

"All packed and ready to go," Anna Mae answered. "The bags and food are sitting there by the door. How did your shopping trip go?"

"You wouldn't believe it," Zach said, shaking his head. "It hasn't even been a full day and the shelves were almost bare. A fight broke out over the last few bottles of water. There was a loud argument over something near the front of the store. Dad and I got in, grabbed a few items, and got out as quickly as we could. It's not much but it will have to do."

"It's already hit Hardeeville," Anna Mae gasped. "Then we need to get out of here."

"I absolutely agree," Zach concurred. "You and Mom carry the suitcases and food out to the car while Dad and I turn things off in here."

Zach opened the refrigerator and stuffed all the perishable items into a large trash bag and set it by the front door. James had pulled the range out and turned the gas valve off.

"Is there anything else?" James asked.

"Don't think... oh wait, the water," Zach answered as he headed for the utility room. He located the gas valve and the water valve and turned them both off. Making quick stops in the bathroom and kitchen, he opened the hot and cold spigots to relieve the pressure and prevent freezing. "I think that's it," he hollered at his dad, waiting by the front door.

Standing at the electrical panel in the kitchen, Zach turned on the flashlight in his hand and switched off the main circuit breaker. James exited the front door first. Zach grabbed Tripp's food bowl, twisted the lock on the door knob, pulled the door shut, and followed James out to the car.

"Come on Tripp. Let's go," Zach urged, trying to hurry the hound who had found something of interest in the yard. "Buckle up everybody,"

Zach advised as he settled into the driver's seat and started the engine. He put the car in reverse, turned around, and sped down the lane, heading for Hardeeville where they would intersect Interstate Ninety-five and head north.

Driving as fast as they dared while watching carefully for signs of riots or unrest, the first three and one half hours of their journey passed without incident. Traveling north on Interstate Seventy-seven, they entered the outskirts of Rock Hill, South Carolina, twenty-seven miles south of Charlotte, North Carolina. Suddenly, everything changed.

"Zach, look up there," James groaned.

"I see it," Zach said.

A large group of people swarmed across the road. Even from a distance, Zach could see many of the rioters carried what looked like baseball bats. Slowing down, he saw two men bash out the windows of a car blocked by the swarm. One of the men dragged the driver out and struck him with his bat. Everybody in the car jumped when they heard gunfire.

"What are we going to do?" Anna Mae wailed, holding Mazie tightly.

"I'll take the exit coming up and see if I can get around them," Zach answered.

Zach yanked the steering wheel to the right and pulled off the interstate onto the exit for Anderson Road. Not stopping at the end of the exit, he turned right, skidding sideways. He jammed his foot on the gas and sped off down the street, having no idea where he was headed. Less than a block away the street was completely blocked by another group of angry protestors. He jammed on the brakes and slid to a stop.

Zach jammed the car in reverse to turn around, but it was too late. The angry mob surrounded the car, shouting threats and insults. Zach and James reached down toward the floor, searching for their weapons.

Thursday, Feb. 12th – 6:59 p.m. ChST
14,000 Feet above the Pacific Ocean
Final Approach to Hong Kong International Airport

As soon as the C-37 aircraft took off from Hawaii and had reached its cruising altitude, Lcdr.Watkins instructed the team to grab some sleep while they had the chance. With just less than two hours left before they were to land at Hong Kong International, the copilot came out of the cockpit and tapped Lcdr. Watkins on the shoulder.

"Sir, just under two hours before we touch down," the copilot advised.

Lcdr. Watkins nodded his head, unbuckled his seat belt, and awakened the rest of the team. The team spent the remaining time looking over their maps and fine tuning their operational plan, then they changed into civilian clothes.

"Everybody back in their seats and buckle up," the pilot announced over the cabin intercom. "We'll be landing in about twenty minutes."

"Double check your gear," Lcdr.Watkins shouted over the noise of the aircraft. "Make certain you do not have any identifying information other than your false passports. No dog tags. No cellphones. No photos. Nothing. We'll get everything we need when we meet our CIA contact. Once we leave the aircraft and enter Hong Kong, we are completely on our own. As far as our government is concerned, we do not exist."

Each team member dug through their backpacks, removing anything personal that could identify them. The personal items were dropped into a bag being passed around. Lcdr. Watkins took the bag and placed it on the seat in front of him. One of the flight crew would lock the bag up as soon as they landed.

The team members watched the gleaming lights of the city of Hong Kong come into view as the aircraft dropped below the clouds. The aircraft banked to the right and began its final approach from the south, lined up on runway Zero-Seven Left. Bouncing in the heavy, humid air, the aircraft passed over the apron and settled out of the air. The wheels screeched as they kissed the runway's surface. The pilot engaged the reverse thrusters to slow the aircraft as it raced down the runway.

At the end of the runway, the pilot steered the aircraft onto the taxiway leading to the general aviation area. An airport ramp worker with a flashlight in each hand directed the aircraft to an open parking space on the parking ramp. The pilot shut down the engines and climbed out of his seat. He opened the forward hatch and waited for the SEAL team to make their way forward.

"Good hunting," he said as he took the bag of personal items from Lcdr. Watkins. "Look for parking area two. White cargo van. Li Fang Catering in red letters."

The SEALs filed out of the aircraft and made their way into the general aviation terminal. The false passports that had been provided worked perfectly. They all passed through customs with no problems. As they walked out of the customs area and into the main terminal, Lcdr. Watkins scanned the area, looking for a man with a blue ball cap. Seeing nothing, he kept scanning the terminal as the team walked toward the exit. Still nothing. He stopped and bent over, pretending to tie his shoe. As he straightened up, he saw a man wearing a blue ball cap rush out of a bathroom to his left. Their eyes locked. The man made a subtle nod to indicate that he had seen them.

"Okay, let's go," Lcdr. Watkins said.

The automatic doorway slid open and the team walked out into the sticky tropical air. A light drizzle added to the oppressive feeling as they headed for parking area two as the pilot had instructed. The man in the blue ball cap followed, lagging behind at a safe distance. The team reached the parking area and walked down the rows of parked vehicles until they located the white van parked at the end of one of the rows. Not far behind, the man in the blue ball cap rushed up and stuck his hand out.

"Ryan Bidwell, CIA," the man said. "Welcome to Hong Kong."

Lcdr. Watkins reached out, shook Bidwell's hand, and asked, "How far to the safe house?"

"At this time of day no more than fifteen to twenty minutes."

"Have you located the target?"

"Yes. He arrived too late to catch the bullet train to Ch'angsha. My partner followed him. He checked into the SkyCity Marriott."

"Do you have what we need?"

"Yes. Everything is at the safe house."

"Good. Let's go."

Bidwell and the SEAL team piled into the van and took off, arriving at the safe house seventeen minutes later. The SEAL team spent ten minutes selecting the weapons they would need. After another five minutes bringing Bidwell up to speed on their plan, they loaded the weapons and supplies into a large, gray SUV and departed for the SkyCity Marriot Hotel.

Bidwell drove the SUV into the hotel's parking lot, dropped Senior Chief Wei off at the entrance, and pulled around behind the hotel. Senior Chief Wei entered the hotel lobby and spoke in Chinese to the man behind the registration desk. He passed by the elevators and rushed to the end of the corridor. Pushing the panic bar on the exit door, he let Lcdr. Watkins and Bidwell in. The rest of the SEAL team stayed out of sight in the SUV.

"My partner said he hasn't left his room. Room eight-twenty-one," Bidwell whispered.

The two men hurried to the elevator and rode up to the eighth floor. Starting down the hallway, they heard a door open and close. They stopped in front of the vending machine. Pretending to look for the correct change to make a purchase, they watched a couple pass by and get on the elevator.

"Quick, before someone else comes," Lcdr. Watkins urged as they continued down the hallway.

Stopping beside the door for room eight-twenty-one, Lcdr. Watkins told Senior Chief Wei to pretend to be hotel management.

Wei rapped on the door three times and called out, "Sorry, is hotel management. Must speak to you." He rapped again. "Please. Is most important."

They heard the sound of the interior door lock being disengaged. The door eased open a crack.

"What do you...,"

Lcdr. Watkins brought his foot up, shoved the door open, and forced his way in. He brought his hand around from behind his back. A bright, blue-white flash lit up the room as he shoved a stun gun into Adam West's chest.

Chapter Twenty One

Thursday, Feb. 12th – 6:45 a.m. EST
Anderson Road
Rock Hill, South Carolina

Several of the members of the riotous mob began banging on the car's fenders with their ball bats, screaming obscenities and demanding food and money. Tripp lunged forward, put his paws on the back of the front seat, and snarled, showing his white teeth. Mazie screamed. Anger boiled up inside Zach as the fingers of his right hand curled around the grip of his pistol. With his other hand he reached over and pushed the gear lever into Park. Then he reached over and began to lower the window.

"Dad, let's make them back up," Zach shouted.

James rolled the passenger side window down, pointed the H&K submachine gun out the window, and fired two quick bursts into the air. Zach followed suit and fired two rounds from his ST1 Lawman .45 caliber pistol. The sudden, and unexpected, explosion of gunfire startled the screaming mob.

James and Zach opened the car door, climbed out, and stood beside the car. He fired at the ground in front of the parting crowd.

"If you do not back off and let us pass, you will die right here, today," Zach screamed. "Do you understand?"

A man that appeared to be the instigator of the mob raised his bat in the air, shouted something, and lunged at Zach. Zach leveled the ST1 Lawman at the man and pulled the trigger. The man shrieked and fell backward, a large red stain spreading down his leg.

"Anyone else?" Zach bellowed, advancing to the front of the car. He fired another shot several feet in front of the crowd. "Dad, they need some more convincing."

James pointed the submachine gun at the ground in front of the crowd and fired a short burst. "The next time won't be at the ground!" James shouted. He raised the barrel up and pointed it directly at the crowd. "Well, who wants to be first? Anyone? How about you there in the green shirt. Do you want to die today?"

James advanced a step and pointed the barrel of the submachine gun directly at the chest of the man in the green shirt. "Prepare to meet God," James shouted.

"No! No!" the man screamed as he turned and ran for his life.

Deciding that whatever the people in the car had was not worth their lives, the crowd folded in on itself and began moving away.

"Let's get out of here while we can," James yelled.

Both men leaped back into the car. While Zach jammed the car into gear and sped away, James hung half out of the window and fired another burst from the submachine gun, in case the crowd might change its mind.

Zach made a u-turn at the first intersection, passed under the interstate, and roared down Anderson Avenue. Speeding down the street, he looked over at James. "Dad, see if you can get GPS on your cellphone and find us a way around Charlotte."

James fished his cellphone out of his pocket and tapped furiously on the screen. "Come on! Come on!" he urged. "Okay, I've got it. We're on Anderson Avenue. Follow that until it turns into Highway Twenty-one. A mile or so after that it intersects with Highway Five. Take that toward the West. That will take us well around the city."

Zach followed his Dad's instructions, barley slowing down for stop signs or traffic signals. Soon, they left the city of Rock Hill and headed west, passing into rural farmland. Only then did Zach slow down and relax his hands on the steering wheel.

"Anna Mae, how is Mazie?" Zach asked, glancing over the seat.

"She's finally beginning to calm down," Anna Mae answered. "Zach, that was crazy. What is the matter with people?"

"They are scared. If they listen to the nonstop lies the media is spewing out, they are convinced the rule of law is breaking down. When the transportation system breaks down, the food supply will dry up. People will become desperate. We already saw that happen in Hardeeville. I'll bet the shelves are completely bare by now."

"What are we going to do?" Anna Mae fretted.

"We've got some food stored at the cabin," James said. "If we are careful, we should be okay for a while. The cabin is hidden deep in the woods. We'll be safe there. We just have to get there."

"Can't happen soon enough," Zach added. "Dad, watch the GPS and keep us on secondary roads. It will be safer if we avoid cities altogether. Everyone else, be alert. We don't want a repeat of what happened in Rock Hill."

Everyone nodded agreement. Tripp licked the back of Zach's neck. Zach reached up his right hand and scratched the hound's neck.

Thursday, Feb. 12th – 9:43 p.m. ChST
Hong Kong SkyCity Marriott Hotel
Hong Kong International Airport

The instant Adam West had opened the door Lcdr. Watkins had overpowered him and jabbed a stun gun into his chest. Senior Chief Wei had quickly stepped behind West and eased West's quivering body to the floor. Lcdr. Watkins closed the door and reengaged the lock.

"Here, put these on his wrists," Lcdr. Watkins said, holding out a pair of handcuffs.

With the handcuffs in place, they dragged West across the room and lifted him up onto the bed. A large black ziptie went around his ankles.

"Do we gag him?" Senior Chief Wei asked.

"No. I want to hear what he has to say. He shouldn't be out too long."

Lcdr. Watkins dragged a chair over beside the bed, laid his pistol in his lap, and waited for West to wake up. A few minutes later West stirred. He batted his eyes open and closed several times as he came out of the high-voltage induced fog.

Realizing he was bound hand and foot, he sputtered, "What is this? You have no right. I'll..."

"You will shut up and listen," Lcdr. Watkins threatened, jamming the muzzle of his M45C pistol into West's ribs. "You are alive only because you may be useful to us. Do you understand?"

"You can't do this!" West howled. "Do you know who I am?"

"Yes, I know who you are Mister Adam West, former assistant to the former president." Seeing the surprise erupt on West's face, he continued, "Yes, I said former. I have been informed that Hayworth and Morgan have resigned, effective immediately, to avoid prison. They were escorted from Washington in shame. Mister West, you are now a nobody and soon you will also be headed to prison for a very, very long time. Unless you choose not to help us. If that is the case, you will die here in China. It's your choice. Decide quickly."

West struggled violently against the bindings, but they did not budge. Panting from exertion and fear, he laid still, looking up at Lcdr. Watkins. "Who are you?"

"That is not important. All you need to worry about is if you are going to help us."

"I won't help you unless you tell me who you are."

"Too bad for you," Watkins snarled as he slowly screwed a sound suppressor to the muzzle of his pistol and placed it against the middle of West's forehead.

"That's going to make a horrible mess," Senior Chief Wei said. "Here, use this." He grabbed one of the pillows from the bed and held it out.

Lcdr. Watkins took the pillow and placed it over West's face then shoved the suppressor against the pillow.

"oomph, mawaw, uhuh,"

Lcdr. Watkins lifted the pillow. "What's that? What are you saying? You want to help us?"

Gasping and sputtering, West cried out, "What do you want?"

"We are going to drive to Ch'angsha and you are going to help us get into the biolab."

"How do you know about the lab?"

"It doesn't matter. We know all about the plan to spread a mutated virus. You are going to help us stop it. We are going to destroy the lab."

"You're crazy," West stammered. "You'll never get away with it."

"Well then, I guess I just as well kill you right now my partner and I will disappear." Lcdr. Watkins pulled back on the hammer of his pistol. "Good bye, Mister West."

"No! Wait! I'll help you," West wailed.

"I'm glad you decided to help. I will see if I can arrange life in prison rather than a needle full of poison. Let's get him up and get going."

Senior Chief Wei grabbed West's shoulders while Lcdr. Watkins slid his feet off the bed. Together, they stood him up.

"I'm going to cut the tie around your ankles. If you try anything stupid, there *will not* be any warning. I *will* kill you."

The two men, one in front and one behind, marched West to the elevator. When they reached the first floor, they pushed West down the hallway and out the hotel's back door. They hurried across the rear parking lot and shoved West into the backseat of the CIAs asset's car.

Ryan Bidwell, the CIA asset, familiar with the roads and Chinese traffic laws, sped out of the parking lot and headed north out of Hong Kong, following Highway S3 on the west side of the city. Avoiding larger cities as much as possible they continued north on the expressway that ran north between Dongguan and Guangzhou.

The speed limit on Chinese expressways was posted as one hundred-twenty kilometers per hour. Having been in the country for over a year, Bidwell knew the Chinese police generally gave a tolerance of around ten kilometers. To be safe, he set the vehicle's cruise control at just six kilometers over the speed limit. He advised the SEAL team member riding in the passenger seat to be on the lookout for the characters *qiao su she xiang*, which indicated a speeding detection camera. As a precaution, Bidwell would switch off the cruise control and slow down to just under the speed limit until they passed by the detection camera.

Thursday, Feb. 12th – 11:49 a.m. EST
Highway 90
Colettsville, North Carolina

Exercising great caution to avoid cities and large gatherings of people, Zach had followed secondary highways that ran north and east of Morganton, North Carolina. Traveling east on Adoka Road, Zach stopped at the unincorporated community of Colettsville's one and only stop sign. He turned left onto Highway Ninety and passed a small general store with an old, beat up pickup sitting out front. A few hundred feet further north he passed a United States Post Office.

Only a handful of the original Gothic design houses that had been built during the "railroad fever" of the late eighteen hundreds still remained. Of that small handful, several stood empty, windows broken out, doors standing open, with yards overgrown with weeds. Most of the town's original houses had been torn down and replaced by wooden cabins of varying designs and sizes. Smoke curled up from several smokestacks, pooling high in the frigid air.

As they approached a faded sign advertising Johns River Valley Camp, James pointed at the sign and said, "Zach, be careful. The turnoff to Globe Road where it intersects with Racket Branch Road is really easy to miss. It's a little over a mile past that sign."

Zach sat up straighter and focused on the road ahead. Just as the road curved, Zach saw the sign and turned left onto Globe Road.

"Be careful, Zach," James piped up. "The road from here on is really rough and crooked and there are a lot of deer roaming the woods."

"Got it," Zach replied.

Driving more slowly, Zach followed the road, first left then back to the right then back to the left again. "Boy, you weren't kidding about it being crooked," Zach remarked.

The road straightened out as it entered the community of Gragg, North Carolina. Calling Gragg a community was quite generous considering it covered no more than a one-half mile radius of land. When they reached the edge of Gragg, the highway ended and turned into Edgemont Road, a dirt road with spots of gravel scattered here and there.

"Another mile and the road changes to National Forest Road," James advised. "After that the cabin is only another quarter of a mile. I'll tell you when to turn."

Back and forth, back and forth the car leaned as Zach followed the switchbacks through the trees. The road turned to the right and became more narrow. The last one-quarter mile was a rough, rock-strewn track more than it was a road. Zach slowed down, picking his way around large pot holes, waiting for his dad to tell him where to turn.

"There. Turn left right after that tree," James blurted out.

"Here?" Zach questioned, stopping in the road. "I don't see anything."

"Right there, just past that tree," James answered, pointing over Zach's shoulder. "I know it looks like nothing but weeds. The snow is covering up the tracks. There is a path there. Trust me."

"Okay," Zach said as he took his foot off the brake and steered the car off the road.

Knocking down fender high weeds, Zach drove around a dense thicket of Eastern Red Cedar trees and plowed through the drift of snow lining the edge of the road. Just as his dad had assured him, there were two tire tracks leading to a small cabin nestled between two large pine trees.

"Wow," Zach exclaimed. "You would never know it was here."

"That's exactly why I bought it," James chimed. "The heavy snow that has started falling will soon obscure our tracks."

Zach pulled up beside the cabin, turned the engine off, and let out a deep sigh. He tilted his head left and then right, trying to relieve the tension in his neck, partly because of the length of the trip and partly because of the narrow, winding roads. What had started out to be just over a six hour trip ended up taking over ten hours. Twice they had had to detour miles out of their way to avoid large crowds of people.

Zach and James worked at unloading the car while Anna Mae and Margaret entered the cabin and searched the pantry for something quick and easy to prepare for a lunch. Once the luggage and the food had been carried into the cabin, James went out behind the cabin and carried in some firewood. In less than five minutes he had a cheery, crackling fire going in the fireplace.

Zach stepped up onto the porch and stomped his feet to clean off the snow. He opened the door and hurried over next to the fire. "Brrr. It's cold out there. The fire feels great."

"Did you get the car out of sight?" James asked.

"Yes. I parked it behind the pile of dead trees behind the cabin. No one will be able to see it."

"Lunch is ready," Margaret Templeton, Zach's mom announced, sliding bowls of hot, steaming soup onto the table.

With lunch finished, Anna Mae and Margaret gathered up the dishes and left them sitting in the sink. Finally able to relax, Zach, Anna Mae, and Mazie settled on the coach beside the fireplace. Tripp circled twice and curled up on the rug in front of the couch. James and Margaret stretched out in the two recliners Enjoying the crackling warmth of the fire, everyone was soon fast asleep.

Friday, Feb. 13th – 8:33 a.m. ChST
Safe House
Ch'angsha, Hunan Province, China

Ten and a half hours from the time they left Hong Kong, Ryan Bidwell and the SEAL team arrived in Ch'angsha and drove straight to the safe house to meet Yijun Guo, the CIA Operative covering Hunan Province, China. The SEALs had been less than enthusiastic at having to ditch their weapons in Hong Kong. After much discussion, Bidwell had convinced them that getting caught with weapons should they get stopped by the police was not a risk they wanted to take. Bidwell assured the SEALs that Yijun would be able to provide anything they needed.

West was hustled into the safe house. His hands and feet were bound and he was gagged, then dumped in a tiny, musty smelling bedroom. The team's plan was to proceed to the biolab at Hunan University late in the afternoon, allowing them to take advantage of the darkness. While Bidwell and the SEALs rehearsed their plan for destroying the biolab, Yijun prepared a spectacular meal of local delicacies.

After finishing the delicious lunch, the team selected the weapons and supplies they would need, then went over their plan again to be certain each man knew his part and the fallback plan if anything went wrong.

With a few hours to spare, the team spread out in the safe house and grabbed some sleep. The mission would be dangerous and depended on each member being rested, alert, and ready for action.

Friday, Feb. 13th – 3:35 p.m. ChST
Safe House
Ch'angsha, Hunan Province, China

Dressed in civilian clothes, Ryan Bidwell, Lcdr. Watkins, and Senior Chief Wei went over their plan one final time. Confident they had all the details firmly in their minds, Lcdr. Watkins went to the bedroom to get Adam West. He cut the plastic tie from West's ankles and ordered him to stand up. After removing the gag from his mouth, he shoved West out the door and directed him into the small living room where the rest of the team members waited.

Looking at Special Warfare Operator First Class Rudy Sanders, Lcdr. Watkins asked, "Sanders, do you have all the explosives we will need?"

"Yes sir," Sanders answered. "I have my pack stuffed with all the Semtex I can carry. Fifty pounds should be enough to level a city block. There won't be anything left after we set it off."

The Semtex plastic explosive in Sanders's backpack was chosen because Semtex was very difficult to detect in a sealed container, and it could be easily molded into different shapes. Those properties made it the first choice of military units and also many terrorists.

"I also added some TBX, a thermobaric explosive," Sanders added. "The enhanced blast explosive will produce a huge, high temperature fireball that will sterilize anything in the containment area of the biolab."

"Good," Lcdr. Watkins responded. "Sanders, you and I will go in with West. Lieutenant Chang, you and Senior Chief Wei will stay outside with Yijun in case we need covering fire. Is everybody ready?"

Getting quick assent from everyone, the team exited the safe house and piled into Yijun's van. Lt. Chang grabbed a RAD M91A2 sniper rifle, chambered a round, and laid it across his lap. Senior Chief Wei shoved a magazine into his M-4 rifle and chambered a round. The M-4 rifles Yijun provided had been highly customized by Heckler and Koch, which included a flash suppressor with an optic site for improved accuracy.

Yijun started the engine, backed out of the driveway, and headed west toward the Xiangya Medical College. Eighteen minutes later Yijun pulled into a parking lot on the north side of the medical college, just a short two blocks from their destination. Lcdr. Watkins slid the side door open and hopped out, motioning for Adam West to get out. West, still handcuffed, swung his legs out and stood beside Watkins. Rudy Sanders climbed out of the back and joined them.

Watkins unlocked the handcuffs, removed them, and tossed them into the van. "I'm warning you, West," Watkins said. "If *anything* goes wrong, I promise you that you will be the first to die. Do you understand?"

"Got it," West grunted.

"Let's go."

In the growing darkness, the three men headed south toward the medical college building where the biolab was housed. They entered through the east entrance and walked up to the security desk.

"I need to see Doctor Tang," Adam West demanded. "It is urgent. I do not have time to waste."

"Doctor Tang notified security that you would be arriving," the security guard replied. "Sign the log and you may go right in. Also sign in your associates."

West snatched a pen from the desk and scribbled his name and two fake names for Watkins and Sanders. He dropped the pen back on the desk and started down the hallway.

"Great job," Lcdr. Watkins said once they were out of earshot of the guard.

At the end of the hallway, West jabbed the elevator's Up button. The door screeched open and the three men walked in and rode the elevator up to the fourth floor. Midway down a dimly lit hallway, West pushed open the door to Doctor Tang's outer office. To the SEAL team's advantage, Doctor Tang's administrative assistant had already left for the day. Crossing the outer office quickly, West shoved the door to Doctor Tang' private office open and strode in, followed by the two SEALs.

"Mister West," Doctor Tang exclaimed. "I not expect you so soon. You not tell me you bring friends."

"They are not my friends. They are experts in handling infectious biological materials. Let's get on with this. Is the virus ready for transport? Doctor Yu informed me it would be ready as soon as I arrived."

"Yes. Is ready," Doctor Tang answered with a puzzled look on his face, knowing Doctor Yu had not talked to West because he himself had informed West the virus was ready.

Sensing something was wrong, Tang became suspicious and backed up toward his desk. "These men not cleared. I not release virus."

West made a facial expression, trying to warn Tang. Frightened, Tang stepped behind his desk, jammed his hand into the top drawer, and pulled out a pistol. Sanders, hand resting inside his jacket, pulled out his M45C, .45 caliber pistol and fired two quick rounds into Tang's chest. Tang collapsed and fell over backward behind his desk. Even though Sanders's weapon had a suppressor screwed to the barrel, it still made a load noise in the confined space.

Watkins shoved his pistol in West's back. "Can you get into the biolab?"

"Yes, I can get in. The biolab is in the basement. It's never locked."

"Let's go," Watkins ordered, shoving West toward the door.

The three men rushed out of the office and headed for the elevator. Watkins kept his hand on West's back and his other hand inside his jacket, gripping his pistol tightly. They ran down two corridors then turned left to the elevator. Arriving first, Sanders jabbed the elevator's down button. With the door half open, Watkins shoved West inside and jabbed West with his pistol. West fished his security card out of his jacket pocket and jammed it into the access reader. The door whooshed closed and the elevator began its descent.

Upon reaching the basement level., the door slid open. As they hurried off the elevator, Sanders's jacket flapped open. Seeing the weapon in Sanders's hand, the security guard became alarmed. He jumped up, pulled his weapon, and fired.

Chapter Twenty Two

Friday, Feb. 13th – 3:20 a.m. EST
Mountain Cabin
Deep in the Woods

Thump. Thump. Thump.

"Zach, what's that noise?" Anna Mae whispered. "It sounds like someone walking on the porch."

Zach sat up in bed and tilted his head, listening for sounds from outside. "I hear it." He slipped out of bed, pulled his trousers on, and grabbed his weapon. He tiptoed across the room and tapped his dad on the arm. "We've got visitors. Someone's outside on the porch."

"Huh?" his dad asked, groggy from sleep.

"Visitors. On the porch," Zach whispered. "Get your weapon."

Jarred awake, James snatched his weapon off the side table, threw on his trousers, and joined Zach at the door.

Tripp, awakened by the activity, stood next to Zach, a rumbling growl emanating from deep within his chest.

"Go out the back door and come around the side of the cabin," Zach ordered, holding up five fingers. "In five, I'll open the door. Take Tripp with you."

James turned, scurried across the room, and slipped quietly out the cabin's back door, holding on to Tripp's collar.

Zach counted to five and shoved the door open. He heard the sound of heavy footsteps running on the porch.

James, breathing through his mouth to cut the sound, stood waiting at the edge of the cabin. As the intruder was about to jump off the porch, James turned Trip loose. The redbone hound took off in a flash and caught the intruder's leg as his foot hit the ground. The intruder lost his balance and slammed into the snowy ground. Tripp let go of the man's leg and lunged at his throat.

Zach jumped off the porch and grabbed Tripp's collar. "Tripp, Down! Down!" Holding the angry hound back, he yelled at his dad, "Cover him and get him up."

James bent down and pointed the barrel of his pistol at the man's face. "I don't want to shoot you, but I will. Get up and keep your hands where I can see them."

Moaning loudly, the intruder, a man in his early thirties with a scruffy beard, rolled to his side, and pushed himself up. Holding his hands up, he turned to face Zach and James.

"I was just looking for some food," the man stammered. "I didn't see a car. I didn't think anyone was here. The grocery stores are plumb out of food. The shelves are completely bare. My kids are hungry. I didn't mean no harm. Honest."

"Dad, What do you think?" Zach asked.

"I say we believe him," James replied. "We know the part about the grocery stores is true."

"Have you got any weapons?" Zach asked, patting the man's coat pockets.

"No sir. I wouldn't have hurt anyone. I'll just go and I promise I won't bother you again."

James shoved his pistol behind his back and shot Zack a knowing look. Zach nodded. "Come inside where it's warm. I think we can spare some food. I hope Tripp didn't hurt you."

"No, but he sure scared the bejeebers out of me."

Together, they stepped up on the porch and stomped the snow off. Zach opened the door and followed his dad and the man inside.

Seeing Margaret, Anna Mae, and Mazie huddled in the corner, Zach called out, "It's okay. This man didn't think anyone was home. He was looking for food for his kids." Zach turned toward the man, "How about a name."

"My name's Jessie Ray Kirby. My wife, Mary Beth, and I live in a small cabin about two miles back up the road."

"I'm Zach Templeton. This is my Dad, James. Over there is my Mom, Margaret, my wife, Anna Mae, and our little girl Mazie."

"Pleased to meet you folks. I'm real sorry if I scared you folks."

"How many kids do you and your wife have?" Margaret asked.

"We got five youngins. Range in age from two to ten. We don't go to the store often. It's hard to find work up here in the mountains. I guess something big must a happened. Got to the little store about a mile from our place this morning and fist fights were breaking out over what little food was left. Craziest thing I ever seen."

"Yeah, we saw the same thing down in South Carolina yesterday," Zach said. "There's been a major political shake up in Washington. Things are probably going to get worse."

Margaret and Anna Mae went through the cupboards and selected some food items and packed them in a box. Anna Mae carried the box over and held it out. "Here, Mister Kirby. I hope this will help."

"After what I done?" Mister Kirby sniffled, barely able to talk.

"We're glad we can help. We've all been through hard times. The Lord has provided for us. We must be willing to share."

"Mary Beth and I surely do thank you folks. This will help. A lot."

With the box tucked under his arm, Mister Kirby walked over and shook hands with both Zach and James.

"Thanks again," he said. "I don't know what we would have done if you folks weren't so kind. I'm sorry for trying to break in."

"Do you need a ride home?" Zach asked.

"No. My car is parked about a half-mile back up the road."

As Mister Kirby put his hand on the door knob to leave, James laid his hand on the man's shoulder. "Don't tell anyone we're here. If you need more food, come back, but do it at night so no one will see you."

"You'll give us more food?"

"I think we have enough to share."

"Thank you so much Mister James, Mister Zach. I promise I won't tell a soul you're here."

"Glad we could help," James said as Mister Kirby walked out the door and disappeared into the darkness.

Zach turned and looked at his dad with a perplexed look on his face. "Are you sure we have enough food to share with a family of seven?"

"Yes, I'm sure," James answered with a twinkle in his eye. "Now let's all go back to bed and see if we can get back to sleep."

Friday, Feb. 13th – 4:51 p.m. ChST
Zhongnan University Level-4 Biolab
Tongzipo Road, Yuelu District
Ch'angsha, Hunan Province, China

Shaking from fear and the massive slug of adrenaline coursing through his veins, the security guard's first shot at Sanders went wide of its target, striking Adam West just below his left eyeball. Dead instantly, West crumpled to the floor at Lcdr. Watkins's feet without so much as a twitch. Special Warfare Operator Rudy Sanders jerked as the round from the guard's second shot tore into his side. Watkins and Sanders both opened fire at the guard.

Each firing multiple times, they riddled the guard's body with rounds. He pitched forward and fell across the desk. Blood soaked the papers scattered on the desk and ran down the side of the desk, pooling on the floor.

"Are you okay?" Watkins asked, seeing the dark red stain on Sanders's side.

"I think so," Sanders gulped, pressing his hand on the wound.

"Quick. Let's go," Watkins urged. "We need to get this done and get out of here."

They raced down the hallway, slammed the door to the biolab's anteroom open, and stopped in the biolab's prep room. On their right, they saw the bulky biohazard suits hanging on their storage hooks.

"I'll go," Sanders panted. "There isn't time to suit up. The sound from the gunfire may have alerted someone." He opened the decontamination room hatch, stepped in, spun the locking mechanism, and pulled the door to the inner high-containment area open. Sanders entered the high-containment area and began hurriedly placing explosive charges and wireless timers in strategic places.

While Sanders was busy in the high-containment area, Watkins placed multiple charges around the biolab's work area. Sanders stumbled out of the biolab's prep room without bothering to pull the inner hatch closed and rejoined Watkins. "All done," he gasped.

"Me too," Watkins said as he lifted a remote out of his pocket and pressed a red button. "Let's get out of here."

On the way back to the elevator, Watkins yanked out his cellphone and tapped a speed dial number.

"I'm ready and waiting," Yijun answered on the first ring.

"Sanders got hit," Watkins blurted. "We'll be coming out the northeast side of the building. Meet us at the first street north of the medical building. We have only five minutes."

Watkins and Sanders rode the elevator up to the ground floor and hurried to the closest exit.

Outside the building, they turned left and hurried for the street where Yijun was to meet them. Yijun was just turning the corner. He saw the two men racing toward the street, screeched to a stop, and waited as they jumped into the back seat. Yijun stomped on the accelerator and headed east, back toward the safe house. Watkins eyes were fixed on the watch on his wrist. "Now," he shouted.

Three seconds later an enormous explosion created by enough explosives to level a city block turned the entire medical building into rubble. A few milliseconds later the thermobaric explosives ignited, creating a monstrous fireball. The building vibrated for a few seconds then fell inward on itself.

The massive shock wave rocked their vehicle as it sped down the street. Already four blocks away from the conflagration, they would be ignored by the emergency units rushing to the scene.

With the biolab, scientists, design documents, lab notes, and the virus itself incinerated, the next objective was to put the SEAL team's escape plan into effect and leave China as quickly as possible.

Epilogue

Mountain Cabin
Near White Rock Trailhead

Not far south of the border of Tennessee, deep in the Pisgah National Forest, the Templeton family's mood was somber. Listening to a radio newscast, they learned that after the first round of news leaked out, there had been another major shakeup caused by the arrest of several dozen more US political leaders. There was one piece of good news. They learned from former President Paul Cantwell that the biolab in Ch'angsha, China, had been turned into rubble. Cantwell informed them that all records, test results, and materials related to the mutated virus were incinerated by the blast as well as the researchers that had been involved. The threat from the mutated virus had been eliminated.

However, the good news also came with some sad news. Zach's good friend and former comrade, Rudy Sanders died before the team could return to the CIA safe house.

The country would be saved the expense of a protracted trial of Adam West as he had died during the siege of the biolab. Unfortunately, any knowledge he had of the identity of other order members died with him.

Deep in thought, Zach flinched when his cellphone buzzed and began to dance. He lifted it off the side table and answered, "Zach Templeton."

"Zach, this is Rear Admiral Jeffers. I thought you would like to know the SEAL team successfully exited China and have arrived back in Pearl."

"That's great news, Admiral.. I'm really sorry to hear about Rudy."

"Yes. We are all deeply saddened. It is a great loss to the team. He will be greatly missed."

"Thanks for letting me know, Admiral."

"There's more, Zach. I can't go into all the details, but I was certain you would want to know that SEAL Team One out of Little Creek, Virginia, with the help of the CIA, was dispatched to hunt down and eliminate any members of the Order of Light they could find."

"I hope they get them all," Zach snapped.

"Well, the last I heard, they only located two of the ten members. They found Schechter and Oates together. Seems they contracted and succumbed to a deadly disease, a bullet in their brain."

"That's too bad, Admiral. What about the others?"

"We believe they have gone deep underground and will probably never be found. Schechter and Oates refused to talk and took whatever knowledge they had to the grave. West is dead. So, that is also a dead end. At this time, there are no other leads that we know of."

"Well, then, what about China's role in this?"

"The Chinese President has contacted President Kistler. China is threatening to declare war over the destruction of the biolab. So far, President Kistler has denied America's involvement. All military forces have been put on alert because President Kistler raised the DEFCON level. Only time will tell if war can be avoided. That's all the news I have for now, Zach. If I hear of anything else, I will let you know. Thank you for what you have done, Zach."

"It was my privilege, Admiral."

"Smooth sailing and calm seas, my friend."

Before Zach could answer, the cellphone went dead. He tapped the End call button and laid the cellphone back on the table. Zach was saddened that he would not be able to attend the funeral. Butte, Montana, Rudy's home town, was just too far away. Traveling even short distances had become dangerous given the turmoil going on in the country.

Zach stood up, stretched, grabbed his jacket, and headed for the cabin's back door. He stepped outside onto the small, rear porch and leaned against the railing, staring off into the woods. James had watched his son while he was talking on the phone. Noticing the grim look come over Zach's face, he decided to follow Zach out onto the porch.

"Bad news?" James queried, leaning on the rail beside his son.

"Yes and no," Zach answered. "All but one of the SEAL team made it back safely. One of the team members, Rudy Sanders, died during their escape back to the safe house."

"That's too bad."

"Yeah, he was a great guy. The only good news is that the criminal Adam West died during the destruction of the biolab. SEAL Team One out of Little Creek, Virginia, with the help of the CIA, caught up with two members of the Order of Light, Schechter and Oates. Unfortunately, they refused to identify any of the other order members. They took knowledge of the other order members to the grave. With West also dead, it is unlikely they will be able to locate any of the other order members."

"All things considered, with the top three order members dead, I think we have to consider it a win."

"Yeah, I guess you're right. Say, Dad, I was wondering about what you said to Jessie Ray Kirby about giving him more food if they needed it. I know we should be willing to share, but can we really afford to do that?"

"Yes, I believe we can," James said, smiling. "Follow me."

Together, the two men went back into the cabin. James pushed the small dinette table out of the way and rolled back the rug, revealing a three-foot square trap door.

"Follow me," he said as he started down the ladder.

"Wow!" Zach exclaimed when his feet hit the bottom. "What is all this?"

"Look back there," James said, pointing to his right. "The cabin has two buried one thousand gallon propane tanks. The heater, extra fridge, and freezer are all propane and there are solar panels on the roof. I bought this cabin a little over a year ago from the wife of a survivalist who died suddenly from a heart attack. She just wanted to get rid of it and sold it cheap."

"You never mentioned it. How come?"

"I hoped to never have to use it, but here we are."

"How long do you think the food will last us?"

"Well, the freezer is well stocked. There are two dozen pails of powdered survival rations that are guaranteed to last twenty-five years and there is also a thousand gallon potable water tank back there. I'd say we could hold out well over a year."

"That long!" Zach whistled. "Does Mom know?"

"Yes, she does. Together, we have been building up the stock of non-perishable food items for the last six months. We were afraid of what we believed was coming. Looks like it was a good thing we did."

"I want to go up and let Anna Mae know. I know she has been worried ever since we got here."

"Sure, let's go."

Zach climbed up the ladder. He reached out a hand to help James as he reached the top of the ladder. While James straightened the rug and replaced the dinette table, Zach went over and sat on the couch beside Anna Mae. Her eyes grew wider and wider as Zach filled her in on what lay hidden below their feet.

Zach stood up and grabbed Anna Mae's hand. "Let's go join Mom and Dad."

Standing around the small dinette table they joined hands and bowed their heads. Zach prayed and thanked God for bringing them safely to the cabin and for the incredible blessings He had provided. With great difficulty, his voice breaking several times, he prayed for comfort for the family of Rudy Sanders and that the Gospel would be shared during the funeral. He finished with a prayer for their beloved country, praying that its men and women would come out stronger after the turmoil was over.

They raised their heads and released each other's hands. Zach and James hugged and kissed their wives, happy to be safe and together.

"Me too," Mazie cried, tugging at Zach's trousers.

"Of course, Sweetie," Zach said as he picked Mazie up and hugged her tightly, planting a wet kiss on her cheek.

"Daddy," Mazie squealed, giggling and rubbing at her cheek.

Only time would tell what lay ahead for the Templeton family.

THE END

GLOSSARY

World Time Zones:

HST – Hawaiian Standard Time - UTC/GMT -11 hours
PST - Pacific Standard Time - UTC/GMT -8 hours
MST – Mountain Standard Time - UTC/GMT -7 hours
CST – Central Standard Time - UTC/GMT -6 hours
EST – Eastern Standard Time - UTC/GMT -5 hours
VST - Venezuelan Standard Time - UTC/GMT -4 hours
CET - Central European Time - UTC/GMT +1 hour
ChST – China Standard Time - UTC/GMT + 8 hours

Gene Editing/DNA Modification Terms:

DNA – Deoxyribonucleic acid, A complex, double-helix polymer made from repeating units called nucleotides
RNA - Ribonucleic acid, a single-stranded biopolymer
CRISPR - Clustered regularly interspaced short palindromic repeats
Cas9 – A nuclease protein enzyme that works as a "scissors" to cut the DNA
Nucleotides – DNA nitrogen bases: adenine (A), thymine (T), guanine (G) and cytosine (C)

The complete DNA genome for a human contains about 3 billion base groups made from various combinations of the nitrogen bases (letters ATGC above), resulting in approximately 20,000 individual genes on 23 pairs of chromosomes.

Brownian Movement: The random motion of particles suspended in a liquid or a gas. This motion typically consists of some quantity of particles that constantly undergo small, random fluctuations. It was named for the Scottish botanist Robert Brown, 1827.

About The Author

Keith Hoar is a writer and former Certified Business Intelligence Expert who consulted for numerous Fortune 100 companies. He designed executive suite business intelligence dashboards and real-time reporting systems. Keith also owned his own consulting company that designed custom software applications and sophisticated data-driven reporting systems.

Keith proudly served his country in the United States Navy for ten years. At Naval Submarine School, New London, Connecticut he assisted in training crews from both Fast Attack and Ballistic Missile submarines that patrolled the world's oceans in defense of freedom.

Keith has published four edge-of-your-seat, hold-your-breath thriller novels: ***Edge of Madness, RAGE***, and ***DEADLY SECRETS***, ***COLD DARK LIES***, a Historical Fiction novel: ***LEAGUE OF TRAITORS***, and the Christian, nonfiction book, ***DECEIVED: The Assault of Revisionist History***.

Thank you for taking the time to read about the author. Keith is most grateful for fans of his books, and would love to correspond with readers like you. If you would like to receive more information, visit https://keithhoarbooks.wixsite.com/home or you may reach him at his author email - kahoarauthor@email.com

www.ingramcontent.com/pod-product-compliance
Lightning Source LLC
Chambersburg PA
CBHW060555310726
48982CB00008B/1131/J

* 9 7 8 1 7 3 6 2 7 6 1 4 3 *